The Tower

Simon Toyne

W F HOWES LTD

LP

This large print edition published in 2014 by
W F Howes Ltd
Unit 4, Rearsby Business Park, Gaddesby Lane,
Rearsby, Leicester LE7 4YH

1 3 5 7 9 10 8 6 4 2

First published in the United Kingdom in 2013
by HarperCollins*Publishers*

A CIP catalogue record for this book is available
from the British Library

ISBN 978 1 47125 067 5

Typeset by Palimpsest Book Production Limited,
Falkirk, Stirlingshire
Printed and bound by
CPI Group (UK) Ltd, Croydon, CR0 4YY

MIX
Paper from
responsible sources
FSC
www.fsc.org   FSC® C013604

To Stan
(Sorry there are no pirates in it)

PART I

All things are full of gods

Plato

PROLOGUE

The basement is dark and quiet.

A figure, stripped to the waist and kneeling takes the blade in his right hand and draws it across the skin at the joint of his left arm and shoulder, tracing the scar of a previous cut. The blade is sharp and the scar opens easily, letting blood run down skin quivering at the bite of the knife.

'The first,' he says, his voice low in the darkness. 'This blood binds me in pain with the Sacrament. As it suffers, so must I, until all suffering will end.'

He switches the blade to his left hand and repeats the cut on his right shoulder.

'The second,' he says, continuing the ritual learned from a hospital worker in the southern Turkish city of Ruin, a man loyal to the cause who had faithfully recorded everything the dying Sancti said through their delirium and suffering. The knife continues to cut, drawing fresh blood from old wounds, carving the same pattern he has seen on the bodies of the sacred monks, captured on a camera phone by the same spy after their suffering had finally ended. It is a ceremony that remained secret and locked in the

3

He slips on his jacket then mounts the stairs back up into the modern world like a man rising from the dead.

Reborn.

Renewed.

Ready.

CHAPTER 1

Merriweather looked up at the bank of screens.

Something was wrong.

He glanced behind him though he knew he was alone in the control centre. Everyone else was at the inter-departmental party they threw each year to mark the start of the Christmas holidays. Merriweather wasn't big on parties. He didn't drink and couldn't do small talk so he'd volunteered for the caretaker watch to garner some points with colleagues on the Flight Ops Team and bag a little heavy-duty processor time to crunch the deep space data he was working on for his PhD.

He leaned forward in his chair and cocked his head to one side, listening to the chatter of the hard drive. Some people could listen to a car engine and tell you what was wrong with it, others might hear one bum note in a symphony played by a sixty-piece orchestra, Merriweather knew computers – and this one definitely sounded hinky. There was a hitch in the processing tone, like a broken tooth on a clock wheel or a fresh scratch on one of the classic 45s he liked to collect. He stroked his knitted tie nervously as he considered what to do. Unlike the other techs at the Goddard Space Center, Merriweather was strictly old school. He wore a tie every day, along with pressed trousers, horn-rimmed glasses and neatly combed hair – just like his boyhood heroes, the Houston mission controllers of the sixties and seventies. He also liked rules and order. He didn't like it when things went wrong.

A tap on his keyboard banished the Pillars of Creation screensaver, the most famous image taken by the Hubble telescope, controlled from this room and currently orbiting Earth six hundred kilometres above Merriweather's head. He ran through the standard checklist of the latest telemetry: temperature normal, speed steady, all systems green, no fluctuation in the solar wind – nothing abnormal.

He typed in a string of commands and the big screen on the wall flashed up an updated image from the main reflector feed. It showed the luminous swirl of Cosmos-Aztec6, thirteen point four billion light years away – the furthest system ever observed from Earth.

The processor crunched again, making Merriweather wince, then something happened that he had never seen before. An application autoloaded on to his desktop, a large window filled with numbers.

'Virus,' he said. 'We have a virus!'

No response. No one there.

The numbers remained on screen for a few

seconds then disappeared. Merriweather tapped the keyboard and shook the mouse. He kicked back, rolling his chair away from the desk and across the floor to another workstation. Same thing: frozen screen, frozen keyboard. The processors chattered feverishly as they continued to feed on whatever digital poison had somehow found its way into the pristine system.

The main screen flickered and Merriweather looked up. The image was beginning to shift and disintegrate. Whatever had locked him out was now taking control of the guidance systems. The telescope was moving.

He fumbled for a desk phone, knocking the receiver to the floor, pulling it up by the cord and stabbing a button marked 'Dr Kinderman – cell phone'. On the screen the image continued to break up as the telescope turned. In his ear the ringing tone began. Somewhere down the hall a Marimba tune rang in synch with it.

Merriweather clamped the phone under his chin and went through every reboot command he could think of to try and unlock the keyboard. Nothing. The ringing tone continued in his ear. He dropped the phone on the desk and launched himself towards the exit.

Outside in the corridor the Marimba was louder. It was coming from Kinderman's office. He arrived at the door, knocked once out of habit then opened it.

The state of the office came as a complete shock:

wrenched-open drawers, papers everywhere, books all over the floor. The cell phone was on the desk. It shimmied a couple of times, vibrating in time to the ring, then stopped. In the silence that followed Merriweather heard the crunch of the pernicious code coming from Kinderman's terminal. He moved cautiously into the room, wading through drifts of paper, until the monitor came into view. He stopped dead when he saw the message on the screen:

MANKIND MUST LOOK NO FURTHER

CHAPTER 2

Shepherd took a deep breath then let it out slowly, trying not to make a sound as he edged forward down the dark corridor, gun first towards the solitary door. It was open slightly, the splintered timbers around the lock evidence of how many times it had been kicked in over the years. Somewhere above him the Virginia winter wind moaned through broken windows, filling the derelict townhouse with whispering voices. It was two below outside, probably colder in here, but he was sweating beneath his body armour.

He stopped a foot short of the door and leaned against the wall, feeling the flex in the plaster-board and timber frame – not much good for stopping bullets. He hunkered down below eye-level like he'd been taught and slipped his scoping mirror from his belt then past the edge of the doorjamb.

Daylight leaked in through high, narrow windows sketching the outline of a room: another door set into the far wall, a table in the centre spilling over with various items – a man and a woman standing directly behind it.

The skin tightened on Shepherd's scalp. The man's eyes, framed by safety goggles, seemed to be staring straight at him. He saw a hand clamp tighter across the face of the terrified woman, held in front of him like a shield, saw the other hand rising up.

He leaped away just as gunfire shattered the cold silence and bullets smacked into the wall where he had been resting. He rolled into a new position further down the corridor and levelled his gun at the door. 'FBI!' he shouted. 'Drop your weapon and come out slowly with your hands on your head. We have the building surrounded.'

Not true.

He was a lone agent following a cold lead that had just gone volcanic.

He heard noises coming from the room, something clattering to the floor then footsteps scuffing away. He moved forward in a crouch, gun just below his line of sight, free hand reaching for a stun grenade on his belt. He pulled the pin and tossed it round the doorframe.

The grenade clattered across the floor, clanged against the metal leg of the table then detonated with a lightning flash that Shepherd saw even behind his closed eyelids. A sharp, percussive boom-shook the wall and he was up and into the room.

No one there. Far door open.

He ran through the white magnesium smoke, performing a quick inventory of the table as he passed: 9-volt batteries, wire cutters, soldering iron, duct tape, vacuum packs of plastique. Bomb-making equipment.

The smart move would be to regroup and call for backup, but the suspect knew he was cornered. He had fired shots and fled, even after Shepherd had identified himself as FBI. He was desperate, and therefore unpredictable.

And he had a hostage.

If Shepherd waited for other units to show, the suspect would probably kill the woman and make a run for it. But right now he was vulnerable, his ears ringing from the pressure wave of the grenade, his eyes useless in the gloom of the basement. Shepherd had the advantage, but it was slight and wouldn't last for more than the next few seconds. He had to make a choice.

He took a breath and swept his gun arm round the edge of the doorframe, following it into the second room. The suspect was in the far corner, backed up against the wall, the hostage still in front of him and terrified.

Shepherd stood square on, maximizing the cover of his body armour, his gun steady in a good two-hand hold, trying to fix the front sight on what he could see of the suspect's face. With his peripheral vision he sucked in the detail of the room: a single mattress on the floor; a low table next to it; a movie poster tacked to the wall with a burnt-orange sun and slashed white lettering. His mouth went dry as buried memories rushed out of his past.

The dank smell . . .

. . . the same sun on the same poster . . .

. . . a room just like this.

He tried to zone it all out, keeping his eyes on the suspect and his mind on the here and now, but the sun kept pulling at him with something like real gravity, dragging him back to that dark, dark place he had done everything he could to forget.

His hand began to tremble. The suspect was shouting but he couldn't make out what he was saying. Then he saw a hand rise up. Something in it. Some kind of button with a wire trailing down to the belt bomb wound around the hostage's neck.

Behind them the sun blazed on the wall like an omen of the explosion to come. Shepherd felt weak. He couldn't hold it together. His whole world condensed to the end of his gun and the suspect's face came into focus along with the words on the movie poster.

Apocalypse Now

He pulled the trigger.

Adjusted for recoil – everything muscle memory now, drilled in deep from hours on the range – squeezed off another round. Saw an explosion of red beyond his gun-sight. Then he watched in silence as both suspect and hostage fell in crumpled slow motion to the ground.

In the stillness that followed, Shepherd felt everything drain out of him. His eyes drifted back to the molten sun, his hand dropped to his side, the red-handled gun dangling from his curled trigger finger. He didn't even feel the instructor take it from him, or register the fluorescent lights flickering into life above his head. In his mind he was still back there, staring at the same poster on a different wall – the room where she had found him and they had saved each other.

'. . . Shepherd . . .!'

The voice seemed to come from very far away.

'SHEPHERD – YOU OK?'

The granite face of Special Agent Williams slid into view, obscuring the poster and breaking the spell.

Shepherd blinked.

Nodded.

'You made some tactical errors.'

He nodded again.

'Get yourself over to The Biograph for a debrief.' The Practical Applications instructor slapped him on the back with a hand made solid from years of pulling triggers and turned to the two actors, already on their feet and tugging wet-wipes from their pockets to clean away the red dye from Shepherd's training pistol. They each had an impact mark on their forehead, just above the eye. Kill shots both.

'Back to initial positions,' Williams barked. 'Next trainee coming through in five.'

14

CHAPTER 3

Shepherd stepped out of the front door of the townhouse into the teeth of a westerly wind straight off Chesapeake Bay and headed away along Main Street.

Hogan's Alley covered ten acres of the Marine Base in Quantico and was built as a microcosm of any-town America with its own bank, drug store, hotel, gas station – basically all the institutions criminals targeted out in the real world. Normally, the whole town echoed with radio buzz, shouted orders and the crackle of gunfire from FBI, DEA and other assorted law-enforcement officers as they learnt the art of urban tactical deployment. Today it was almost deserted, like everywhere else, as the whole base wound down for the Christmas holidays. Shepherd noticed a stuffed Santa dangling from an upper window of the Coin-Op Laundromat swinging in the strengthening wind like a hanged man. Someone had shot him in the ass with a paint-round: so much for the Christmas spirit.

He hunched his shoulders against the chill and looked up at the night sky out of habit. The evening star had already risen in the west and, as he looked at it, a huge flock of geese streaked across the sky, their loud honks making him pause. The ancients would have read much into the direction of the birds' flight and the position of the wandering star in the sky. But Shepherd knew it was just nature and that the shifting star was actually the planet Venus whose brightness had always been a comfort to him, even in his most desperate and lonely nights.

He turned the corner just as the streetlights flickered on in response to the creep of night. At the far end of the block, more light leaked on to the sidewalk from the foyer of The Biograph, named after the movie theatre in Chicago where John Dillinger had been gunned down in the mid-thirties. The marquee above the entrance advertised *Manhattan Melodrama* starring Clark Gable and Myrna Loy, the last movie Dillinger had ever seen. Shepherd reached the unmanned ticket booth and pushed through the door into the space where the foyer should have been.

The classroom held a hundred students seated in concentric rows around a large screen that could be patched in to a number of audio-visual teaching aids as well as any of the sixty-two security cameras set up around the town. Right now it was showing the basement room of the townhouse with Shepherd in the middle of it, frozen in his two-handed stance, his gun pointing at the crumpled bodies on the floor. A man in a black suit stood before the screen, head to one side as if studying an exhibit in an art gallery. 'You see a ghost in there, Shepherd?' he asked without looking round.

'No, sir, I was just . . . it was a high-pressure situation.'

The man turned and gave Shepherd the same hard scrutiny he'd been giving the screen. 'They're all high-pressure situations, son – every one of 'em.'

Special Agent Benjamin Franklin was one of two active field counsellors permanently attached to Shepherd's class, there to give a practical dimension to each lesson, answer any questions and tell the new intake how it really was out in the real world. He was one of those solid, square-jawed types seemingly minted in a different time when men still called women Ma'am and cars were covered in fins and chrome. His short blond hair was receding and fading to ash above pale blue eyes like chips of ice that somehow still managed to convey warmth whenever he smiled, which he did now. 'Might I ask,' he said, 'would you fire again, given the same scenario?' His Carolina drawl gave his words a slow courtliness.

Shepherd thought back to the blur of action as he'd squeezed the trigger, the suspect in his sights but the wrong person ending up dead on the floor. 'No, sir.'

'How do you figure that?'

'Because . . . because I hit the hostage.'

Franklin started up the aisle towards him, buttoning the jacket of his suit and flashing an old, steel Timex. 'Take off your body armour Shepherd and walk with me a while.'

The night seemed darker after the brightness of the classroom and the wind had picked up. It was blowing leaves down the street and into Shepherd's face as he fell into step beside Franklin.

''Bout twelve years back,' Franklin said, peering at the darkening forest ahead as if he could see the lost years among the trees, 'I was part of a six-man task force running an investigation into a string of hit-and-run bank jobs across the Ohio–Indiana state line. In each case a lone, masked gunman stormed into a small out-of-the-way bank, grabbed a hostage – always a woman – and threatened to shoot her if anyone tripped an alarm. He was smart to a point because the size of the banks meant security wasn't top of the line so we didn't have any decent security camera footage. Also he never got greedy so was always out and away within a couple of minutes. And he always took the hostage with him, saying if he heard so much as a car alarm he would kill her.

'As you can imagine the local press shook up a hornets' nest of fear about it all but there was also a bigger concern: none of the hostages were coming forward afterwards. For about a week or so we lived in fear of getting a call from some hunter or dog walker who had stumbled upon the silenced corpse of one of our unfortunate bank customers. Then he hit another bank, third in a month, and we got fresh footage.'

Franklin directed Shepherd away from Hogan's Alley and towards the path through the forest that led to the main building complex beyond.

'This is how it went down. Woman walks into the bank, talks to the door guard; gunman comes in and disarms the guard while he's distracted, grabs the woman, robbery ensues then perp leaves with a hostage. We could see by comparing the clear images of the new footage with the fuzzy older stuff we had that it was the same woman every time. Turns out she wasn't a hostage at all, she was one of the crew. That's why no one was coming forward afterwards.

'We quietly spread the word among the state banks, so when they pulled another job ten days later in Des Moines, a teller tripped the alarm and the cops got there in plenty of time to pick 'em up. When he was cornered the gunman tried to pull the same hostage routine, said he was going to kill her if they didn't give him a car and a free pass. Cops just told him, "Go 'head, shoot her." All of which brings us back to your little situation. Tell me what you knew about your suspect from the mission brief?'

Shepherd dug his hands deep in his pockets and tried to focus on something other than how cold he was. 'The intel said he was on several international watch lists as a known terror suspect. Believed to be a Jihadist, trained in Afghanistan by Al-Qaeda.'

'And from your reading and case studies do

terrorists and other religiously motivated individuals tend to give themselves up to officers of
an enemy state they believe they are conducting
a holy war against?'

'No.'

'No they do not.'

The trees parted to reveal the Quantico Hilton
rising up in front of them, all square lines, slit
windows and concrete. This was where the labs
and active case teams were housed; proper
on-going, messy cases with as-yet undiscovered
solutions, not the clean textbook ones Shepherd
was being weaned on. It could easily have passed
for a small mid-western high-school campus had
it not been for the sound of gunfire crackling out
of the forest behind them. The next recruit must
have made it to the basement. Shepherd hoped
he or she was doing better than he had. Hearing
the shots reminded him of all the paperwork he
needed to fill out back at the briefing room. The
forms for discharging your weapon during an
exercise were thorough, tedious and in triplicate
for very good reason: it stopped the recruits from
getting trigger-happy.

'Don't worry about the admin,' Franklin said,
apparently reading his mind. 'I'll square it with
Agent Williams. You can fill it in and file it after.'

After what? Shepherd wanted to ask, but Franklin
was already halfway towards the glass doors of the
main building.

'Never forget that you are a highly and expensively

trained officer, son. In the currency of law enforcement that makes you an asset to Uncle Sam and a much-valued target to a terrorist. If you don't take the shot, odds are the bomber will push the button anyway and there will be three bodies to scrape out of that basement instead of two. The hostage dies either way. And, given the little story I just told you, how do you know the hostage was even friendly?' They moved from the frigid night into the brightness and heat of the executive building. 'You have to wonder what that woman was doing at dusk in a rat-hole basement with a known terrorist in the first place. I can understand you being upset that you shot someone who might be innocent, it's a credit to you, but don't lose sleep over it. You made the right choice, Shepherd. Though you do need to work on your marksmanship.'

They passed the honours board that dominated the glass atrium with the name of every top-of-the-class graduate written in gold, dating right back to 1972 when the doors first opened. Shepherd doubted his name would ever grace it. He was a good few years older than the average intake, which showed in his fitness scores, and his shooting was clearly letting him down. The things he really excelled at were not part of the five areas of ability that went towards his final mark; his expertise had not even been thought of when the FBI first came into being.

The elevator door opened and Franklin stepped inside, waited for Shepherd to join him then pushed button number 6. Shepherd's mouth went dry. The sixth floor was where the most senior personnel lived.

'You cannot have doubts out in the field,' Franklin said, his soft voice sounding conspiratorial in the confines of the elevator. 'Because if you hesitate in a situation like that, you die, or, worse still, your partner does and you end up carrying it around with you for the rest of your life. They don't put this sort of thing in any of the manuals but I'm telling you how it is, for your own sake and for mine – especially if we're going to be working together.'

The door swished open before Shepherd had time to respond and Franklin headed down the silent corridor, checking his watch as he passed all the heavy doors belonging to the sub-division chiefs. The corridor was arranged according to rank with the lesser chiefs nearest the elevator. Franklin swept past them all, heading straight for the door at the very end with Shepherd close behind, feeling like he was back in high school and had been summoned to the principal's office. Only here the 'principal' was one rung down from the Director of the FBI, who himself was just one down from the President of the United States of America. Franklin stopped outside the door, checked his watch one last time then rapped twice above a nameplate spelling out: ASSISTANT DIRECTOR.

In the softened silence of the corridor they sounded like gunshots.

'Come in,' a deep voice rumbled from the other side.

Franklin gave him the smile, only this time the warmth wasn't there and it occurred to Shepherd that maybe he was nervous too. Then he opened the door and stepped into the room.

CHAPTER 4

Assistant Director O'Halloran was a thin blade of a man worn sharp by a lifetime in the Bureau. Everything about him was hard and precise: the steel rims of his spectacles; the pale grey eyes behind them that looked up as Franklin and Shepherd entered the room; even his gunmetal hair appeared to have been parted with a scalpel rather than a comb. He was sitting at the same immaculate desk he had been photographed behind on the recruitment literature that went with the application form Shepherd had filled out almost a year ago: same flatscreen monitor, same keyboard, same desk phone and framed photograph. The only things different were the two files on the desk in front of him: one plain, the other with Shepherd's photograph printed on the first page. Shepherd's pulse quickened when he saw it.

'You have quite the impressive resumé,' O'Halloran said, tapping a thin finger on the file with the photograph. 'Mathematics major with computer science at the University of Michigan. MSc in physics from CalTech. Best part of a PhD in theoretical cosmology from Cambridge

University in England – though you never finished that one, did you? Even so, I imagine you could be making six figures and upwards in the financial sector, yet you chose to sign up as a GS-10 with a basic starting salary of $46,000. Why is that I wonder?'

Shepherd swallowed drily. 'Money's not that important to me.'

'Really, you a Communist?'

'No, sir – I'm a patriot.'

'OK, Mr Patriot, tell me about your PhD, why didn't you finish it?'

Shepherd glanced down at the file, recalling the psychiatric evaluations and background checks that had formed part of his recruitment screening. All of it would be in there, at least everything he had told them. But this was the Assistant Director he was talking to so there could well be other things in there by now – things he had hoped to keep hidden.

'It's all in the file, sir.'

O'Halloran regarded Shepherd from the centre of his stillness. 'I want to hear it from you.'

Shepherd's mind raced. He was being tested and Assistant Director O'Halloran was far too senior for it to be about something trivial. If it was to do with the parts he'd left out of his past then Franklin could easily have questioned him about it back at The Biograph, which meant it had to be about something else. He should stick to the story he'd already told, volunteer no new information, and

25

hope things became clearer over the course of the next few minutes.

'I had been in academia all my adult life,' he said, saying the same lines he had spoken to his recruitment officer. 'It was everything I knew but not everything I wanted to know. Some people like to gather knowledge just for knowledge's sake, I always intended to apply mine.'

'NASA.'

Shepherd nodded. 'A large proportion of my education was funded by Space Agency scholarships. I also spent a lot of research time on various NASA projects, which is pretty standard for anyone on one of their scholarships: they get extra brain power, we get our feet under the table and gain practical experience of the work we will hopefully end up doing.'

'So what happened?'

'9/11 happened – sir. Homeland defence and the war on terror became the number one priority. It took a big bite out of everyone's budget. Almost the entire space program was shelved. I suddenly found myself with no grant and no job to go to even if I did manage to complete my studies. It was . . . like hitting a wall.'

'So you dropped out.'

'That's one way of putting it, sir.'

'How would you put it?'

'At first I felt cheated, like something had been taken away from me. It seemed pointless to carry on studying for a job that was no longer there.

There were plenty of private companies offering to fund the remainder of my studies but they all wanted me to sign my life away in exchange. Work for them as soon as I graduated, study stock markets instead of stars. It wasn't what I wanted. So I took off and went travelling to clear my head and try and work out what I was going to do with my life now NASA no longer appeared to be an option.'

'Where did you end up? There's a gap in your file of almost two years where you seem to have disappeared off the face of the earth: no social security records, no job history, no credit card records.'

'I was off the grid mainly – Europe first then Southeast Asia and eventually Africa, travelling from place to place, working cash jobs in bars and as migrant labour on farms, staying in backpacker hostels that charged by the night. They don't take credit cards in most of those places. I'd been a student for most of my adult life so I knew how to live cheap.'

'Then what, you saw the light and decided to rejoin society?'

'Yes, sir. I realized I was squandering an opportunity. What happened on 9/11 changed my life – but almost three thousand other people lost theirs. My future had been altered; theirs had been taken away. My intention had always been to pay back the money for my education by devoting myself to public service and working for NASA.

I came to realize that just because that particular opportunity had been closed to me didn't mean I couldn't pay my dues in other ways.'

'So you signed up for the FBI?'

'Not immediately, sir.'

'No, that's right.' O'Halloran opened the file for the first time and flipped to a page near the back. 'First you worked as a volunteer for various aid agencies, setting up computer networks and fund-raising pages and teaching computer skills to homeless people and the long-term unemployed.' He looked back up. 'You really weren't kidding about money were you?'

'No, sir – it's never been something that has particularly motivated me.'

O'Halloran pursed his lips and studied Shepherd like a poker player deciding which way to bet. 'I'm not entirely happy that the Bureau I have served all my adult life seems to be some kind of conso-lation prize for you, Shepherd, but I can't afford to turn away a candidate with your qualifications.' He closed the file and laid a hand on the second one. 'Are you familiar with the Goddard Space Flight Center?'

'Yes sir, I spent a few summers there running test data off Explorer 66.'

'Is that anything to do with the Hubble Space Telescope?'

'Not really. They both collect data from the furthest edges of the universe, at least they did – Explorer is pretty much used as a test satellite now. Hubble does everything Explorer used to and has a much greater reach.'

The lips pursed again. 'Not any more.' O'Halloran opened his desk drawer, removed a badge wallet and handed it to Shepherd. 'I am not in the habit of sending trainees out in the field before they have completed their training or spent at least a year in a field office, but apparently, out of more than thirty thousand currently active Bureau personnel, you are uniquely qualified for a situation that has arisen.' Shepherd opened the wallet and saw his own photo staring back from an FBI ID card. 'That will *temporarily* entitle you to carry a concealed weapon and transport it onboard commercial airlines. You can collect your Roscoe and a box of shells from Agent Williams on your way out.'

Shepherd read the name printed next to a date that expired in a month. 'My middle name is Thomas,' he said, turning the badge to O'Halloran.

'There's already a Special Agent J. T. Shepherd in the Memphis office and, as no two agents can have the same ID,' he raised his hand and made a small sign of the cross in the air, 'I now baptize you J. *C.* Shepherd. That's your Bureau name, and you will answer to it. I am placing Agent Franklin in full command of the investigation and you are to follow his lead exactly. You have been assigned to this investigation solely because of your unique and considerable expertise in the field of astronomy. You will use it to assist Agent Franklin in this investigation and give your opinion only when it is requested. The rest of the time you will look upon this as a valuable opportunity to learn on the job from a well-seasoned and highly regarded agent. Once your usefulness to the investigation has been exhausted, your temporary status will be revoked and you will report back here to finish your training, understood?'

'Yessir.'

'I trust you know your way to Goddard from here? There's a car signed out to you in transport.' He took the plain covered file from the desk and held it up. 'Agent Franklin can brief you on the way.'

CHAPTER 5

Shepherd and Franklin drove for the first ten minutes in total silence, the *whump* of windscreen wipers and hiss of tyres over wet tarmac punctuated only by the rustle of paper as Franklin read through the file. Occasionally he jotted a note in a pocketbook lit by the glow of a small Maglite clamped in his teeth. Shepherd sensed he was unhappy about the situation. That made two of them.

After his performance on Hogan's Alley the last thing Shepherd wanted was to be heading out into the real world with a loaded gun tucked into his jacket. As promised, Agent Williams, the firearms instructor, had been ready and waiting in the armoury with an oiled SIG 226, which he made Shepherd speed-load from an open box of 9x19 Parabellums while he looked on. Shepherd's Catholic education had hammered enough Latin into him to know that *para bellum* meant 'prepare for war'. He tried to push the thought from his mind as he slotted fifteen shells into the magazine, fumbling two, before smacking it home and looking up into the pained expression on the instructor's face.

'Do yourself a favour,' Williams had said, as Shepherd signed for the gun and the spare shells, 'try not to put yourself in any situation where you may have to draw this weapon. Just keep it in your holster and come back as quickly as you can to finish your training.'

Shepherd checked the rear-view mirror. Behind him he could see the lights of the grey panel van that had followed them out of the gates at Quantico. It was a tech wagon, loaded with forensics equipment and two Physical Science Technicians ready to process the crime scene his former workplace had now become. They were on I-95, heading north: the bright lights of DC spread across the horizon ahead of them like a luminous stain, lighting up the low cloud that was spilling monsoon-level rain over everything. The weather was slowing them down but at least it would be too late for commuter traffic to be a problem when they eventually hit the capitol. He figured they would be in Maryland in twenty minutes, though he still had no idea why they were heading there.

The Maglite twisted off in the passenger seat and Shepherd heard the creak of the vinyl seat as Franklin turned to him. 'That little story you span back there,' he said, 'your tale of travel to the far corners of the world to find yourself – I just want you to know, I ain't buying it.'

Shepherd felt heat on his cheeks and was glad it was too dark for Franklin to see. 'I don't follow you, sir.'

'I've spent over twenty years talking to people who have done everything from write bad cheques to kidnap children so they could torture them for fun, and you know what every single one of 'em had in common? They all tried to lie to me. Now you may have all your highfalutin' degrees in astrophysics and rocket science and whatever else, but I got a degree in people and I know when someone is spinning me a line. I can smell it on them, and right now, Agent Shepherd, you stink.'

Shepherd said nothing and kept his eyes on the road.

'Now I don't really care all that much why you're lying or even what it is you're hiding, what does concern me, however, is having a partner I can't trust. Having a partner you can't trust is like having no partner at all, and that's dangerous, Agent Shepherd, as you just discovered down in that basement. So if at any point you feel like kicking a piece of the truth in my direction – man to man, partner to partner, in the knowledge that, felonies aside, it will go no further – then we'll get along a whole lot better. In the meantime, operate on the assumption that I'm apt to doubt every single goddam word that comes out of your mouth, understood?'

'Sir, I promise you . . .'

Franklin raised his hand and turned his head away. 'Don't make it worse by lying to me again. I'm being honest with you, Agent Shepherd, I'm just asking for you to do the same.'

33

The seat creaked as Franklin turned back to the briefing documents. 'OK, now I've put it out there so you know where we stand you can make yourself useful and explain to me the wisdom behind spending over a billion tax dollars putting a telescope into space that then costs over forty million dollars a year to run.'

Shepherd stared ahead through the spray and considered the question, relieved to be back on safe, familiar ground. He thought about the unimaginable distances the Hubble Space Telescope could penetrate compared to the relatively puny ones achieved by terrestrial instruments. He thought about the light from dead stars it could gather from the pure nothingness of clear space, carrying information all the way back from the beginning of time. But in the end he kept it simple. 'How many stars can you see tonight?' he said.

Franklin looked out into the wet, black night as a Big Rig hooned by, going way too fast for the weather and throwing up so much spray you could hardly see the edge of the freeway let alone the sky. 'OK, fair point, but why not just build a telescope on top of a mountain in Mexico or somewhere the sun always shines. Hell, why not just wait for a clear night, be a lot cheaper.'

'They did all that. There's a fifty-metre dish on top of the Sierra Negra volcano in south Mexico that can observe both northern and southern skies. It's pretty impressive. Trouble is the earth keeps turning, so it can only study a piece of sky for a

34

few hours at a time. A space telescope like Hubble can lock onto a distant object and keep it in its sights for months, years even, while the earth turns beneath it.'

'And that costs forty million a year?'

'It's a very complicated process.'

Franklin grunted. 'Sounds like a scam to me.'

Shepherd considered letting it go but didn't want to slip back into the uneasy silence. 'How good a shot are you?' he asked.

'Better than you, *Special* Agent.'

'You think you could hit a tin can on the side of the road from a moving car?'

'Depends how fast the car is going.'

'Say it's doing thirty.'

'Nine times out of ten.'

'What if the car was doing eighty-five?'

Franklin considered. 'Maybe three out of ten.'

'OK, now imagine the car is doing eighty-five thousand miles an hour and the tin can is on the other side of the country, perched on top of the Hollywood sign. Think you could hit it then?' Franklin didn't reply. 'Hubble could. It could lock onto that can and take a picture of it so steady you could read the label. It's orbiting the earth at around seventeen thousand miles an hour, and the earth is orbiting the sun at sixty-seven thousand miles an hour. That's a total of eighty-four thousand miles an hour and yet Hubble can still fix onto a tiny patch of sky nearly fifteen billion light years away. It's one of the greatest miracles of modern technology, the pinnacle of man's achievements in science. That's why it cost so much and needs all that money to run it.'

'And all of that is controlled out of Goddard?'

'Yes.'

Franklin shook his head. 'Not any more – right now your gold-plated telescope couldn't hit a barn door with a banjo. It's spinning around up there like a bottle at a frat party. Someone managed to upload a virus that knocked out the guidance system and shut down all communication.'

'Really? That would be – very difficult.'

'How difficult?'

'When I was working at Goddard they had a small systems security scare. One of the ground operating stations for another satellite was left wide open via an email account and some kid hacked into it. He didn't do any damage but some of the ops systems got infected with internet junk that flowed in through the hole he'd made. It was picked up pretty quick and fixed but it prompted a review of the whole system. How much do you know about government cyber security?'

'About as much as you know about firing guns.'

'OK, so all state owned and operated computer operating systems are rated according to the Orange Book scale drawn up by the Department of Defense. This lays out specific security criteria for all government systems ranging from a D grade for non-sensitive, clerical stuff all the way up to beyond A1 for things like the NSA, the FBI and the military systems that launch the nukes. Following the scare at Goddard all the operating systems had to be upgraded to at least an A1. That means the prospect of Hubble's ground-based operating system being breached by any kind of regular cyber attack is extremely unlikely. It would be like a junkie with a twenty-dollar pistol knocking off Fort Knox. Whoever did this must have known exactly what they were doing.'

'You think it's an inside job?'

'Has to be. We should talk to Dr Kinderman, he's in charge of Hubble and helped redesign the new system. He'll be able to give us the names of everyone with the right kind of technical knowledge and any ex-employees who might have an axe to grind.'

'Good thinking, Agent Shepherd,' Franklin said, 'only problem with your otherwise flawless plan of investigation is that Dr Kinderman is AWOL. Right now he *is* our number one suspect.'

CHAPTER 6

EIGHT MONTHS EARLIER
Badiyat Al-Sham – Syrian Desert
Northwestern Iraq

When Gabriel Mann pointed the horse towards the horizon his only wish was to get as far from the compound as possible before he died.

He headed northwest, into the empty heart of the desert, with the heat of the rising sun on his shoulder and the scent of oranges strong in his nostrils. He tried not to think about all he was leaving behind because it only made it harder for him to go, and that was what he had to do – he had to leave her.

Instead, he tried to focus only on staying alive long enough to be far, far away when the disease took him. He didn't want to risk infecting others or falling where circling buzzards might draw human scavengers who would steal his clothes and weapons and risk carrying away something far more deadly. He needed to die where no one would ever find him, somewhere the desert sun could dry and purify his flesh and the wind could scatter his dust over the sterile ground where nothing grew and everything perished and was forgotten.

He travelled for nearly four hours before the fever struck. The heat had been building for some time, though it was hard to tell how much of it was coming from the sun and how much from him. He was in the scant shade of a low, dry wadi, keeping the hot wind away from his horse, when his skin started to prickle as if biting insects were suddenly swarming all over him. At the same time a sensation welled up inside him like a feeling of uncontrollable grief. Despite his efforts to put her from his mind he had been thinking about Liv, picturing her face, the green of her eyes and how her hair had spread bright and golden over the pillow the last time he had seen her, sleeping in the sick bay. This sadness of leaving her, fuelled by the fever, now spilled out of him and tears rolled through the dry dust on his cheeks. He raised a shaking hand to wipe his face and it came away bloody.

A blight – the monk from the Citadel had called it – a strong smell of oranges followed by a sudden and violent nosebleed.

It's over, he thought, with something close to relief. Now I can lie down.

He steered his horse to an overhang that formed a small oasis of shadow amid the blinding white. This was it, the place his whole life had been heading towards, this dark nook that looked like a vertical grave.

This was where he would die.

CHAPTER 7

Liv spent most of the first day hiding at the top of one of the compound's empty guard towers, keeping to the shadows, out of the heat.

She had woken in the sick bay to find Gabriel gone and an unsteady peace rippling through the camp. She found the note he had left for her, trapped beneath the tablet of stone known as the Starmap.

> *My darling Liv,*
> *Nothing is easy, but leaving you is the hardest thing I have ever done. I know now what pain my father must have felt when he had to leave. I hope to return when I can. In the meantime, do not look for me, just know that I love you. And keep yourself safe – until I find you again.*
> *Gabriel*

She clutched the note in her hand now, as though it were a spell that might summon him back to her. Her attention shifted between the vast emptiness of the Syrian desert and the fenced-in drilling compound below where arguments flared up in guttural, rapid-fire Arabic that she could somehow understand.

Most of the angry exchanges were about money and the lack of it now the oil had gone, but some were about her. Angry whispers drifted up like smoke from a smouldering fire, calling her names in a variety of languages —

حواء
   Hawwāh
       Ishtar
          Lilith

Some spoke in her defence, but most did not. The majority denounced her as a witch who had conjured water where oil had flowed and brought ruin upon them all.

Liv remained motionless as rock as she listened to the voices, as if stillness might make her invisible to all the milling men, like hornets disturbed from a nest. Peering down through the gaps in the heat-shrunk timbers of the tower, she studied the wreckage of the battle that had liberated the compound but not her: the hulk of the broken-down military heli-copter that had spluttered and died when the water appeared; the lake with the drill derrick at the centre spewing water now from deep, deep underground – and everywhere rust-coloured stains on the ground where men had fallen and bled. She was pretty sure no one had spotted her when she had crept up here but she held tight to the scalpel she had taken from the sick bay, just in case. She was only too aware that she was the only woman in an isolated community of volatile and hostile men – and she knew how that tended to work out. If she could stay hidden until night she could steal down, take one of the horses that drank at the water's edge and slip away.

It was late morning when she heard the first clang of boots climbing the metal ladder. She rolled silently across the floor, her heart jack-hammering, the scalpel slippery in her sweat-slicked grip. She positioned herself by the trapdoor, her legs drawn up tight to her chest, ready to kick hard at whatever appeared in the gap.

The footsteps rose, heavy and loud, stopping just below the trapdoor. 'Hello,' a deep, syrupy voice called up in English.

She didn't reply.

'I bring you water and food.' Very slowly a hand raised the trap and pushed a canteen and a pack of K-rations through the gap, then a pair of eyes appeared. 'No need to fight,' the man said. 'You are safe here. You have my word.'

'And who are you?' Liv replied, now there was no point in keeping silent.

'I am Tariq al Bedu. I rode with Ash'abah – the Ghost. I will watch out for you as he did, in the memory of his name. You must drink. I will bring more in a while.'

She glanced at the canteen, still wet from being dipped in the pool of fresh water below. 'Thank you,' she said, then – because she had once written an article on victim survival and remembered it was harder to harm someone if you knew their name – added, 'My name is Liv Adamsen.'

The man smiled and she could see the warmth of it spread to his eyes. 'I know who you are,' he said, and was gone.

Liv listened to his steps ringing away down the ladder, melting into the taunting hiss of fresh water spewing out of the ground below. She dragged the canteen towards her with her foot, still wary of going too close to the trapdoor, unscrewed the cap, sniffed the contents and then took the tiniest of sips. She figured a small amount of any kind of drug wouldn't be able to knock her out, so she sat for as long as her thirst would allow, analysing how she felt, waiting for something to happen. When nothing did, she took another drink, then another, until the whole contents of the canteen were slipping down her dry throat in thirsty gulps. Within the hour the man was back, bringing more water and an apple to eat, then he left her in peace and made sure everyone else did the same. Then, just before dusk, the soldiers came.

They rolled into camp in a cloud of dust and well-drilled purpose, American marines on a single-minded mission. Armed sentries surrounded the broken helicopter and others quickly winched it onto a flatbed loader while someone else addressed everyone in Arabic offering a ride back to Al-Hillah for anyone who wanted one. Liv used the distraction of their arrival to steal down the ladder, careful not to make a sound, and ducked into the shade and cover of one of the metal-sided buildings. Much as she wanted to leave the compound, she knew the US military were actively looking for her and, after all that had happened, she wasn't inclined to trust the reasons for their search or whoever had ordered it. She scanned the gathered crowds, looking for Tariq. A shadow fell on her and she turned to discover a stocky man in oily overalls glaring down at her with hate in his eyes.

'A curse be upon you,' he said, spitting on the ground at her feet, his hand drawing back to strike. Liv gripped the scalpel ready to fight back when Tariq stepped between them. 'Go, if you are going,' he said to the man, 'and take your grudges with you.'

The man's hand dropped to his side. For a moment he looked as though he was about to say something but he just spat on the ground again and hurried off towards the American convoy.

'That's Malik,' Tariq said, his eyes fixed on the man. 'He was in charge of transport here until the fuel turned to water and killed all his engines. He thinks you are responsible.' They watched Malik join a line waiting to board one of the troop carriers. 'He's leaving, along with all the others who now think this place is cursed.'

A marine stepped up to the waiting men and ushered them into the vehicle then hit the switch to seal the rear hatch behind them, ready to move out.

'I can take you anywhere you want to go,' Tariq said, 'or you can stay here a while, for there is much work to be done, is there not?'

The din of revving diesel engines rumbled through

the air as Liv considered his strange question. She stepped from the cover of the building as the convoy started to pull out, figuring she could still sprint after them if she chose to, but instead she just stood there, watching the dust cloud drift away until the sound of the engines faded to nothing.

She turned and looked at the people who had stayed. Most of them were riders but there were a few compound staff too, their white overalls singling them out. They gathered around her now, all faces turned towards her. She could feel the expectation coming off them like heat. 'What do they want?' Liv whispered.

'They want to know what they should do next.'

She laughed. 'And who put me in charge?'

The ring of faces smiled back at her, reflecting her good humour. It was as if the soldiers had taken all the anger away with them, leaving just a few relics of the violence behind – some bullet holes in the skin of the buildings, the rust-coloured patches of earth. 'What happened to the dead?' she asked.

'We put them in a refrigeration truck to keep the flies away,' Tariq replied, 'though with no fuel, the cooler isn't running.'

Liv nodded. 'OK,' she said, 'then that's what we do first – we bury the dead.'

CHAPTER 8

Gabriel had no idea how long he had been lying in the shade of the dry wadi when the sound of engines drifted down to him on the wind.

Instinctively he rolled onto his front, adrenalin flooding through him despite his raging fever and the well-drilled operational part of his brain taking over.

He couldn't be spotted now, not with the blight burning inside him.

He grabbed the trailing reins of his horse to keep it close and listened out, trying to locate the sound. The hot wind moved it around making it hard to pinpoint, which was a good sign. It meant it must still be some way off.

He used the reins to haul himself to his knees then moved the horse into the sliver of shade, stroking its flanks to calm it and tethering it to a rock. He forced himself up the side of the bank, choking down on the sobs that still battled to burst from him, the scratch of the dry earth blissful against his screaming skin. He reached the top and listened again.

The sound was closer now, coming from the west.

The itch crawled over him like fire ants and he rode the waves of it, clamping his arms to his sides to stop his hands from clawing at the prickling skin. When the itch subsided a little he tipped his head on one side to keep his profile low and slowly raised his eye above the line of the bank.

Two white, flat-bed pick-ups were kicking up dust as they bounced across the desert a couple of hundred metres to his left. Their windows were smoked black and the 50-calibre guns mounted on their backs were manned by soldiers wearing red-and-white-checked keffiyeh around their faces. They were Syrian Army – border patrol.

He slid back down the bank, shaking with the effort of just staying silent. All he wanted to do was lie down and rest and never get up again. But he couldn't. The patrol had changed everything.

He could backtrack, move away from the border to reduce the risk of being found by the patrols; but that didn't mean he would be hidden from the people they were seeking. He could try and find one of the alluvial caves that honeycombed the desert and crawl deep underground into a tomb of his own making; that would deal with the buzzards at least. But it wouldn't account for the human traffic. Other people would seek the same shelter, hiding from the heat and the men with guns. And he could not risk being found.

He lay there for a long while, shaking from the fever, as the inevitability of what he must do grew in his mind. There was only one place he could go, one place on earth where the blight would pose no threat.

He waited a long time, until he was sure the patrol had gone, then led the horse along the gulley, keeping low, looking for better cover. The sun was at its full height now and burned mercilessly into his agonized skin. After a few hundred feet that felt like miles he found a partial cave scooped out of the softer rock, big enough for him and his horse, and fell into the stifling shade, clenching his whole body against the blazing itch. He waited out the worst of the day, preparing himself for the journey he must make. Somehow, he had to evade capture and the company of others and find his way back to where the blight had first started and where he knew it already prospered.

He had to get back to the Citadel. He had to go back to Ruin.

CHAPTER 9

Liv chose a spot a good distance outside the perimeter fence and led by example, working by hand now the earthmovers were no use, breaking through rock and dirt baked hard as brick. It felt good to disappear into mindless work after all that had happened to her. Her previous life seemed like an abstract collection of memories now, something she could as easily have read in a book, not experienced herself. It was hard to imagine herself as that person now, the career journalist, subway-surfing through the morning rush hour with a skinny latte in one hand and a smartphone in the other, on her way to yet another assignment, another deadline, flicking through the IKEA catalogue and the Sunday supplements at the weekend. It was an existence she had spent a lifetime building, only to have fate dismantle it in a matter of days.

They finished digging the graves as the afternoon sun was dipping low in the sky and carefully placed the bodies in the bottom of the hole, enemy next to enemy, united in death – all but one. While most of the men had been busy with the communal grave, some of the riders had dug another a little way off and it was to this that they now carried the body of their leader, the one they called Ash'abah – the Ghost. They laid him to rest, said their silent prayers.

After the graves were filled, most of the riders left too, taking their horses and melting away into the desert.

Liv stayed by the grave of the Ghost. She had known him for less than a day and yet in that short time he had taken considerable risks on her behalf and ultimately laid down his life to protect her and Gabriel. She looked down at the mound of dirt and felt a rush of terror at the oblivion of it all. She looked around for something to mark the grave, anything that might signify that someone noble and important had died here. The larger grave was marked by a pile of broken rocks taken from the ground during the digging but she wanted something more distinct for the Ghost, something that had clearly been put there by man, not nature. She tried to think what Gabriel would do and when she re read his note she had her answer.

'You OK?' The voice surprised her and she turned to find Tariq close by, his AK47 assault rifle resting across his crossed legs.

'Yes,' she said. 'Come with me. I might need your help.'

The Operations Room had been looted since the last time she'd been there. The large topographical map still filled the back wall but all the smaller maps and anything else portable or valuable enough to take had gone. The solid block of carved black

50

granite where she had found Gabriel's note lay where she had left it, half-buried in discarded paperwork and scrolls of seismic data printouts. Liv swept them aside, revealing the carved letter T in the centre of the stone with smaller symbols surrounding it: the dots outlining the constellation of Draco; a symbol of a tree; a simple human figure. Someone had taken a rubbing of both sides of the stone and she was momentarily distracted by it, picking up the curl of paper and staring at the dense symbols lifted from the other side of the stone. There was something in them, something calling to her like a distant voice. She folded the sheet, slipped it into her pocket and grabbed hold of the chipped edges of the stone, hauling it across the table with arms that were already exhausted after an afternoon of hard digging.

'Let me,' Tariq said, taking it from her and hugging it to his chest.

'Thanks,' Liv said, 'follow me.'

The Starmap thumped down onto the Ghost's grave, the weight of it pressing into the loose earth, the carved T-shaped cross standing out in the centre of the stone. It seemed appropriate somehow, marking his grave with the Tau, a religious symbol from before the great religions had even been born. There would be no mistaking the significance of this grave now, or the importance of the person who rested here.

'I need to go and see to the horses,' Tariq said. 'You should come inside the compound, it's getting dark and it's not safe for you out here.'

'I'm fine. I'll just be a minute.'

Tariq nodded and drifted away, leaving Liv alone by the grave.

She stared down at the stone. Most of the text was on the other side of it, but she reached into her pocket and pulled out the rubbings she had found in the comms room, her eyes seeking the sheet containing the symbols that were now hidden.

The text was written in two languages. One was the lost language she had been able to understand when she was carrying the Sacrament. She concentrated on the symbols and discovered that, even though the Sacrament had left her now, she could still understand it:

The Sacrament comes home and The
Key looks to heaven
A new star is born with a new king on Earth to
bring order to the end of days

She frowned and felt a coldness creep over her. The first line was clear enough because she had lived it: she was the key that had unlocked the Sacrament, carried it out of the Citadel and brought it home to this lost place in the desert. But that was where her understanding ended. The second line suggested something else entirely, something still to come – something ominous that would be heralded by the arrival of a new star. She looked up at the evening sky, still too bright for the first stars to show. All the other prophecies, the ones that had brought her to this place, had outlined the future in ambiguous terms and with various possible outcomes. This one seemed too absolute, a star would appear and that would be it, the end of days – whatever that meant. There had to be something else here, something in the second block of symbols.

She studied them now, strange icons that looked like no language she had ever seen with the lines of different constellations weaving in and out of them: Draco, Taurus, the Plough.

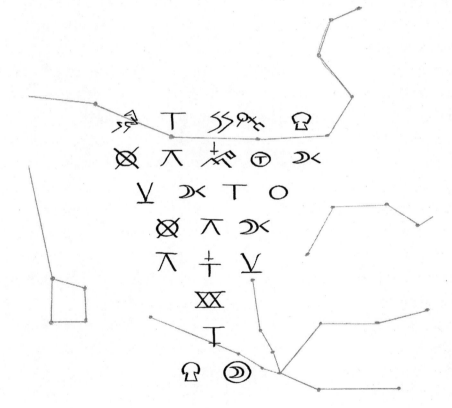

The symbols were crude and simple but when she concentrated on them the strange facility she had with language, her parting gift from the Sacrament, did not reveal their meaning. Instead, her head filled with impressions of things and feelings, some of them hopeful, some of them disturbing. She considered each symbol individually – a river, an eagle, a skull – trying to link them together into some kind of narrative, like piecing together fragments of an ancient truth she had once known and now forgotten. But though she felt she understood something of what each symbol individually represented, their collective meaning continued to elude her.

She spent a long time studying the symbols, but in the end, the earth turned, the sun set and the symbols faded to darkness before her eyes. And though Liv had not pinned down anything close to a translation, the emotions they had summoned remained. And the overriding thing they had left her with was a sense of foreboding. Whatever was coming, whatever was written on the ancient stone, she could feel its power and she feared it.

CHAPTER 10

They arrived at the Goddard Space Flight Center a little after ten, just as the storm got about as bad as it was going to get. Rain gusted into the car as Shepherd cracked a window to flash his pristine ID. The guard handed him two security passes and a visitor's map and directed him to one of the smaller executive staff parking lots by Building 29, the huge hangar-like structure that sat in the middle of the complex. Shepherd hadn't been here for almost ten years but as he slid the Crown Vic into gear and hissed through the puddle under the raised barrier, it looked like nothing had changed much at all.

Building 29 rose out of the howling night, a huge white block of a building with two strips of darkened windows on the ground and first floors and none at all on the other four. Most of the offices and control centres inside Building 29 didn't need windows, drawing their views from deep space rather than the Maryland countryside.

Shepherd slowed as he drove past the entrance. There were lights on inside but he couldn't see anyone. Maybe it was the late hour, or the weather, or the fact that the Christmas holidays were just around the corner – but the whole place seemed deserted. He eased the car round the edge of the building and the headlights lit up a figure wearing a rain slicker, the hood pulled right over his head in a way that made him appear almost monastic. An arm extended from beneath the wet folds and pointed to two empty parking bays with signs in front of them showing they were reserved for senior project directors. Shepherd drew the car to a halt and the figure glided over to Franklin's side of the car, producing a NASA golfing umbrella and popping it open just as Franklin opened his door.

'Mike Pierce, Chief of Security,' a voice rumbled from beneath the hood. He held the umbrella up for Franklin as he got out of the car and glanced at Shepherd as he did the same. Shepherd saw the eyes take him in, make a quick decision based on seniority and logistics then turn to usher Franklin away beneath the cover of the umbrella, not bothering to wait for the junior agent. The van that had followed them all the way from Quantico pulled in next to him, sending a wave of cold water arcing onto the back of Shepherd's legs. He locked the car and splashed across the tarmac after the umbrella. He figured if the techs could find fingerprints on cotton and microscopic traces of DNA in a sterile room, they could probably find their way into a building without his help.

Stepping through the open service door into the clean, white-walled corridors of Building 29 was like jumping through a time-portal back to a previous life. Because there were no pictures on the walls and no unnecessary furnishings – to help maintain the sterile conditions required in the 'clean rooms' at the heart of the building – everything looked exactly as it had the last time Shepherd had set foot here.

'Mike Pierce.' The hooded man crushed Shepherd's hand in a wet grip. 'We met before?' The eyes studied him from within the frame of a too-large face made bigger by the absence of hair. He looked like a weightlifter gone to fat but who still had some steel at his core and clearly felt a need to prove it whenever he shook another man's hand.

'I was here for a few months back in spring '04,' Shepherd said, letting go of Pierce's hand to prompt him to do the same.

Pierce shrugged out of the rain slicker in a shower of water and draped it over a seat by the door. 'I don't recall any kind of Bureau investigation back then.'

'Don't be fooled by the lines around the eyes,' Franklin cut in. 'Agent Shepherd here is still wet behind the ears as far as Bureau work goes. He's just here to help walk me through the tricky science parts.'

'I worked on Explorer for a while,' Shepherd explained as a bang behind them announced the arrival of the others heaving various boxes of gear out of the rain and in through the narrow service door.

57

'Looks like the gang's all here,' Franklin said. 'Lead on, Chief Pierce: tell us what you know.'

'Well pretty much everything is in the report,' Pierce said, closing the door behind them then swiping a card through a lock to gain entrance to an inner hallway. 'At 20.05 this evening the main system network servicing the Hubble Space Telescope was subjected to a sophisticated cyber attack. Merriweather, the technician who was on duty when it happened, is waiting in the control centre to go through all the specific details for you.'

'What about Dr Kinderman?'

'Still no word. I've tried contacting him on all his numbers, sent emails, even got Merriweather to ping him on Twitter and Facebook. Nothing. His cell phone was found in his office, which appears to have been ransacked.'

'Anyone else been in there since Kinderman went missing?'

'Just myself and the technician who found it.'

'OK, let's start there.'

Pierce swiped them through another security door and pointed to an office door halfway down the corridor.

Shepherd had been in Kinderman's office a few times before, once when he had started working here and again on the day he left. It was something of a tradition at Goddard, being paraded in front of the chief on your way in and out for a chat and a pep talk. He remembered being struck on both occasions by Kinderman's extraordinary neatness and precision, a memory that jarred heavily with the chaotic mess of files and paperwork now covering most of the floor.

Franklin surveyed it all from the door while he pulled on a pair of blue Nitrile gloves he'd produced from his jacket pocket. Shepherd felt hot blood rising up his neck as he realized he'd left his own back in the car.

Franklin stepped into the office and made his way through snowdrifts of paperwork towards the centre of the room. He stood for a moment, turning slowly, taking it all in: the neat, uncluttered desk; the crooked photos on the wall of various presidents standing next to the same neatly-pressed man; the same man shaking hands with the King of Sweden as he received the Nobel Prize for his work in measuring the rate of universal expansion. In the world of astrophysics Dr Kinderman was the closest thing you could get to a rock star and Shepherd was finding it very hard to think of him as a suspect.

He felt something soft and cold press against the back of his hand and looked down to discover a pair of fresh gloves held low so Franklin wouldn't see them. He smiled his thanks at the PST who had come to his rescue and quickly pulled them on just as Franklin finished his silent appraisal of the room and looked up. 'OK boys,' he said, 'get to work.'

The two techs swooped into the room, one shaking open various-sized evidence bags, the other scoping every surface with a high-end camera that took both stills and video. Franklin joined Shepherd and Pierce back in the corridor. 'Looks like someone left in a hell of a hurry.'

Pierce nodded. 'When I first saw it I thought it was a break-in.'

'You still think so?'

He shook his head. 'Not when I saw that.' He pointed to a small book lying open next to the terminal keyboard. It was photographed and handed out to Franklin. It was a standard appointments diary, a double page to a week, every blank space crammed with small, precise handwriting. 'I was trying to find out where Dr Kinderman might be, but as you can see it wasn't much help.'

Franklin flicked through the pages until he arrived at the current week where the writing just stopped. The last entry was in today's date:

T

end of days

The rest of the diary was blank, as if nothing was going to happen ever again.

Franklin looked up. 'You said no one has been in this room apart from you and the person who found it like this.'

'That's right, just me and Merriweather.'

Franklin handed the diary over to one of the techs for processing. 'Why don't we go and say hello to Merriweather.'

CHAPTER 11

The Space Telescope Operations Control Centre was roughly half the size of a tennis court and smelt of warm circuitry and ozone. There were no windows in the room and therefore no daylight. The only illumination came from the occasional desk lamp and the combined glow of a few dozen flat-screen monitors facing a larger central screen. All of them were displaying the same message:

MANKIND MUST LOOK NO FURTHER

A man stood as they entered, his clothes and horn-rimmed glasses making him look like he had beamed in from the fifties.

'Merriweather, these are Special Agents Franklin and Shepherd from the FBI.'

They shook hands. Franklin nodded at the big screen. 'That the same message you found on Kinderman's computer?'

'Yes, sir –' He cleared his throat and stared up at the screen rather than anyone in particular. 'Well, I mean it was part of the program that did it – I think. Or rather – this message was the last thing that uploaded and now it's everywhere and we can't take it down. The whole system's locked.'

'Any idea what it might refer to?'

Merriweather blew out a breath and raised his eyebrows. 'Hubble's a telescope, all it does is look at stuff – it could refer to anything.'

'It's not looking at anything any more though is it?'

Merriweather shook his head and Shepherd felt for him. He knew how attached people got to the projects they were working on, how they often became the most meaningful relationships you had. Hubble had just been attacked, possibly put out of action for months, and Franklin was talking about it like someone had dented a car.

'Talk us through the sequence,' Shepherd said, trying to steer the conversation back to the investigation. 'What was the first physical manifestation of the virus?'

'It hit the guidance system first. That was when I knew it was serious and went looking for Dr Kinderman. I found his office in a mess and this message on the screen. Actually no, first there was a command box with what looked like a decaying googolplex in it, *then* the message popped up.'

'Tell me about the googolplex.'

'Wait a second,' Franklin jumped in, 'would you mind translating for those of us who flunked Physics.'

'A googolplex is a mathematical term for a

62

particularly long number,' Shepherd said, his eyes staying on Merriweather. 'It's where we get the word "Google" from. All those zeros you get when a search comes back refer to the googolplex. And the fact that it was decaying simply means it was getting smaller.'

Franklin nodded. 'OK, got it.' He turned to Merriweather again. 'So a big number flashed up on the screen followed by this message?'

'Yes, sir. I think the googolplex was probably something to do with the initialization of the malware and I just happened to be there to see it.'

'And you were alone in the control room when all this happened?'

'Yes.'

'Is that standard practice?'

'No. I mean usually there are at least . . . everyone else was at the party.' He looked at Pierce for support.

'Merriweather volunteered to man the graveyard shift,' Pierce said. 'I checked on the staff rota. He was the only one here.'

'Mighty public spirited of you, staying back here to watch the store while everyone else gets to go off and party. Not so great that that's when the store got knocked off though, huh?' Franklin stared hard at Merriweather for a long few seconds then smiled in the way Shepherd was fast getting used to. 'Don't worry, son. I reckon you're too smart to hang yourself out to dry by throwing a spanner in the works on your own watch. Tell me about Dr Kinderman, when was the last time you saw him?'

Shepherd recognized the interview method Franklin was using. He was moving the questions around, rapidly changing topic and tone to give the subject no time to think and shake away any subterfuge they might be clinging to. It was a technique you used on someone you thought might be lying.

'He was still in his office at around five thirty. I walked past on my way to get a snack before everyone else left.'

'Did you speak to him?'

'No. He was at his desk, working.'

'Did he seem anxious to you?'

'Not that I could tell.'

'Did you notice him acting strangely at all in the past few days?'

Merriweather shrugged. 'I can't really say. Dr Kinderman doesn't exactly conform to conventional notions of behaviour.'

Franklin took a deep breath and seemed to double in size. 'Listen, son, you can either choose to help us or you can choose to be obstructive, and one of those options is a Federal offence and comes with jail time. Just answer the question.'

Merriweather's face went blank, like a shutter had just come down and Shepherd realized Franklin had taken a seriously wrong turn. Threats wouldn't work with someone like Merriweather. His loyalty to the project would be fierce and

64

would far outweigh any personal agenda or self-regard. NASA was like a religion, and the faithful did not abandon their beliefs just because someone threatened them.

'Listen,' Shepherd said, cutting across Franklin to try and rescue the situation. 'I know what you're thinking: there's no way Dr Kinderman would do this, am I right?' Merriweather looked at him blankly, the shutters still down. Shepherd was aware of Franklin glaring at him, furious that he had broken rank and taken over the questioning. 'I know exactly what you mean about him being unconventional. I crunched some data here on one of the last Explorer missions, remember that?'

Merriweather nodded. 'They shut it down a while back.' His voice sounded hollow, like he was talking about someone who had died. In that moment Shepherd knew exactly where all his nervousness was coming from and it wasn't guilt: it was fear for what would happen next. 'Tell me what happens if you can't re-establish contact with Hubble?'

Merriweather looked up, locking eyes with Shepherd for the first time. 'The only way to reboot it would be to manually restore the system.'

'So you'd have to launch a mission. Someone would have to physically go into orbit to fix it?'

Merriweather nodded.

'And is that likely?'

Merriweather took a deep breath and let it out slowly. 'No.'

'Why not?'

'Because of James Webb.'

'Anyone mind telling me who the hell James Webb is and what he's got to do with any of this?' Franklin said, directing the question to the room.

Merriweather took off his glasses and rubbed at the indentations they'd left on the bridge of his nose. 'James Webb was the architect of the Apollo programme, the one who put a man on the moon. But in this case it's not a *who* it's a *what*.' He sank down at the laptop he'd been working on and typed something. The screen filled with an image of what looked like a wide flat coffin with a golden satellite array on top like a sail. 'Say hello to Hubble's successor, the James Webb telescope. It's bigger, will have a much higher orbit and will see much, much further. They're building it right now. My guess is if we can't fix Hubble from down here then they won't bother fixing it at all. They'll just shut us down and wait for James Webb to come online.'

'And you'll most likely be out of a job?' Shepherd said, knowing exactly how painful that felt.

Merriweather nodded.

'Is that why you think Dr Kinderman couldn't be involved,' Franklin said, picking up the line of questioning, 'because he wouldn't sabotage his own project and betray his colleagues?'

Merriweather shrugged. 'Why would he do it? Why turn his back on his life's work, all of our work? It doesn't make any sense.'

Franklin pulled out a chair and sat next to Merriweather, bringing his eye level down to his. 'People do all sorts of things for all sorts of reasons, son.' His tone had softened considerably. 'But if Dr Kinderman was coerced in some way, if someone put him in a situation that forced his hand in this then we can help him. If he's in danger we can bring him to safety. So anything you can give us, anything at all that might help us understand what has happened here will be a great benefit. And you won't be being disloyal, you'll be doing him a favour.'

Shepherd had to hand it to the old bastard. He might have pitched it wrong at the start of the interview but he was playing it pitch-perfect now.

Merriweather balanced his glasses back on his nose and ran his thumb along the line of his lower lip. 'OK,' he said, punching a new command into the laptop. The image of the James Webb telescope was replaced with streams of code. 'I've been trying to pin down the virus ever since it was uploaded but whoever designed it knew what they were doing and covered their tracks unbelievably well. The only way I can see anyone getting a program big enough to do what it did past the network security would be by junk streaming it.'

Franklin glanced at Shepherd, one eyebrow raised in a question mark. 'Junk streaming is when you attach tiny bits of code to genuine traffic. They're too small to be picked up by the firewalls so they pass through it and then activate and clump together when they're on the other side. It's a bit like sending component parts of a bomb onto a plane one piece at a time then building it on board. But in the same way, if one piece doesn't get through or gets corrupted in transit then the whole thing won't work.'

Merriweather continued to tap commands into the keyboard. 'But uploading the virus is only part of the story,' he said. 'What it then managed to do was very sophisticated and precise. It didn't just knock out the comms and send Hubble spinning off into space. It actually reprogrammed the guidance systems causing the onboard rockets to fire and carefully move Hubble out of position.'

'Dangerously so?'

Merriweather glanced up at him. 'Sir?'

'I mean has it been effectively weaponized? Is it currently hurtling towards Manhattan or Washington?'

'No, no – nothing like that.' He turned back to the laptop, finished his sequence of commands and hit *Return*.

High on the wall next to the main screen four rows of red LED numbers flickered into life.

'See that top figure – 569, that shows the telescope's current altitude in kilometres. As long as the number doesn't start getting smaller there's no danger of Hubble crashing back to Earth. So far it hasn't changed. The next two readings are the relative long and latitudinal positions and the fact that they are changing shows that Hubble is drifting, but in a very controlled way. But it's the last reading that's the most interesting and seems most relevant to the message. That shows us where Hubble is pointing. Before the attack it was in the 270-degree range, locked onto a piece of thin space in the constellation of Taurus. But now it's shifted round to dead zero where it's remained ever since. Zero degrees is the home position. It means Hubble is now pointing directly at Earth.'

Shepherd glanced at the message shining out from every screen – MANKIND MUST LOOK NO FURTHER – its meaning more resonant and emphatic now the instrument of man's furthest gaze had been turned inward.

'You think this could be some kind of cover up?' Franklin asked. 'Maybe Hubble saw something out there and Kinderman didn't want anyone else to know about it, so he put up this warning and turned the telescope around so no one else could see it?'

'Maybe. Hubble's not like a conventional telescope where you look through an eye-piece and see stars, it builds up images from the data it collects. People like me work on specific batches of gathered information and just see a tiny part of the puzzle. Dr Kinderman's the only one who gets to see the whole picture.'

Franklin turned to Pierce. 'Any chance we can take a look at the archives?'

'No,' Merriweather replied, hunching over the laptop and rattling in new commands. 'After the crash I initialized a system check to isolate any infected files. That's when I discovered this.'

A new directory opened listing dates running back for weeks. Merriweather clicked today's date and a new window opened.

It was empty.

He clicked another, then another, working his way back through the week, each file as empty as the one before. 'All the recent data has been wiped. I checked the backups too. There's no trace of anything Hubble has been looking at for the last eight months. It's all gone.'

Franklin nodded. 'So maybe Kinderman did see something – the only question is what?'

Shepherd's eyes flicked between the telemetry and the biblical message shining out of the screens. 'You said Hubble was investigating a piece of thin space before the attack.'

'In Taurus, yes.'

'Were you looking for something specific?'

'Not that I was aware of, I was just looking at edge radiation – Heaven data.'

Franklin turned to Shepherd. 'Could you kindly translate?'

'Sorry. The known Universe was created by a single event, the so-called Big Bang, which happened around fourteen billion years ago. Since then everything has been constantly expanding outwards. Thin space is where the edge of the Universe is closest to Earth. Beyond it lies whatever was there before everything else came into being. Some think this is where God resides.' He frowned as a new thought struck him.

'When the Hubble project was launched wasn't there a lot of noise and protests from various religious groups?'

'Yes,' Pierce answered. He stepped forward out of the shadows and into the light. 'I'd just started working here, had to run through protest lines to get to work sometimes: people waving doom and judgement placards in your face, calling it all a heresy, daring to gaze so far into heaven.' He stared hard at the message on the screen, his mind ticking behind his eyes. 'I didn't really connect all that with this until just now, but –'

He snapped to attention. 'Come with me gentlemen, there's something I need to show you.'

CHAPTER 12

Cold neon tubes *tinked* into life in the visitors' centre as Pierce held the door and Franklin and Shepherd hustled in out of the weather. It was a big, rectangular space large enough to accommodate the busloads of school kids who came here every day to look at the old rockets and dream of riding them to the moon. Shepherd had been one of them once.

'In here, gentlemen,' Pierce said, shrugging out of his rain slicker and punching a code into a door next to the ticket desk.

His office had none of the romance of the public areas. There were no pictures on the walls of man's extraordinary exploration in here, no forming galaxies or wonders of creation, just a framed photograph of Pierce in his State Trooper days wearing a dress uniform and looking a little more lean and a lot more mean than he did now. A coffee pot sat in the corner. The heating plate was turned off but the smell of burnt coffee still filled the room with a smoky aroma that twisted Shepherd's gut. He hadn't had time to eat before leaving Quantico and they hadn't stopped anywhere on the way. Franklin didn't seem to need food.

Pierce fitted a small key into a large filing cabinet and heaved open the bottom drawer. 'We get crank mail here all the time, mostly reports of UFO sightings and/or conspiracy theorists and moon-landing deniers who think Hubble is NASA's latest hoax and all the images are done in Photoshop. Most of it comes in as email but we still get some the old-fashioned way.' He lifted a well-stuffed hanging divider out of the drawer and started sorting through it. 'This past year it's gone nuts. I don't know if it's all this weird weather we're having, or the business in Rome that knocked the Church on its ass or what it is but something sure got the doom and damnation crowd all worked up. 'Bout eight months ago we started getting these.' He took a clear plastic wallet out of the divider and handed it to Franklin. It was full of postcards, all variations on the same theme – old-master style paintings showing a monumental tower under construction. 'They're all pictures of the Tower of Babel. We got the first one in May, then a new one on the first day of every month since. We date stamp everything when it comes in so you can see what order they arrived.'

Franklin snapped his Nitrile gloves back on and carefully tipped the cards out onto the desktop. He picked one up, stared at the strange painting for a second, one stone coil inside another cork-screwing up into the clouds, then flipped it over to read the handwritten message on the back:

73

And the Lord came down to see the city and the tower, which the children had builded.

The words transported Shepherd straight back to the oak-panelled horror of his school where his Latin master had started each term by reading the same passage from a well-thumbed leather Bible. 'The quote is from Genesis,' he said, 'the Tower of Babel story.'

'Yep, and they were all sent directly to Dr Kinderman,' Pierce added. 'The postmarks are from all over but the writing looks to me like it's the same person. I didn't know what to make of them when they first started coming in but we keep everything on file, just in case. Each month there was a different quote, always from Genesis and always referring to the Tower of Babel. Then last month we got this.' He pulled a single brown envelope from the file and handed it to Franklin. It too was addressed to Dr Kinderman only this time with a printed label. Franklin shook out a single sheet of folded paper and opened it to reveal a typed note:

Build not a tower into heaven for the glory of man.
Nor seek to gaze upon the face of God
For His judgement shall be upon you,
Thou Sodomite and member of the occult tribe,
And that right soon.
The servants of the Lord are watching.
You must destroy your tower

74

And avert your gaze from heaven
Lest your blasphemy bring destruction upon you
And upon all of the earth.
Sacrifice the tower or the faithful servants of the
  Lord
Shalt sacrifice you
And your blood shalt stand payment for your
  sins.

Novus Sancti

Franklin looked up at Pierce. 'You report this to State PD?'

He nodded. 'Fancy language aside it's still a serious threat. There's a crime reference number in the file.'

'Novus Sancti,' Franklin muttered. 'Does that mean anything to you?'

'It's Latin,' Shepherd said, 'it means "new holy" but by the context I would say it's being used here as a name.'

Franklin turned back to Pierce. 'Did the State-ies follow this up at all?'

'They registered the complaint, told Dr Kinderman to be extra vigilant, asked me to keep them updated on any new developments.'

'That'll be a "No" then.'

Pierce bristled. 'There were over four hundred murders in this state last year; they've barely got the manpower to investigate those, let alone divert resources to every crazy with an axe to grind.'

Franklin pointed to the fourth line. 'What does that mean – *Sodomite and member of the occult tribe* – are they saying he's a devil worshipper?'

'Not necessarily,' Shepherd replied. '"Occult" actually just means "hidden" or "secret". It could just as easily mean he's a freemason.'

'What about "Sodomite"?'

Pierce cleared his throat. 'Well that's a reference to . . . Dr Kinderman was – I mean I don't think he is now, but in the past he had . . .'

'Dr Kinderman is gay,' Shepherd cut in to put Pierce out of his misery. 'It's no big secret, it's mentioned in his Wikipedia entry. When he was a student he apparently had a brief fling with some guy who outed him when his star began to rise. There was a mild bit of tabloid interest at the time but it didn't fly very far. Dr Kinderman just made a statement confirming it and saying something like we all do foolish things when young. He also stated that for the past twenty years his only committed relationship has been with his work.'

'That true, do you think?' Franklin addressed the question to Pierce.

'Who can say? What Dr Kinderman did in his own time is nothing to do with me. He certainly spent a whole lot of time here. He was always around – he practically lived here.'

'Did he seem particularly concerned or surprised when this letter arrived?'

'Like Merriweather said, Dr Kinderman wasn't what you would call the conventional type. He didn't seem scared or anything like that. He listened to what the State Trooper had to say about being careful then got straight back to work.'

'What about religion – is Kinderman a man of faith?'

'No, at least not that that I'm aware of.'

'And how many other people are working on this project?'

'About forty or so.'

'Yet they only targeted him.'

'Dr Kinderman is the most high-profile and generally these kinds of stunts are for publicity, which is exactly why we try and play them down.'

Franklin nodded. 'We're going to take these away with us and run them through our labs, see if the paper or the ink talk to us at all. The guys in Kinderman's office are also going to have to remove his hard drive so we can go through it and see if there's anything there. Any security codes you know of that will make it easier for us to gain access would be much appreciated.'

'Of course.'

'You said Dr Kinderman spent most of his time here. Does he have an apartment on site?'

'No, but he has the next best thing. He has a house in Presley Park, just the other side of the road you came in on. You could walk it in less than five minutes.'

Franklin glanced through the window at the rain-whipped night. 'Thanks, Chief, but if it's all the same to you I think we'll take the car.'

CHAPTER 13

Shepherd drove. Franklin stared ahead, facing down the stormy night and saying nothing. Since voicing his suspicions about Shepherd's missing two years he had barely spoken to him at all. Shepherd guessed he was sore at him for butting in on his interrogation of Merriweather too. The silence had become an almost tangible thing between them, taking on presence and weight.

When he had applied to the FBI he had counted on the gap in his record not being a problem. He had not been arrested or done anything in those missing years to put him on any of the databases they checked when screening new candidates. As far as the standard computer searches were concerned he was clean. But Franklin was a duty-hardened agent with instincts honed by years of dealing with people in all their broken forms. He'd sniffed out the shadows in his story immediately. But trust worked both ways and he didn't know nearly enough about Franklin to risk telling him the truth.

Ahead – Turn left.

The flat voice from the sat nav punctured the

silence. Shepherd reached out and tapped the screen, broadening the scale of the map until the Space Center appeared directly North of them. Proximity to Goddard had obviously been way up on Dr Kinderman's wish list and the usual status symbols of cars and big grand houses didn't really matter to him. As Pierce had suggested, you could probably cut through the woods and walk to Presley Park faster than Shepherd had just driven it.

Turn right in twenty metres, then you will have reached your destination.

Shepherd turned into a narrower road and head-lamps swept across a row of evenly spaced houses, slightly smaller than those on the main drag.

'There!' Franklin pointed at a one-storey, brick-built rambler set back a little from the road. Shepherd pulled into the empty drive next to it and cut the engine.

The Kinderman residence was entirely unassuming. There was a small patch of grass in front, a tree planted in the centre and neat borders filled with utility plants that would pretty much look after themselves. There was nothing modern about it, no additions, no carport or garage. It still had the original steel and glass porch over the front door. Behind the low building a wall of tall trees surged and flowed in the wind. There were no lights on inside.

'Let's see if the good doctor is home.' Franklin popped open his door and stepped into the rain. Shepherd killed the headlights and followed.

The distance from the car to the house was barely ten metres but Shepherd was more or less soaked by the time he made it to the porch. Franklin was already leaning on the doorbell, listening to its chimes echoing inside the house through the loud drumming of rain on the glass overhead. He pressed it again and they listened out, standing uncomfortably close in the slender shelter of the porch as they waited for movement inside or a light to come on behind the pebbled glass surrounding the front door.

'Nobody home,' Franklin said after a suitable wait. 'Watch the street.'

He dropped down, stuck his Maglite between his teeth and started probing the lock with a pick he had taken from his pocket.

'Shouldn't we get a warrant first?'

'And wake up some poor old judge on a night like this?' The lock clicked and Franklin stood up. 'If we find anything we'll get a warrant, then we can find it all over again: no harm no foul.' He swapped the pick for his gun and held the Maglite in a fist-grip so the beam shone where the barrel was pointing. Shepherd automatically did the same, months of simulations on Hogan's Alley kicking in as adrenalin and muscle memory took over and the words of Agent Williams whispered in his head: *try not to put yourself in any situation where you may have to draw this weapon.*

So much for that.

Franklin took up a position by the door and

gestured for Shepherd to take the other side. 'Remember this is not a drill, Agent Shepherd. This is the house of a suspected terrorist we are entering and, though I don't think we'll find anyone inside, I'd rather be prepared than dead. So nice and slow, just like you were taught and do not move until you are covered.'

Shepherd got in position. Franklin reached forward, turned the handle and threw open the door in a single smooth movement.

Time stretched slow as the door swung wide revealing a yawning darkness beyond. Shepherd tensed, his pupils full wide, watching for movement. Franklin moved forward, gun first, the beam of his Maglite probing the dark in a sweep from left to right. Shepherd followed, keeping close, going right to left until the beam of his torch crossed Franklin's in the centre of the hallway.

No one there.

They moved quickly and silently through the rest of the house – cover and move, cover and move – until they had satisfied themselves that Dr Kinderman was not here and neither was anyone else. It didn't take them long. The house was not that big.

Franklin hit the lights and they stood in the middle of the modest living-room-slash-kitchen-slash-dining-room taking in what they had previously only glimpsed by torchlight.

If anything, the inside of Dr Kinderman's home was even less impressive than the outside. A small oak-floored hallway led away from the front door to three others: a small bathroom, a bedroom, and some wooden stairs leading down to the basement. 'Tell me, Agent Shepherd,' Franklin said, 'you ever seen inside a safe house or a terrorist cell?'

'No, sir, I have not.'

'Well, look around, they look exactly like this. Functional, clean, unlived in.'

'We don't know that he's a terrorist.'

'No, but the evidence is stacking up wouldn't you say?' He nodded at the large picture of Christ the Redeemer hanging above the fireplace, arms outstretched and looking down at the sprawling city of Rio de Janeiro. 'Pierce didn't think Kinderman was religious.'

'Maybe he just likes big statues, or Brazil.'

'Or maybe he found God on the quiet and felt so bad about sticking his telescope up the Almighty's nose that he switched it off and ran for the hills.'

Shepherd shrugged. 'I guess anything's possible.'

'I guess it is.' Franklin pointed at the bedroom. 'Take another look, see what you can find, I'll check the rest.'

The bedroom was as plain as the rest of the house, the picture hanging over the neat double bed the only clue as to the person who slept there. It showed The Pillars of Creation from the Eagle Nebula, clearly a favourite image for the man who had been responsible for discovering them. Shepherd felt odd standing here, in the private space of one of his heroes. It seemed like an intrusion and his presence implied a degree of complicit agreement in Dr Kinderman's as yet unproven guilt. He put it from his mind, swapped his gun for the blue Nitrile gloves and got to work.

The wardrobe held lots of white shirts, pressed and cleaned and still in their laundry wrapping, a few suits of the tweedy, academic kind Kinderman favoured and four pairs of identical black, wing-tipped shoes, polished and lined up on newspaper, ready to be stepped into. There was a gap where a fifth pair would fit, presumably the ones Kinderman was now wearing.

The drawers contained more clothes but no answers. There were no new death-threat letters stashed away at the back of the sock drawer, no drugs or guns or dubious pornography or bundles of money or anything else that implied a secret, dangerous life. Everything was neat, tidy and unremarkable. He finished his search and stood for a moment in the centre of the room, taking in its incredible ordinariness. It felt like Kinderman might have just stepped out for a late supper and be coming back soon. Part of him hoped he would, but the chaos of his office at Goddard told a different story. Shepherd flicked off the light and closed the door on his way out.

He found Franklin in the living room, hunkered down by the fireplace. 'Take a look at this.' He pointed at a fire basket containing a few logs, some sticks and several old newspapers. 'Notice anything funny about the papers?'

Shepherd picked one up. It was a copy of the *New York Post*, a relatively unusual paper to find in Maryland. On the cover was a picture of a man dressed like a monk, standing on top of a dark mountain with his arms outstretched, looking just like the statue in the picture above Kinderman's fireplace. Shepherd checked the date. The paper was eight months old. The story of the man climbing to the summit of the Citadel in the ancient city of Ruin had been more or less a front-page fixture in the spring. Recently Ruin had been in the papers again, this time because of the sudden outbreak of a viral infection that had resulted in the entire city being quarantined.

He picked up another paper, a copy of *USA Today* dated a few days after the *New York Post* and showing a photo of the same mountain, this time with smoke pouring out of a hole in its side, the headline read:

TERROR ATTACK CRACKS CITADEL WIDE OPEN

The other newspapers were the same, all covering versions of the same story and dated around the same time. Some showed the monk on top of the Citadel, others showed the moment he fell to his death, or pictures of bloodied monks being stretchered out of the mountain following the explosion, their bodies stripped to the waist by paramedics to reveal strange networks of ritualized scars from multiple cuts deep in the skin.

'Lots of people have old newspapers in their fire baskets,' Shepherd said, scanning one of the articles to remind himself of the details.

'Yes, but not normally a collection of different titles all covering the same thing. The Bureau got involved in this in a small way trying to help locate a couple of the terror suspects who were American. One was a female journalist from Jersey, the other an ex-army guy: Liv Adamsen and Gabriel Mann.'

'They're mentioned here.' Shepherd held up one of the papers and showed him a mugshot of a handsome-looking man in his early thirties with short dark hair and blue eyes and a pale, blonde woman with eyes so green they glowed beneath the poor print quality of the paper.

Shepherd picked up the last newspaper. On the cover was a photograph of a plump Cardinal looking imperious in his red and black robes beneath the headline:

CHURCH BANKRUPT: POPE'S RIGHT-HAND MAN IN SUICIDE SHOCK AT THE VATICAN

He remembered that one too, the biggest scandal to rock the Church in a long time. Something to do with mortgaging all the Church's treasures and buildings in order to fund some doomed oil venture in Iraq. Some of the more lurid tabloids had even suggested they were drilling for oil where Eden used to be.

'All from eight months ago,' Shepherd mused, dropping it in the basket with the rest, 'the same time the postcards started arriving.'

Franklin stood up and stretched the kinks out of his back as he paced the Spartan living room. 'So how does any of this link up? Does any of it link up? We've got an attack on government property that may or may not be connected to the attacks outlined in these newspapers. We got a missing person who's our number one suspect. We got a potential religious angle, which could shake out either as Kinderman seeing the light and going rogue, or somebody else putting the frighteners on him to do God's work for them – maybe even the same guys who were involved in these attacks eight months ago. What else . . .?'

Shepherd dug his notebook from his pocket. 'There's the Tower of Babel references and the death threat written in biblical tones and signed *Novus Sancti*. We also have the missing data, which also dates back eight months, though that could just be a coincidence.'

Franklin shook his head and wandered into the kitchen. 'I'm not a great believer in coincidence.' He stood by the sink with the lights off, staring out into the night. The ambient light from the street picked out a small strip of grass and the line of storm-shaken trees that marked the edge of the property and the beginning of the woods.

'Maybe we're massively overcomplicating things. Nine times out of ten it's about money. Look at this place, it's not exactly a palace.'

'But you heard what Pierce said, he was always at work, this is just where he slept.'

'Maybe, but he wouldn't be the first smart person in history who dug himself into a deep hole and then got bought by someone offering him a ladder.'

Shepherd thought about it and shook his head. 'I don't think it can be money. Dr Kinderman never struck me as the material kind and he won the Nobel Prize nine years ago.'

'You get paid for that?'

'You get a cut of how much money the Nobel Foundation made that year. It's usually something like a million – million and a half. If there's more than one winner they share it. Dr Kinderman won it on his own.'

Franklin whistled through his teeth. 'Man, I should have paid more attention in science class. Still I reckon I could easily burn through a million bucks in nine years. Maybe pick up some expensive tastes along the way and get myself in some situations that a blackmailer could get his hooks into.' Franklin took a last long look at the meagre, anonymous home. 'Come on, we're wasting time here. Let's head back to base, see what the techs have come up with. I might even buy you a burger on the way back – but that still don't mean I trust you.'

CHAPTER 14

The cross-hairs followed Franklin until he left the kitchen and disappeared from sight. The finger in the nonslip glove relaxed on the trigger and an eye flicked up from the scope.

Carrie Dupree was in the trees, back from the house a little and low enough on the trunk not to be shaken too much by the wind. She had been in position since way before the storm hit, waiting for Dr Kinderman to come home. She watched the lights in the house go out and listened through the surf sound of the wind-tossed branches until she heard the front door bang shut then a car start up and drive away.

She probed the darkness, everything glowing a phosphorescent green in the night-sight. The house remained dark and silent.

Nothing moved.

She felt a slight vibration in the sleeve pocket of her camouflage jacket and swung the rifle round ninety degrees to a neighbouring tree. She could just make out the slim outline of Eli, the hand holding the phone that had sent the alert making a chopping sign across his throat.

Time to pull out.

Exfiltration was fast and practised. She capped the scope and powered it down, slung the rifle crossways over her back then dropped down from her tree. Eli joined her and stood sentry while she broke the rifle down further and bagged it so it could be stashed quickly in the trunk of the car once they made it back to the road, then they headed away through the woods. Occasionally, they came across the stacked branches and litter of a den built by the neighbourhood kids who slunk from their houses and went feral in these woods. There was no one around now, the late hour and weather had seen to that.

They drew close to the edge of the trees and Eli stopped. The dark yard they had passed through earlier was now bright with light spilling from several rooms in the house and a TV was blaring loudly somewhere inside. Too chancy to go back that way and risk being seen.

Eli pointed right and moved off, keeping the boundary lines of the properties in sight as they moved through the trees looking for another way out. They found a quiet house, no lights on, no movement inside, no car in the drive, and no security lights pointing out at the yard ready to light up anything that moved across it. There were no toys or trampolines in this garden, just a lawn surrounded by a wooden fence running all the way round the property. Carrie wondered if it had been put up to keep the neighbourhood kids out. Either way, it wouldn't stop them.

She went first, springing over the fence and landing in a crouch, her hands feeling the cold, wet earth through her gloves. She heard the creak of the fence and squelch of Eli's boots as he followed her, crouching down behind her, so near she could feel him. She savoured the delicious closeness, a momentary distraction that made her slow to react.

The dog appeared out of the dark in an explosion of noise and teeth. It launched itself straight at her, a large, angry animal, black as the night, all muscle and rage. She turned and raised her arm to protect her face from the claws and the bite, but the dog did not reach her.

Eli's boot caught it just behind the head, turning the snarl into a yelp and sending it spinning away. It landed on its side, rolled and scrabbled to get to its feet but Eli was already on it, grabbing its rear legs and heaving it up, flipping it high with an arch of his back then down hard, smashing its head against the ground. Another yelp squeaked from it as the soft earth stunned it but did not knock it out. The dog clawed at the ground again, weaker now, its back legs kicking free from Eli's grip, desperate to get away from the source of its pain.

Eli stepped forward, his trailing leg whipping through the air, connecting with the dog's throat in a wet thud that snapped the dog's head back.

This time it did not yelp at all because its wind-pipe had been crushed. Its tongue lolled from its mouth, bloody and twitching as it fought for breath. Casper moved over it, raising his boot high and bringing it down hard, stamping the life out of it repeatedly in fury until Carrie laid a hand on him, pulling him away and past the house to where the streetlights swayed in the wind.

They vaulted the chain-link gate with the BEWARE OF THE DOG sign on it, keeping in the shadows of the trees until they made it back to the little league baseball park where they'd left the car, well away from the street lights.

Eli got in the passenger seat. Carrie drove, the heater on full, filling the car with dry air and noise, neither of them speaking until they were a couple of miles down the road.

'You OK, baby?'

Eli didn't reply.

Carrie let it slide and settled into the roar of the heater and the rumble of the road, worrying about what lay beneath his silence.

She had never seen him kill anything before tonight and there had been something magnificent and terrible about the way he had done it. Eli wasn't physically imposing, if anything his height made him appear slimmer than he was, but there was something about the way he carried himself, some-thing lean and dangerous, like an old-fashioned razor – and she knew where it came from.

Like all true lovers, part of their intimacy lay in

the secrets they shared. Eli had confessed his in the mission military hospital where he'd been released after being locked up for seven months for *nearly* killing someone. One by one he had detailed, in a quiet expressionless voice, all the people he had killed in his relatively short life. It had started with the kid in Juvie who had tried to touch him somewhere he shouldn't. He hadn't expected the skinny, younger boy to fight back and had been caught off guard when he did, slipping on the tiles in the shower block and cracking his head. Eli told her how he had jumped on top of the boy, grabbed his hair and hammered his skull against the tiles until someone else found them and dragged him away. Eli's tormentor had died in the infirmary two days later.

I just wanted to make sure he stayed down – he told her – *but then I couldn't stop.*

This first homicide kept him institutionalized until he got a release into the Army where his country turned his aggression to good use. Carrie had listened as he listed all the people he had killed while in uniform, stroking his head and letting him talk them all out like he was exorcizing demons. Killing was his gift, but also his curse, and she knew his true secret, whispered to her alone in the quiet of a psychiatric cell he'd been sent to after killing a sergeant in a fight over a toothbrush:

I like it – the killing. I like it. It's the only thing I ever been good at. But killing is a sin, so I must be damned to all hell for liking it so.

92

She looked across at him now, the muscle in his jaw working in that way it did when something was eating him up inside.

'Hey baby, it's OK, honey – you were only looking out for me,' she told him. 'Saving someone you love from hurt is a righteous thing to do. And some poor dumb animal don't have no immortal soul.'

He shook his head. 'Animal or a man,' he said, 'it's all the same for me.' He stared ahead, his face lit by the wash of oncoming headlights, his eyes focused on something darker than night.

She wanted to stop the car and hold him, stroke his head, but they needed to get away. Stopping a car by the side of the road in this weather was just inviting some do-gooder or a highway cop to come snooping, and they couldn't afford to be seen.

'You want to make the call? Tell Archangel what we saw at the house,' she said. 'I'll look for a motel where we can rest up.'

Eli dug a phone from his pocket, the screen lighting up his face as he searched for the number. He switched it to loudspeaker and the sound of dialling and connecting chirruped in the enclosed space.

Carrie had never been concerned with killing or death the way Eli and many other men like him seemed to be. She had heard all the arguments against the deployment of women in theatres of war and thought most of it was just horseshit. The first time she had watched an Iraqi tank commander's head snap back after she squeezed the trigger of her M24 she'd felt nothing, nothing at all. Never lost a single moment's sleep about it neither. And it was the women who gave birth, and then watched their sons and husbands go off to war. Living on when everything you'd loved had been taken away, that was the really tough stuff. Killing was easy.

The ringing tone purred amid the rumble of the road. Someone picked up and Archangel's voice joined them in the car.

'Is it done?'

'No,' Eli said, 'he wasn't there, but someone else was. Cops of some sort I think.'

'Did they see you?'

'No.'

There was a pause on the line. 'He can't have gone far. Let me see what I can find out. Go somewhere safe and wait for my call, until then God bless and keep you both.'

Then the phone went dead.

PART II

Blessed is he that readeth, and they that hear the words of this prophecy . . . for the time is at hand.

Revelation 1:3

CHAPTER 15

EIGHT MONTHS EARLIER
Badiyat Al-Sham – Syrian Desert
Northwestern Iraq

Liv woke just as dawn was starting to bleed into the eastern sky. She was lying on the ground next to the grave of the Ghost, her head full of strange symbols and the sky full of fading stars.

She had been dreaming she was back in her old apartment, watering the hundreds of plants that lined the walls. She had grown plants since she was small, squeezed between her father and her brother as they potted and seeded like other kids baked cakes with their moms. It was her dad's way of spending time with his kids and getting them to help out with his gardening business. He taught them the names of everything, though he also let her make up some to keep her amused. Some of them had stuck. To this day she still called **Physillis** an orange eyeball tree.

She opened her eyes and the loamy smell of the earth escaped from her dream and drifted across the desert. It took her a few moments to recall where she was as she hung for some blissful heartbeats suspended between the past and the present before she remembered. The apartment was gone, incinerated along with everything in it by someone who had been looking for her. Her father was dead, so was her brother – and Gabriel was gone. It all struck her like a fresh loss, so hard that she just wanted to curl up again, go back to sleep and escape into the bliss of her dream.

Then she heard the noise, like the soft hiss of a huge snake.

Instinctively she rolled away from it, right across the grave, coming to rest so she was staring across the stone at the source of the sound.

Tariq was curled up and sleeping on the ground nearby, his AK47 cradled in his arms, his mouth forming words that escaped as sibilant whispers from his dream.

– *Saa'so Ishtar – Saa'so Ishtar –*

She watched him twitching in his sleep, whispering the words over and over until the lightening sky woke him too.

'What is Ishtar?' She fired the question at him while he was still blinking awake. He rubbed his eyes with the heels of his hands then looked over at her, his forehead creased in a question. 'You were saying it over and over in your sleep – what is it?'

'Ishtar is a goddess,' he said, pushing himself up and automatically checking his rifle for sand, 'an ancient goddess from the time when all these lands were green. She was the goddess of fertility, and love, and war. It was she who made everything grow and gave names to every living thing.'

Liv remembered her dream and the memory of naming plants by her father's side. 'I heard people calling me that – amongst other things.'

Tariq unwrapped the keffiyeh from around his neck, shook it out and carefully laid it on the ground. 'There is an old tale,' he said, as well-practised hands removed the magazine from his rifle, ejected a shell from the breach then began taking it to pieces. 'It is a nomad tale from the ancient times. It tells how Ishtar was tricked by jealous men and made prisoner in the caves of the underworld. She was kept in darkness, away from the sun, to make her weak. Her powers were stolen so that the men who had imprisoned her might live as gods, never ageing and never falling ill. And because of this the lands that had been nourished by her dried up and everything died.' The top cover of the rifle and the recoil spring were carefully laid in turn on his keffiyeh.

'But the story also tells that when time reaches the end of its long road Ishtar will escape from the darkness and return again, bringing back the water so the land may be reborn.' He blew hard into the firing chamber, inspected inside then did the same with the other parts he had removed. 'And you brought the water, that is why they call you Ishtar.'

Liv laughed. 'I'm an unemployed, homeless reporter from New Jersey. Does that sound like a goddess to you?' She stood up and stretched the kinks out of her back. 'Listen, you said yesterday you could take me anywhere I wanted to go. You think you could take me as far as the Turkish border?'

'If you wish,' he said, snicking his rifle together again with impressive speed and smacking the magazine into place. 'But first, let me show you something.' He rose from the ground and slung the rifle over his back, heading around the perimeter fence to where the holding pits had been dug. They had been intended to catch the overspill of crude oil from the central well but were now brimming with water. Tariq helped Liv up the side of one of the banks and pointed past the edge of the second pit. 'There,' he said. 'You see it?'

From her elevated position Liv saw how the water had breached the holding pits in several places, creating rivulets that snaked away across the baked earth, carving new channels as they went.

'The blood is flowing back into the land,' Tariq said. 'And see –' he pointed along the edge of the water '– the land is starting to live again.'

All along the banks of the new rivers, green shoots were bristling. 'See there, we call that Ya'did or skeleton weed. And there, you see those tiny yellow flowers?'

'Groundsel,' Liv said. 'And that is Artemisia, or some other sort of ephemeral grass; and that looks like a tamarisk seedling.'

Tariq turned to her smiling. 'You see, you know the plants, you can name them all.'

Liv shook her head. 'Don't read too much into it. My dad was a horticulturalist and I had no mother so I grew up digging and planting instead of playing with dolls, I got dirt in my blood.' She followed the lines of the water to where the heat rippled the air. In the distance a column of dust was rising, another illusion to raise her hopes that Gabriel might be returning. She stared at it, waiting for it to melt away like her hopes always did. Only this one didn't. 'Someone's coming,' she said, hope swelling in her chest.

Tariq looked up and saw it, his chin rising too as if he was sniffing the air. 'Horses,' he said, 'many horses.'

'Yours?' Liv gazed at the distant dust as if her eyes were the only things keeping it there, hoping maybe that the riders had gone looking for Gabriel and were now bringing him back.

'Maybe,' Tariq said, his hand unconsciously drifting to the shoulder strap of his rifle. 'We should get back to the compound — I have a bad feeling about this.'

CHAPTER 16

By the time Liv and Tariq made it back inside the compound the approaching dust cloud was clearly visible in the sky and everyone had emerged from the silver-sided buildings and gathered by the central pool, all eyes looking in the same direction, waiting for whatever was heading their way to arrive. With everyone gathered together like this, Liv realized how few of them were left. She counted thirteen including her – a mixture of oil workers and a couple of the riders who had stayed along with Tariq.

'Thirty riders!' a voice called from halfway up the steps to one of the guard towers. 'Maybe more.'

'Ours?' Tariq called back.

There was a pause as the man reached the top and raised a pair of field glasses to his eyes. 'No,' he shouted down, 'not ours.'

Tariq snapped to attention like a shotgun being closed. 'Close the gates.' He barked at a startled-looking rigger still wearing his white work overalls. 'NOW!' He watched the rigger scurry off then called back up to the watchtower. 'How long until they get here?'

'Five minutes, maybe less. They're riding pretty hard.' The man paused again and stared through the field glasses. 'They have guns.'

Tariq turned to the assembled few. 'Who knows how to operate the fifty-calibre cannons?' He was met with silence and a ring of frightened faces. 'What about rifles – can anyone fire a rifle?' A couple of drill technicians put their hands up nervously. 'Good, go and get weapons from the locker in the transport hangar and push some of the vehicles outside to give us cover. We'll use that as a fallback position and try and keep them at bay using the tower guns if we need to.'

Liv looked on with a sense of detachment. Part of her felt anxious about the approaching men and what their intentions might be, but another, stronger part felt that preparing to meet potential violence with more violence was the wrong move. The land wasn't even theirs and neither was the water running out of it.

'Stop!' she said. 'This is wrong, this is not how it is supposed to be. We should not fight. We should welcome them.'

Tariq looked at her as if she had gone mad. 'But they are riding here at speed and they are armed. Their intentions are clear I think.'

'And what of our intentions – if we meet them with closed gates and pointed guns, what does that say about us?'

'It says we are strong and we are prepared to defend what is ours.'

'But this isn't ours. A few days ago I had never even set foot here and neither had you. And now you are prepared to take men's lives and risk your own for it? Doesn't that strike you as insane?'

'It is the way of things. It has always been the way of things.'

'But things can change. People can change. Open the gates and put down your guns. Whatever happens is meant to happen. Nothing here is worth fighting for. And nothing here is worth dying for either.'

CHAPTER 17

Shepherd drove through the barrier and back into Quantico a little after midnight, just as the storm was finally blowing itself out. Franklin had been on the phone most of the way. He'd called O'Halloran first to give him a pared down headline account of what they'd discovered at Marshall, then spent the rest of the time liaising with the tech guys who had finished processing Kinderman's office and were now heading back. Shepherd drove squinting through the spray and the darkness, trying to glean what he could from Franklin's half of the conversations and wondering what would happen when they got back to base.

The van was already parked up by the laboratories when Shepherd pulled up next to it and shut off the engine.

'Thank you, driver,' Franklin said. 'That will be all.' He slid out of his seat and was already halfway to the entrance before Shepherd managed to fumble his own door open.

'What do I do now?' he called after him.

Franklin didn't look back. 'I want your report

105

on my desk by 0800. After that you're free to return to your training.'

Shepherd got a sinking feeling in his guts. He had suffered Franklin's disdain all the way through the few short hours he'd been on this investigation that he hadn't wanted to be assigned to in the first place, but now, as it was about to be taken away from him . . . he desperately wanted to remain part of it.

He took a step forward, aware that Franklin was about to walk through the door. 'Maybe I should take a look at Dr Kinderman's hard drive.' Franklin stopped but didn't turn round. 'I can help sort through the data. Sift through the emails and the technical stuff to look for anything unusual. It's bound to be full of astronomical terms and acronyms that could easily confuse someone unfamiliar with the jargon.'

Franklin grabbed the handle, pulled open the door and stepped through without saying a word.

Shepherd watched it slowly swing shut: closing on his last chance. He was about to turn and walk back to the dorms when Franklin reappeared round the edge of the door. 'Report on my desk by 0800, Agent Shepherd,' he said. 'Until then your time is your own. So if you'd rather spend it staring at a computer screen than getting some shut-eye then maybe there's hope for you yet.' Then he shot him *the smile* and was gone.

CHAPTER 18

Liv felt the ground tremble as the riders poured through the open gates and quickly surrounded them on all sides. She kept her eyes fixed on the lead horseman who halted the line with his upheld hand and trotted on alone on his pale horse. He removed his keffiyeh as he approached, revealing a dust-rimed face burnt almost black around the eyes by years in the fierce desert sun.

'See who is with them,' Tariq whispered.

Liv scanned the line of riders and saw Malik smiling back at her. It was he who probably brought them here, though for what reason she could only guess at. She stepped forward, opened her arms and smiled. 'Welcome,' she said in fluent Arabic that surprised the rider. 'You must be thirsty after your long ride, your horses too.'

The rider looked down from his lofty position and circled her slowly, scrutinizing her down the curve of his long nose. She could smell the dust and dung of his panting horse, feel the heat radiating from its damp flanks as it was brought to a halt in front of her. The rider turned to his men. 'I was hoping Ishtar would have more meat on her,' he said loudly.

The riders erupted in laughter, Malik included.

He turned back, his lined face now split in a smile of his own to reveal an incomplete set of long, broken teeth. 'You don't look much like a goddess to me.'

Liv smiled, her eyes flicking to Malik then back to the rider. 'You shouldn't believe everything people tell you.'

'Are you calling me a fool?'

'No. Why don't you tell me your name, then I can call you that.'

He leaned forward, his worn saddle creaking beneath his shifting weight. 'They call me Azra'iel. You know what that means?'

It was an odd quality of her new fluency with language that she often saw images rather than meanings, and felt the words rather than interpreted them. Azra'iel. A picture formed in Liv's head of huge black wings and she felt fear. 'It means "Angel of Death".'

The broken smile returned. 'Maybe you are a goddess after all.' His hand passed across strips of bright ribbons on his chest and in a movement too fast to register Liv found herself staring down the barrel of a pistol. 'Maybe I put a bullet in your brain to find out.'

Before Liv could react Tariq stepped in front of her, shielding her body with his. 'Take it,' he said. 'It's the water you want, you do not have to kill to get it.'

'Do not tell me what I want. No one tells Azra'iel what he wants.'

'It's OK,' Liv said in English, moving from behind him, doing her best to ignore the gun as it swung back to point at her.

'What are you – American? English?' The rider said, picking up on the switch in language.

'American. I'm from New Jersey.'

Azra'iel sat high in his saddle and swept his arm across the desert landscape. 'This is where I am from. My family has lived on this land for two thousand years. We have seen the great Caliphs come and go, then the Mongols, and then the Turks.' He jabbed the barrel of his gun at the ribbons on his chest. 'Saddam Hussein gave me these himself for defending his Republic against the American invaders, but he was an idiot and now he is dead. I was not fighting for him, I was fighting for the land. And now the land belongs to me.'

Liv held his gaze and slowly shook her head. 'The land does not belong to any man,' she said. 'It is we who belong to the land.'

'You are wrong, goddess. It belongs to any man who will fight for it – this is what my people have learned – and you did not fight.'

'No. We welcomed you. We invited you to share it, in peace. Isn't that a better way?'

The jagged smile returned. 'Better for me.' He turned away and raised his voice so all could hear. 'This oasis is ours now. I give you a choice. You can leave or you can die. You have two minutes to fill your canteens. I advise you to take as much as you can. The desert is not as friendly or as welcoming as your goddess.' He turned his horse and started walking away.

'We could fall back to the transport shed,' Tariq whispered. 'There are guns there. We could make a stand. Or if we make a diversion when we head through the gates I think I might be able to make it to the top of one of the towers and turn the big guns on them.'

'Then what? Bury the bodies, wait for the next lot of people to show up and kill them too?'

'What else can we do? We won't last two days out in the desert without water. Better to fight and maybe die here quickly than slowly out there in the furnace.'

'Better not to die at all,' she said.

'You have something else in mind?'

She swept her hand through the water, her fingers dragging through the cool, wet earth at the bottom, remembering the symbols on the Starmap. 'No,' she said, watching the swirls of earth eddying in the clear water, turning it a dusty red. There was something familiar about all this, she had seen something like it in the stone. She tried to concentrate on it and bring it to the front of her mind but it continued to elude her, like something glimpsed at the edge of her vision. 'If you want to go, then go,' she said, turning to Tariq. 'I'm sure you could make it to Al-Hillah on foot before the thirst takes hold.'

'What about you?'

She glanced up at the gravesite, visible through the line of riders and the chain-link fence. 'I'm staying here,' she said, 'or as close as I can manage without getting shot.'

Her hand passed through the water again, sending larger clouds of red mud spreading in the water as she stood and walked towards the riders.

'Goodbye, Malik,' she said, as she passed through the line.

His smile faltered and he made as if to reply but she was already gone, striding towards the open gate and out into the desert without once looking back to see if anyone was following her.

CHAPTER 19

The National Cyber Crime Task Force was buried deep in the Maryland bedrock and housed a huge bank of central databases that fed the entire law enforcement network as well as hard drives and backup files relating to hundreds of thousands of cases – everything from simple internet scams and corporate fraud to online paedophile rings and major terrorist networks.

The main machine room was practically deserted by the time Shepherd stepped into its air-conditioned gloom. He had stopped to splash water on his face and grab something to eat after Franklin had failed to make good on his offer to buy him a burger, wolfing down a doughnut and a cup of coffee on his way over. No food or drink was allowed in the cyber crimes labs. A seated figure was silhouetted against three large flatscreen monitors on the far side of the room, his fingers punching code into a keyboard so fast it sounded like tap dancing. He turned at the sound of Shepherd's approach and smiled a greeting. 'Agent Franklin said you'd be along.'

Agent Smith was one of the senior instructors in the cyber crimes division. There was a rumour that did the rounds each year that the Agent Smith of the Matrix movies had been based on him and there was certainly more than a passing physical resemblance – same dark hair receding from a widow's peak, same sharp features on top of a whip-thin frame – but that was as far as the comparison went. The real Agent Smith was just about the friendliest instructor in the building, generous with his time and endlessly patient with those who were never going to pound the cyber beat but needed to understand enough to pass the module anyway.

'I've set you up with a ghost file,' he said, nodding at the terminal to the right of his.

Shepherd sat at the desk and assessed the data. In cyber crime there are two types of evidence: physical and digital. Physical evidence is the actual hardware itself. Often in the chain of evidence it has to be shown that a suspect has used a certain computer, so fingerprints or even microscopic flakes of skin beneath the keys of keyboards are sought to prove it. Digital evidence is different. Files and directories can be cloned or copied and worked on by several teams of people at once to crunch the data faster. These clones are called ghost files and Shepherd was looking at one now, an exact copy of everything on Dr Kinderman's hard drive. 'Find anything yet?' he asked.

Smith continued to machine gun code into his

terminal. 'The most interesting thing I've found so far is nothing.' He hit a key and folders started opening, rippling down his main screen like a deck of cards, every single one of them empty. 'Everything you would expect is there up until eight months ago, then there's nothing at all. No directories, no sub-directories, no caches. Whoever cleaned this out really knew what they were doing.'

Shepherd had been hanging on to the hope that Smith would find something in Dr Kinderman's personal files, an email, or a virus that had originated elsewhere with a pathway that might give them a new lead. But the efficiency and skill with which the drive had been forensically wiped just threw more suspicion on Kinderman. 'You want me to start checking through the older data, see what I can find?'

'You can if you want but I think it will be a waste of time. Anyone this thorough is unlikely to have left anything behind – I'm pretty sure anything incriminating on the drives would have been in the chunk of data that's now missing. I was just about to run it through CARBON, see what that throws up.' He hit *Return* and a progress bar popped up on the screen, then he sat back with a small grin on his face that had '*ask me*' written all over it.

'What's CARBON?' Shepherd obliged.

'*That* is something very confidential that I can only divulge to you now you are a serving Special Agent. But what I am about to tell you does not

get mentioned in the classroom, understood?'
Shepherd nodded.

'Back in the typewriter days, before photocopiers
even, the only way you could get an exact copy
of a typed document was to sandwich carbon
paper between two blank sheets. The force of the
typewriter letters striking the top sheet would leave
a carbon trace on the bottom one, producing a
copy. This application does a similar thing. It
records keystrokes, only the user doesn't know
anything about it. In fact very few people do.

'After 9/11, when homeland security became the
number one priority and the usual concerns for
civil rights and privacy went out of the window,
the US Government cut a very high-level deal with
all the major computer chip manufacturers. Not
sure if you know this but 99% of all the world's
microchips are made in South Korea. So you can
imagine, having the American government in your
corner when you've got North Korea as a neigh-
bour must have been a powerful persuader in the
discussions. Anyway the deal was simple. All they
had to do in exchange for Uncle Sam's undying
gratitude and future unspecified favours was to
modify their product a little. Ever since then, each
new chip produced has an extra partition of
memory built into it that doesn't show up on any
directory and can only be accessed by certain
approved law enforcement agencies with the right
software.' He pointed at the progress bar on the
screen as it closed in on 100%. 'CARBON.

Basically, they created the ultimate in Spyware. Normal virus protection doesn't even see it because it's not code, it's built right into the hardware.'

The progress bar disappeared and a document opened, crammed solid with words and numbers. 'The data is pretty raw,' he said, his fingers resuming their tap routine, 'and because of the covert nature of the technology the memory cache is relatively small to keep it hidden so it has to constantly dump old data to keep recording new stuff, just like media disks on security cameras. Usually it holds about a week's worth of activity. I'm just going to run a filter to split the data out a little and pick out any hot or unusual high-frequency words.' He executed a new command and another window popped open. 'This is where you can make yourself useful.'

Shepherd leaned in as words started to appear in the window, gleaned from the raw data. He recognized almost all of them. 'Ophiuchus is a constellation,' he said, working his way down the growing list. 'Andromeda is a galaxy and all those long numbers beginning with PGC are from the Principal Galaxy Catalogue. Red-Shift is an astronomical term for what happens to distant light . . .'

They continued in this way for several minutes, Smith highlighted everything Shepherd recognized until they reached the bottom of the list and Smith hit *Delete* to get rid of all the isolated words. There were now just two remaining:

MALA
T

Shepherd fished a notebook from his pocket and flipped back through the entries he had made at Goddard. There was the T again in the last entry Dr Kinderman had made in his diary:

T
end of days.

A thought struck him, something about the T and what it might mean in relation to Hubble. He found the contact numbers he had taken down and dialled one, checking the time as he waited for it to connect. The line clicked a few times before a ring tone cut in. Shepherd held his breath as he waited for someone to answer.

CHAPTER 20

Two floors above Shepherd, Franklin sat in a small office, door closed, his face illuminated by a different computer screen.

During his more than twenty years' service in the bureau he had learned a lot about himself. He knew he wasn't the most instinctive of investigators, didn't have the genius he had seen in some to ask exactly the right question at exactly the right time and had never been the one in a midnight incident room to make the single connection that pulled everything together. But he was dogged and he knew people. He could tap them like a tuning fork and listen to the sound they made. He always knew when the note was wrong and right now, with Shepherd, it was screeching like nails on a blackboard.

On the screen in front of him were Shepherd's Bureau application forms and resumé. He had been scouring them for the last twenty minutes, cross-checking the missing two years against social security records, credit-scoring agencies, anything that might give him a steer on where Shepard was and what he had been doing. So far the only small discrepancy he had found was on the standard

118

Questionnaire for National Security Positions. There was a new addition to the form, a declaration of faith, added by a Republican government riding high on the wave of post 9/11 hysteria. The Democrats had fought it, citing it as a dangerous erosion of the Constitution and its separation of religion and state, but the Republicans maintained that it would help identify Muslim candidates whose background and cultural knowledge could prove insightful in the war on terror. The bill had just squeaked through, but only after a compromise had been agreed that the new section should be optional and no candidate could be penalized for not filling it in. Shepherd had exercised that option and left his blank.

This in itself was unremarkable, but in Franklin's experience the only people who chose not to fill in the faith section were atheists. Shepherd's resumé showed he had spent several years at a hardcore Catholic boarding school and yet he hadn't ticked the box declaring himself to be Catholic. It was a small point but it added to Franklin's distrust of him. There was something hard-wired into his DNA that could not allow himself to entirely trust anyone who did not, in one way or another, have a healthy fear of God. It was one of the central tenets of the Irish, whispered down to him on whisky breath by his father and uncles when they were swaying with patriotism for a country none of them had ever set foot in: never trust a man who does not have God in his heart, and never trust a man who will not take a drink with you.

He sat back in his chair, reaching for his phone.

Thinking about his da' had tugged at something inside him. Maybe it was Christmas and the usual guilt that came with that. It was too late to call so he scrolled down the contacts list to the entry for Marie and opened up a blank text:

Something's come up. Got to work tomorrow so wont be able to make it home. Will call when I know when I can get away. Say sorry to Sinead for me.

He pressed *Send* and watched the message go. It was odd that he still thought of the house as home even though he didn't live there any more.

He closed all the files, shut down the terminal and was pulling his jacket off the back of the chair when his phone buzzed. Marie had got straight back to him.

What about saying sorry to me?

Franklin read the words and felt the ache inside him twist a little more. She was right of course but he'd got tired of apologizing to her a long time ago. He slipped his jacket on and headed for the nearest exit, swapping the phone for a crumpled packet of Marlboro. Another bad habit he had been trying for a long time to quit.

CHAPTER 21

'Hubble Flight Team.'

The line was noisy and Shepherd covered his other ear so he could hear better. 'Merriweather?'

'Speaking.'

'It's Agent Shepherd. Where are you?'

'I'm at Goddard. I've stepped out for some air and patched my calls through to my cell in case anyone needed me, how can I help?'

'Before the attack you said Hubble was exploring a piece of thin space in the constellation of Taurus.'

'That's right.'

'What do you use as shorthand for Taurus?'

There was a pause. 'If I was writing it down I'd use the astrological sign, a circle with two horns.'

'Not the letter T?'

'No.'

'What if you were typing it?'

'If I was typing it I would put in the whole word, or maybe just the first few letters and then predictive text would do the rest.'

Shepherd wrote T and TAURUS in his notebook

and added a large question mark after them. 'What about MALA?' he spelled it.

'Nothing, sorry. What are these in relation to?'

'They showed up in some raw data we recovered from Dr Kinderman's computer. It's probably nothing but we have to check.' Shepherd wrote MALA in his notebook and added a question mark after that too. 'Thanks, Merriweather. Sorry to have bothered you.'

'No problem. Listen, if you find anything else let me know, I'm as eager to get to the bottom of this as anyone . . .'

'I'm sure you are.'

'. . . and you can always get me on this number. I'll keep it patched through to my cell and leave it switched on just in case, though I'm planning on sleeping at my desk until either Hubble comes back online or someone forces me out of here at gunpoint.'

Shepherd smiled. 'I'm sure of that too. You take care, Merriweather. We'll sort this thing out, one way or another.' He put the phone down just as the door opened on the far side of the room and footsteps approached.

'Found anything?' Franklin's voice boomed across the empty space.

No – Shepherd thought.

'Yes,' Smith said, cheerful as ever. 'We recovered some CARBON data, and Agent Shepherd has been helping me sort through it.'

'Good for Agent Shepherd – anything useful?'

Shepherd looked down at his notes. 'We found a couple of unusual words. I think the T might refer to Taurus but I have no idea what MALA means.'

'Interesting.' Franklin leaned forward in a wash of coffee and cigarette smoke. 'Watch and learn, rookie.' He clicked on Google and typed MALA into the search window, hit *Return* and pages of results popped up. 'Sometimes the simple, direct route gets the best results.' He clicked on the top hit and a Wikipedia page opened up.

Mala: [*mala*] Name given to several historical anti-establishment groups and more recently a clandestine anti-religious terror organization.

Shepherd turned to Franklin who was smiling his trademark smile. 'If you'd paid a little more attention you would have seen the Mala mentioned more than once in those old newspapers we found back in Kinderman's pad. I told you the Bureau got involved. They were the terrorist group blamed for the attacks on the Citadel in Ruin.'

Shepherd turned back and continued to read.

The Mala are one of two pre-historic tribes of men whose combined history underpins the emergence of modern civilization and religion. The other tribe – the Yahweh – were victorious in a struggle to possess

123

and control a powerful ancient relic known as the Sacrament, which is believed by many to still exist inside the Citadel fortress in the southern Turkish city of Ruin, where it has been kept and protected since pre-history by the spiritual heirs of the Yahweh, a brotherhood of monks known as the Sancti.

Shepherd bristled at this last word. 'The letter sent to Kinderman was signed *Novus Sancti*.'

Franklin nodded. 'Looks like the religious angle is starting to fly. Read on.'

The Mala, having lost the Sacrament, were branded as heretics by the emerging Church and driven into hiding where they became synonymous with other anti-Church organizations such as the Illuminati. Because of the secretive nature of the Mala, little is known about them but many famous scientific figures are believed to have been members. These include Sir Isaac Newton, Galileo Galilei and many others, particularly in the field of astronomy, who often suffered persecution because their theories and discoveries challenged the teachings of the church. The church, in turn, continues to portray the Mala as terrorists, Satanists and worshippers of the occult.

Shepherd sat back in his chair. 'The letter also called Kinderman a member of the occult tribe.'

'Which would explain why Kinderman was targeted by religious freaks, though not why he would sabotage Hubble.' Franklin turned to Smith. 'Can you dig anything else out from Kinderman's drive? Maybe the context of these words will give us something to go on.'

Smith hammered in more commands, so hard that Shepherd wondered how many keyboards he went through a year. He hit *Return* and the program went to work.

Shepherd looked down at the question marks in his notebook, feeling that his usefulness to the investigation was slipping away. He was already thinking of the report he would have to write before dawn and getting through the next day of classes having had no sleep.

'Looks like he was talking to someone,' Franklin said.

Shepherd looked up and read the new messages.

408 Finished calculating co-ordinates for the **Mala** star, will send separately for you to check

408 Not much time left. May be needing our friends in **Mala** sooner than I thought.

'It's network mail,' Shepherd said, recognizing the repeated number as a directory code. 'It's an encrypted, stripped down version of email they use to share data between different departments and facilities. He was talking to someone else at NASA.' He grabbed the desk phone, hit redial and put it on speakerphone so everyone could hear. This time it barely rang before being picked up.

'Hubble Flight Team.'

'Merriweather, Shepherd again. Do you have a network mail directory handy?'

There was a pause punctuated by the muffled rattle of a keyboard. 'Yeah, I got it.'

'Could you tell me who has the directory code 408?'

Three muffled taps then a louder one. 'That's Professor Douglas.'

Shepherd felt the ground fall away beneath him. 'Joseph Douglas?'

'Who else.'

'OK, thanks.'

'You need anything else?'

Franklin leaned over. 'This is Agent Franklin. Please do not mention this conversation to anyone. Not even Chief Pierce, understood?'

'You got it.' Franklin disconnected before Merriweather could say anything else, picked up the handset and dialled the number for transport. 'Looks like I'll be heading back to Goddard with an arrest warrant.'

'Professor Douglas isn't at Goddard,' Shepherd said, 'he's at the Marshall Space Flight Center in Huntsville, Alabama. That's where they're testing all the components of the James Webb Telescope prior to launch. Professor Douglas is in charge of the whole project.'

Franklin's face went dark as he registered the implications. 'This is Franklin,' he barked down the phone at whoever answered. 'I need a ride, soon as humanly possible, to fly me as close to Huntsville, Alabama as possible.' He covered the mouthpiece. 'Make yourself useful Shepherd, find me the name of whoever is head of security at Marshall and get him on the phone.'

'You should take me with you.'

Franklin looked genuinely amused. 'Really? And why's that?'

'Because I know Professor Douglas,' Shepherd replied, sensing that the door closing on his part of the investigation might just be starting to open again. 'I used to be his student.'

CHAPTER 22

Carrie perched on the edge of one of the sunken motel beds watching Eli sleeping on the other. There wasn't much to the room: a bulky air-con unit built into the window; a fifties-style table with cuss words carved into it and two mismatched chairs swamped beneath their drying cammo jackets. They were pushed up against the solitary wall heater, steaming slightly and filling the trapped, mildewed air in the room with the fresh, wet smell of the forest.

The phone lay next to her on the worn counterpane. She could never sleep when she was waiting on new orders. It was a limbo state she had never relaxed into, something which came with command. The grunts could always sleep like babies, but the officers and NCOs were like parents, with all the responsibility and worry that came with that.

Outside the rain had settled into a steady drumming, like the noise Humvee tyres made over a decent blacktop. The only other sound came from an antique TV set bolted high on a wall. When they had first come into the room and switched

128

it on it had been tuned to a porno channel, the unmistakable fake panting making her fumble for a button to cut the sound or change the channel. She hadn't been quick enough. The screen had briefly flashed pink with the urgency of flesh before she managed to turn it off. Neither of them mentioned what they had seen, though she knew it had chimed with something unspoken in both of them. The TV was now tuned to a local news station with the volume low, in case anything came up that might be relevant or useful.

She glanced at Eli's sleeping form, feeling the frustration that, even though they were alone in this seedy motel room with the caved-in mattresses whispering of all the things they denied themselves, their still unfulfilled mission was keeping them apart. She just wanted it to be over so they could get married and finally be together, to face the coming judgement as man and wife, blessed in the eyes of God.

Eli let out a small sound, like a frightened animal. Eight times out of ten he would jolt himself awake, staring around for the horrors that came out to play when he slept. When she'd first met him in the mission hospital outside Kandahar, he couldn't sleep at all without screaming himself awake so this was an improvement. He was getting better and it was she who was making him so. If she had enough time she would heal him completely, but she wasn't sure how much time they had left.

The phone rang and she pounced on it, rising

from the bed and moving away to the furthest corner of the room.

'Hello.' She faced the wall and kept her voice low so as not to wake Eli.

'You were right about the people you saw,' Archangel's voice hummed in the earpiece. 'They were FBI.'

Carrie let this sink in. It would make their job harder, but not impossible. They just needed to find Kinderman before the Feds did, and Archangel would help with that. She was still in awe of the reach of the network she was only one tiny part of. Archangel had contacts like you wouldn't believe. She turned and saw Eli, his eyes open now and looking at her with the glassy mix of fear and suspicion he often carried with him from his dreams. She smiled and blew him a silent kiss. 'You want us to keep our ear to the ground, see what we can find out?'

'No. I want you to get a few hours' sleep and then pull out. The Lord has many enemies and the Devil never sleeps. But I have a new target for you, a new sacrifice to make, one just as important as the one that got away.' Carrie leaned forward, anxious to hear what he had to say, a calmness flowing through her like it always did when she finally got a new mission. 'How quickly do you think you can get to the Marshall Space Centre in Huntsville Alabama?'

CHAPTER 23

The C-130 bumped and lurched as the wheels lifted from the tarmac of Turner's Field. Shepherd was strapped tight into a jump seat facing inward in the paratrooper position, the sound of the twin props filling his ears and vibrating through his entire body as they struggled to grab hold of the slippery air.

They were in what was known as a Bubird, part of the Bureau's varied and colourful fleet of mostly confiscated aircraft. The C-130 was generally used for transport rather than passengers, but this had happened to be the one gassed up and ready to go when Franklin put in the call. It had previously belonged to a Mexican drug cartel, the pilot had cheerfully told Shepherd as they were prepping for take-off. The Mexicans had obviously stripped the interior to the bare fuselage in order to cram in as much product as possible. So far no one had deemed it necessary to put any of those little comforts back in again – things like sound-proofing or heating or padding for the sharp, metal-edged seats that were already cutting off the circulation below his knees. He adjusted his position in a vain attempt to get more comfortable, hugging to his chest the field laptop Agent Smith had given him and wrapping the shoulder strap round his hand for extra security.

They started to bank to starboard, into the weather over Chesapeake Bay, and the plane shook in protest, dipping and yawing as the wind batted it around like a kid's toy.

Franklin was strapped into an identical chair directly opposite. He had the visor down on his flight helmet, so Shepherd couldn't tell whether he was looking at him or not. Shepherd felt pretty sure Franklin would can him from the investigation at the first opportunity and send him straight back to Quantico, exhausted and way behind on his work. At least it was nearly Christmas, so he could catch up over the break when everyone else went home.

Home

He closed his eyes and did his best to zone out the hellish flight, remembering back to a time when the word *home* had almost meant something to him. His folks were already old when they had him – a mistake, his aunt had said, but then she said a lot of mean things. They died within months of each other when he was five years old. What little he could still remember of them played out like scratchy fragments of old newsreel: his father, cowed and frail, sitting alone at the dinner table, his weak eyes magnified behind foggy glasses, always fixed on an open book in front of him; his mother, staring out of the kitchen window, a slender cigarette pointing out at who knew what, looking like she envied the smoke for being able to drift away and escape. They were aged beyond their years: she from the cigarettes she could never give up, he from a life of worn-down disappointment.

Shepherd got his brains from his dad who had burned through books as fast as his mother went through Virginia Slims. His father always worked several jobs at once and one of them was always a night-watchman position, so he could do his rounds and then read in solitude and quiet. When his heart gave out, a couple of months after his mother's lungs had done the same, it was discovered that he had been smart enough to hide some of his income from his wife and stick it in policies in his son's name. The will made his aunt his guardian and stipulated that all of the money – bar a small lump sum for his aunt – was to be held in trust and used only to pay for his education. Furious perhaps at the sum her brother had managed to save and the relatively small amount left to her, the aunt sent him – the son of her atheist brother – to the strictest religious institution she could find, an overly-fancy boarding school, which took him away from what blood relatives remained and introduced him to a new kind of loneliness.

There is something particularly cruel about tossing a poor boy into a moneyed environment. They called him 'The Nigger', though he was as white as they were – which told you as much about them and their world as it did about him and his situation.

There had been nothing nurturing about St Matthew the Apostle: no kindly headmaster who saw and encouraged his potential; no tight-knit group of friends looking out for one another and bound together by their otherness. He had been on his own from the moment he stepped through the grand, arched doors.

He had withdrawn into his studies, the one area where he could take them on: in maths and science in particular it didn't matter how much money your daddy had, only whether you got the questions right. There was also much less chance of being cornered and beasted in the study rooms because there was – almost always – a tutor present. But for all this misery, there was one good thing that had come out of St Matthew's. It was here that he had discovered and fallen in love with the stars.

In the summer he would crawl out onto the flat lead roof of the dormitory building, away from the 'night patrols' of his tormentors, and sleep there instead. Lying with his back against the soft metal, still warm from the heat of the sun he would gaze up at the speckled dark, picking out patterns in the distant points of light. Study time from then on had new material to fill it. When the classwork was done he scoured the library for books on astronomy and devoured their contents, putting names to the patterns until he could lie on the cooling roof, look up at the night sky and name it all. That had felt something like home to him: warm and safe and far away from people, taking comfort in objects that were millions of light years away while the trapped heat of the nearest star warmed him in the cold night.

The true extent of his aunt's revenge only became apparent when he started looking at colleges. It was then that he discovered the fees at the hateful school she had chosen for him had been so high he had already burned through all the money that should have seen him through college and beyond. This was when he found NASA's Graduate Program.

College was the first time he'd encountered a tribe of people who didn't all seem to hate him. This had felt like home, for a while – though whenever the holidays came around and everyone went back to their real homes he was reminded of how temporary it all was. He started volunteering for every graduate work placement going just to keep himself busy in the quiet times until NASA became a sort of home too, with its womb-like control centres and extended family of obsessives.

But in truth he had only ever experienced what he imagined *home* was supposed to feel like just once in his life. And the truly surprising thing was, it turned out not to be a place at all. He pictured her now – *Melisa*. Meeting her had been like coming home. Only with her had he ever felt able to let his carefully constructed defences down. Only with Melisa could he truly be himself, with no apology and no pretence. She made him feel better as a person than he knew he really was. And then she had gone.

The C-130 rose up into a cloudbank and the shaking increased as furious turbulence took hold of the tin-can plane. Shepherd's eyes opened in instinctive alarm. Franklin was smiling straight back at him. The smile broke and his lips moved, the scratchy sound of his voice cutting through the howl of the engines and rumbling through the comms into his head. 'Anytime you want to share your confession with me, Agent Shepherd, I'll be more'n happy to listen.'

Shepherd looked away.

God damn if he wasn't a mind-reader too.

He hugged the laptop tighter as the bucking plane continued to try everything it could to jerk it free. Right now it was the most precious thing in his life, that and the opportunity fate had given him. He had thought it would take months even years before he would get proper access to the vast resource that was the FBI Missing Persons File. So when Agent Smith had handed him the field unit and set him up with a temporary Bureau user ID it was like getting the keys to the kingdom. Every single law enforcement agency worth a damn, domestic and foreign, was linked in on some level to the FBI's MPD database. In terms of looking for someone who had slipped off the map it was like going from pinning photocopied sheets to a community notice board, to sticking a full-page ad on the front cover of every newspaper in the Western world.

But he would have to be very careful: usage was strictly monitored. He would have to try and work his way around the monitoring software if he wanted to avoid getting canned from the Bureau before he had barely stepped through the door. And abusing Agency privileges and access was also a felony. But there was another problem. The level of clearance he had been given by Smith was directly linked to the urgency and importance of the investigation he had been assigned to. The moment he was taken off it, all those privileges would be removed. His window of opportunity was very small and closing fast. It might take him years to regain this sort of clearance, by which time Melisa's trail would be colder still. He felt closer to her now, bouncing around in this cloud, than he had in long months.

He turned his head to the front of the plane in time to see the nose break through the clouds revealing the stars in the clear night. The turbulence melted away almost instantly and his arms relaxed around the laptop – but only a little.

He could sense that Franklin was still smiling at him but he did not look in his direction. He might tell him the story of his lost years one day, but not yet. Not until he had learned the ending for himself. Until then, he would do his level best to stay on the investigation for as long as he could. So he closed his eyes and sifted through what he knew, trying to work out the links between a missing Nobel laureate, nearly a year's worth of lost space data and something that had happened in the city of Ruin eight months earlier.

CHAPTER 24

EIGHT MONTHS EARLIER

Gabriel slipped across the Orontes River marking the border between Syria and Turkey just after midnight on the fifth day. He had walked his horse for much of the way, resting it during the heat of the days and wary of the dry dust kicked up by galloping hooves. Several times he had spotted patrols in the distance and pulled the horse to the ground, lying beside it until they had passed, shivering despite the desert heat and the fever that rose and fell inside him like lava.

During the nights he had shivered from real cold as the chill of space settled back on the earth, the crackle and boom of distant battles showing him where the civil war raged so he could steer a course around it. He rode harder then, his way lit only by the stars and his desire to keep going.

At the height of his fever, rocked almost unconscious by the movement of his horse across the vast desert, he had imagined his father riding with him, pointing out the spots of long-ago battles and bringing forth the ghosts of those that had died here. Ottoman sultans, Persian caliphates, Roman emperors, Alexander the Great, they had all fought for a land no man could ever really own. St Paul had walked here too, converting to Christianity on the long road to Damascus, moving away from the very place Gabriel was trying so hard to get to.

By the time he reached the river marking the end of Syria and the beginning of Turkey, he was half dead from the disease that consumed him from within and half frozen from cold. He found a spot between two checkpoints and slipped into the dark night river, clinging to the swimming horse as if he were crossing the Styx and the horse was the only thing stopping him from drifting away into the underworld.

Not yet – he told himself and held on tighter – just a few more hours, then death could have him.

He rose with the horse, throwing his body over it so it lifted him clear of the river, then lay across its back, dripping and shivering, letting the horse drink for a long while before finally spurring it forward one last time.

The civil war had brought battalions of troops to the border, so he moved slowly at first, picking his way carefully past the military posts, before galloping the last seventy kilometres along the long dusty tracks that ran for miles through the olive and pistachio groves.

He entered the city of Ruin as dawn was lightening the sky and the city was beginning to stir. Ahead of him he could see the Citadel rising sheer and black at the centre of the city, so high the summit was lit by sunlight that had yet to rise above the rim of the surrounding mountains.

He kept to the centre of the great wide boulevard running straight to the heart of the city and away from the early risers who stared mutely at this lone horseman moving past the cars and souvenir shops. He knew the Old Town, locked each night behind its portcullises and seven-metre-thick walls, would be preparing to let the first tourists of the day inside. As soon as the sun peeped above the mountains and bathed the Old Town with light the gates would open and he would charge straight at them, relying on his appearance and the flying hooves to scatter the tourists. He would then ride to the top of the hill and ring the ascension bell at the Tribute dock, demanding that they pull him up and into the mountain. The monk Athanasius would know why he was there. They had to let him in. Just a few more minutes and his journey would be over.

He reached the end of the boulevard and cut across Suleiman Park towards the main public gate. It was the widest of all the entrances and would, he hoped, allow people to get out of his way when he charged at them. He didn't want to hurt anyone and certainly didn't want to touch anyone and risk passing on the fever that burned inside him.

He passed under the final tree, the foliage parting to reveal the Old Town wall. Then he saw them, two ghosts standing sentinel in shrouds of white. In his delirium he thought they must be visions of death, waiting to claim him, but as his horse carried him closer he saw that they were real.

The skull-like eyes of one turned to him then motioned to the other.

He heard the rustle of their sterile suits as they moved towards him, saw the HazMat chevrons and quarantine sign behind them, and realized – as exhaustion and defeat finally dragged him from his horse – that he was too late. The disease he had carried out of the Citadel, and travelled so far to bring back again, had already spread.

CHAPTER 25

The transport plane dropped below the cloud barely two hundred feet above a field of whiteness so bright Shepherd had to squint to make out Redstone Army airfield with the space centre beyond stretching all the way to the horizon.

'Pilot, you sure this is Alabama and not Alaska?' Franklin's voice crackled through the drone of the engines.

'They got weather like this all over the South,' the pilot replied, 'biggest dump since records began. Christmassy though, ain't it? If it's nice weather you wanted we should have flown north. Apparently they got a heat wave in Chicago. World's gone crazy.'

'End of days,' Franklin muttered loud enough for Shepherd to hear. 'Maybe Kinderman was on to something.'

The tyres squealed against the frozen tarmac as they touched down on the cleared runway and the smell of scorched rubber seeped into the hold, making Shepherd feel slightly sick. He hadn't slept all night, had barely eaten anything and the flight had been so bumpy he felt like he'd been beaten up.

'You think NASA might stand us a little breakfast?' Franklin asked, demonstrating again his uncanny knack of sniffing out a raw nerve and tweaking it.

'I can take you to the canteen,' Shepherd said, breathing in freezing air that smelt of rubber and trying hard not to think about the greasy piles of bacon and hash browns laid on each morning for the seven thousand space centre personnel.

Franklin smiled. 'In that case I'm actually glad I brought you along.'

The plane jerked to a stop with the same lack of grace as the rest of the flight and freezing air flooded the hold as the rear-loading ramp began to lower.

Outside, a Ford Explorer was waiting for them, its engine running and sending thick clouds of exhaust fumes past the NASA logo on the side. A man in a dark blue parka with a security badge stitched on the sleeve got out of the passenger door and stood with his hands crossed in front of him. He was a carbon copy of the Security Chief at Goddard: same solid weightlifter's build; same flat face; Shepherd bet he had the same neat office with a picture of his youthful self on the wall.

'Dave Ellery,' the man said, extending his hand to Franklin who led the way down the ramp. 'I'm Chief of Security here.' He wore gloves against the cold and didn't bother taking them off when he shook hands. Not friendly at all. It was a territorial thing stemming from the fact that the FBI had cross-state jurisdiction and could take over an investigation if they decided to. No one likes meeting a bigger fish, especially in law enforcement. Ellery gestured to the rear doors and got back into the front passenger seat without saying another word.

The inside of the basic Explorer was like five-star luxury after the plane. It was super-heated, the seats were padded and Shepherd felt an ache in his fingers and toes as blood started working its way back into them.

'You fellas sure picked a day for it,' Ellery said, staring out from behind black shades at the white landscape.

'From what I heard they done hijacked your weather and shipped it off to Chicago,' Franklin said, subtly upping his southern accent to match Ellery's. It was a technique they taught at Quantico called subject mirroring that implied kinship and helped promote trust, though Shepherd suspected it might be somewhat lost on the frosty Security Chief, who had probably done the same course anyway.

'I didn't mean just the weather,' Ellery said without elaborating.

'Bad day already?'

'I'll say. I'm running short-staffed and we've had to evacuate one of the research facilities because of a helium leak. You can't mess with that stuff. Had to shut the entire building down.' He removed a box file from an attaché case by his feet and handed it to Franklin in the back seat. 'I dug out those documents you asked for.'

The word **THREATS** was written on the file in thick marker pen. Franklin opened it and slid out twelve clear plastic folders, each containing correspondence from a different month. *January* contained a one-page note typed on an old-fashioned typewriter that said:

Dear NASA,

Quit wasting tax dollars shooting junk up into space. The army needs equipment bad. Spend money on that you assholes or I will personally shoot the man pushing the launch button. I am deadly serious.

A Patriot

''Course that's just the physical stuff,' Ellery said. 'We get ten times as much mail over the internet. I can show you that in my office if you want.'

Franklin sorted through the plastic folders until he found one marked *May*, the month Dr Kinderman had received his first card.

'Is it true what I heard, Hubble got knocked offline?' Ellery asked.

'That's classified information. And whatever you heard we would 'preciate you keeping it under your hat, sir. You know how rumours can get in the way of an investigation.' Franklin's accent was travelling down through Georgia and getting further south all the time.

He handed *January* through *April* to Shepherd and popped the fastener on *May*, carefully sliding out the contents to keep them in order. May had clearly been a bumper month for the crazies. Top of the pile was an almost illiterate letter written in crayon with some photos of astronauts stuck to it with their faces burned out by a cigarette. Below that was a photo of the *Challenger* shuttle exploding, with a future date and I WILL MAKE THIS HAPPEN AGEN written on it. The next item was a postcard with a Renaissance painting of the Tower of Babel on the front. Franklin showed it to Shepherd then flipped it over. On the back, in a familiar neat hand was written:

"And they said, Go to, let us build us a city and a tower, whose top may reach unto heaven; and let us make us a name."

'You get any more like this?' Franklin held up the card and Ellery's head swivelled round to see it.

'One a month since May, reg'lar as clockwork.'

'Was the Professor bothered by them?'

'Not especially.'

'But he did see them?'

'Sure, they were addressed to him.'

146

'Did you mention them to Chief Pierce over at Goddard?'

Ellery snorted. 'Why would I do that? Chief Pierce has his own fair share of nut-jobs to deal with I'm damn sure he don't need any of mine.'

Franklin handed the remaining files to Shepherd leaving himself with *December*. 'Did you get another one this month?'

'No. Matter of fact we did not.'

Franklin popped the fastener. 'Don't tell me, you got a letter instead, one that was typed but similar in tone.'

Ellery paused. 'How did you know that?'

Franklin didn't answer. He had already found the twin of the A5 manila envelope that had been sent to Kinderman. It was in its own plastic folder next to the letter it had contained. Franklin held it out so Shepherd could read it. It was identical to the first one except for one small detail.

'Least he didn't call this one a Sodomite,' Franklin said so only Shepherd could hear. 'You follow this up?' he asked Ellery.

'Of course. We take threats seriously here, no matter how strange, vague or misguided they may appear. I sent the original up to Langley, that one there is just a copy. I sent one of the postcards too.'

'They find anything?'

'Who knows? These things don't rank too high on the "hurry up" scale. Anything more important comes along – which is just about everything – stuff

147

like this gets bumped to the bottom of the pile. Here we are, gentlemen.'

Shepherd looked up as the Explorer eased off the main road and approached the front of a mirrored building that reflected the sky making it seem like it was hardly there. Beyond it in the distance the launch towers rose above various research facility buildings that sprawled across the campus. One of them had a small crowd of people outside it wearing white, clean-room suits and was surrounded by parked emergency vehicles, their lights turning slowly.

'Is that where the helium leak happened?' Franklin asked.

'Yup, that's the cryo lab – biggest vacuum testing facility in the world. They got a test room there where they can suck every molecule of air right out of it and freeze it down to space temperatures. We use it to test all the expensive hardware before it gets launched, make sure it won't break up in space.'

Something tightened in the pit of Shepherd's empty stomach. 'What are you testing in there now?'

'Mirrors.'

'What for?'

'Same thing we've been testing all year – James Webb.'

Franklin jerked forward in his seat. 'Driver, you need to take us over there right now.'

'Now wait a second.' Ellery swivelled round.

'This is my facility. You can't just come here and start ordering people . . .'

'Yes I can,' Franklin cut him off. 'That's exactly what I can do. Start driving, son.'

The driver obeyed, throwing the wheel hard over and sending the Explorer into a sharp U-turn. Ellery opened and closed his mouth like a landed fish but said nothing. Ahead of them the cryo lab swung back into view, leaking thick clouds of helium vapour like the whole place was ready to blow.

'When did the leak happen?'

'The alarm went off 'bout a half hour ago.'

'And had you spoken to Professor Douglas by then?'

'Excuse me?'

'Had you told him we were coming?'

'No. I'd spoken to him but I didn't say what it was about.'

'What did you say exactly?'

'I said some people had been asking for him, but I didn't say who.'

'And when was this?'

'Just as soon as I got off the phone to you.'

Franklin shook his head. 'Driver, you need to get us over there as fast as you can.' The Explorer lurched, pushing everyone back in their seats as the driver floored the accelerator.

'What the hell is this about anyway?' Ellery growled, trying to claw back a bit of authority.

'Those mirrors you've been testing, are they

expensive by any chance, difficult to replace if they got broken?'

'They cost about fifteen million dollars apiece. They're precision-engineered and coated in gold. We got six of them in the chamber at the moment.'

'Really? Well there's a very real chance that right now, while everyone else is standing around outside, Professor Douglas is inside using his car keys to scratch his name on them.'

CHAPTER 26

The speeding Explorer crunched to a stop just short of the building, sending the crowd of bunny-suited lab techs scattering. Franklin was out of the door before it had even stopped. Shepherd had clipped his safety belt on out of habit and was now cursing as he fumbled to release it. He opened the door and ran round the car, the freezing air like razors in his lungs.

Franklin stood to the side of the main entrance, listening. Shepherd noticed he was holding his gun. He undid the buttons on his coat and reached for his own, falling in line behind Franklin and standing slightly away from the wall like he'd been taught. Franklin turned and beckoned Ellery over.

It all felt so familiar to Shepherd from his recent intensive training that he had to remind himself this was not a simulation and the bullets in his gun would not fire paint. Also, the man they were looking for with drawn guns was his old professor, a man he respected more than pretty much any of the long procession of people who had lined up to cram knowledge into his head. Professor Douglas, with his sharp, kind eyes and his boy-scout enthusiasm. Professor Douglas who was a vegetarian because he couldn't bear the thought of a living thing having to die on his behalf. Professor Douglas – suspected terrorist, wanted by the FBI.

Ellery joined them in a rustle of goose-down parka, his eyes darting around. Nervous. 'Tell me about the building,' Franklin said, keeping his eyes on the door. 'Where are the exits?'

'There's this one and a fire exit out back.'

'You need to get someone round there to cover it. What about inside? Tell me about the layout?'

'The layout is kind of tricky.'

'Then you'll have to come with me. I don't want to get lost in there. Shepherd, you cover the rear exit.'

'We're going inside?' Ellery looked like he was going to pass out.

'I can guide us,' Shepherd said. 'I worked in this building for a while. There's a door leading away from the lobby to a changing room. From there you pass through a scrubbing station and an airlock to get to the central chamber. The coolants are fed into it from storage silos on the far side of the building. They come in through deep underground pipes to aid the insulation. If there's a leak then it will probably be in the main chamber.' He looked at Ellery for confirmation. He badly wanted to go inside and be there when Franklin confronted Douglas, for the Professor's sake as much as anything.

Ellery nodded, all his earlier bravado now gone. 'That's about the size of things. You'll need access codes for the doors but they'll all be the same because the system is in evac mode. It's star, four zeros then the hash key.'

Franklin nodded. 'OK. You go organize your men to cover the exits. We'll go in the front and try and flush him out.'

Ellery nodded and hurried away. Shepherd watched him go, taking in the crowd beyond him – the emergency vehicles, the shivering people – his senses made sharp by adrenalin and fear. In the distance he noticed that the trees were heavy with snow and what looked like black fruit. A car door slammed and the fruit took flight, rising in the air like a column of living black smoke, thousands of migratory birds flying out of season and resting on trees that had never known snow. Nature turned on its head.

End of days.

'Ready?' Franklin said.

No – Shepherd thought. 'Yep,' he said, turning back to the entrance and raising his gun.

'Good, 'cause you're on point.' He stepped around and behind Shepherd so the front of his body was tight to his back – *nuts to butts.* 'Cover and move,' he murmured, 'just like in Hogan's Alley.'

Except the bullets are real – Shepherd thought. *The bullets are real.*

Then he stepped forward and opened the door.

CHAPTER 27

Shepherd went in low, sweeping the entrance lobby from left to right while Franklin stayed high and swept in the opposite direction. It was exactly as he remembered it, a row of five chairs stretched along the far wall below a huge picture of the space shuttle, a water cooler in the left corner with a waste bin next to it half full of paper cups, a heavy door to the right with a thick window built in at head height and HazMat and Radiation symbols below it. Nothing else.

He stepped forward and moved across the foyer, heading for the door and repeating the training mantra over and over in his head: *Check and move, check and move.*

Franklin stayed close enough to make them a single entity with two sets of eyes and two guns.

Star, four zeros then the hash key. Through the door. It swung shut behind them with the suck of rubber seals, cutting off all sounds from outside. In the quietness they heard something new, a low, steady hiss as though a huge snake was waiting for them somewhere inside the building.

Shepherd stepped to the side of the door – gun

in front, heart pounding – and scoped as much of the room beyond as he could through the small window. The gowning room was all white tiles, bright lights and shelves full of rolled-up suits and gloves. There were some full suits hanging like ghosts on the wall, which made his finger tighten on the trigger.

He glanced up at Franklin who had taken a position on the other side of the door. Nodded once. Reached out with his left hand and punched the code into the door. The lock clicked. Franklin twisted the handle. Shepherd pushed it open from the hinge and followed it low, just as before, left to right, corner to centre, while Franklin stayed high and swept the opposite way. A movement made Shepherd's gun twitch round. One of the hanging suits had moved. He blew out a long breath realizing it was only the air from the opening door that had shifted it.

The hissing sound was louder now. It was coming from beyond the air shower that led into the main chamber.

They moved towards it, their shoes catching on the sticky mats there to pull impurities from the soles of lab boots before they entered the high-pressure air shower that would blast off the rest. Shepherd stopped as he reached the clear screen that marked the entrance. 'Let's go,' Franklin said, joining him by the door and seeing there was nothing inside.

'We should be suited up before going in there.'

'Really?' Franklin turned and opened the door.

'Wait!' Shepherd ducked in after him just as a tornado of wind rushed at them from all sides sounding like a thousand hand dryers going off at once. Franklin ducked and crabbed over to the far door, leading with his gun as if the noise was some kind of attack. The racket lasted for ten seconds then cut out. Franklin turned back to Shepherd. 'What were you saying?'

'Never mind.'

The window in the final door revealed little of the large chamber beyond. The entire upper part of the room was hidden behind a thick wall of white vapour, like someone had captured a cloud and was storing it here. 'Helium,' Shepherd whispered.

'Poisonous?'

He shook his head. 'There's a danger of oxygen starvation if you inhale too much. Other than that it just makes your voice sound funny. It's the same stuff you get in party balloons. Biggest risk is frostbite and cold burns. It boils at minus four hundred and fifty degrees Fahrenheit and in the pipes it will be liquid, so even colder. The Professor won't be in there if it's a liquid spill. Not unless he's dead. No one can survive long in cold like that.'

Franklin smiled and stepped behind him. 'You first.'

Shepherd looked again through the window at the gas cloud and took a breath. He felt the grip of the gun pressing into his palm as he held it tight in one hand and punched the code into the door with the other. The lock clicked, he pulled it open and stepped inside.

It was beyond freezing inside the room and the hissing was sinister and loud. Above him the underside of the cloud shifted as the opening door stirred the air, making it look like something was moving inside it.

He swept the room the same way as before. The vapour in the air reduced visibility but he could make out the lower third of the circular door to the vault in the centre of the room. This was where the hardware was tested and where the leak would most likely be coming from. He moved toward it, keeping low and well below the freezing cloud. It had been cold outside in the freak winter weather but nothing compared to this. His breath was frosting the moment it passed his lips. He glanced up at the thick cloud above his head, formed by the lighter than air helium filling the chamber top down like smoke. There was something wrong about it being there. He dredged his mind for what he knew about the facility. Fragments came back to him, bits of technical information about how it worked – then it hit him.

Laminar flow.

He looked back up at the cloud. The room kept itself clean using laminar flow, air blown constantly in parallel streams from top to bottom to sweep particles down to the filters in the floor. But the cloud was not being blown downwards. It just sat there, filling the upper part of the room with freezing vapour. He remembered how it had shifted when he had opened the door. There was no airflow in the room at all. Maybe it had been damaged by the leak. Maybe not.

He spotted something else that was wrong. In the clinical environment of the clean room, nothing should be out of place, everything had to be stowed away and locked down to prevent dangerous and potentially costly accidents: but there was a laptop lying on the floor over by the vault door. He moved closer to it, squinting through the thick air to get a better look. Shifting hardware in and out of the cryo unit was incredibly precise. Even a scrubbed glove could leave contaminants on a component, so it was all done by computer-controlled robotic lifting arms. The laptop was hardwired into the control panel of one of these. The arm was extended, the gripping claw disappearing into the dense cloud above his head. Shepherd took a step towards it, moving sideways to bring the screen of the laptop into view. There was a number on it, two zeroes followed by a one and an eight. As Shepherd watched, the eight turned to a seven. Then a six. Then a five.

Countdown.

He darted forward, grabbing one of the high-pressure hoses used to clean components and pointed it up at the cloud, pulling the trigger at the spot where the top of the arm had to be. The hiss of air joined the shushing sibilance of the room as the cloud parted above him, just long enough for him to see what the arm was holding.

He dropped the hose and span round, grabbing Franklin by the arm. 'GET OUT!'

In his mind he was already sprinting back to the entrance, dragging Franklin with him, but the world had gone into slow motion.

How long left before the counter hit zero? Not long enough and he dared not turn to look. Say ten seconds at most. Ten seconds to get as far away as possible.

Something tugged on his arm, holding him back. He looked back and into Franklin's face, confused and angry. 'RUN!' he screamed, pulling him towards the door. No time to explain. No time for anything.

He counted every step, imagining each one corresponding to the countdown on the laptop.

. . . nine . . .

. . . eight . . .

Until now, Shepherd had not been fully committed to the idea that his old Professor was in here somewhere, sabotaging key components of Hubble's successor.

. . . seven . . .

. . . six . . .

But everything was so deliberate and planned. He made it to the door and yanked it open, heaving Franklin through and charging after him.

. . . five . . .

. . . four . . .

The roar of the air shower kicked in and for a second he thought he'd got his timings wrong. He carried on running, straight through the second door with Franklin right next to him.

. . . three . . .

. . . two . . .

So clever.

Evacuate the building so no one gets hurt. . . . flood the upper part of the chamber with freezing gas . . . lift a reserve tank of coolant into it with the arm so the gas keeps it cool . . . until the countdown tells it to drop the tank onto the hard, relatively warm floor . . .

. . . One . . .

In front of him, Franklin was halfway through the final door and Shepherd threw himself forward, bundling him out of the scrubbing station and down onto the floor of the entrance lobby.

Down.

Stay down. Helium is lighter than air. Helium rises.

. . . Zero . . .

Shepherd heard a muffled crump then the percussive wave of the explosion ripped through the building, turning the world into torn metal and broken glass.

And then darkness.

PART III

What man is there that hath built a new house, and hath not dedicated it? Let him go and return to his house, lest he die in the battle

Deuteronomy 20:5

CHAPTER 28

EIGHT MONTHS EARLIER
Old Town, City of Ruin
Southeastern Turkey

Gabriel died shortly after noon on the same day he rode into Ruin.

A man in a HazMat suit appeared over him, his visor fogging with hurried breath, drawn by the cardio alarm.

'Over here!' His voice was muffled by the hermetic suit, lost amid the wail of the alarm and the howls of other patients. 'HERE!' He reached out a gloved hand and placed it on Gabriel's chest, pumping hard on the breastbone to massage the still heart beneath it, cursing the fact that his other hand was strapped tight to his chest by a sling.

Another suited figure looked up from another bed and started to walk over, any urgency blunted by the now commonplace nature of death. It was the third time a cardiac alarm had sounded that day and, with so many infected and suffering so hideously, it was hard not to see the release of death as something of a blessing.

'Do something,' the man at the bed said, still pumping rhythmically on Gabriel's chest with his one good hand.

The new arrival glanced at the monitor, the heartbeat flat-lining. He looked down at the still form, bound to the bed. 'He's gone,' he said, flicking a switch to silence the alarm.

The man at Gabriel's side looked up, anger lighting his face, his breath fogging his visor as he spoke. 'What's your name?'

'Dr Kaplan, I'm the senior physician in charge, why do you ask?'

'Because I want to spell it right when I write up the charge of medical homicide by neglect.'

The doctor's eyes dropped to the ID displayed in the clear pocket on the front of the man's suit and read the name: Chief Inspector Davud Arkadian, Ruin City Police. Pushing Arkadian's hand away he moved up to the bed and continued the CPR on Gabriel's body. His bulky helmet turned back towards the other doctors. 'Over here,' he shouted, loud enough to be heard above the din. 'Make it fast and bring the crash unit with you.'

Gabriel felt like he was floating upwards, flying in a bright sky. Below him he could see fields and rivers rushing past, flitting between clouds that grew thicker the higher he flew. He felt weightless, peaceful – free.

Through the clouds he saw the land fall away and the vast mirror of the ocean stretch out. Huge flocks of birds flew past him, all heading in the same direction towards land. Even at this great height he could see other things moving across the water below. They left lines behind them, long straight, white wakes like scratches on the surface of the sea. Ships. Thousands of them, all heading back to land, the lines of their wakes slowly converging the closer they got to port.

He continued to rise, as if some force was pulling him up to the bright sun that warmed and welcomed him. No. Not the sun, more vast somehow and indistinct. It continued to grow the closer he got, bigger even than the ocean below though he could not see the edge of it. Moving towards it required no effort, it was as easy as falling. But there was something about the ships and the birds that plucked at something inside him. They were all going in a different direction to him, and it made him feel uneasy. He felt like he should be going the same way too, back to the land, away from the soothing sun that filled the sky.

He tilted himself downwards, his head pointing back towards the earth and swept his arms through the air, pulling himself down and away from the light. The steady rise stopped, just a little, then started again, pulling him up like he was a cork bobbing in water. He fixed on a spot of dry land far below him, reached out with his arms again and pulled forward, kicking hard with both legs.

'Clear!'

Two of the three HazMat suits stepped back from the bed. The third held the defibrillator paddles to the smears of conductive gel on Gabriel's chest and pressed the twin fire buttons.

Gabriel arched upwards, his bound hands twitching into claws at his sides.

Dr Kaplan stepped forward, checking the ECG monitor and resuming CPR. The line on the screen jumped then settled back to nothing. 'Nearly had him. Give him another milligram of epinephrine and get ready to try again.'

The second suit fumbled a syringe into the cannula fitted to Gabriel's arm, the urgency and his gloved hands combining to make this simple task ten times more difficult. He emptied the plunger and sent a milligram of adrenaline into Gabriel's veins. Inside his inert body the peripheral vascular system responded, constricting to send a shunt of blood to his core, thereby raising his blood pressure. The doctor placed the syringe on a stand and pressed a button on the defibrillator unit to prime it again.

'Charging,' he called out. The insectile whine of building electricity cut through the air.

Dr Kaplan continued to pump Gabriel's heart with his interlaced hands, forcing blood through veins while Arkadian made himself useful as best he could with his usable arm. He stayed by Gabriel's head squeezing the bag valve mask fixed to his face, sending a steady pulse of oxygen to his immobile lungs. He watched the line on the screen flicker but stay flat, the heart still not beating on its own. The second doctor got ready with the paddles, placing one high and one low with the heart in between.

'Clear!'

Gabriel arched. On the screen the ECG jumped.

They moved back to their positions, three people working together to carry on functions that were normally automatic, keeping him alive by hand while the ECG continued to dance but refused to settle.

'We can't keep on with this indefinitely,' Dr Kaplan said between pumps. 'CPR and artificial respiration only go so far in keeping a patient viable. His brain is already being starved of oxygen. Any longer than a few minutes and it becomes increasingly pointless.'

'Then you'd better get a move on,' Arkadian said.

Kaplan nodded. 'OK spike him up with another mil of epinephrine. Let's go again.'

Arkadian focused on the bag in his hand, squeezing and releasing it steadily at the same pace Gabriel would breathe if he could. 'Come on,' he whispered, dipping his head down level with Gabriel's ear. 'Don't go out like this. Not like this.'

Gabriel could see the land beneath him getting closer but the effort to reach it was exhausting. Occasionally a gust of wind would help him out, blowing him downward in a sudden surge, but it never lasted long and the upward force would start to pull on him again, working on his mind too, telling him to give up, let go, relax and float away.

The land was also taking form and he continued to focus on it, using it as a hook to pull him down, fixing on a patch of green in the middle of a vast, dry desert. He continued to kick and pull with his arms, swimming in the air like he was trying to get to the bottom of a crystal-clear lake.

He could see more now, trees and rivers and a lake at the centre of the green, reflecting the bright sun behind him. And there was something else, a person, a woman, standing by the edge of the pool and looking around as though she had lost something. She was calling out but he was still too high to hear her. He could feel weariness flooding his whole body and again the voice from above told him to just let go. Then another gust of wind pushed him down, halving the distance so he could finally see who it was and hear what she was calling.

'Gabriel!' Liv hollered into the same wind that had pushed him close to her. 'Where have you gone? Why have you left me here?'

Gabriel kicked harder, the sound of her voice and the sight of her pulling at him now with far more strength than the light in the sky. 'I'm here,' he called out. 'My love, I'm here. I'm coming for you. I'm coming back.'

Then he kicked once more and something seemed to snap. The lights went out and he was suddenly falling through darkness, down to the earth that he could no longer see, and down to the woman he could no longer hear.

'Heartbeat steady at eight nine, BP 100 over 80.' Kaplan stood back watching the proof on the heart monitor that it had taken over the job he had been doing for the last five minutes.

Arkadian continued to pump the air bag, too scared to stop in case it was the only thing keeping Gabriel bound to this earth. 'You can stop that now,' Kaplan said, 'he's breathing on his own.'

Arkadian stepped back, suddenly aware that he was drenched in sweat inside his spacesuit. 'Congratulations, Doctor,' he said, managing a smile, 'you just saved a good man's life.'

The doctor looked down at the figure on the bed. The infected and blistered skin already starting to sheen again with sweat as the fever came back to life too. 'Yes,' he said. 'But for how long?

CHAPTER 29

The heat hammered a headache into Liv before she had even made it out of sight of the compound. She was following the line of one of the larger streams that flowed out from the holding pits, tracing it through the contours of the land. She did not stoop to drink from it despite her thirst. She knew the riders would be watching and she did not want to give them the satisfaction. She felt uneasy walking away, though she knew she had no option: each footstep seemed heavier than the last, like her whole body was rebelling against leaving this place. It was as though her heart was physically bound to it and each step made the bond tighter as it tried to pull her back.

After nearly two hours' walking, the land started to fall away and she came across a shallow depression in the ground where the water had pooled. She stopped still the moment she saw it and sank slowly to the ground.

An eagle stood on the far bank of the pool, dipping its curved beak into the water, sending gentle ripples across the surface while its powerful talons gripped the wet, red earth like soft flesh. It saw her, held her gaze with its huge amber eyes. She sensed no fear in it, or surprise at her presence, it just stared at her, so intently that she felt it must see right through her. Then the crunch of a foot on dry earth behind her made the bird take flight in an explosion of feathers and water droplets.

Liv spun round and saw Tariq standing over her, his eyes following the bird upward as it rose into the sky. 'Hey,' she said, 'you followed me.'

He looked down at her and smiled. 'We all followed you,' he replied, and stepped aside to let the rest of the refugees file past. Liv watched in silence as they walked down to the water one by one. She felt like crying.

Since Gabriel had gone she had been almost overwhelmed by feelings of loneliness. It gave her hope to see these strangers now, people who had chosen to follow her into the unknown rather than seek their own salvation. There was something happening here – bigger than her, bigger than any one person – and she knew they must feel it, as she felt it, or else why would they be here?

'This is a good omen,' Tariq said, looking up at the eagle. She followed his gaze to where the outspread wings gyred high above them, forming the shape of a T in the sky. She'd seen this before.

She grabbed the folded piece of paper from her pocket and opened it to reveal the rubbing of the

Starmap, her eyes focusing on the first line of symbols.

The river
An eagle
A T-shaped cross
Her eyes slid across the remaining symbols and her heart thumped in her chest.

'Stop,' she called out. 'Don't drink it, don't drink the water.' Faces turned to her and she could see questions and doubt in their eyes.

She focused her mind on the symbols that followed the T.

The river again, a man kneeling next to it, his head hanging down and dripping, then the skull – symbol of death.

Liv looked back along the stream towards the distant compound, now just a shimmering smudge in the distance. For most of its length it ran clear, but even as she watched she could see a change. Far in the distance a current was swelling and surging down the stream towards her. It stirred up the mud as it went, turning the water the reddish colour of the earth – the colour of blood.

How long before it reached here? Ten minutes? Five maybe. Then the water in the pool would be spoiled too. Unless. She looked at the land, the way the river split, half of it flowing down into the pool.

'We must dam the stream into the pool,' she called out.

She moved quickly without waiting for a response, heading back to where the water split in two. Most of the flow was coming towards her, down a shallow, two-metre wide stream that was feeding the pool. She picked up one of the boulders that littered the broken ground and stumbled forward, the weight of the rock dragging her down. She reached the fork and the boulder splashed into the water, sinking almost without trace beneath the surface despite the shallowness of the stream. The water continued to flow around it unimpeded. She cast around for another rock and scrambled over to a large, brittle stone that fell apart as soon as she tried to pick it up. She grabbed the two largest chunks and hauled them back to the stream, dropping them next to the first one. Again they sank with barely a trace – and so did her spirits. She was already exhausted; she couldn't possibly dam the stream on her own. It was hopeless.

A rock hit the surface in an explosion that covered Liv with water. She turned and saw Tariq behind her, brushing dust from his empty hands. He looked at her and smiled. 'I'd get out of the way if I were you.'

She looked beyond him and saw something that made her laugh in pure shock. All eleven of the exiles were staggering towards her, each carrying a rock. She jumped away as the first plunged into the stream in a depth-charge of water. Another joined it, then another. They were already piling up, a few rising above the surface and visibly slowing the flow. Liv dropped down into the water, scooping the red earth up from the riverbed and jamming it into the gaps between the rocks.

Tariq issued more orders in Arabic, and a curved wall began to form, extending across the stream that had run into the pool and diverting the flow to the other fork.

'Look,' the cry came from one of the workers. He was pointing upstream. Everyone's eyes followed – everyone's but Liv's. She knew what they were looking at because she had already seen it – first on the stone and then in the hazy distance. The river was turning to blood.

'Quickly,' she called out, continuing to scoop mud into the wall of rocks. 'We haven't got much time.'

The sight of the river turning red electrified the weary group. Some rushed to collect more stones, others joined Liv in the water, frantically shovelling mud with their hands to seal the gaps.

Tariq dropped down and shovelled mud next to her then a hiss like a huge snake drew all eyes up as the red wave closed in.

'Out of the river, everybody!' Liv shouted.

Those in the stream leapt out as if crocodiles had suddenly appeared in it. Some scrambled down the rapidly drying riverbed to help Liv and Tariq fill gaps in the dam wall, others stood back, awed by the sight of the swollen river arriving in a surge of red.

It hit the wall with a slap and slopped over the top

of the dam. Liv and Tariq dropped back, digging a reservoir in the mud of the rapidly drying riverbed to catch the overspill. She looked up. Leaks had sprung out on the upper part where the mud had already been washed away. One more breach and the whole thing could collapse. Others sensed this too and everyone joined her in the mud, bolstering the wall with armfuls of silt and whatever rocks they could still find close by.

A stone tumbled down from the top of the dam and a cascade of red water followed it. Without stopping to think, Liv splashed through the water towards it, grabbing the stone and jamming it back in place. She held it there, feeling the sickening flow of red-tinted warm water over her hand, as though it really was blood.

From her new position she could see over the top of the dam and beyond. The trickle that had been the second fork of the stream was now a solid red flow. But if the wall broke, all that water would quickly revert to its natural course and find its way down to the pool.

Liv leaned against the dam and braced it with her whole body, arms outstretched, willing it to hold. She could hear the slop of water on the other side of the wall, feel it running over her from the numerous gaps. She could almost sense the whole dam moving, feel the stones slipping out of place under the pressure of the raging river.

Then something shifted.

A stone she had tried to jam back in place moved

forward, seating itself tighter into the wall, and the flow became a trickle around it. She looked over the top of the wall, her eyes wide. The water level had dropped. It was still dropping, leaving red tide marks along the lengths of the banks. The surge had ended.

They worked quickly and silently, all energy focused on filling any holes in the dam. But Liv never moved. She remained where she was, crucified on the wall and mired in red, her mind running through the symbols that had predicted all this and wondering what greater terrors might lie in the future, until Tariq laid his hand on her shoulder and told her 'It's OK. The dam held. You can let go now.'

CHAPTER 30

Shepherd opened his eyes to a world of silence. For a few moments he had not the slightest idea where he was, or even who he was. He could see a floor strewn with debris and a wall that disappeared in a jagged line three feet up from the ground. Beyond it was a whiteness that hurt his eyes and low grey cloud.

The cloud.

His mind hooked onto the word – and he remembered.

He felt the cold all around and sinking into him – but not from beneath. There was something warm underneath him.

He forced himself up, willing his disconnected arms to move and push him up from the floor so he could see what it was. He feared it might be blood, his blood, but it was just Franklin, unconscious and unresponsive. He felt cold, everything felt cold. He needed to get them both away from here and into the warm.

He tried to stand but dizziness surged through him, driving him back down again. He focused on the chewed metal edge of what had once been the outer wall, trying to fix on something long enough to stop the world from spinning.

A face appeared above the wall, shouting something his ears could not hear. He tried to raise his hand and call the man over. He tried to push himself up so the man could see Franklin. But in the end these thoughts went no further than his brain and just the effort of thinking was enough to let the darkness back in. His eyes closed. The coldness pressed down. And the whistling whine in his damaged ears faded back to silence.

When Shepherd woke again it was with a gasp that hurt his throat.

He was lying on a bed in a white room, all wipe-clean linoleum and health awareness posters. One listed the symptoms of radiation sickness, another the toxic properties of various chemicals. He had been here before. The same posters had graced the walls in his research intern days when he had come to the sick bay to be treated for a mild helium burn.

Helium.

Burn.

The words pierced the bubble surrounding his brain and it popped in sudden and painful recollection.

'Franklin!' He sat up in bed and the room shifted as though it was floating.

White-coated figures surged through the door. They were all talking to him, at him, he could see their mouths moving but all he heard was a *waa-waa* sound, their voices muffled and indistinct like his ears were waterlogged. He worked his jaw and they popped, his hearing returning as suddenly and painfully as his memory had.

'Please,' he said, closing his eyes against the headache brightness and holding his hand up against the noise. 'Could someone tell me what happened to Agent Franklin.'

'Nothing.' Shepherd opened his eyes at the familiar voice and looked past the white coats who were now checking his blood pressure and other vital signs. Franklin was leaning against the door-jamb, hands deep in his pockets, the smile back in place like nothing had happened. 'Well, I got blown up – there is that – but apart from that I'm pretty good. Better than you leastways, but then you did take more of the blast than me.' He turned to the medical personnel. 'Now if you gentlemen are sure he ain't gonna die in the next few minutes, might I trouble you to leave us in private for a moment or two?'

Shepherd watched the medics leave and close the door. What was left of his coat was hanging on the back. It looked like cattle had stampeded over it. The laptop case was propped against the wall next to it, untouched because he had left it behind in the Explorer. Franklin sat down by the bed. 'Looks like you saved my life back there. Guess I owe you a drink.'

Shepherd swallowed, his mouth still parched

from the dry air he'd breathed so long in the cryo chamber. 'I don't drink.' He swallowed again, missing the look of mild disapproval that flitted across Franklin's face. 'What about Douglas?'

Franklin shook his head. 'Missing. If he was anywhere in the facility then he's dead for sure, but we haven't found anything yet. The explosion tore everything to pieces. Place looks more like some kind of modern sculpture now than a building. My feeling is he wasn't in there.' He leaned forward and dropped his voice low. Shepherd could hardly hear it through the whine in his ears. 'That thing you saw on the computer before you dragged me out of there, I caught a glimpse of it myself, looked like some kind of countdown.'

Shepherd nodded. 'I think it was primed to make the loading arm drop the helium tank once everyone was clear of the building. Was there a fire?'

'No, just an almighty bang.'

Shepherd remembered the *crump* and the cold, solid wave sweeping over them. 'It was a pressure bomb. Helium doesn't burn. It's inert. It's one of the reasons they like using it as a coolant in facilities like this – much less dangerous. But if it's cooled to liquid form and you heat it up quickly it expands in an explosive manner.'

He looked down at his battered body stretching away on the examination table. At least he was in one piece. They were very lucky, considering. 'I'm guessing the Webb telescope mirrors that were in the testing chamber . . .'

'Destroyed,' Franklin nodded. 'I doubt you could find a piece big enough to comb your hair with.'

Shepherd closed his eyes and let out a long breath. 'They killed James Webb,' he said out loud, as though mourning a friend.

'What?'

'The project, it's dead. They won't restart it again after this. The only reason it had managed to keep going so long was because of existing commitments to the manufacturers. It was already billions over budget.' Something occurred to him and he sat up in bed, steadying himself as vertigo swam through his head. 'We should issue warnings to all the major ground telescopes – the VLA in New Mexico, the Keck II in Hawaii; and not just here but globally. If there's some kind of "end of days" cult at work here, targeting anything that's staring at the sky, then it won't be restricted to space telescopes or confined to the US.'

'Cool your jets, rocket man, already been done. There's a high-level alert out on all international security networks with copies of the postcards and details of the two attacks. All potential targets have been advised to beef up their security and report to us if they have received similar threats.'

Shepherd swung his legs off the bed and down to the floor. He still felt dizzy but it was getting better. 'What about telescopes under construction? There's a big one out in Arizona somewhere. I think the Europeans just started one somewhere in Chile. They could be targets too.'

'The alert went out to all national and private observatories, both operational and under construction. I may not have all your fancy degrees, Shepherd, but I'm not an idiot. Oh by the way – who's Melisa?' Shepherd felt like he'd been punched in the gut. 'You were talking while you were out. Kept saying that name over and over, like you were calling for her, like maybe she was lost. She got something to do with your missing two years?'

Shepherd looked at Franklin's chest rather than his eyes.

Maybe he should just tell him. But then he knew so little about Franklin. He had no idea if he would honour his word or just feed anything he told him straight back to personnel and end his career before it even got started. His eyes lit on the ID pinned to Franklin's jacket, his name written in full beneath a stern photo: Agent Benjamin Franklin.

'What's your real name?' he asked.

'What?'

'Your name. I'm assuming that when you became an agent you got baptized just like I did.' He looked up and finally met his gaze. 'Or were your parents very patriotic?'

'Only people who know my real name are my family and a handful of people I trust.'

Shepherd smiled. 'Give and take. You say you can't trust me, but trust is a two-way street, Agent Franklin. How can I trust a man who won't even tell me his real name?'

The door opened behind Franklin but neither of them turned to look.

'I got something,' Ellery said, oblivious of the atmosphere in the room. 'Best if I show you in my office.' He pointed back over his shoulder.

'Be right there,' Franklin replied, the chair legs scraping as he stood up. 'After you, Agent Shepherd.'

Shepherd stood and the room shifted a little but not enough to make him sit down again. He grabbed the laptop bag from the floor and his battered coat from behind the door. 'No,' he said. 'You first.'

CHAPTER 31

Shepherd walked into Ellery's office and smiled to himself when he spotted what was hanging on the wall. It was a photograph of the Chief's younger self, glossy and framed and staring out from beneath the sharp brim of his County cap at a small wooden crucifix hanging on the opposite side of the office. The only other attempt at decoration was a potted cactus on the desk that looked like it was shivering.

'Take a seat, gentlemen.' The man the photograph had become was two-finger pecking at a keyboard, his reading glasses forcing his head to tilt back and making him seem old. 'After what you said about the situation at Goddard I got the guys to run some background and give me the headlines. I got them to pull up the Professor's email correspondence for the last week, see if there was anything there that might be relevant.' He turned the monitor round so they could see it. An email program filled the screen with an empty inbox. 'Somebody, and I'm assuming it was the Professor, wiped everything going back months. I had them check his work files too and it's the same story.'

'How many months exactly?'

'Right the way back to May.'

Eight months.

'If you hand the hard drives over to us,' Franklin said, 'our own tech guys might be able to retrieve some of the lost information.'

Ellery shrugged. 'Whatever you need: guess this thing is federal now so it's your call.'

Shepherd felt sorry for him, this worn-down version of the proud young man in the photograph. He'd been so full of piss and vinegar when he'd met them off the plane, now he seemed powerless and defeated in his own office.

'There's something else.' Ellery leaned back in his chair, swiping the reading glasses from his face and reaching for a drawer. He pulled out a thin sheaf of printed paper held together with a clip. 'That letter you were interested in. I called up the labs, dropped your name and had them put a rush on it.' He handed the documents to Franklin.

It was a report from the Questioned Documents Unit. The top sheet displayed a unique file number and brief description of the items under scrutiny. The next few pages were filled with various test results: pen identification, video spectral comparisons, thin layer chromatography, Raman spectroscopy, paper tests. The final sheet took all these results and translated them back into something the field agents could use. The results for the letter were peppered with the acronym CS/WU, which stood for Common

Sample/Widespread Use, basically meaning the item was too commonplace to be of any use in an investigation. But the results for the postcard were more interesting.

The card is a CS/WU low-grade high-acid paper pulp mass-produced item sold in multiple outlets online. However the thicker card-like material has rendered excellent nib impressions revealing much about the type of pen used.

Cross-referencing the chromatography results shows the sample was written with a fountain pen using something like a 33 Reverse Fine Oblique nib by someone who is either left-handed or fluidly ambidextrous.

The ink is Parker Quink Black Permanent (CS/WU); the pen is also most likely a Parker make, possibly from the 75 range.

Running this sample through the database resulted in 2 hits.

Signature on petition from Operation Fish.

Signature on letter to the Governor of South Carolina objecting to the building of a mosque in Charleston.

In both cases the signatory was the Reverend Fulton Ronald Cooper, head of the Church of Christ's Salvation, based in Charleston, South Carolina.

'The TV preacher?' Shepherd looked up at Franklin. 'He's our suspect?'

'So it would seem.' Franklin turned to Ellery. 'Thank you for this Chief, most helpful. Now, if you wouldn't mind giving us a moment here.'

The effect was crushing. Ellery rose from his chair and left the room without another word, the door banging shut like a coffin lid as he closed it behind him.

'Couldn't you maybe go a little easier on him?'

'You mean old hitch-up-his-pants, "I'm the Sheriff round these here parts" who gave us such a warm welcome? I *am* going easy on him.'

'Well go easier.' Shepherd glanced nervously up at the photo like it was listening. 'He gives us a lead and you humiliate him by sending him out of his own office to stand in the hall.'

Franklin looked amused. 'Ah, he deserves it for letting us walk into that exploding building while he stayed back and hid behind his pension. And the reason I sent him out is not because of some badge-related pissing contest, it's because I need to talk to you in private.' He turned so he was facing him. 'How you feeling, Agent Shepherd – any concussion, anything broken?'

'I'm OK.' He wondered where this was going.

'Want to carry on with this investigation? See where it goes? Help your Professor if you can?'

Shepherd tried to read his mood. If anything his tone seemed conspiratorial, which at least hinted at a degree of inclusion. 'Yes,' he said. 'Yes I would.'

187

'Good.' Franklin rose and moved behind Ellery's desk, settling in his empty chair and pulling the desk phone towards him. 'Let me tell you the facts of life, son.' He held up the documents from the Questioned Documents lab. 'Ellery did us a favour by chasing these up because, even though he used my name, I doubt anyone has linked it to this investigation yet. If they had they would already have handed the information to someone in the field office in Charlotte to go apprehend the good Reverend and have a little talk about his penmanship. Do you want that to happen? Of course you don't want that to happen.

'But there is another way to play this. The way I see it, by the time we've brought another agent up to speed, we might just as well have gone to Charleston ourselves. We can fly there as fast as they can drive it and be first on the scene. So providing you're not seeing double or deaf in both ears, I say we keep on with this thing and follow this lead.'

'What about Professor Douglas?' Shepherd said, sensing a trap. 'Shouldn't we head over and check out his home address like we did Kinderman's?'

'You think we'll find him there? Man blows away billions of dollars' worth of space hardware, you think he's going to just head home and wait around for a knock on the door?'

'Probably not, but we might find something.'

Franklin drummed his fingers on the desk, something Shepherd had seen him do in class when he was getting annoyed with a slow candidate. 'OK, let me put it this way,' he said, smiling through his evident irritation. 'Do you think whatever we *might* find there will be more or less useful than talking to the man who sent these cards?'

Shepherd said nothing. He still wasn't entirely convinced this wasn't some kind of test designed to make him incriminate himself and give Franklin an excuse to can him from the investigation.

'Tell you what,' Franklin smiled and opened his hands like he was closing the deal on a car, 'why don't we get Ellery to follow up with the search of Douglas's home.' He pointed to the picture on the wall. 'He has the local connections, he'll probably do a better job than we would. That way he can claw back some of the self-esteem you think I've beaten out of him and it leaves us free to stay on the trail. We got the scent of this thing now, and if Cooper is behind all this, then I want to look him in the eye and know it.'

Shepherd thought it through. The correct protocol for any geographically spread investigation like this was to share any leads on new suspects with the field office nearest to the target to enable swift response and arrests and minimize the chance of the subject getting away. The nearest field office to Charleston was Charlotte and, despite what Franklin said, agents from there would still arrive faster than them because they could fly too if they thought it necessary. He couldn't work out why Franklin, the seasoned, strictly-by-the-book agent, was suddenly bending the rules and cutting him in on it. It didn't add up. But he also badly wanted to stay on the investigation. One of his tutors had once told him that when considering any unknown you should always remove emotion from the equation because if you know the answer you're trying to reach you'll skew your formula to get there. A chill slid down his spine as he remembered who it was – Professor Douglas.

'How are you planning on flying to Charleston?' he said, reaching for the laptop case.

Franklin smiled, picked up the phone and started to dial. 'Same way we got here,' he said.

Shepherd took the Questioned Documents results from Franklin and slipped them inside the case. Just this simple task made his battered muscles creak and complain. He thought of the cold hard seats in the hold of the C-130. 'That's what I was afraid of.'

CHAPTER 32

Assistant Director O'Halloran put the phone down and listened to the yawning silence stretching out beyond his door. All the other section chiefs had gone – some on leave, the rest God only knew where – leaving a long corridor of empty offices and darkened windows. He'd never heard the building so quiet, even at Christmas when everything generally wound down. He could feel the absence of other people like the lack of a coat on a cold day.

He hit a function button on his computer to turn the sound back on from the CNN news feed. Like most people in the intelligence community he was addicted to information and the twenty-four-hour news cycle helped feed his addiction. It was also useful to keep up-to-date on what was being reported, just in case a breaking story compromised an on-going investigation. The Hubble/Marshall story had yet to break. At the moment the lead story was still the freak weather sweeping the nation. He watched for a while, distracted by the novelty of seeing people building snowmen on Miami Beach and New Yorkers in shorts and T-shirts paddling and splashing around in front of the huge Christmas tree outside the Rockefeller Center where the ice rink usually stood. Strange days.

He nudged the sound down a little and turned his attention back to an open file on the screen, condensing everything Agent Franklin had just told him into a few bullet points that he added to the Hubble case notes, highlighting the name Fulton Cooper. The Reverend's high-profile Christian charity work, particularly in relation to wounded servicemen and women, had turned him into something of a media favourite. He was an outspoken advocate of what he called a 'new crusade' which favoured a stronger and more aggressive military, particularly in relation to non-Christian countries. It was a stance that had made him much beloved of the Republican Party, who often brought him in to lend moral weight to various anti-government rallies whenever military spending came under review.

The tone of the newscaster shifted up a little as he introduced the next story and O'Halloran glanced up in response. The summery scenes from New York had been replaced by cold grey images of warships and sailors in black uniforms. A Chinese battle fleet had unexpectedly pulled out from around the disputed Senkaku islands in the East China Sea and headed home. The Japanese were claiming it as a victory but the Chinese, true to form, had so far refused to comment. The news anchor listed other unconfirmed rumours of further large-scale troop and military withdrawals elsewhere in the world, name-checking Syria and Somalia before the picture cut again to footage of the US air force base at Baghram in Afghanistan. O'Halloran leaned forward, feeling the usual tightening in his gut at the mere mention of the place. It looked like someone had kicked an ant's nest over there was so much swarming movement. Thousands of personnel were pouring out of troop carriers and onto massive C-5 transporter planes that then lumbered into the sky. It looked like the whole US presence was packing up and coming home. O'Halloran frowned. He was usually kept up to speed on stuff like this. He opened another window on his monitor and checked the internal mail, scrolling back through the military dispatches. Nothing. Maybe the news had got it wrong. Or maybe someone higher up had kept him out of the loop because of his personal history.

He picked up the framed photograph from the desk taken two Christmases ago, just before Michael had been posted. His son stood between him and Beth, a solid slab of a boy who towered over them both and looked like he was still in uniform even in his button-down shirt and jeans. Perhaps it was because he was tired, or that Christmas was round the corner and Michael wouldn't be home for it, but O'Halloran felt tears drip down his cheeks and glanced up at the door, nervous that someone might come in and find the big chief weeping like a sentimental drunk. He removed his glasses and placed them on the desk, wiping his eyes with the back of his hand. What the hell did it matter if anyone saw him like this, there was no one here anyway. He'd signed more leave forms over the past few weeks than he had all year and had to deny even more. It was like everyone wanted to go home.

He stared at his wife in the picture, leaning against the boy who dwarfed her: his Beth, smiling and radiant in the midst of the family she had created. He hadn't seen that look in a long time. It had started to slip the moment Michael shipped out to Afghanistan with his unit and he had seen it melt from her face entirely the day they got the news that he had been killed and was never coming home again. He felt a sudden tug to be with her, to hold her in the silence of the home they had built and where their son had grown up. He could easily grab a quick lunch and be back before anyone missed him.

He closed the files, logged out of the system and grabbed his jacket from over his chair. Just as he made it to the door his desk phone rang but he ignored it. He locked the door and walked away down the corridor, leaving the phone still ringing and getting quieter with every step as he headed back home.

CHAPTER 33

The river did not rise again. It settled back down to its previous level and the dam held fast. The only visible difference was the colour of the flowing water and the red residue it had left high on the banks, as though a massacre had taken place along its entire length.

Once they were sure the dam was solid and the danger was over, everyone shuffled back to the pool, exhausted and thirsty. Liv brought up the rear. She imagined what they must look like, trudging across the desert, caked in red mud like a procession of unfinished clay people, chunks of it falling off the exhausted line ahead of her, turning the sun-bleached desert a dusty pink. She reached the place where the land dropped away and saw the pool again, clear and glittering below her. All she wanted was to fall face first into it and drink forever, but as she saw the man at the head of the line draw close to the water's edge, she realized she could not – none of them could.

'Stop,' she called out, breaking into a shambling run. 'Stop. We must not wash in the pool.' She could see irritation in the faces that turned to her. 'We must not drink either, not until we are clean.'

'We must drink.' The man at the head of the line wore white driller's overalls so splattered with red mud he looked like a butcher. He turned away and made for the water.

'Wait!' Liv ran to intercept, stepping in front of him to bar his way. 'What's your name?'

The man looked furious. 'I am Kasim Barzani.'

'Kasim, I need a drink as much as you do, but after all we did to keep the pool clean we must be careful not to contaminate it.' She pulled at her shirt and a cloud of red dust shook loose and drifted to the ground.

'It is just mud. What difference will a little bit of mud make?' Kasim turned to everyone. 'How do we even know the water is poisoned?' He turned back to her. 'How do you know?'

Nods rippled down the line of exhausted faces. Liv could sense the thirst raging inside them. It wouldn't take much for them to trample her into the dust in their rush to get to the water. She thought about telling them of the symbols on the stone and what she had read there but it sounded crazy even to her as she voiced it in her head. 'I don't know if the water is poisoned, not for certain. But if you are so sure it isn't, then drink some, but not from the pool. Go drink some of the red water on the other side of the dam – then we will see if it is poisoned or not.'

Kasim's face flushed and Liv instantly regretted losing her temper. 'I'm sorry,' she said. She felt like the sun was boiling the brains in her head. She was too tired for this, and she hadn't asked these people to follow her into the desert – but that didn't stop her feeling responsible for them.

'I can wash everyone,' Tariq said, stepping out of line. All eyes turned to him. 'I was working away from the dam when the surge hit.' He held out his arms to show his clothes. 'I do not have so much of the red clay on me. I can clean myself with water from my canteen, then fetch more from the pool to clean the mud off everyone else.'

Kasim's small black eyes darted between Liv and Tariq as if this might be some kind of trick. 'Who goes first?' he asked.

'Does it matter?' Liv said, in a voice more breath than substance. She was so exhausted she could barely stand let alone speak. 'If it makes you feel any better then I will go last.'

'I will start with the cleanest,' Tariq suggested, 'that way I will soon have someone to help me.'

Kasim looked down at himself and nodded his agreement as he realized there were plenty more filthy than he was. Liv looked down at herself painted red from head to foot by the silty water as she had clung to the dam. She looked up at Tariq. 'Like I said –' she managed a smile '– guess I'll be going last.'

Liv observed the cleaning process from a distance, huddled in a thin blade of shadow created by one of the larger boulders that littered the land. After the confrontation with Kasim she didn't want to risk causing any more tension. She watched Tariq gently pouring water over the heads and bodies of the group, like an Old Testament prophet baptizing the faithful in the desert and studied the Starmap with fresh eyes. She had hoped that, now the events predicted in the first line had been revealed, it would shed new light on the rest of the prophecy. But even though symbols like the skull were repeated elsewhere in the text, their meanings seemed to shift depending on the symbols around them. She knew now that it meant poison in the first line but when it appeared again in the last that meaning did not seem to fit. It was like each symbol was a mirror, identical in form but reflecting something entirely different depending on where they were placed.

When the last man was clean and had gone to join the others by the main pool she tucked the paper into her pocket and shuffled stiffly across the dust to the red muddy puddle they had left behind. By now her headache was monumental, hammered hard by dehydration, heat and stress and made worse by the torment of seeing everyone else now gathered at the edges of the water, drinking.

'You might want to spread the word subtly that they should maybe go easy on the water,' she said to Tariq as he held out a canteen of water for her. 'I'm not sure how long it's going to have to last us. I'd tell them myself but I don't think I'm exactly Miss Popularity at the moment.'

Tariq looked over at the others. 'I think they have more respect for you than you know.'

'Even Kasim?' Liv poured the water over her face,

allowing the last few delicious drops to run into her mouth.

'He followed you into the desert didn't he? Don't worry – I'll tell them we should ration the water, at least until we know what we're doing.' He exchanged a full canteen for the empty one. 'What **are** we going to do?'

Liv took another drink of water then let out a long weary breath. 'Honestly?' she said. 'I have no idea.'

'But you made the water come. You knew the river was going to run red.'

She shook her head. 'The water came from the earth, not from me.'

'But you knew it was going to happen. How?'

'You really want to know?' Liv pulled the folded sheet of paper from her back pocket, now stained red. 'This is carved on the Starmap – the rock we laid on the Ghost's grave.' She pointed to the first line. 'See here – a river, an eagle, a skull. These are what made me think the water was about to be poisoned. Except . . .' She frowned as again she tried to express it. 'It was more like I felt it.'

'Like a premonition?'

'Something like that, only one that has somehow been captured in these symbols and written down. Not exactly scientific, is it? And please don't tell the others. The way things are at the moment they might lynch me if they realized I put them through all this because of some ancient warning scratched on a stone.'

Tariq smiled. 'Our culture is different from yours; we place more importance on the past and are not

199

so fixed on the future. The wisdom of the ancients is revered, and so are those who can interpret it. Many believe our ancestors saw our future more clearly than we see it ourselves. Did you know writing was invented here?' Liv nodded, remembering her conversations with Gabriel when they had been seeking the Starmap. 'Our belief is that the ancients invented the written word precisely so they might record these things, so they could speak to us and pass on the divine knowledge they carried. May I see it?'

Liv handed him the facsimile of the Starmap.

Tariq studied the document, his brow furrowed in thought, while Liv poured water over her hands, watching it run red on the ground.

200

'This crescent symbol with an arrow next to it,' he said, pointing to the end of the second line. 'It is still used by the Bedouin.'

Liv studied the symbol and noticed it was repeated again in the third and fourth lines.

'It refers to the phase of moon,' Tariq explained. 'In the desert we use the moon to measure the passing of time. Each phase is twenty-eight and a half days. That arrow next to it is the Bedu number nine, so together it means "nine moons".'

Liv did a calculation in her head. 'Two hundred and fifty-six nights – eight months.'

Tariq pointed to the very last symbol, another crescent enclosed by a circle. 'That also refers to time. It is the moon inside the sun, representing a day and a night together. It is more generic. It means "days".'

Liv looked at it in the light of this new information and something clicked in her head.

'"Days,"' she repeated, her eyes drawn back to the skull. 'That makes more sense. Whenever I look at this second skull I get a sense that something is ending, like a death. Death of days – sounds pretty apocalyptic.'

Tariq nodded solemnly. 'Every culture has its own account of the coming apocalypse. In mine we are taught the Sumerian myth of the god Marduk, who will return one day and destroy the earth. The Sumerians were incredibly advanced in their knowledge and understanding of science and cosmology in particular. Modern scholars believe that Marduk may actually be a planet whose orbit will one day make it crash into the Earth. There are many accounts in the past of near misses. The flood myth for example, present in every culture on earth, is believed by some to have been the result of a heavenly body passing close enough for its gravity to upset the flow of the oceans. Even the Christian nativity, with its bright travelling star has been attributed to Marduk. Sometimes it is represented as a bull with a sun between his horns, just like this is.' He pointed at the large star on the map, directly between the horns of Taurus.

'Eight months,' Liv mused, 'then Marduk returns to destroy the world. And the first line of this prophecy has already come to pass, so I guess we're already on the clock.'

Tariq handed the document back to her. 'I better go tell the others to go easy on the water,' he said. 'Otherwise we won't even make it to eight months: and I would hate to miss the end of the world.'

He bowed slightly then turned and headed away. There was something very comforting about the old-fashioned courtliness of this man. He was like someone from another time. He reminded her of Gabriel a little.

Liv looked back down at the symbols, focusing on one in particular.

Though many of them danced before her eyes, this one remained steady and clear. The sword above the crude horse figure was Gabriel – the warrior, the rider, sword of justice and liberator of the Sacrament. It was the one symbol that gave her hope because the sword also appeared towards the end of the prophecy next to another.

$$\underset{\rule{0pt}{1.2em}}{\overset{\rule{0pt}{0.3em}}{+}}$$

It meant two things to her: first, Gabriel was still alive, he had to be if he was to figure in events that would come to pass eight months from now; and second, before those eight months had run their course he would be reunited with the one who was represented by the T: the Sacrament, the Key – her.

CHAPTER 34

Gabriel woke to haunted moans echoing off stone walls. He opened his eyes and saw a vaulted ceiling high above him, a host of frozen angels bound to the stone, faces fixed in sorrow, as if in lament for what they saw below.

He twisted his head to the side and saw rows of beds stretching away to the nave of a church. They were filled with the writhing figures of men and women, straining against thick canvas bands that bound them, their skin a riot of boils that burst under the stress of their contortions. Doctors in contamination suits moved between the beds, tending to the worst cases by giving them shots that instantly calmed them. On the far wall he saw images of demons pulling tongues from the damned and devils boiling others in vats of oil and realized where he was. It was the Public Church in the Old Town of Ruin, close to the base of the Citadel. He had made it, but too late. The church was now a howling sick bay full of the infected.

The disease was spreading.

Gabriel gritted his teeth as a wave of fever rolled over him followed by an excruciating urge to scratch violently at his skin, but he was bound to his bed like the others so he could not. He heard footsteps approaching across the stone floor and closed his eyes, quelling the urge to writhe against his bindings and feel the ecstasy of relief from the growing itch. He felt hot, was getting hotter, and sweat tickled down his burning skin making it worse.

The footsteps stopped by his bed and he battled hard just to remain still. He didn't want to be knocked out with a dose of strong sedative. He needed to think and for that he needed to be conscious, no matter how agonizing it might be.

'You've looked better.' The voice took him by surprise. He recognized it. 'Don't worry,' the voice came again. 'I haven't told anyone who you are. You still have a number of serious outstanding warrants on your head and to be perfectly frank I just can't face the paperwork.'

'Arkadian!' Gabriel opened his eyes to a figure in a complete HazMat suit, one arm in a sling and a familiar face smiling behind a plastic visor.

'I heard some lunatic had ridden in here on a horse,' Arkadian's voice was muffled behind layers of material that kept him isolated from the infected air. 'How you feeling, better than you look, I hope?'

'I feel like I'm dying. I probably am dying.'

'Nonsense. You're the picture of health compared to some of these people.' He glanced up and across the huge empty space of the church. 'Most of them have been driven insane by this thing. They have to be heavily sedated just to stop them howling and weeping and tearing at their own flesh.'

Gabriel shuddered and clenched every muscle as a new prickling blossomed and spread inside him. He could see how easy it would be to give in and be driven mad by this unbearable sensation. 'How many cases?' he managed, between gritted teeth.

'Twenty-eight confirmed so far, eighty-four more being held in quarantine. They're all here in the Old Town too. So far it's only adults, children seem to have some kind of immunity and everyone's hoping to God it stays that way.'

'How many dead?'

Arkadian hesitated. He watched Gabriel snatching shallow breaths and guessed he was mindful of attracting the attention of the doctors. 'How many?' Gabriel repeated once the spasms had eased.

'Nine.'

'When was the first?'

'Two days ago, a waiter working at his aunt's café on the embankment. She was the next to die.'

Gabriel closed his eyes. He thought back to the two figures with breathing masks he had seen as he approached the Old Town wall; the paper suits and HazMat signs. If they had reacted fast enough to put a quarantine in place and isolate the infected then perhaps it had been contained. Maybe he wasn't too late.

'Have all the people infected worked close to the Citadel?'

'Yes – all except you. You have been the cause of

206

much excitement, and also concern. Concern because you're the only one with the Lamentation who hasn't originated inside these walls, excitement because it seems to have affected you differently. Most people are driven incoherent by it and die within forty-eight hours of the main symptoms appearing. But you can still talk. How long have you had it now?'

'I don't know. Days.'

'More than two?'

'Five, I think.'

Arkadian's eyes misted a little behind the visor as he imagined five days of this kind of suffering. 'Why did you come back?'

Gabriel shivered, freezing again despite his burning skin. 'To protect Liv. I wanted to bring it back where it came from. I wanted to return it to the Citadel.'

'Well – you have done.'

Gabriel shook his head. 'Not quite.'

Arkadian looked on until Gabriel had ridden out another spasm. 'Listen,' he said, leaning closer. 'I'm going to have to let the doctors know you're awake. They need to ask you some questions and run more tests. Right now you're the best chance they have of finding an antidote to this thing.'

'OK. Just don't tell them who I am.'

Arkadian managed a smile. 'You take me for a fool? You'll be no good to anyone if I have to throw you in jail.'

'But I want you to do something for me first. Send a message to the Citadel. Try and persuade them to open their doors and allow the sick inside.'

207

Arkadian stared down at him as though he had genuinely lost his mind. 'They're not going to do that.'

'Why not?'

'Because it's the Citadel, they don't let anyone inside.'

'Things change. This infection started in there, it must be decimating the population of the mountain. They probably need medical help more than anyone. Tell them doctors will come too, along with all the medical equipment they need to study this thing and try and find a cure. It's airborne. That's how I got it. I breathed it in when I was there. And all these people here worked on the embankment closest to the mountain, that's why they got it. So we need to return it to where it started and keep it contained. Just imagine if this thing spread.'

A sudden noise made Arkadian look up. A woman was fitting and bucking so hard against her bed it started to shift and move across the floor. Three suited medics converged, obscuring her from view. One of them struggled to push the bed back into place while the others fought with the woman who was now howling like a banshee. They were trying to sedate her but she was thrashing so hard they couldn't get the needle in her arm. The disturbance started to spread and others, tied and bound in the surrounding beds, began to rouse from their chemical slumbers. Then, as quickly as it had started, the thrashing stopped. The woman gave one last howl that sounded like the life was being physically torn from her, then was still.

The three medics stood for a moment, staring down at the body. Then one drifted away to calm another patient, and so did another, leaving only one remaining at her bedside, loosening and unwrapping the tight canvas bindings that were no longer needed.

'Ten,' Gabriel said.

Arkadian looked down at him and nodded. 'Who shall I contact in the Citadel?'

Gabriel closed his eyes, exhausted from the sheer effort of keeping it all together. 'A monk called Brother Athanasius. He helped me get inside the last time. He is the one who will help us again.' He opened his bloodshot eyes and stared up at Arkadian. 'Always assuming he's still alive.'

CHAPTER 35

For the second time that day the propellers of the C-130 clawed their way into the cold air and slung the plane up into the low, buffeting clouds.

Inside, strapped in the same painful jump seat as before, Shepherd's battered body felt every judder and lurch. He consoled himself with the knowledge that the flight to Charleston would be marginally shorter than the inbound journey had been.

He and Franklin were studying the background files on the Reverend Fulton R. Cooper, fruits of Shepherd's first real test-drive of the laptop and its ability to probe deeply and effortlessly into the databases of the FBI. He hadn't had long but even so the speed and range of information it had managed to spit out had been impressive. Of course it didn't hurt that Fulton Cooper was a public figure.

Shepherd read through the documents chronologically, starting with Cooper's humble beginnings in the seventies selling bibles on the road alongside his father after his mother ran out on them. It was his father who had encouraged his son to preach at fairs and small town chapels, realizing that his son had a rare gift to engage a crowd and that business was always brisker whenever he spoke. At fifteen, Cooper had already started preaching on TV, first as a guest of other televangelists then on his own show where his lively blend of infomercial techniques, personal appeals and assertion that modern Christianity was exemplified in the American dream caught on so fast he was nationwide in less than three years and pulling in half a million dollars worth of pledges per show. Then it all came tumbling down.

His wife suddenly left him and appeared on a *Primetime Live* exposé accusing him of being a habitual drunk and wife beater. The file contained copies of photographs and medical records going back years showing the black eyes and broken fingers Cooper had inflicted on her, as well as screen grabs taken from a security camera, which showed him kicking her repeatedly in the driveway of their house after returning home from a fundraiser. She filed criminal charges, his TV shows were immediately cancelled, and he ended up going to jail for criminal assault.

Cooper staged a press conference the day he was released re-pledging his life to Jesus and begging forgiveness for all the sins he had committed while Satan had taken possession of him. He had spent his time in the wilderness, he claimed, and had put the temptations of the devil behind him now the Lord had revealed a new path for him as a modern crusader. The last few pages of the file showed exactly how this had manifested itself. There were extracts from his sermons against other religions, details of his various media campaigns outlining his opposition to the construction of non-Christian places of worship anywhere in America and his call to pass a law making Christianity the only religion that could be legally taught in American schools. But by far the most powerful component of his new mission was a charitable initiative called 'Operation Saviour' which, according to the literature, gave 'spiritual help and healing for warriors on the frontline of the holy wars'. It raised money to send medical help and psychiatric counsellors to servicemen and women fighting in religiously sensitive war zones such as Afghanistan and the Middle East and helped them get jobs when they returned home again. It had won Cooper some very high-powered admirers. There were pictures of Cooper smiling and waving on stage at various political rallies, standing shoulder to shoulder with senators, congressmen and members of the cabinet from several administrations.

The buzz of static cut straight through Shepherd's head as Franklin flicked on the comms. 'What d'you think?'

Shepherd stared at the most recent photograph of Cooper, beaming for the cameras at a Presidential primary. 'He seems an unlikely terrorist.'

'They're generally the most effective sort.'

'Also, Dr Kinderman and Professor Douglas are two of the smartest people I've ever met. I'm not sure I buy it that someone like Cooper could persuade them to sabotage their life's work.'

'Maybe he had something on them, every man has his weak spot and every man has his price. Or perhaps they found the Lord and then Cooper found them.'

'Professor Douglas had already found Him.'

'Really?'

'Not all scientists are Godless heathens. I heard him deliver a lecture once on the relationship between religion and science where he said studying the stars was just another way of trying to get closer to God. He equated it with saying a prayer. So I'm having trouble seeing how he could destroy the very thing that enables him to do that. It would be like persuading the Pope to blow up St Peter's.'

Franklin chewed over this last piece of information. 'How much do you know about Operation Fish?'

Shepherd flicked back to the top sheet and re-read the Questioned Documents results that had thrown up Cooper's name in the first place. 'Wasn't it some kind of religiously motivated witch-hunt?'

'It was if you believe certain sections of the press. It was an inter-departmental internal investigation prompted by whispers that various offices of government had been infiltrated and were now being run by a large Christian network whose agenda didn't necessarily coincide with the national interest. Part of the investigation was a data-catching initiative to flush out radical Christians: it's not just the extreme Islamists the government wants to keep its eye on, dangerous and crazy is still dangerous and crazy no matter which God you bend your knee to. Anyway we put out a story that Darwinian evolution was going to be made a mandatory subject of study in all schools then set up a petition to collect the names of people who were violently opposed to it, which is how Cooper fell into the net. Guess he sees himself more of a "made in the image of God" kind of way than just some high-functioning monkey.'

'What happened to the investigation – did they ever make any arrests?'

Franklin shook his head. 'A combination of pressure from both houses and an effective press campaign claiming it was an attack on the first amendment got it shut down before it could bear any fruit.'

'But isn't that exactly what a powerful secret network working inside government would do to prevent itself from being discovered?'

Franklin shrugged. 'I just obey orders, and there was no political desire to keep the investigation going. Targeting Christians in an overwhelmingly Christian country is never going to win many votes, particularly post 9/11 with Islam becoming the new communism. The average guy on the street would probably be quite happy to discover a group of powerful Christians were quietly running the country. But here's a thought for you, this network was supposed to extend far and wide, not only in central government but also in law enforcement, the judiciary – NASA. So if, as you say, Professor Douglas was a man of faith maybe he was part of this network, maybe Kinderman was too. And people of strong faith will do anything if they believe it's God's will. So whatever preconceptions you have about the Reverend Cooper, or your Professor Douglas, you need to be under no illusion that whoever we are chasing down here are powerful and very motivated people. We need to tread carefully, Agent Shepherd, there's nothing more frightening than an enemy who thinks death is just a gateway to something better.'

CHAPTER 36

The Postillion Gate swung wide and the slow clip of hooves on cobbles echoed across the Public Square as the tribute cart emerged from the seminary complex in the Old Town of Ruin.

Riding up front were two seminaries, dressed all in black apart from the white of their surgical masks. Usually the weekly spectacle of delivering provisions to the Citadel was witnessed by large crowds of tourists who would gather along the route, cameras in hand, ready to get the best view of this timeless ceremony. Today there was no one.

The cart passed through the stone arch onto the embankment encircling the base of the Citadel, heading towards the wooden bridge spanning the moat of waving grass that grew where water once rippled. The wind flapped and tugged at the black cassocks of the two seminarians, ruffling the cellophane round the many floral tributes that still covered the spot on the flagstones where the monk had fallen.

The sound of the wheels changed to a deep rumble as they moved off the flagstones and onto the wooden bridge spanning the dry moat. It jerked to a halt by the waiting wooden platform, secured at each corner by thick ropes that soared up the side of the mountain and disappeared into the dark of an overhanging cave high above them.

Normally, the unloading would take four men about ten minutes to complete. Today it took the two of them less than five. The amount of food had been drastically cut over the past few weeks, suggesting there were far fewer mouths to feed. The only things they had requested more of – much more – were medical supplies.

The weekly bundle of correspondence was the last thing to be loaded. It was placed into the wooden box built into the corner of the platform before one of the seminarians pulled hard on a thin, hemp rope, causing a bell to sound high in the mountain above.

They watched as the ropes creaked and tightened and the platform started to rise, relieved that there were still arms strong and healthy enough to pull it up.

The platform rose steadily, three hundred feet up into the gloom of the tribute cave where it jerked to a solid stop. Hooded figures wearing surgical masks peeled away from the shadows to unload it, stacking the crates of food in various stone shelves cut into the walls and handing the medical equipment straight to the waiting brown cloaks who took it down into the darkness of the mountain where the distant sounds of suffering could be heard.

Brother Osgood watched from the edge of the cave, fiddling nervously with the straps on his face mask. He had only recently been elevated from the lowest order of monks within the mountain to the brown cloaks of the Administrata, not that the old system of apprenticeship had much bearing since the first case of the blight had struck. He waited until most of the supplies had been unloaded then stole forward, feeling the platform rock beneath his feet as he plucked the correspondence from its box and scurried quickly away again, glad to be away from all the people in the tribute cave.

He moved through the dark corridors, clutching the bundle to his chest, probing the blackness ahead for signs of anyone else coming his way. Since the blight had struck, the Apothecaria had advised everyone to minimize contact with others and movement inside the mountain had been severely restricted.

Osgood passed a padlocked door with a handwritten sign nailed to it saying Cave Robigo – Beware Blight. Similar signs barred routes all through the mountain, remnants of the initial attempt to contain the disease by sealing off different areas as each new case occurred. No one had bothered to take them down, even though they were no longer relevant. There were far too many other things to occupy the monks and everyone knew to ignore them anyway, at least the ones who were still rational.

A low, guttural moan wormed its way out of the darkness and the cotton mask sucked in and out of his mouth as his heart rate rose. Even after a year he had still not got used to the dark of the mountain, and still had nightmares from time to time in the quiet midnight of the dormitory. He would imagine the tunnels closing in on him, or dread creatures pursuing him down the labyrinthine corridors, the sounds of their inhuman grunts getting closer and closer until he woke, breathless and slicked with sweat. And now the nightmares had escaped into this waking world.

He clicked the latch on the heavy wooden door that led into the garden, shielding his eyes in preparation for the blinding daylight about to hit him.

The garden filled a large central portion of the mountain and was surrounded on all sides by high walls of sheer rock, It was the sunken crater of a long-extinct volcano that had bequeathed such rich and fertile soil that it had sustained the men of the mountain for thousands of years, through drought and famine and siege. For so long it had been the living jewel at the heart of the black mountain.

But not any more.

Osgood blinked as his eyes adjusted to the daylight and made his way past vegetable beds filled with the decaying remains of beans and tomato plants, lying black and shrivelled among the sludgy remains of pumpkins that looked like rotting heads. The vines that had covered the rock walls hung in withered curtains and broken branches littered the ground, buried in drifts of brown leaves bearing the black spots that had first heralded the arrival of the contagion. And all around, the air that had once smelled so strongly of earth and loam and life, now carried the bitter tang of wood smoke mixed with something Osgood would not forget for the rest of his days.

Through the broken trees he could see the source of the smell as well as the group of monks who presided over it. It was the firestone, piled high with tangled branches through which hungry flames licked, and on top of them – three bodies.

They had started to burn the corpses on the third day of the contagion when they began to run out of places to store them and panic had already started to gnaw at the edges of the ordered life of the mountain. It had been decided that diseased corpses posed too much of an additional danger to health and they had to be either buried or burned. Burning was quicker. The fire had been burning constantly ever since, as the bodies kept on coming.

'Brother Athanasius!' Osgood called to the group, coming to rest as far from the heat and stink of the fire as he could manage. 'I have brought the dispatches.'

A monk turned to look at him, his bald head and face marking him out in the otherwise long-haired and bearded community of men, the pain and trauma of the last week, carved deep into his face.

Athanasius nodded a greeting and stepped forward, holding his hand out for the bundle of dispatches, sensing the novice's reluctance to come closer. Traditionally the letters could only be seen by the Abbot but the blight had swept through the mountain with no regard for age or rank and most of the senior clerics and heads of the various guilds were now either dead or strapped to beds in one of the many isolation wards set up throughout the mountain. The only ones left of any authority were Father Malachi, the head librarian, Father Thomas, also one of the group by the fire, and Athanasius himself who, as the Abbot's chamberlain, had now assumed his duties.

He took the bundle and was about to return to the fire when he spotted his name written on the top letter. He tore open the envelope and read the hand-written note inside.

> *Brother Athanasius,*
> *The disease you told me about when last we spoke has spread. I have it and so do many others. I'm sure many in the Citadel have it too. We must find a cure and stop it spreading further. In order to do this I ask you to allow the sick and their carers into the Citadel. The more patients the doctors can study, the quicker they will be able to find a cure and by bringing the sick into the mountain we can concentrate the infection and contain it. I understand the magnitude of what I am asking but I hope you can help me again, as you once did before – for all our sakes.*
> *Yours,*
> *Gabriel Mann*

Athanasius handed the letter to Thomas, his mind buzzing as he waited for him to finish reading it. In the entire history of the Citadel, no one had ever been allowed inside the mountain who had not been strictly vetted and ordained. Even though the circumstances they found themselves in were exceptional in the extreme, there were still those who would rather die than break with tradition. And this would mean bringing women in too.

Thomas finished and looked up, his intelligent eyes registering the shock of what he had just read. 'What do you think?' Athanasius prompted.

Thomas stared into the flames now steadily consuming the latest victims of the terrible blight that no one had so far been able to stop. 'I think we need to talk to Father Malachi,' he said. 'We cannot sanction this without him, or the support of those he represents. Unfortunately, I'm fairly certain I know what his response will be.'

Athanasius nodded. Malachi was as traditional and conservative as any in the mountain and the seemingly endless parade of recent calamities that had plagued the Citadel had only made him more rather than less so. He would be a hard man to convince, but the letter in Athanasius's hand offered the first real glimmer of hope he had encountered in some time and he was not about to let it go.

'Then we will just have to convince him,' he said, and smiled for what seemed like the first time in days as he strode away across the blasted garden, heading towards the Great Library at the heart of the mountain.

CHAPTER 37

The Great Library spread like a maze through forty-two chambers of varying sizes, deep in the heart of the mountain. It was one of the greatest treasures of the Citadel, the most valuable and unique collection of books and ancient texts anywhere in the world, gleaned from thousands of years of acquisitions and donations. It was also one of the reasons for the mountain's millennia-old tradition of isolation and secrecy. There were texts housed in the library's restricted sections containing knowledge so dangerous that few had ever been allowed to see them, even inside the cloistered and secretive world of the Citadel.

Athanasius approached the entrance, a steel-and-glass door cut into the solid rock of the tunnel that looked like it belonged more in a hi-tech science facility than an ancient monastery. He placed his hand against a scanner set into the wall and a cold blue light swept across it to check and verify his identity.

'Don't show him the letter,' Father Thomas said, arriving breathless at his side. 'It is an appeal for us to help save lives. Malachi cares little for people. All that matters to him are his precious books.'

'Agreed,' Athanasius nodded.

The door into the airlock slid open in a hiss of hydraulics. It was only large enough for one person at a time and Athanasius took the lead, stepping inside and waiting for the outer door to close behind him. A light blinked above a second scanner and a down-draught of air swept over him as impurities and dust were cycled down to filters built into the floor. The library was climate-controlled: a constant sixty-eight degrees Fahrenheit and a dry, 35 per cent relative humidity to protect all the precious paper, papyrus and vellum from moisture and the attendant damage it could wreak. The light stopped blinking and Athanasius placed his palm on a second scanner that controlled the final door into the library.

Nothing happened.

The blue light that should have crept down his hand did not appear and the door leading into the library remained closed. Athanasius peered through the window set into it but saw only perpetual darkness beyond.

'Try it again,' Father Thomas shouted from outside, his voice muffled by the door, his face framed in the window and frowning at the dead scanner as if its failure to do its job was a deliberate act of mutiny. Father Thomas had designed and updated all the security and control systems in the library and took any faults, no matter how small, very personally.

Athanasius placed his hand back on the glass. This

time something did happen. The door behind him opened again, allowing him back out into the corridor.

'Someone's tampered with the entry system,' Father Thomas said, looking as if he was about to explode with anger. He glared past Athanasius at the mutinous locking system then focused on something over his shoulder. 'Malachi,' he said.

Athanasius turned and saw what had caught his attention. Through the window of the closed door a small orb of light had appeared in the distant dark of the library, growing larger as it wobbled towards them. This was another of Father Thomas's genius innovations, a movement-sensitive lighting system that followed every visitor and illuminated only their immediate surroundings as they made their way through the library leaving the vast majority of the precious collection in almost permanent darkness. The frequency of light even changed as one progressed further into the collection, turning through soft orange to red when the older and more delicate surfaces and inks were reached.

'Remember our mission here,' Athanasius whispered. 'Do not let your anger overshadow our greater purpose.'

Thomas grunted and fumed quietly as the orb of bobbing light drew closer and revealed the bearish, hunched figure of Father Malachi like a tadpole at the centre of a luminous orb of spawn. He shuffled along, taking his time as he followed the thin filament of guide lights set into the floor to lead people through the maze of the library.

'Can I assist you?' he said as he finally reached them, his voice rendered flat and robotic by the intercom that was thankfully still working.

'What have you done to my entry system?' Thomas asked, the peevishness in his voice clearly evident.

'It is not your entry system. It belongs to the library and I have locked it.'

'Why?'

'Because I do not want just anybody to be able to gain free access here: I'm sure, with everything the way it is in the mountain, you understand that.'

Father Thomas opened his mouth to respond but Athanasius held his hand up to silence him, mindful that they should choose their battles and this was not the one they needed to win. 'That is why we have come to talk to you,' he said. Malachi's eyes darkened behind the thick pebbles of his glasses and his bushy eyebrows beetled above them. 'We have been contacted by the outside,' Athanasius continued. 'They have requested that we help develop a cure for the blight.'

'They have a cure?' Malachi took an involuntary step forward, his glasses magnifying the hope in his eyes.

'No. Not yet. They are working on one, and they would like us to help.'

The shadows on Malachi's face settled back into guarded suspicion. 'How?'

Athanasius took a breath and ran his hand over the smooth dome of his skull. He had hoped the carrot of a cure might have been enough to tempt

Malachi away from his entrenched and long-held suspicion of the world beyond the walls. He should have known better. 'We are all united in suffering,' he said, 'and in our desire to prevent others from suffering as we have.' Malachi said nothing. He just continued to stare through the window like a glowing, malevolent ghost. 'We have been asked to allow medical teams into the mountain so they might treat our infected and study the disease at its origin.'

Malachi's eyebrows shot up in outrage. 'Outsiders? Inside the mountain? I hope you are not seriously considering this lunacy?'

'Is it lunacy? To want to try and arrest the spread of this creeping death?'

'We have weathered plagues in the mountain before. You should read your history, Brother Athanasius. We suffered and survived our trials then and we shall do so again, and without the need to welcome the world in to gawp at us and what we guard here – our sacred order is more robust than you give it credit for.'

'The plagues of the past are nothing compared to what we face now,' Father Thomas cut in, stepping into the narrow airlock to join Athanasius. 'Historically there has always been greater medical knowledge inside the mountain than outside, so there was never any need to look further than these walls for cures and treatments. We have also historically enjoyed rude health, have we not? But with the march of time and the loss of the Sacrament neither of those things are now true.'

'Yes,' Malachi replied, his fierce eyes turning back to Athanasius, 'and whose fault is that? Had the Sacrament remained here then none of this would have happened. If you want to cure this blight that you have brought upon us then I suggest you concentrate on returning the Sacrament to the mountain where it belongs. That is my answer. Bring back the girl and what she stole and we shall see then how things change.'

Athanasius was not a violent man but if the thick glass of the airlock door had not stood between them he may well have struck Malachi right then and there in the middle of his narrow-minded face. The whole world could wither and perish for all Malachi cared, just so long as his precious library remained unsullied and safe. His act of sabotaging the entry system so he could prevent people freely entering his dark kingdom merely proved it: he had effectively pulled up a drawbridge to create a state within a state, with himself and all the other librarians inside and everyone else without.

'Do you intend to stay locked up in there indefinitely?' Athanasius asked, the hint of a plan starting to form in his mind.

'I do indeed, both to protect the library as well as shield my staff from the dangerous tide of lunatic liberalism that seems to be sweeping through the corridors of the Citadel.'

'So I take it you will not even consider this letter or the proposal it contains?'

Malachi looked at the envelope in Athanasius's

hand as if it were a viper about to strike. 'I will not even touch it,' he replied.

'Very well,' Athanasius took a step back and rejoined Thomas in the passage. 'As you have effectively removed yourself from the community of the mountain you have also disqualified yourself from its governance. Therefore, Father Thomas and I will now vote on this matter ourselves.'

Malachi looked like he was about to explode. 'You can't do that. Any change in the constitution must be voted on and agreed unanimously by all the guilds. And for that you need me.'

Athanasius shook his head. 'If you read the Citadelic statutes closely you will see that in fact a consensus is required from all **active** guilds, as voted for by their chief representatives. And as you have just made abundantly clear, you and your members are no longer an active part of the mountain. So as sole representatives of the still active guilds within the mountain Thomas and I will consider the merit of this proposal alone. We shall inform you of our decision once it is made, of course, out of courtesy. Good day, Father Malachi.'

Then he turned and walked briskly away before Malachi had a chance to respond.

CHAPTER 38

The C-130 dropped through violently churning clouds and banked hard to bring it into the wind and onto its approach heading.

'Jesus, would you look at that,' the pilot's voice crackled through the comms.

Shepherd peered across the cargo space and through the tiny windows opposite. He caught small glimpses of the city of Charleston below, frozen solid and blanketed with snow. He wondered why the pilot sounded so surprised after what he had told them about the weather earlier. It was like this all over the South he had said. A section of midtown slid into view, the higher buildings looking like huge ice crystals that had punched up through the ground, then the plane shifted again, bringing a new view into the windows.

Below him the broad Cooper River snaked through the heart of the city. It seemed low, just a narrow channel winding its way through flat, snow dusted banks. The USS *Yorktown*, a World War Two museum ship at permanent mooring just down from the Ravenel Bridge, looked like it was beached on the white flats. Then Shepherd saw cracks in the white that surrounded it and realized what it was. The river wasn't low at all and the white flats not the banks, they *were* the river. The whole thing had frozen solid leaving just a trickle of water running down the centre.

The plane levelled off, bringing more of the city into view and Shepherd finally saw what the pilot had seen. It wasn't the snow or even the extraordinary sight of a frozen South Carolina tidal river that had drawn the exclamation from his lips – it was what was on the river.

East of the bridge and beyond the cracked edge of the ice sheet where the fresh water met the salt of the sea were more ships than Shepherd had ever seen before in one place. Closest to land were smaller vessels and fishing boats, all crammed together so tight it looked like you could almost walk across the river using them as stepping-stones. Further out in the deeper water were bigger ships: container vessels, tankers, cruise liners, military ships and even the immense outline of an aircraft carrier. It was an astonishing sight and there was something both impressive and deeply unsettling about it. Just before the plane started its final descent and cut the view entirely Shepherd realized what it was. They all had their bow inward. Every single one of the hundred or so ships was pointing towards land.

CHAPTER 39

Father Malachi surged through the library in his halo of light.

Following his meeting with Athanasius and Father Thomas he was in a state of total shock. A month ago, when the Abbot and the Prelate still lived and the Sancti still held sway within the mountain, Athanasius would have been executed for even considering the heresy he was now proposing. Secrecy and isolation were how the mountain had kept its great secrets for so long. Now that damned fool with his weak, liberal ideas was going to allow a bunch of total strangers inside – civilians, doctors, women! – all of them carrying this filthy disease. How quickly the solid walls of his world had started to crumble.

He passed through an arch and strode through the Renaissance section, his follow light becoming steadily dimmer as he travelled back through the great archive of man's learning. While others in the Citadel turned to God in their time of need, Malachi always found divinity and peace in the written word. Every great thought and every profound event mankind had ever had or experienced was written and recorded somewhere in this vast network of caves. There was an answer for everything here somewhere.

When that damned monk Samuel had jumped to his death and the Abbot had confided in him that his body may have contained clues as to the identity of the Sacrament, he had come to the library and taken solace in the chronicles of the Rides of the **Tabula Rasa**. These recorded every historical instance where the identity of the Sacrament had been threatened. Each time the knights had ridden out and each time the traitors had been found and silenced and the Sacrament's secret had remained. Later when the blight had appeared he had found records detailing outbreaks of other contagions throughout the Citadel's long history. Again, the mountain had always recovered and prospered. It would do so again. He had to believe that. Whatever lunacy Athanasius was considering it was up to him to maintain the true spirit of the Citadel. And with the Sacrament gone it was the library that now held the greatest secrets. He would keep the door locked and the world outside, even if the mountain beyond was awash with strangers. The soul of the Citadel was in these books, and so — somewhere — was the answer to the question now running though his head. 'What should be done about Athanasius?'

CHAPTER 40

Liv and Tariq stood by the edge of the pool, staring down at the muddy dish of water. They had only been in the desert half a day but already the water level was down by half.

'You did tell everyone to go easy?' Liv murmured.

Tariq nodded and squinted up at the sun, dropping low in the afternoon sky. 'It's not the people who are the problem.'

The combination of fierce desert sun, the dam stopping the river from replenishing the pool and the natural leaching away of water into the dry ground meant the pool was emptying so fast they could almost see it happening.

Liv looked up at Tariq. 'We can't stay here long. Where's the nearest town or settlement?'

He nodded back towards the compound. 'Al-Hillah is half a day's ride in that direction, so maybe two days' walking.'

Liv imagined walking for two days in this heat. The few hours it had taken to get here had been hellish enough. 'How much food do we have?'

'Hardly any: the riders didn't give us much time to pack and everyone was busy filling their canteens with water. Certainly not enough to feed everyone on a hard, two-day journey.' He looked at the lengthening shadows stretching across the land. 'I will go alone, one person alone will need less food. The heat is fading so I could travel all night and cover a lot of ground. I will take as little as I need and bring back horses and supplies. The water here should last another day.'

Liv shook her head. 'If you're going I'm coming with you.'

'No. You should stay.'

'With Kasim and his barely disguised looks of hate? I don't think so. Besides, what if something happens to you out there and we're stuck here, slowly dying of hunger and thirst while we wait for your return?'

'Nothing will happen to me.'

'Not if there's two of us it won't. Come on, let's go check the food supplies and break the happy news.' She turned and walked away before Tariq could argue.

The food had been collected and stored in a large backpack that was kept in the shade of one of the rocks to protect it from the worst of the heat. They had been rationing it, handing out just a handful of dried dates or a small piece of an energy bar every few hours to make it last. Liv wasn't sure how much was left but figured she and Tariq would need to take the lion's share to give them the energy they would need for their journey. She scanned the patches of shade beneath the larger boulders looking for Kasim, figuring if anyone was going to object to their plan it would be him. She felt relieved when she couldn't see him.

She made it to the boulder where their 'larder' was kept and reached into the gap beneath it for the pack. She knew something was wrong the moment her hand closed around the shoulder strap and pulled the bag towards her. It was too light. She dragged it out, unsnapped the cover and looked inside. Empty.

She looked around in panic, her exhausted mind knocked sideways by the discovery. The flat stone and pocket knife used for cutting the energy bars was on the ground beside her. She *was* in the right place – so where was the food? No one had said anything about it running low the last time the rations had been handed out.

Then she stopped dead, remembering the last person who had done it.

It had been Kasim.

Kasim had handed round the last rations about an hour ago.

And now Kasim was missing.

CHAPTER 41

Joint Base Charleston served as both a civil and a military airport, hence the blunt utility of its name. It was also shared by different branches of the armed forces and the C-130 pulled to a stop now between the drooping wings of two massive C17 military transports, one painted in Army camouflage the other in Air Force blue.

'Agents Franklin and Shepherd?' Their welcoming committee snapped to attention as they walked down the loading ramp into a freezing wind that was whipping off the river. He was a two-chevron Petty Officer with a clipboard and a pink, scrubbed-looking face that appeared to be suffering in the cold. Franklin flashed his creds, Shepherd fumbled his from the coat he'd borrowed from Marshall after his had been destroyed by the helium blast, the PO ticked something on his clipboard and gestured towards a waiting Crown Victoria with base markings on the side and its engine running. 'Sorry gentlemen, you just got me. We're kind of short-staffed here. And I can't hang around or let you have the car either. I can take you off base and into town but that's about all. Traffic is hellacious today for some reason. You'll have to find your own way back. I'm real sorry.'

'Don't worry about it, son – we're grateful for any help.' Franklin showed him Cooper's address and the PO whistled through his teeth. 'Fancy. That's south of Broad in the old town, where the tourists go and the rich folks live. Like I say, I can take you there but I can't wait.'

Franklin held up his hands in surrender. 'No problem – we can hook up with the local PD once we're off base and take it from there.'

Franklin moved towards the passenger seat leaving the back for Shepherd. He didn't speak again until the car was rolling.

'Your staffing situation got anything to do with that floating traffic jam out in the river?'

'You got that right, sir. We've had unauthorized ships arriving here for the past twenty-four hours. The Port Authority is in meltdown. They've drafted us in to help deal with the situation but it seems to be getting worse. We put out a general call twelve hours ago advising all shipping that the port is now embargoed but no one seems to be taking any notice. They just keep on coming.' The PO eased out onto a broad boulevard lined with piles of greying snow. 'Did you see the carrier when you came in?'

'Hard to miss it.'

'That's the USS *Ronald Reagan*. It's supposed to be out on patrol in the Atlantic but it showed up here about an hour ago. There's all hell breaking loose over at command. They're talking mutiny and all kinds of stuff.'

'Anyone spoken to the captain?'

'If they have, I don't know about it. What I do know is that none of the ships – military or civilian – have responded to communications. We can track them coming in on radar so we know they're headed here, but all attempts to contact them and divert them elsewhere have been met with radio silence. It's like a fleet of ghost ships coming in to anchor.'

'What about the crews, they sick or something?'

'They're all fine. Everything's fine. There's no engine failure or nothing like that. They get here, drop anchor and start disembarking. That's why we're short-staffed, everyone's on double duty trying to deal with all the paperwork. By rights all the military personnel should be arrested for dereliction of duty and held in the brig but we haven't even got the capacity for that. The brig holds around three hundred men and it's full already. There's six thousand on the *Reagan* alone. We also got a cruiser and a destroyer out there and a coupla frigates heading this way. I heard talk they were gonna commandeer Fort Sumter out in the bay and use it as a holding pen, but then the National Park Service got all bent out of shape because it's a civil war monument and all. You ask me, the whole thing's a mess. A big crazy mess.' He shook his head.

Shepherd watched the PO's eyes in the rear-view

mirror. They were edgy, flicking left and right, fixing on the road then checking the mirrors like someone might be following them. His fingers tapped on the wheel as he drove, like he was nervous or scared. 'Can't you send some of these ships off to another port, take the pressure off here a little?' he asked.

'Well that's the thing, sir – we got Kings Bay and Jacksonville south of here but they're having the same problem. They got ships showing up there too.'

'Any port in a storm,' Shepherd muttered, looking out of the window at the frozen edges of the city as it started to snow again.

'What's that, sir?'

'Nothing.'

'I tell you one thing.' The PO's hands continued to drum anxiously on the wheel. 'The one thing all the ships have in common.' He checked the rear-view mirror one last time before whispering his secret. 'They're all American. American registered and American crews. And the funny thing is, when we interview the crews, and ask 'em why they put in here, they all keep saying the same thing: "We just needed to get home", that's what they're saying – "We need to get home".'

Home

That word again, taunting Shepherd with a meaning he had never really known. Outside his window the parking lots and business units of northern Charleston began to disappear as they headed Downtown. The PO had been right about the traffic. Lines of cars packed solid with people and possessions, inching forward through the drifting snow. The vast majority of them were from out of state. Shepherd even spotted one with Canadian tags.

Shepherd's phone buzzed and he checked the caller ID before answering.

'Hello, Merriweather.'

'I just heard about the explosion at Marshall. Is it true?' He sounded about as tired as Shepherd felt.

Shepherd glanced at Franklin before answering. 'Unofficially, yes. We're trying to keep a lid on it at the moment, though, so don't repeat that to anyone.'

'What about James Webb? Was it badly damaged?'

Shepherd looked out of the window at the frozen city. 'It was totally destroyed, or at least all the components in the cryo testing lab were.'

The phone went silent and Shepherd watched the lines of traffic slip by as the PO made good use of his lights and siren to thread his way through it.

'What about Professor Douglas?' Merriweather said. 'Is he – was he?'

'He's fine so far as we know. We haven't found him yet. He wasn't at the facility. We're trying to track him down now. But no-one was hurt, which is the only good news. Well, that and the fact that your job probably just got a little more secure. It will probably be cheaper to fix Hubble now than rebuild James Webb, so I guess every storm cloud has a silver lining.'

'Yeah I guess.' He didn't sound particularly happy.

Outside, the lines of cars thinned a little as they reached the older part of town with its grander, prettier architecture: Colonial-style mansions, Federal, Georgian – all sliding past behind a veil of snow like ghosts of the city's history.

'How is Hubble – any change?' Shepherd asked, trying to lift Merriweather's mood.

'Yes actually there is.' He brightened a little. 'It's still pointing straight down to Earth but at least it hasn't started losing altitude or anything worrying like that. If anything, it appears to be settling into a new orbit.'

'What about Taurus, anything new appearing there?'

'Not that I know of but I'm a bit blind at the moment. I'll do some asking around with some people I know with telescopes that still work.'

'Thanks, Merriweather. I appreciate it. Try and get some sleep.'

'Ah, sleep is overrated. I can sleep when I'm old.'

Shepherd smiled. 'Take care, Merriweather.' He hung up.

The tyres rumbled as they hit the old cobbled roads built with discarded ballast stones from British sailing ships when Charleston was part of its expanding Empire.

'Take a right over there,' Franklin said, pointing to a turn up ahead, 'otherwise you'll get caught up in the one-way system.'

'You been here before, sir?' the driver said, making the turn.

'Coupla of times.'

They were in the heart of the tourist district now and every store served either food or nostalgia. The driver slowed as they passed a mule-drawn carriage with a few brave tourists huddled in the back, heads down against the driving snow, looking back to where the harbour was framed at the end of the long street. You could just see the ships through the snow, clustered together in the same waters where sails once billowed and cannons boomed as the British were driven out.

'Here you go, gentlemen.'

The Crown Vic turned a corner and pulled up to the kerb by a classic red-brick Charleston Single House with chocolate-brown shutters framing tall sash windows. Bright lights burned inside making the windows glow, and steam rose from a vent in the basement. On street level two broad steps led up through an arch to an iron gate that served as the front entrance. A Christmas wreath was hanging above a rectangle of polished brass with THE CHURCH OF CHRIST'S SALVATION engraved on it.

'Sorry I got to dump you,' the PO said, like a cab driver desperate to get rid of his last fare before home. 'Just bad timing with all the craziness.'

'Don't worry about it and thanks for the ride.'

They got out of the car and Shepherd felt the cold wrap itself round him as it drove off, the snow swallowing the sound of its engine and leaving them in crystal silence. Franklin pressed a button by the side of the locked gate but if it made a sound inside the house the snow swallowed that too. 'You think we should sing Christmas carols?' he said.

The sound of a bolt cracked through the silence, making Shepherd jump.

Halfway along the side of the house a door opened and a woman stepped out and started making her way towards them. She looked to be about thirty or so, her black hair cut short and matched by a black two-piece trouser suit worn over a grey turtle-neck sweater. She didn't smile as she covered the ten or so feet between them, merely looked at them both, sizing them up, her breath clouding in the cold air. Shepherd noticed she had a slight limp and, as she drew closer, he saw a thin pale scar cutting across her left cheek. She stopped a foot short of the closed gate and regarded them through the bars. 'Can I help you, gentlemen?' The scar puckered a little when she spoke.

'Yes, I think you probably can,' Franklin held up his ID. 'Is the good Reverend at home?'

Her grey eyes flicked to the badge then back again.

'The Reverend Cooper is on air at the moment.'

'That's OK, we can wait.' Franklin smiled. The

woman did not. Neither did she make any move to open the gate.

'What's your name, miss?'

'Boerman. Caroline Boerman.'

'Well, Miss Caroline from the Carolinas we can wait out here if you'd like.' He kicked his shoe against the wall to clear the snow from it. 'But I should tell you I'm a Southern boy and the cold makes me awful grouchy.'

A small smile finally cracked the mask of her face, puckering the scar even more but going nowhere near her eyes. 'Of course,' she said, unlocking the gate and stepping back to allow them past. 'Where are my manners?'

CHAPTER 42

The front door of the Church of Christ's Salvation opened into a warm, high-ceilinged entrance hall running the entire width of the building. It was plainly decorated in white that caught the glare from the tall windows looking out onto the snow-covered street. Three sofas, also white, were arranged in a horseshoe around a low coffee table with leaflets and small booklets on the surface next to a jar filled with multicoloured plastic key rings. The only real clue as to what went on in the building was coming from the television fixed above the bare brick fireplace.

Now you have watched me on TV today.

The Reverend Fulton Cooper said, his eyes burning from the screen.

I've taken my own step of faith to come in front of the camera and talk to you across America. But now you need to take a step of your own. YOU need to do something for Him.

'Please take a seat,' Miss Carolina said, 'the Reverend will be with you soon. Can I get you some coffee?'

'That would be fine,' Franklin settled into the sofa opposite the TV.

I want you to look out of your window. Do it right now and see what is happening in the world. I know you have terrible floods out there in Texas and in New Mexico. I know you have drought in Illinois and Indiana. These are the signs of His coming.

The Reverend moved across the screen to a window and the camera followed showing the swirling blizzard over the rooftops and the distant ships in the bay.

Here in the holy city of Charleston we have snow where no snow ought to be. Maybe Hell has frozen over too, my friends, because Carolina sure has. And so has Florida. And so has Georgia. Is this not evidence that mankind's sins have sorely displeased the Lord and that His great reckoning is upon us?

The camera swept back to him, eyes still blazing down the lens, challenging the viewer.

You need to make a vow of faith to make your peace with the Lord and you need to make it fast. If you have wandered from the flock then now is the time to return. Be reconciled with your Lord and do it now, for time is running out. The true Church will always welcome you. Call the number on the screen right now. Salvation is waiting.

A graphic of a dove flew across the screen, wiping the Reverend from view and dragging an infomercial in on its tail.

Franklin reached forward and fished a key ring from the jar. It had a phone number stamped on it next to a website address, the same ones that were now scrolling across the screen beneath images of American soldiers marching on dry foreign soil. The picture changed to a group of wounded servicemen and women gathering together in a field hospital, some with bandages round their heads, others with limbs missing – all of them praying.

A caption crashed onto the screen:

OPERATION SAVIOUR
Saving the souls and rebuilding the lives of those destroyed in the Holy wars

The door opened behind them and Miss Boerman reappeared. 'Reverend Cooper can see you now if you'd like to follow me.'

The first room they passed through was divided into small cubicles, each containing a computer terminal, a phone and an operator. There must have been twenty of them, all fairly young, all talking and tapping, filling the room with the hum of overlapping conversations.

The next room contained two parallel lines of people stuffing envelopes with the same books and key rings they had seen on the coffee table. One was in a wheelchair, another had a prosthetic hand and Shepherd put it all together – the youthful demographic, the discipline and order, even the limp and the scar on Miss Carolina's face – these must be some of Cooper's Christian soldiers, rescued from wherever they'd been fighting and now doing the Lord's work for the Church that had saved them.

They followed Miss Boerman up some narrow stairs and through a heavy door into a different world. Gone were the utility desks and bare brick walls. Everything on the upper floor was plush and expensive. They were in some kind of salon with deep red velvet furniture and wood panelling on the walls that had been painted a soft, expensive, chalky grey. There was a fire in the hearth and split logs piled neatly to one side of a carved marble surround.

'Let me see if he's ready,' Miss Boerman said, disappearing through a hidden door in the panelling.

Franklin leaned in to Shepherd, keeping his voice low. 'Looks like the good Reverend lives above the shop, you know why he does that?'

Shepherd shook his head. 'Because in the state of South Carolina religious organizations are exempt from property tax. It means he can live in all this luxury, right in the heart of town, without paying a dime to do it.'

He stood back up as Miss Boerman stuck her head round the edge of the hidden door.

'The Reverend Cooper will see you now,' she said.

CHAPTER 43

By the time the sun dipped low enough to touch the horizon, Liv and Tariq were ready to leave. Following the discovery of Kasim's theft everyone had decided they should try and get to Al-Hillah as planned, food or no food. They didn't really have much choice.

They filled as many canteens as they could carry and drank freely from the pool to fully hydrate themselves before the long march ahead. One small consolation of Kasim's clandestine departure was that he had not been able to take much water as filling the canteens at the pool would have been too obvious. As a result Liv and Tariq had plenty of spare water containers for their journey. They were heavy but Liv consoled herself with the thought that the more they drank, the lighter they would become.

The two of them set off with the sky still bright but the sun now gone, rising out of the depression in the ground like the dead coming back to life. Tariq led the way, past the dam and along the line of the river back towards the compound. Al-Hillah lay directly beyond. They had talked about taking a wide route to avoid the compound entirely, but with hunger already gnawing at their stomachs and the extra miles this would add to their journey they had decided to risk taking the direct route instead, timing their march so they could creep past it as close as they dared under cover of darkness.

Night fell quickly and so did the temperature. Liv pulled her clothes tight against the creeping cold but could still feel it slowly taking hold of her feet, numbing them as they trudged forward. Ahead of them the compound glowed into life as the battery-powered security lights switched on automatically, using power collected by solar panels during the day. She felt drawn to them, a moth to the light. 'They seem brighter tonight,' she said.

'It's because they're getting closer,' Tariq whispered, then pressed his finger to his lips. 'We should keep quiet. Sound travels further in the still of a desert night.' It felt good to be moving again and she found the tightness that had tugged at her as she walked away from the compound was lessening again with every step she took back to it.

For the next hour they walked in silence, settling into a steady pace, stopping occasionally to adjust anything on their packs that made a noise. It was in the soft silence of one of these stops that they heard it, a steady, rhythmic sound, rising and falling as the night breezes shifted it around. Liv titled her head towards it and Tariq did the same. Through the whisper of the wind they heard it again, the unmistakable thrum of a diesel engine.

'Generator,' Tariq whispered. 'That's why the lights

are so bright. They must have fresh supplies of fuel and have switched on the main perimeter lights. Someone else must be there.'

Liv listened harder, trying to pick out any other sounds of life. She was listening so hard that when the new sound came, close and loud, it made her spin round in alarm. It had come from behind, a haunted, moaning sound from over by the river. The sound came again, rattling and wet and she saw what had made it. It was a man, shuffling up the bank, his breath coming in gasping, laborious moans.

Kasim.

Liv started to back away as his eyes locked onto her, so wide and staring that they seemed to glow in the night. A thick, viscous rope of dark drool leaked from his mouth and he raised an arm to point directly at her, his hand bent into a claw.

SaHeira, he said, his voice ragged and raw.

Witch.

Then he coughed, a fierce racking sound that brought him to his knees and sent him into convulsions. He rolled onto his back, fighting for air. Then his eyes rolled up into his head and he started to spasm. Liv jumped as a hand fell on her shoulder. 'Don't look,' Tariq said, trying to turn her away from the death throes.

Liv shrugged away, her eyes transfixed by Kasim, bucking and twitching on the ground, fighting for his final breath. He gave one last long shudder then was still.

'Look,' Tariq said, pointing past his body, 'you were right.'

Kasim's canteen drifted in the water where he had stopped to drink, driven by thirst and lack of supplies. Tariq stepped over the body and retrieved his backpack lying on the bank. Inside were the missing rations. 'We need to get away from here,' Tariq said, shouldering the bag. 'He made too much noise. People will be coming to see what it was.'

Liv turned to the compound glowing brightly in the night, close enough now to pick out details. She could see the spindly structures of the guard towers, the shiny-sided buildings, the drill tower in the centre still throwing water high into the air; but no movement, and no people. She started walking towards it, following the line of the widening stream to its source at the centre of the compound. She did not want to look upon the agonized death mask of Kasim any more. But most of all she did not want Tariq to see the tears that had started to run down her cheeks. She wasn't even sure why she was crying. Maybe it was exhaustion – or guilt. Wherever she went it seemed, people died – and she was weary of death. It seemed to walk alongside her, taking the lives of everyone she touched and driving others away. She couldn't shake the growing feeling that it was she who was at the heart of all this misery – that she was the cause and the curse.

'What are you doing?' Tariq said, drawing level with her, his voice a low whisper so it would not carry.

'I'm going back,' she said, her eyes fixed on the compound. 'And if they shoot me then they'll be doing me and everyone else a favour. You go on to Al-Hillah if you want. I'm tired of running scared.'

She marched on, feeling relieved more than anything as the tension continued to unwind inside her. The adrenalin of the incident with Kasim burned away leaving a gnawing sickness in the pit of her empty stomach and her muscles feeling heavy and weak. Ahead of her the compound opened up a little as her perspective shifted. She could see past the main building now into the wide central area where the derrick rose from the main pool of water. There was still no sign of life, no horses, no people. Maybe they had realized the water was poisoned and ridden away.

The compound opened up a little more and she saw two vehicles parked by the main transport hanger that hadn't been there before: a jeep and a transport truck. It explained the fresh supplies of fuel. She was close enough now to read the registration plates and make out the logo on the side of the truck – a flower with the earth at its centre. The heat of hope warmed her exhausted muscles and she broke into a shambling run. It was the symbol of the international aid agency ORTUS – the charity Gabriel worked for. He had said he would come back. He had promised. Maybe he had . . .

She made it to the gate too exhausted from her sprint even to call out his name. She rattled the gate then found a stone on the ground and started banging it against the steel frame. The anvil clang echoed in the night like a chapel bell and she kept at it, beating the stone against the metal until it splintered in her hands.

A door opened on the side of the transport hangar, framing the silhouette of a man and Liv crumpled to her knees, all her energy spent. The figure hurried out of the door towards her and another followed. She could not make out details of their faces because of the bright lights shining behind them. She watched them draw closer, clinging to the gate to keep herself vaguely upright as hope drained steadily out of her. The way they moved, the slope of their shoulders, other tiny things told her, long before they reached the gate to open it, that neither man was Gabriel.

She let go of the gate and allowed herself to slump down the last few feet to the cold earth. The smell of the earth filled her nostrils as her head made contact with the ground. Then she gave in to the welcome relief of oblivion, closed her eyes and let the darkness take her.

CHAPTER 44

The Reverend Fulton Cooper was shorter than Shepherd had expected but he displaced the air like a much larger man. He was standing in the middle of a large room that had been converted into a TV studio, talking to a tall reed of a man clutching a clipboard and wearing headphones. The studio was basic, just three cameras on wheeled tripods with wireless transmitters plugged in the back feeding a signal directly into a large iMac in the corner. Including the laptops the telephone operators were using there was maybe less than twenty thousand dollars' worth of technology on display. No wonder the Reverend could afford to base his church in a million-dollar mansion. He was broadcasting to the world with a miniscule overhead and no taxes to pay.

'Gentlemen.' Cooper finally turned his attention to them, all smiles and open arms. 'My apologies for the wait. As you can see I am rather busy, but I am more than happy to be of assistance if I can.' He stayed where he was, inviting them to come to him, establishing the power structure.

Franklin didn't move. 'And we surely appreciate

that,' he said. 'Is there maybe somewhere more private we could talk?'

Cooper's smile widened. 'I have nothing to hide from any of these people: we can talk about anything right here in this room.'

'All right,' Franklin said. 'How's your catching?'

The smile slipped a little. 'I don't get your meaning?'

'Your catching,' Franklin repeated, then his arm shot forward sending something arcing through the air. Cooper took a step back, his smooth veneer further ruffled by the unexpected move and swatted the object away with his left hand, sending a plastic key ring skittering across the floor of the studio.

'You'll never make the team catching like that,' Franklin said, finally taking a step forward. 'Did you know only around ten per cent of the population are left-handed? Also most people use the same hand to do everything like throw, catch – write threatening postcards to NASA.'

The smile returned but it didn't quite make it to Reverend Cooper's eyes. 'Take twenty minutes, everyone,' he announced to the room. 'Gregory, can you run infomercials on a loop until I'm finished with these gentlemen?' He turned back to them. 'Why don't we sit down,' he gestured towards two sofas in the middle of the studio arranged around a low table with a laptop on it. 'Miss Boerman, if you would be so kind as to bring us a large pot of coffee.'

'Coffee!' Franklin said. 'Now there's an idea.'

They settled in the sofas and sat in silence while the room emptied, Cooper busying himself with his cell phone in a way that suggested whatever was on his phone was far more important and deserving of his attention than they were. Shepherd didn't mind. It gave him the chance to study him up close: he found him vaguely fascinating. His head seemed too big for his compact body and every facial gesture seemed amplified. He also hummed with a restless energy that combined with his carefully combed silver hair and expensive colour-matched suit to make him come across like a high-powered corporate executive or a senator with his eye on higher office.

'If you could switch your phone to silent and leave it on the table while we talk,' Franklin said, 'I would appreciate it.'

Cooper looked up.

'This is an informal interview but an important one and I don't want you to be distracted while we talk.'

Cooper obeyed, reluctantly laying his phone down next to the laptop.

'Mind if I smoke?' Franklin asked, producing his pack of cigarettes.

Cooper's frown deepened. 'I believe smoking inside any public building is illegal.'

Franklin tapped a cigarette out and popped it between his lips, reaching a finger inside the pack to fish out his lighter. 'That's true but I believe

259

the deeds to this house are in your name, which makes it a private residence. A man can do whatever he likes in his own home.'

'I'm afraid I must still insist that you do not smoke.'

Franklin shrugged, returned the cigarette to the pack and laid it on the table next to Cooper's phone. 'Your house, your rules.'

The door closed as the final person left and Shepherd reached into the laptop case to pull out copies of the postcards sent to Kinderman and Douglas.

'Recognize these?' Franklin asked.

The Reverend took them and studied them, his eyes struggling to focus, his vanity preventing him from wearing reading glasses. 'Of course I recognize them.' He looked up and smiled. 'Those are the shining words of Genesis.'

Franklin returned the smile but there was no warmth in it. 'Do you recognize the handwriting?'

'Of course I do.'

'And why is that?'

'Because it's mine.'

Silence stretched out in the empty room. The sofa creaked as Franklin leaned forward. 'Care to tell us why you sent them?'

Cooper opened his mouth to reply but the door opened and Miss Boerman reappeared carrying a tray of coffee. She moved the laptop to one side and placed it on the table, careful to avoid the documents and other items on the table. Cooper waited until she had left. 'Do you believe what is written in the Bible, gentlemen? Are you men of faith? Because if you know your Scripture then you will not be blind to the clear signs that judgement day is upon us. I saw that those telescopes were an insult to the Lord, modern-day versions of the Tower of Babel, symbol of man's pride in seeking to gaze upon the face of God, and I prayed to Him saying, "Lord, I know we have offended you, what would you have me do in your blessed name to make amends?"'

'And he told you to send death threats?'

Cooper smiled like a gambler with an ace in the hole. 'Death threats? I sent no death threats.'

Shepherd reached into the case and handed over copies of the final letters sent to both Kinderman and Douglas. 'Then maybe you can explain these.'

Cooper took them and held them at arm's length taking his time to inspect them before handing them back. 'If you recall I admitted I did write those cards. But these are *letters*, and they have been *typed* not written.'

'So you're saying you did not send these?'

'I did not.'

Franklin leaned further forward, his voice dropping in a way that was both conspiratorial and menacing. 'Quite a coincidence, though, don't you think, them both making reference to the exact same thing.'

Cooper chuckled. 'I don't think I am the only

one who has read the Bible and paid heed to the teachings of the good book. Let me ask you something, gentlemen. If you were aware that a heinous crime was being committed would you not seek to prevent it from taking place? Are you not, as law enforcement officers, duty bound to uphold the law? Well I follow the highest law there is, a law that is second to none. So, yes, I will admit I did send those cards, I saw it as my duty to remind those people of the danger of what they were doing, but I did not threaten anyone, as God is my witness I did not do that. Nor am I responsible for the events that have succeeded in toppling these towers.'

Franklin stiffened. 'What events?'

Cooper looked surprised. 'Well now, surely you know.'

'Know what?'

Cooper leaned forward and tapped something into the laptop. 'I don't know if you were trying to keep a lid on it but I'm sure you are aware, news travels awful fast these days.' He turned the screen round for them to see. It showed a Twitter feed, new tweets appearing almost every second, all using the same hashtags:

WDW Kate @WebbieWorld349
Explosion at Marshall Space Center. James Webb telescope destroyed? Latest. ow.ly/c5mK #NASA #HUBBLE_WEBB

Letitia Potorac @metaevolve
#NASA $8bn space telescope sabotaged?
fb.me/1B49ZI2yW

Ira Upinski @eyeupinsky
#NASA #HUBBLE Space Telescope knocked out of orbit, several sources confirm: bit.ly/wRNi0c

'It appears my prayers have been answered and the good Lord has once again confounded the vain attempts of mankind to know His mystery. Your prompt appearance here and the nature of your questions merely confirms to me that these rumours must be true. They are true I take it – the Hubble telescope has been disabled and its successor destroyed?'

'Yes,' Shepherd said.

'Well how about that. Thank you, gentlemen, thank you kindly. You have just given me the theme for the second part of today's show. Now if you have no further questions I'm afraid I'm going to have to ask you to take your coffee elsewhere. I am in the middle of a live broadcast here.' He began to rise.

'I have a question,' Shepherd said. 'Why didn't you sign the cards?'

'Because I was quoting the Bible: I would not presume to sign my name after the words of the Lord.'

Shepherd nodded. 'Also I'm wondering why the cards all have different postmarks?'

Cooper shrugged. 'I travel a lot. I guess I must have posted them wherever I found myself to be.'

'Could we see a copy of your schedule going back to May?'

'For what purpose exactly?'

'It would help us match your whereabouts with the postmarks and confirm your story.'

Cooper hesitated. 'I'll get the office to send you over a copy.' Franklin produced a card and handed it over. The Reverend took it and flipped it over in his soft, manicured hands then fixed the smile back in place and gestured towards the door.

'It's been a pleasure, gentlemen. I'm sorry I could not be more helpful.'

The gate clanged shut behind them on the snow-covered street. 'You think he sent the letter?' Shepherd asked.

Franklin reached into his pocket, pulled out his rumpled packet of Marlboros and tapped out a cigarette. He cupped his hand against the cold and fired up a battered Zippo that looked like it had been rescued from a car wreck, sucked the flame into the cigarette then let out a long stream of smoke. Despite everything they had been through in the last twelve hours or so this was the first time Shepherd had seen him smoke. 'If it wasn't him then he knows who did.' Franklin took another deep draw, the cherry glowing bright and red against the soft, silent white of the street. 'I got an instinct for these things. That's why I wanted to come here and look the man in the eye. That was a nice touch at the end there, by the way, asking him about the cards.'

Shepherd shrugged. 'I was just yanking his chain a little.'

'It showed good instincts. Pushing a man's buttons, knocking him off centre, sometimes that's all it takes to start cracks forming, and the cracks show you where the weaknesses are.'

Shepherd looked out into the street. 'Didn't get us anywhere though, did it?'

Franklin took a final deep pull on his cigarette then dropped it to the ground, crushing it with his shoe. 'Not yet.' He studied the building, spotted a gap between the mailbox and the wall and crammed his empty pack of cigarettes into it. 'But you can't just toss in a line and expect to haul out a fish straight away. You need to learn a little patience, Agent Shepherd.' He stepped into the snow, heading for the corner.

Shepherd followed, tilting his head down against the weather. 'Where we headed now?'

'Police station up on Westside, but we'll need a ride there. You got your phone handy?' Shepherd pulled it out of his jacket pocket. 'Call a cab and get it to pick us up at the Fast and French on Broad Street in twenty minutes.'

'What's that?'

'The nearest place we can get some goddam coffee.'

Reverend Cooper watched them leave, following them with his eyes until they disappeared in the snow. Behind him he heard the door to his private office open and he listened to the approaching footsteps. He waited until they were close enough then turned suddenly, shooting out his arm to catch Miss Boerman's face hard with the back of his hand. She was knocked sideways by the force, crashing against his desk and knocking a phone to the floor as she scrambled to recover. Cooper was already on her, grabbing her throat with one hand and pulling the other back to strike her once more.

'Don't you EVER do something like that again.'

She closed her eyes but made no move to get away. Cooper's hand curled into a fist as his rage balled up inside him. He wanted to break her nose and see her spitting teeth through split lips. He wanted to hear the snap of her fingers and her cries of pain. He wanted to . . .

He stepped away, breathing heavily as he fought to master the demons that used to be the master of him. Now was not the time to let the devil back in.

'Get out,' he said. She stood up, straightening her suit jacket, the red marks of his fingers already rising up on her white cheek. 'Tell the studio to be ready to broadcast in five minutes and close the door on your way out.'

He waited until she had gone, then picked the phone up off the floor and dialled a number from memory. Outside in the street the footprints of the FBI agents were already being rubbed out by the steady fall of snow. If only the men who had made them and the threat they posed were as easy to erase. Then again – maybe they were.

The phone clicked as it connected. Then Carrie's brittle, little-girl voice answered.

CHAPTER 45

Gabriel was one of the last to be evacuated from the Public Church. Arkadian had stood by his bed the whole time, a guardian angel in a spacesuit, giving a running commentary on what was happening: equipment being packed up and shipped out, patients being transferred from beds to stretchers so they would fit on the ascension platform and be easier to carry through the narrow tunnels once they were inside the mountain. He kept laying his gloved hand on Gabriel's chest, like a father reassuring his son, finding the one spot where there were no electrodes or tubes coming in or out of him.

And then it was Gabriel's turn to go.

Arkadian stepped back as four suited orderlies got to work on him. They gave him a shot to settle him and undid the straps that bound him to the bed, clearly in a rush to get this thing over with. Gabriel felt himself slipping into a half slumber.

'You hang in there, OK.' Arkadian's face appeared over him, his voice muffled by his contamination suit. 'I'll buy you lunch when you come out.'

Gabriel tried to respond, say something flippant

and brave like they did in the movies but his mouth was no longer working and his eyes flickered shut.

He felt and heard the clatter of wheels over the flagstoned floor as they moved him then the air cooling as he neared the door. He forced his eyes open and saw the vaulted ceiling and ecclesiastical paintings slide away above him to be replaced by night skies and stars. He picked out Draco, the constellation that had led him and Liv to the lost place in the desert, the place where he had last seen her. He wondered if she was still there, waiting for him, looking up at the same stars. As he stared up he spotted something else, a new star, brighter than all the rest, travelling across the sky. He watched it sliding across the night then a beam shot out from it, blinding him, and making his stretcher-bearers turn their heads away. It held on them for a few seconds, long enough for the news cameraman in the helicopter to get a good shot, then it moved away, the sound of the rotors chopping the air and sending cold air down onto Gabriel's burning skin.

They passed through another stone arch onto the embankment and the Citadel came into view, a monumental darkness that blocked out the stars as they drew closer. The hollow bang of wooden boards replaced the scuff of feet on stone as they reached the bridge leading to the ascension platform. The mountain was so close now it blocked out half the sky. Tears leaked from Gabriel's eyes as they placed him on the platform. Arkadian appeared above him, his mouth forming words that he couldn't hear, then he disappeared, ushered away by the orderlies.

The sound of wooden battens banging into place echoed through the night as the guardrails on the edge of the platform were put back in place then a bell rang high in the mountain. The ropes securing each corner of the platform creaked then the platform lurched and lifted off the ground.

Gabriel looked straight up at the night, half-filled with stars and half black. He could see the tribute cave high above, dark and wide like a huge black mouth, growing larger as it sucked them closer. He thought of what he was leaving behind, all the sorrow and regret: his father found and gone, his mother gone too, and the woman he cared most for in the world, the one he felt bound to protect at all costs, abandoned and alone like he was. And all because of this mountain, this hateful mountain.

The ascension platform rose higher, lit from time to time by the searchlight from the hovering news helicopter, then it passed into darkness as it entered the tribute cave and banged to a halt.

The last time Gabriel had been here was in the dead of night, alone, unannounced and armed. Now he was strapped tight to a stretcher, his senses dulled by the sedative, his body wracked with a disease that had robbed him of both strength and freedom. And there were people everywhere.

Two monks loomed over him, their surgical masks looking sinister against their cowled and bearded faces.

270

'Bring the patients this way,' a voice commanded from somewhere inside the cave. 'We have a place prepared.'

The two monks hoisted him up and carried him off the platform, the air closing in on him and the sound deadening as they moved out of the cave and deeper into the mountain.

They began to descend, bumping down narrow corridors. Gabriel could feel his temperature climbing in the trapped, stuffy air and sweat trickled down inside the tight bindings, further torturing his already screaming skin. Something started to disconnect inside him. He had held on for so long, using the focus of getting here to drive him; now that he had finally made it he had nothing left. A small part of his lucid mind registered the relief of it. He took a breath and whispered something, too quiet for anyone else to hear: 'Goodbye, Liv.' Then a howl erupted from him as he finally let go and was carried screaming into the heart of the mountain.

PART IV

. . . and behold a pale horse: and his name that sat on him was Death, and Hell followed with him.

Revelation 6:8

CHAPTER 46

Brother Athanasius stiffened as the first stretcher appeared out of the darkness and was carried through the door. He was standing in the centre of the cathedral cave, the largest chamber in the Citadel and the only one large enough for the entire population of the mountain to congregate in one place – though this had not happened for some time now to minimize contact and help prevent the spread of the Lamentation.

The monks walked the stretcher down the central aisle towards the huge window set high into the wall behind the altar. Brother Gardener had walked this same path, dragging the dead branch from the garden and unwittingly spreading the infection among the congregation. It was one of the last times they had all gathered together: one of the last times the mountain had been whole.

He turned and looked at the beds stretching away where the monks who had once stood here to worship now lay suffering and dying.

More people were emerging through the door, carrying stretchers and crates of medical supplies. He locked eyes with one of the newcomers, easily distinguishable from the monks by his anti-contamination suit, and walked over holding his hand up in greeting.

'Welcome,' he said, smiling though his mouth was hidden behind a surgical mask, 'my name is Brother Athanasius.'

'Dr Kaplan,' the man replied, raising his own hand to return the non-contact greeting.

Athanasius gestured towards lines of beds filled with the infected. 'I have arranged our sick on this side of the aisle. Those you have brought with you can be housed in the empty beds on the other side. Not much of a gap, I grant you, but it seems pointless to try and separate everyone in an enclosed environment such as this. We have certainly had no success in containing it ourselves.'

The doctor surveyed the large space, the beds, the patients, the monks moving around between them, busily guiding the newcomers in. 'Is this everyone?' he said, surprise evident in his voice.

'Not quite all, some of our number did not agree with letting outsiders inside the mountain. The traditionalists have locked themselves away in another part of the mountain. What you see here is what remains. There are fifty-seven sick and thirty-two still unaffected. As you can see we are somewhat overwhelmed.'

'How many dead?'

Athanasius took a breath as a rush of faces crowded his mind: friends, colleagues, enemies and rivals all

276

now bundled together into the same anonymous statistic. 'One hundred and four.'

Kaplan nodded, mentally adding them to the number he held in his head.

'And what have you observed to be the life expectancy once someone is infected?'

'About forty-eight hours.'

'No longer?'

'Sometimes, but no one has survived more than three days. The Apothecaria – the medical guild of monks within the mountain – kept records of the initial infection and its subsequent spread, which may be of some use, I have them over here.' He walked across the floor, weaving between empty beds steadily filling with bound figures on stretchers. He stopped by a long refectory table that was covered with medical equipment from inside the Citadel, some modern, some crude and home-made, evidence of the severe strain the infection had put on the community's resources. Athanasius hunted through piles of sheets that had been shredded to serve as bandages and bindings until he found a sheaf of papers and handed them to Dr Kaplan.

Kaplan looked at the carefully handwritten notes through his plastic visor. 'Can I not speak to one of the doctors?' he asked.

'I'm afraid all the medical brothers succumbed to the infection early on. Next to the gardeners they were amongst the first to contract the disease.'

'Why the gardeners?'

'There is a garden at the heart of the mountain and

a blight struck the trees first. The gardeners worked hard to cut it out and the infection seemed to pass to them first and then anyone they had been in extended contact with. The doctors naturally fell into this category and succumbed shortly afterwards. Consequently, there is no one left here in the Citadel qualified to do anything other than provide comfort to the dying. The best way we can help now is by assisting you to find a cure. All the data we have is in these notes. This entire chamber is at your disposal as am I and all my staff.'

Dr Kaplan nodded, scanning the notes as he listened. 'I would like to take blood samples from all of you, sick and healthy. You have been exposed to the disease in confinement and yet have not been infected. There may be something in your blood, some natural immunity, that has protected you. If I can compare samples and isolate whatever might be doing it I can start working on an antidote.'

'Of course, I will pass word for everyone to present themselves to you as soon as you are set up and ready.'

They stepped back as another stretcher was carried past, the occupant moaning and writhing against his bindings. Athanasius glanced at the contorted face of the patient then looked again when he realized who it was. 'How long has this man been ill?' he asked, following the stretcher to an empty bed.

'That's a good question,' Kaplan replied. 'He's the one variable in this whole equation. He's the only one so far who has remained lucid, or semi-lucid.

We're not sure how long he's been infected, but longer than anyone else certainly. He claims it's been five days and that he caught it here in the Citadel.'

Athanasius stared down at Gabriel's tortured sweat-drenched face, hair plastered to his forehead by fever. 'He's telling the truth,' Athanasius said. 'He was here, eight days ago, just when the disease first appeared. He could well have been infected then.'

A howl rose from Gabriel as he bucked against his restraints, desperate to free his hands and scratch at his tortured skin. Dr Kaplan looked down at him, ravaged by the disease and driven half out of his mind by it.

'Then this man may well prove to be the saviour of us all.'

CHAPTER 47

The Westside Charleston Police Department building sat on the upper shoulder of the old town like an epaulet. It had a nice view of the Ashley River and a baseball diamond over to one side that made it look more like high school than a police headquarters.

Franklin and Shepherd stepped out of the cab and picked their way along the narrow path that had been cleared in the snow all the way up the two flights of steps to the main entrance. They opened the door and both looked up as the noise hit them. It sounded like every phone in the building was ringing.

'Think we might have caught them at a bad time,' Franklin murmured as they moved towards a solid desk sergeant who was pushing buttons and juggling the phone.

'You here to help or hinder?' the sergeant asked before either of them had even produced their IDs. He was old-school and well padded and wore a thick grey moustache that made him look like a walrus in uniform.

'Neither, really,' Franklin said, flopping his

creds open. 'We're just a couple of fellow law-enforcement agents looking for a port in a storm. We need to borrow an office for a few hours.'

The sergeant shook his head and reached for the phone. 'You got the storm bit right.' He punched a button and stood up straight, his shirt buttons straining against the impressive girth of his stomach. 'Shit storm is what we got going on here. Only we got a ton of shit and only a couple of shovels to clear it with. Half the force didn't turn up to work this morning and the other half are having to deal with this.' He nodded at the thick snow falling outside.

The phones continued to ring throughout the building. Someone, somewhere picked one up. 'Bryan, we got a couple of Feebies down here dripping snow onto the floor –' he peered at their open IDs through his reading glasses '– Special Agents Shepherd and Franklin.' He squinted at Franklin's and covered the mouthpiece with his hand. 'Ben Franklin, that for real?'

Franklin nodded. 'You may have seen my picture on a hundred-dollar bill.'

The sergeant shook his head like a disappointed uncle. 'You better come quick, Bryan. One of them's so damn funny I'm in danger of peeing my pants.'

He put the phone down and nodded at a row of chairs. 'Sergeant Freeman will be down directly. He's in charge of the pencils round here so he'll fix you up with whatever you need.' The phone rang again. He snatched it up and turned away.

'Well he's a character,' Franklin said as they settled in their seats.

'I kind of like it,' Shepherd replied. 'Beats the hostility we usually get.'

'An example of which appears to be heading our way.'

Shepherd looked up at a stocky man with thinning brown hair bustling across the entrance hall. He offered his hand, introduced himself then hustled them into the back of the building with a minimum of charm and maximum speed. They passed through a door into an open-plan office empty but for the sound of phones.

'This OK?' he said, pointing to a desk in the corner.

'Not really,' Franklin said with a smile. 'Too public. Have you maybe got somewhere a little more private? The case we're working on is classified.'

'Sure,' Freeman said. Then he smiled and pointed to a row of solid doors with small windows in them set into the back wall. 'I got just the thing for you.'

'Cosy,' Franklin said, the moment the door closed on the interview room.

'You kinda asked for it.' Shepherd surveyed the white, anonymous walls. It was soundproofed at least, so they could no longer hear the clamour of ringing phones. The only noise was the hum of the building's air conditioning belting out dry heat and making the claustrophobic room even stuffier.

Shepherd stepped over to the metal table in the centre of the room and tried to pull the chair out from under it. It was bolted to the floor. The table was bolted down too. He sat down, slid the laptop from the case and fired it up.

'Local law tend to regard us with the same sort of suspicion as criminals, so sticking us in here probably makes sense to them,' Franklin said, doing a circuit of the room and reading the desperate graffiti scratched into the walls. 'Freeman is probably spreading word round the building right now that we're in here. The first tourists should be coming by in the next few minutes to gawp at us through the two-way mirror.' He nodded at the side wall then sat down in the other chair and Shepherd felt a moment's discomfort as it dawned on him that he had unwittingly sat in the 'suspect' seat.

'Anything you want to confess before I start beating on you?' Franklin said, reading his mind.

'I confess that I could do with some more coffee,' Shepherd said, studying the screen and clicking the menu to hook up to the station wi-fi.

The sound of phones burst in on them again as the door opened and a weasel-faced cop stepped into the room. 'God damn,' he said, staring straight at Franklin. 'I thought it might be you. What the hell you doing back here? You anything to do with the ships and the mass migration?'

'Hi,' Shepherd said, getting up from his seat and

shaking the man's hand. 'Joe Shepherd. You already seem to know Agent Franklin.'

'Dan Jackson,' the man said. 'Yeah I know Franklin from way back.'

'Why don't you show me where the coffee is,' Franklin said, moving to the door, clearly anxious to get the guy out of the room.

'What do you mean "mass migration"?' Shepherd butted in.

'I mean everyone seems to have got it into their heads to hop in their cars and drive someplace. We got almost solid traffic heading into town. People from all over just packing their cars and heading for the city. We got people leaving too but that's not so much of a problem. It's the in-bound traffic that's the headache. It's blocked up all the main roads into the city and, what with the weather on top, we got a major headache and hardly any manpower to deal with it. I thought maybe that's why you were here.'

''Fraid not,' Franklin said, grabbing Jackson's shoulder and easing him towards the door.

'How come you're so short-staffed?' Shepherd asked.

'Beats me, half the squad didn't show up this morning.'

'And these no-shows,' Shepherd persisted, 'are they local guys?'

Jackson considered the question then shook his head. 'No. As a matter of fact they're all out of towners: all the local guys showed up.'

'Listen, Dan,' Franklin cut in, 'why don't you show me where you keep the coffee and I'll tell you why we're here.' He turned to Shepherd. 'See if Smith has managed to dig anything new out of the Kinderman files. I'll be right back.' Then he practically pushed Jackson out of the room.

Shepherd stood for a second, staring at the spot where they had both just stood, wondering about Franklin's strange behaviour. Then the screen flickered, drawing his attention and he sat back down, his fingers drumming the keyboard as he typed in the ID and password Agent Smith had given him earlier. A directory loaded up on the screen, different icons representing all the various databases he now had access to. Any new information Smith had found would be archived in the ghost file, listed in the directory under a Pacman ghost icon – something Smith always maintained proved the FBI did have a sense of humour. He dragged the arrow over to it but did not click on it, his eyes drawn to another icon, lower down in the directory, with MPD written beneath it – the Missing Persons Database.

Shepherd had been rehearsing this moment for the past seven years. All he had to do was click on it, type in a name, a few details then sophisticated algorithms and search spiders would scuttle out across police networks covering more than half the world.

He clicked on the icon and a simple command box opened. It had spaces for key search data:

name, DOB, age, height, weight, hair and eye colour. His fingers moved over the keyboard, finding keys on their own.

Name: Melisa Erroll
Date of birth: He never knew it and she would never say
Age: She would be about thirty-six now
Height: Around one sixty
Build: Slight
Hair: Black
Eyes: Brown

He paused and took several deep breaths. The room smelled of sweat and fear, though that could just as easily be coming from him. The MPD had primarily been designed to locate people fast to rule them out of investigations. Consequently the search engines were programmed to trawl through death registers first. If he got a hit back quickly it would mean her name had been found amongst the roll call of the dead – and, even after seven years of unanswered questions, he wasn't sure if he was prepared for that. But there was also something else that made him pause. The misuse of FBI resources for personal ends was pretty high on the list of prosecutable offences, for obvious reasons, and every search on the MPD was logged and could be checked. Then again, he wasn't searching for any more sensitive details, like bank accounts or passport activity. Not yet at least. But pressing the button would still be crossing a line. And despite everything that had happened in his life, he still believed in rules and obeying them.

He re-read the words he had typed into the search criteria, the barest thumbnails of a human life, and wondered what Melisa would do in his situation. She would probably have instigated a search the moment she got her hands on the laptop. Melisa was passionate and impulsive, a do-er.

Love is a verb – she used to say – *Love is a doing word.*

A single tear slid down his cheek. Then he hit *Return.*

And the search went live.

CHAPTER 48

O'Halloran sat in the den of his house, his eyes fixed on the old bulky TV in the corner that had once been the main family set. The American military exodus from Afghanistan was now the lead story, confirmed by several sources and top of a lengthening list of similar military stand-downs. As well as the Chinese withdrawal from the Senkaku Islands there were now additional reports that the British were also pulling their troops out of Afghanistan, the North Koreans had pulled away from the border with the South, Israeli tanks had done the same from Palestine and government-backed troops in Syria had ceased many of the ongoing assaults on rebel-held cities, leaving artillery batteries deserted. It was as if the over-riding imperial and destructive impulse of thousands of years had been cured overnight by a simple, universal human desire to return home.

In his own small way, O'Halloran had felt it too. His desire to come home had been unexpected and almost primal in its intensity. Twice now he had gone out to his car to head over to the office but both times just the thought of putting the car in gear and driving back to Quantico had filled him with such a feeling of panic that he had ended up sitting there, sweating despite the cold, the engine running and his hand resting on the gearshift. Just the few steps down the drive had made him feel as if a rope was wound around his heart, pulling tighter with each step he took. Both times he had ended up turning off the engine, getting out of the car and walking back to the house, the pressure and panic easing with each step until, by the time he crossed the threshold back into the warmth and comfort of his home, it had gone entirely.

His cellphone buzzed, cutting through the low burble of the news. He stiffened in his chair and the springs creaked as he snapped back into professional mode.

'O'Halloran.'

'Sir, it's Squires. You anywhere near a TV?'

Squires was one of the section chiefs who lived in an office down the hall from his. He was also working from home today, O'Halloran recalled. 'I'm watching the news now.'

'You watching CNN?'

'BBC World, you catching all this about troop movements?'

'Yes, but that's not what I'm calling about, sir. Turn to CNN. You're going to want to see this.'

O'Halloran plucked the remote from his desk and flicked quickly through the channels. On CNN a reporter was standing next to a chain-link fence talking directly to camera. Beyond the fence a field of white snow stretched away to a rocket-launching tower and a building complex surrounded by emergency vehicles. One of the buildings was a mass of twisted metal. The strap line read:

BREAKING NEWS – Suspected Terrorist Attack on NASA Facility.

'Guess the lid just came off this one,' Squires said.

O'Halloran took in the story. Normally a news channel breaking a story on one of his on-going cases would send him into a quiet rage. 'It was only a matter of time,' he said, surprising himself as much as Squires with his calm attitude and detached tone. 'Better prepare a statement to throw some bones to the press. Confirm everything they already know and give them the Hubble information too if they haven't got it already. And leak the names of the missing persons. Maybe if Kinderman and Douglas's pictures are all over the news we might run them down a little faster –'

The picture cut to a shot of Agents Franklin and Shepherd sitting on a sofa in what looked like a daytime chat show.

'*Earlier this afternoon,*' the reporter said underneath the pictures, '*two government agents confirmed rumours that the attack on the Marshall Space Center testing facility was not an isolated event.*'

The sound faded up on the clip.

'– *They are true I take it – the Hubble spacecraft has been disabled and its successor the James Webb telescope has been destroyed?*'

'*Yes,*' Shepherd confirmed.

'Get to work on that statement and get it out fast,' O'Halloran said to Squires, tuning out from the rest of the report. 'Now it's out there I don't want it to look like we're trying to hide anything.'

'What about Franklin and Shepherd? You want me to assign someone new?'

O'Halloran thought about it for a moment. 'No, let me talk to them. I want to hear how this happened and right now I doubt we have the men to spare anyway.'

'I'm happy to come in if you want me to, sir,' Squires replied, his voice a little guarded.

'No, it's OK – you stay home with your family, that's the best place right now. Call me if you hear anything new.'

O'Halloran put the phone down and listened to the familiar creak of the house he had lived in for over twenty years. He could hear Beth in the kitchen clearing up the lunch things.

Stay at home with your family.

Damn right.

He found Franklin's phone number and hit the button to dial it.

CHAPTER 49

Jackson had been thankfully called away almost as soon as he and Franklin had left the interview room. They'd swapped cards and promised to catch up before Franklin left town but in truth neither of them really meant it. They had never been that close and Franklin didn't have time to shoot the breeze about 'back in the day'. He had more pressing things on his mind and other situations to deal with.

He couldn't explain the feelings he'd been experiencing for the last few days or the things they were making him do. All he knew for sure was that they were getting stronger, swelling inside him like the slow intake of a deep, deep breath. Over the years he had listened to enough strung-out junkies talk about how it felt to crave a hit and that was the closest he could get to describing what this was like for him. It was an urge that steadily filled his mind and body, slowly pushing everything else aside until he could think of nothing else. It had taken over everything, driving him to do whatever it took to try to satisfy the craving. He blew out a long breath as he stalked through the empty offices, his footfalls on the stained carpet tiles silent beneath the constantly ringing phones.

Not long now.

He found a coffee pot in a kitchen on the second floor. It was sitting on a hotplate with a layer of thick black sludge on the bottom. Bottomless, twenty-four-hour coffee pots were standard issue in any police department but they usually got continuously topped up by the various shifts. This one had clearly been left to stew overnight and no one had noticed, further evidence of the staffing crisis Jackson had mentioned.

He did his best to scrape the gloop from the bottom of the pot then found some fresh coffee in a container in the icebox and some filters in a drawer and set a new pot bubbling. He was just scouting around for some clean mugs when his phone buzzed in his pocket. He answered it without looking to see who it was, expecting that it would probably be Marie giving him a hard time about not being home.

'Franklin!' He jammed the phone into the crook of his neck, continuing his search through the cupboards.

'You mind telling me why you're making unauthorized statements to the press about your on-going investigation?' Franklin nearly dropped the phone as he recognized O'Halloran's voice.

'Sir?'

'I've just seen you and Shepherd on CNN chatting to the Reverend Fulton Cooper.'

Franklin flashed back to the empty studio – empty but for the cameras. He heard the phone creak as his hand tightened round it. 'He must have taped the interview.'

'You spoke to him in a TV studio?'

'He was –' Franklin closed his eyes and shook his head. He had been stupid. His mind wasn't on the job the way it usually was since the urge had taken him over. 'He was in the middle of a broadcast, sir. We didn't think it should wait.'

'You get anything out of him?'

'A little.'

'You think he's our guy?'

'Yes sir, I think so.'

There was a pause. Franklin stared ahead. A *World's Greatest Detective* mug mocked him from inside the cupboard.

'Stick with it, Agent Franklin. Keep a tighter lead on Shepherd and get more on Cooper fast so we can turn this thing around and make this little PR stunt blow up in his face.'

'Yessir.'

'And Franklin?'

'Sir?'

'Keep me directly informed.'

Franklin waited for more, expecting some kind of explanation or further instructions, but all he heard was a soft click as O'Halloran put down the phone and cut the connection.

CHAPTER 50

For the second time in a week Liv woke up in the windowless room of the sick bay. She looked across to the other bed. It was empty, the sheets and mattress stripped off. On the wall behind it a row of cupboard doors hung open revealing bare shelves.

She tilted her head towards the door and listened. No sound at all came from the hallways beyond it, not even the generator, which suggested it was daytime. She tried to sit up and felt something snag painfully in her arm. There was a shunt strapped to her forearm attached by a tube to a clear bag hanging high on a stand by the bed. She had a moment of panic, wondering if it was doing her good or harm.

Footsteps outside.

Her heart rate stepped up a few beats.

There was nowhere to hide and she didn't have the energy to run. She swallowed drily and watched the door swing open, wishing she'd had the presence of mind to grab something heavy.

'Hey, you're awake.' The man was blond and tanned and somewhere in his late twenties. He looked more like a surfer than someone intent on doing her harm. He also looked drawn and tired, as though he hadn't slept for days. 'How you feeling – like shit I bet?'

He spoke English with an Australian accent. He popped a digital thermometer in her mouth and checked her over with the relaxed and practised eye of someone who had done this a million times before. She could smell coffee and soap.

'Who are you?' she said, the moment the thermometer was removed.

'Name's Kyle.' He frowned as he studied the read-out. 'You're still running a bit of a fever. You should take it easy. Get some more sleep if you can.'

'Don't drink the water,' she said, voicing the alarm that was clanging in her head.

'The water's fine,' Kyle replied, checking her drip bag then smoothing down the plaster holding the shunt in her arm.

Liv sat up and felt the room shift around her. 'No. It's not, it's poisoned – I've seen men die from drinking it.'

'Me too,' he said, and she understood his tiredness. She swung her legs off the bed and pulled at the tube. 'Hey!' Kyle reached out to stop her.

'Show me,' she said, turning away and yanking the tube from her arm.

'You need to –'

She stood, wobbling slightly then headed for the door.

'OK, OK – wait a second, I'll show you.' He grabbed the loose tube and turned the valve to stop the contents of the drip bag emptying onto the floor. 'Just let me sort out that shunt so you don't end up bleeding all over the place.'

Daylight blinded Liv as she stepped through the door into the transport hangar, so bright she had to turn her head away for a few seconds and let her eyes adjust.

The bodies were lying on the far side against the wall, their arms and legs twisted and frozen in the agonized moment of their death. She drifted over, drawn by the horrible tableau. The sickly smell of death was already hanging over them like a cloud. She moved along the line, checking the faces of the dead. Malik was there, his face covered in filth, his eyes staring and sightless and ringed by hungry flies.

'Where are the horses?'

'We didn't find any.'

She frowned. The horses had drunk the water too, but that was before she had left – before it had turned bitter. Maybe the animals had known there was something wrong with it, their superior sense of smell saving them from a similar fate to their riders and they had run away when the water turned and their masters died. She reached the end of the line. Twenty-two bodies in total. Azra'iel was not among them. 'Where are the others?'

'There's a couple still alive. They're in the canteen. When we arrived it had been set up as a ward, I guess because they needed more room for all the sick.' Liv nodded. That explained the bare cupboards in the sick bay. 'They're the only two left, though, and to be honest – I reckon they'll soon be out here too. There's not a whole heap we can do for them.'

The first thing that hit Liv when she walked into the canteen was the smell. Sweet and putrid and so strong it made her head swim and she had to reach out to steady herself against the wall.

'You should really go and lie down again,' Kyle said. 'You're still too dehydrated to be off the drip.'

'I'll go in a second,' she said. It felt hot in the room and unbearably stuffy. A long line of refectory tables had been pushed against one wall and haphazardly stacked up to make more room on the floor. It looked like it had been done in a hurry. She imagined the panic that had played out as people started falling sick. The floor was covered with mattresses and sheets, dragged in from the dorms. Some of them had been stripped, though the dark stains of death were soaked into the fabric of the covers. Only two of the beds were still occupied. A man was stooped down by one of them, gently washing brown filth from around the mouth of one of the riders.

'That's Eric,' Kyle said. 'He's a qualified medic so he's been playing nursemaid.' The man turned and nodded a greeting. He was another version of Kyle: tanned, lithe, coloured string bracelets and leather thongs round his wrist. 'Mike's around here some-place too, but I think he's outside the fence with your lot.'

Liv turned to him. 'Is everyone OK?'

'Oh yeah, they're all fine. Your man Tariq went out with Mike in the truck and brought them all back. They just needed food and rest – and water of course. They're all on grave-digging duties now. Can't have that lot lying out in the heat much longer.'

A sudden movement brought both their attentions back to the man on the floor. His whole body had started to shake and heave. He bucked on the bed, struggling to breathe then coughed and more of the brown stuff spluttered from his mouth. Eric held the man's head as he vomited in a bowl, talking calmly to him the whole time, trying to soothe him. Liv marvelled at his dedication.

'You're right about the water, by the way,' Kyle said, quiet enough that even she could hardly hear him. 'When we first arrived and found all the bodies and a few still alive we thought it might be a virus, or maybe even a chemical weapon-related accident – you know, all those WMDs they didn't find. But the ones who were still alive all said the same thing – they got sick after drinking the water. So I tested it. It's been part of my job out here so I had all the right kit with me. When we first got here there were massive traces of arsenic trioxide in it. Ground water often contains high levels of this compound but these were off the scale. Probably got washed out of some underground deposit by the pressure of the water. Basically it makes your organs fail which results in vomiting, diarrhoea and fits – just like this poor bastard.'

The man on the floor calmed a little and his lips

pulled back in pain revealing a jagged line of teeth. It was Azra'iel, the angel of death, very close to meeting his namesake. 'The land does not belong to anyone,' Liv whispered, 'we belong to the land.'

'What's that?'

'Nothing.' She turned away. 'Where did you come from, Kyle?'

'Melbourne originally.'

'No, I mean how did you come to be here?'

Kyle stared at a spot on the wall, his forehead wrinkled in thought. 'That's a good question.' Fresh movement drew his attention as Azra'iel began to fit again. He leapt forward, grabbing one of his arms and holding him down while Eric tried to get a sedative into him. Liv watched as they fought with him, then – as quickly as it had started – it was over. Azra'iel arched one last time, let out a long rattling sigh and was still.

Kyle looked up at her. 'I need to help Eric clean up here. Why don't you go into the kitchen, get yourself something to eat – if you can stomach it after all this. I'll come find you when we're done and try and tell you how we ended up here.'

CHAPTER 51

The laptop pinged and Shepherd sat up, his stomach hollow with dread.

It was too soon.

The search had only been running for about a minute, two at most. It would still be deep in the death registers. He sat perfectly still in the bolted-down chair, not daring to move, as if remaining motionless might stop the world turning and keep her forever alive.

A single search result was showing in a pop-up, just a string of numbers and a suffix locator, BPD – Baltimore Police Department. As far as he knew Melisa had never been to Baltimore, she had no connections there: but then there were lots of things he didn't know about her, like where she'd been for the last eight years.

He stared at the result.

Could this be it – the end of the road? The end of hope?

It felt hot in the room all of a sudden and sweat trickled down the ridge of his spine. He clicked on the single result and held his breath as it opened in a new window. His eyes scanned the dense text, raw information gleaned from the police report, his mind too wired to take in more than fragments:

. . . DOD: 12th August 2011 . . .

She had been dead for over a year

. . . thirty-six years old . . .

Right age

. . . gunshot wound . . . black female . . .

Black?

Melisa wasn't black – olive-skinned, yes, but not black. She looked more Italian than African. But some cops were pretty binary about these things: anyone who wasn't white was automatically black – it could still be her. At the bottom of the file there were other case-file numbers, each with a different date stretching back ten years from the date of death. This person had a rap sheet, which didn't sound like his Melisa.

His eyes lit on a PDF file attached to the bottom of the document and his finger clicked on it before his mind had a chance to reconsider. A new window opened containing three sets of mug shots and a head-and-shoulders shot of a woman with her eyes closed, lying on an autopsy table. Despite the sombre and tragic image Shepherd nearly wept with relief.

Whoever this Melisa, was she wasn't his.

He watched the hourglass icon spin slowly as sophisticated algorithms continued the search.

Don't find her here among the dead – he thought – *not my Melisa.*

But the ping rang out again, mocking his silent prayer, just as Franklin burst back into the room carrying two mugs of coffee.

CHAPTER 52

'God damned Reverend pulled a fast one,' Franklin said, slopping the coffee on the metal-topped table in his haste to put the mugs down.

Shepherd was barely listening, his hands working fast, heart pounding as he closed all the windows on the screen. There was no time to check out the new search result with Franklin in the room.

'Cooper filmed our interview and leaked it to CNN. Apparently the world just saw us confirm the attacks on Hubble and James Webb.'

Shepherd looked up, his mind racing ahead, wondering what this would mean for the investigation and for them. It was bad. Really bad. Because of this mistake they would undoubtedly be taken off the case, which meant he stood to lose all the access he had only just started to explore – his lifeline to Melisa. That snake of a reverend had ruined everything. He must have been straight on the phone to the news networks the moment they had stepped out of the studio.

He dug into his pocket and fished out the key ring Franklin had thrown at Cooper in the studio as he realized the network news wouldn't be the only place the interview would be running. He opened a new window and copied in the web address printed on the key ring.

The homepage was as slick and professional as the man it was built to promote. Shepherd found a media section in the drop-down menus and clicked on a link to a live stream of the TV show.

The video buffered fast and Shepherd's jaw tightened when he saw himself sitting on the couch next to Franklin, like guests on a talk show. The clip had been cut to make it look as though Cooper was interviewing *them*. It showed the moment when he surprised them about the breaking news stories on Twitter about Hubble and the explosion at Marshall, demanding to know if the stories were true, then a close up of Shepherd's face as he said 'Yes'. It cut back to Cooper live in the studio.

Now you have seen how agents of the government came to this house of God to try and silence me and intimidate me, because they know the truth I speak. They would rather you remained blind and in darkness than have your eyes opened to what is coming. For it is their arrogance that has brought these things to pass, it is the towers they have sought to build in the form of these telescopes in space, reaching up to try and glimpse the face of God that has triggered His wrath. And they fear your judgement and your rightful anger if you were to

305

learn of this truth. But the spirit is strong in me. And when they came to silence me I spoke loud with the voice of the Lord, as I speak to you now.

Turn on the news and see the truth of what is happening. See how the world is quaking and readying itself for the time that is told in the great Book of Revelation of how the righteous shall be gathered and the sinners shall be cast into the pit of Hell. And be in no doubt that the time of His reckoning is close for the signs are all around.

Franklin's phone rang and he took the call. On screen Cooper was walking over to the window again and pointing out at all the ships in the harbour.

See how the great armies of men are trembling before His approach and the great ships of all nations are returning to their ports, as was predicted by St John.

'Thanks,' Franklin said, ending the conversation. 'That was Ellery. They checked out Douglas's home. Found nothing – big surprise. So now we have two suspects to chase down.' He drained his coffee, allowing himself a smile as he set his mug back down. 'Sounds like Ellery was having the worst day of his life, he's now got every crazy conspiracy theorist in the country converging on Marshall convinced that the destruction of Hubble and Webb along with everything else that's going on is the first step of some kind of alien invasion.'

Shepherd picked up his coffee and stared at his reflection in it. 'Maybe they're right.'

'Seriously?'

'Why not – I find it as easy to swallow as the idea that Dr Kinderman and Professor Douglas did it.'

'That's because you're letting personal sentiment cloud your judgement. You can't ignore the evidence.'

'OK, so let's look at the evidence, all of it and not just what happened at Marshall and Goddard. What is making all the ships sail home, or snow fall in Miami, or the birds fly to their nesting grounds out of season. What's making so many people get in their cars and start driving?'

'You think it's aliens!?'

'OK maybe not aliens but something extra-terrestrial in the literal sense of the word – something outside the earth. Something that's affecting everybody. Again, let's stick to the evidence. We know for a fact that the rhythms of life are directly affected by cosmic phenomena, right? And by that I'm not talking about Capricorn rising and Leo on the cusp or any of that crap, I'm talking birds migrating using the magnetic fields of the earth to navigate and the tides linked directly to the phases of the moon.'

Franklin nodded. 'All right I'm listening. What do you think might be causing it – and please don't say aliens.'

'OK, so while I was working at NASA I realized

that the things that get reported are only a tiny fraction of what actually gets discovered. NASA is very prickly about its standing in the scientific community and is very careful to keep a lid on anything that might attract the wrong kind of headlines. A few years back, while I was working there, Hubble picked up the trail of some immense gravity wash. It was never reported because no one could work out what had caused it, but one of the theories was that it might have been created by a planet travelling on an erratic, millennia-long orbit that would make it vanish for thousands of years before it swung back to sweep right through our solar system. There are plenty of records of events like it in ancient civilizations, suggesting that people may have witnessed similar fly-pasts thousands of years ago. With the intersection of orbits and the combined gravity pulls of massive celestial objects a collision would not be out of the question. It would be cataclysmic, the end of everything, the end of days – just like Kinderman wrote in his diary. So perhaps he and Professor Douglas did see something coming, like a meteor or this huge planet the ancient prophets warned us about. And maybe that's why the whole world has gone nuts.'

'Then why not go public with it?'

Shepherd shook his head. 'I don't know.' He pointed at Cooper still preaching from the live feed. 'And I can't work out how he fits into all this either.'

'Maybe he doesn't,' Franklin said. 'Perhaps the whole Tower of Babel, hell and damnation thing is just a coincidence, another symptom of whatever's going on.' He took a breath and blew it out in a long stream. 'OK, confession time. This . . . what you're describing, this feeling or whatever it is that's making people behave strangely – I feel it too.'

'Since when?'

'A few months maybe.'

'And getting stronger.'

'Yeah.'

Shepherd nodded. 'Like that feeling you get when you're running late. A sick feeling almost – half physical and half an emotion – like you're in the wrong place and need to be somewhere else.'

Franklin nodded. 'You feel it too.'

'For the last few months and getting stronger.'

'OK, so just for instance let's assume everyone is experiencing the same thing, only Cooper comes to the conclusion that it's all down to God's impending judgement and decides he's the man to try and do something about it. So he sends the cards, maybe even sends the letters.'

'Agreed, but it still doesn't follow that it made Kinderman and Douglas effectively take hammers to several billion dollars' worth of space hardware.'

The laptop beeped loudly, drawing Franklin's attention. 'What's that?'

Shepherd felt blood rush to his face and was about to launch into a lie when he realized that the alert had sounded different from the previous ones. It had not come from his MPD search but from the ghost file. He opened it up and found a note from Smith.

Managed to recover a few more bits of data. Two terms pop up a few times: **Göbekli Tepe** and **Home**. Let me know if it's astronomy jargon or not. Smith

'Anything useful?' Franklin asked.

'Maybe.' Shepherd dug out his phone, scrolled to the recent calls list and called a number. It clicked a few times then connected.

'Hubble Control center.'

'Merriweather, it's Shepherd. We found something else. Does Göbekli Tepe ring any bells?'

'How you spelling that?'

Shepherd told him.

'Never heard of it, where's it come from?'

'We found it on Dr Kinderman's hard drive. You don't think it's something he might have been studying?'

'If he was, he never mentioned it to me.'

'OK, thanks.'

'Sorry I wasn't more help. Oh, by the way after we spoke last time I called a buddy of mine over at Keck in case he'd seen anything weird in Taurus. He said there's nothing there that shouldn't be.'

'OK, thanks, Merriweather.'

'Anytime. How's the manhunt going?'

'Still hunting.'

'Good luck with that. Anything I can do, I'm here all week.'

'Thanks.' Shepherd hung up. 'According to our man on the inside it's not a star or anything like that.' He leaned forward, his fingers fast-typing GOBEKLI TEPE into Google and hitting *Return*, half expecting no response at all. What he got was almost two hundred thousand hits. The top one was a Wikipedia entry.

Göbekli Tepe Turkish: [gøbękli tępɛ][2] ("Potbelly" or "Home Hill" [3]) is a Neolithic (Stone Age) hilltop sanctuary erected at the top of a mountain ridge in the south-eastern Anatolia Region of Turkey. It is the oldest known wholly human-made religious structure and also the oldest observatory believed to have been constructed by the proto-religious tribe known as the Mala [4] c. 11,000 years ago – pre-dating its more famous British counterpart Stonehenge by around 8,000 years.

'God damn,' Franklin said, 'another observatory.'

The site contains 20 round structures that were deliberately buried sometime in the 8th century BCE. Four have so far been excavated. Each has a diameter of between 10 and 30 meters (30 and 100 ft) and is made up of massive limestone pillars arranged in the exact shape of certain constellations.

Shepherd clicked on the *Images* option and a selection of thumbnails cascaded down the screen. Most showed an especially large stone monolith capped by a smaller one to form the unmistakable shape of an elongated letter T.

The T

Shepherd checked back through the notes and there it was again on the first list CARBON had found on Kinderman's drive. He returned to the Google search and clicked one of the images, opening it up large so the carvings on the main column were now visible. There was a snake, a scorpion, and a bull on the side of it – constellation signs – but it was the caption beneath that caught Shepherd's eye.

The main pillar, or Home Stone, is the largest monolith and also the only one that does not correspond to an existing star.

Home

Shepherd stared at the screen, his eyes flicking between the various open windows – the Home Stone, Cooper silently preaching from the live feed and gesturing out of the window at the flotilla of

ships in the harbour, Smith's last message with the word "Home" highlighted.

'Home,' Shepherd said. He sat up in his chair as the idea took hold. 'That guy who picked us up from the airfield said the sailors were all saying the same thing – that they just needed to get home. So if there is some extraordinary event happening out there in space, some kind of game changer, maybe Dr Kinderman and Professor Douglas felt it too.'

'But we checked Kinderman and Douglas's homes already.'

'Did we though? If I say "home" what does it mean to you?'

'Where my family is, I guess.'

'Exactly. Only Kinderman doesn't have any family and neither does Douglas. So home for them must mean something else. Probably the place where they were born.' Shepherd sat bolt upright in his chair.

'I think I know where Professor Douglas is,' he said.

CHAPTER 53

Sergeant Beddoes drummed his gloved fingers on the wheel of the cruiser. He was parked behind a billboard on the verge of the main road into town, waiting for speeding cars, not that he expected any today.

The snow had taken everyone by surprise. They were used to it up here in the mountains, but not like this and not without warning. It had come down so fast that he hadn't had time to put the snow chains on his car and twice now he'd nearly slid off the road. On top of that the world had gone crazy overnight. He'd been called out to a near riot at the Wal-Mart on the edge of town after people started panic-buying everything in the store. He'd gone in to help break it up and seen people who'd known each other all their lives, fighting over bottled water and canned food. He'd had to pull his gun at one point, but at least he hadn't had to use it. He'd heard stories of full-scale riots in some of the bigger cities, police firing on civilians, law and order breaking down as the gas pumps ran dry and the stores ran out of food because the delivery trucks had stopped rolling.

It had made him wonder if Reverend Parkes had been right and that judgement day was just around the corner.

For the last few months the Reverend had preached nothing else, telling his small, devoted congregation how a new Tower of Babel had brought it all about and that demons were already walking the earth in the shape of men to cause chaos and inspire sin that they might be damned and claimed by Satan when the time came. He had told them to stockpile food, batteries and water – and he had been right. He had also talked to him in private, telling about the secret army that was in place, Christian soldiers drawn from every walk of life ready to fight the forces of evil when they came.

'We can all fight for the Lord,' the Reverend had said, 'each of us in our own small way.' And he had told Beddoes how he could help, using his position as a police officer to watch out for the signs and report them to those who would know their significance. Beddoes had nodded and agreed to do whatever the Reverend thought he should, though he didn't quite understand how he could be of much use.

Beddoes reached up and held the crucifix he kept on a chain round his neck along with the St Christopher his mother had given him when he first qualified as a patrolman. 'To keep you safe and bring you home,' she had said. He'd been thinking about home a lot lately, though home wasn't the same now she had gone. The church filled some of the gap left by her passing, but not all of it. Nothing ever could.

A *ping* sounded on the dashboard. He looked up to find the LoJack receiver had activated but there was nothing on the road. There was a stolen car in the area, heading north by the looks of it. He grabbed his radio to call the dispatcher then paused. He pulled his glove off with his teeth and fumbled in his pocket for the prayer book the Reverend had given him to keep close by, a weapon in the coming war, and flipped to the back. There was an alphanumeric code next to a cell phone number. He compared it to the one on the display and felt his mouth go dry.

They were the same.

He took out his own personal phone and dialled the number written in the prayer book.

Demons in human form – he thought, just as the line connected.

CHAPTER 54

'OK, we're off the air.'

The Reverend Fulton Cooper held his final gesture of prayer for a few beats then opened his eyes, dropped his hands to his sides and smiled. 'Good show, everyone,' he said, casting smiles around the room. The bright studio lights cut out and across the room he saw the pale moon face of Miss Boerman framed by her severe haircut and suit. She was standing by the door, looking straight at him. She nodded when she saw she had caught his attention then turned and slipped back outside.

'Take a break but don't go far,' he announced to the room as he moved towards the exit. 'The Lord has much work for us yet to do. We're live again in an hour.'

He passed through the door and felt the relative cool of the outside air on his skin.

'They're in the chapel,' Miss Boerman said, the thin scar on her cheek puckering when she spoke. The mark of his hand from earlier was no longer visible. She handed him a small plain envelope. He opened it and studied the contents.

'This up to date?' he asked, slipping the note back in the envelope and tucking it into his jacket.

'As of five minutes ago.'

'Everything else set up?'

'Gassed and ready to go.'

'Anyone needs me, tell them I'm at private prayer and not to be disturbed.' He moved past her and headed down the stairs, the leather of his Italian shoes clacking first against the wooden steps, then against flagstones as he arrived in the basement and passed through a solid wooden door in the shape of an arch.

The chapel had been built in the old cellars, making good use of the existing vaulted brickwork and stone floors. It was small with three rows of wooden pews either side of a narrow aisle leading to a lectern which stood before a large stained-glass window that was artificially lit from behind so God's light could permanently shine through it. Cooper occasionally recorded segments of his shows down here, but he also used it for meetings because it was quiet and out of the way and there was another door hidden behind the altar, a requirement of the fire department regulations that also allowed people to enter the chapel without anyone in the main part of the building knowing they were there.

Eli and Carrie were kneeling at the altar, their backs to him, their heads bowed. Eli jumped as the door banged shut – still fighting his demons. Carrie reached out to him with a gentle, calming hand that had killed eighteen people to Cooper's sure knowledge. He caught her profile as she turned; the slightly upturned nose that made her seem younger than she actually was and inclined people to underestimate her, just as they did with him, only with her it was often the last mistake they ever made.

'Praise God for watching over you and delivering you safely,' Cooper said, smiling down at them as they turned round. He beckoned them over to the tech desk set up at the back of the room, which they used when they recorded down here. He turned on the monitor and heard the scuff of Eli's steps approaching, but he didn't hear Carrie's. She was the only person he knew who could walk up the two-hundred-year-old main wooden staircase inside the house without making a single sound.

They were showing a re-run of the morning show. After a few minutes the picture cut to a recorded section and Cooper pointed at the two men in suits sitting on the sofa opposite him. 'Are these the people you saw in Dr Kinderman's house?'

'Yes,' Carrie confirmed.

'They came here asking about all kinds of things but left with nothing. I trust you were careful in your observations of the good doctor's house?'

'No one saw us,' Eli said, his voice flat and empty as always. 'I guarantee it.'

'Good. That's very good.'

Carrie and Eli exchanged a look. 'We seen it on

the news,' she said, 'about the telescopes. We was thinking, now that the mission you set for us is over, now that those telescopes are no longer –'

'We want to get married,' Eli said. 'We want you to marry us. Right now.'

Cooper turned and smiled at them. 'And so I shall,' he said. 'So I shall.' He moved past them, walking back up the aisle towards the fake sunshine streaming in through the window. He stopped in front of the lectern and stared up at the cross. 'We've come a long way, the three of us, from that hell in the desert – a long, long way. And our journey is nearly over. But it is not over yet.'

'But the towers have fallen,' Carrie said, her voice small and unsure. 'The telescopes . . .'

Cooper turned to face them. 'They may have been destroyed but the wrath of the Lord is still evident for all to see, is it not? He is still greatly angered by the audacity and insult of those that built them. Destroying them was only part of His plan. The architects of the heresy must also be made examples of. For if I destroy the temple of mine enemy yet suffer the priest to live, will not he go forth and build a temple anew?

'The sacred mission I gave to you both will not end until those who fashioned this great sin are made to atone for their actions. Only by making an example of them can we warn others of the dangers of sin.

'Now I know you two love each other with a passion that is strong and pure: and I would not seek to stand between something as beautiful as that. But God sent you to me for a purpose, just as surely as He spoke and told me in that still small voice the service He would have you do in His name.

'Remember how I found you in the desert, broken by the sins you had been made to perform. Now I want you to remember what I said to you back in that field hospital in Iraq, I want you to recall for me the piece of Scripture I gave you to speak of your higher purpose and remind you of who you are.'

Carrie answered in her tiny voice. '*Therefore, take up the full armour of God, that you may be able to resist in the evil day, and having done everything, to stand firm.*'

Cooper nodded. 'Ephesians, chapter six, verse thirteen. And you see now how the evil day that was prophesied is upon us, and that now is the time to stand firm. When Jesus was tempted in the wilderness He prevailed by keeping His mind on His calling, on His mission on Earth, and saying, "*Get thee behind me Satan: for it is written, Thou shalt worship the Lord thy God, and him alone shalt thou serve.*"'

He reached out and took their hands and held them in his. '"Him alone shalt thou serve." Believe me I would like nothing better, nothing better in this world than to unite you two warriors of God in the blessed union of marriage.' He let go of their hands and took a step back. 'But His work is not yet done. And only when it is completed will we be free to pursue our own desires.' He reached into his jacket pocket and pulled out the envelope Miss Boerman had given him. 'But never forget that you are not alone in your service of the Lord. You will see from this information that there are many others engaged in the good fight, many others who are part of the same brother and sisterhood who would also see His will be done. Our reach is long for He sees all.'

Carrie took the envelope and opened the flap with the stiletto of her finger. Inside was a printout showing a section of map with a town in the centre called Cherokee. There was also a time, an alpha-numeric number, a compass heading and a note saying: *approximate distance to target, four miles.*

'Some people sympathetic to our cause did me the courtesy of installing LoJack devices to the cars of Dr Kinderman and Professor Douglas. I figured it might be useful to know where they were in case they managed to evade us. Dr Kinderman's car has been in the long-term parking lot of Dulles International airport since early yesterday evening. I think it's safe to surmise that he is no longer in the country but we have others looking into where he may have gone. The signal from Professor Douglas's car, however, was picked up by a State Trooper in Swain County, North Carolina about a half an hour ago.' He pointed at the piece of paper. 'That gives you a rough idea of where he is. It's about a five-hour drive from here on good roads, so it will probably take you a little longer today, the weather being the way it is. If you head off now you should get there before dark.'

He closed his eyes and looked up, one hand on his heart, the other raised in front of him like a benediction. 'I pray you, God, watch over these, your servants, along the righteous path so they may do your work, and bring these foul sinners to swift and rightful atonement so that their souls may finally be freed from the burden thou hast given them, Amen.'

He opened his eyes and smiled at them both, as though something wonderful had just happened. 'You should make a start. Daylight is burning. If you leave the way you came in, Miss Boerman will give you everything you need. We will have more accurate information by the time you get to Cherokee. Remember, we need to send a message to anyone else who would dare to stare upon the face of God. I'm counting on you to send that message, loud and clear. And if anyone tries to stop you in this sacred mission, anyone at all, be they civilian or officer of the law, then they must also be sacrificed in the name of the greater glory.'

CHAPTER 55

Shepherd burst from the interview room and headed across the almost empty office with Franklin following close behind. 'It was during summer break at the end of the first year of my master's,' he said, bundling the laptop back in its case as he walked. 'I was at Marshall working as a lab monkey in data analysis, cataloguing all the new stuff that was pouring in from Hubble. James Webb had just been green lit and Professor Douglas was in charge, though he hadn't put his team together yet. It was really hot that year and everyone else seemed to be on holiday. Me and a couple of other research students were the only ones doing any work.'

They pushed through a set of double doors out to the main stairway and started heading back down to the reception area. 'One Friday a few weeks into our placement Professor Douglas popped his head round the door and told us all to go back to the dorm we were staying in and pack for a two-day trip. We had no idea what he had planned but he was the boss so we did as we were told.

'He picked us up in his old jeep and we headed east. We thought maybe he was taking us to one of the other launch areas but we drove right past them and kept on going. He said it was good to go back to basics every once in a while, remind yourself what it was all about, and that was what we were going to do: no hi-tech, no computers, just a simple reflector telescope, a few beers and a clear sky.

'We wound up late in the afternoon heading up into the Smoky Mountains just north of Cherokee, North Carolina. He had this log cabin there, way up on a ridge. It looked like it was straight out of a Western: three rooms, potbelly stove, fresh water you had to pump out of a well. It even had a porch with a rocking chair on it. I guess it was just far enough away from anywhere so that the sweep of the modern world kind of passed it by. And because it was miles from anywhere it got so dark that the whole sky lit up at night. You could see more stars there with your naked eye than you could with a good telescope in a light-drenched town or a city. He had a telescope set up near the cabin in a hunter's hide built on a rocky ledge and we spent two days up there, tracking the planets, looking at the stars, talking about Galileo and Copernicus and Kepler, where it all came from and where we thought it was all going. He was fired up about James Webb even then. Talked about how it was going to see right to the edge of the universe, right back to the beginning of time.'

They reached the bottom of the stairs and the desk sergeant looked up wearily.

'We need a car,' Franklin said.

'Sure, no problem,' the walrus replied, wearily picking up his phone and punching a button. 'I trust your stay with us has been a pleasant one. Please let me know if you used anything from the mini-bar. I'll let you know when your cab is here.'

'I don't mean a cab. We need to borrow a car. One that's going to be able to cope with the weather out there.'

Shepherd frowned. 'Why do we need a car? I mean, much as I hate to say it, but wouldn't flying be quicker?'

'I doubt anything will be taking off in this,' Franklin said, pointing outside at the thickening snow. 'We might get lucky and make it to Charlotte, always assuming they haven't got worse weather there. But then it's still about a three-to-four-hour drive to Cherokee on mostly mountain roads. It's maybe five hours from here but mostly on dead-straight, flat plain roads. Trust me, I know this area pretty well. We'll be better off driving.'

Franklin steered Shepherd away from the main desk and over to the row of seats by the wall. 'Tell me why you think Douglas is there.'

'There was something special about the place. The professor had history there, real history, why else would he drive all that way when there are plenty of mountains much closer to Huntsville? It had all these photographs of people in frames tacked to the walls, some going way back, including one of the Professor as a kid standing on the porch and squinting into the sunlight as he held a model plane over his head. He must have been about five or six but you could still see the man he would become.'

Franklin looked over at the desk sergeant who was now resolutely ignoring the constantly ringing phone. 'How we doing with that ride?' he shouted over.

The sergeant looked at them over the top of his reading glasses. 'We're just having a Caddy waxed and polished for you now.'

Franklin turned back to Shepherd. 'Funny guy. He should be on Comedy Central.'

Shepherd glanced outside at the swirling white. 'What about the roads – the traffic's all snarled up already, we saw it coming in.'

'Exactly. We saw it coming in to town. The roads heading out will be pretty clear. So long as we get a decent car, driving's going to be our best option. Trust me.'

Shepherd nodded, but for the first time he wasn't sure whether he did.

CHAPTER 56

Liv sat in the kitchen eating dried fruit and salt crackers she'd found in one of the food lockers. Kyle pulled a stool from beneath a stainless-steel counter top and sat down wearily opposite. 'You should drink some of this,' he said, pulling a bottle of water from a thermal box on the floor. 'It might taste a bit funny because it's got rehydration salts in it.' He poured half of the bottle into a glass and slid it over to her. 'I made up a batch for your friends. Don't worry, it's clean. In fact all the water's clean. I've been running tests every hour and the ground water's flowing pure again. The pressure must have blown away the contaminants, though I'll still keep checking it. Go ahead – drink.'

Liv drank, forcing herself not to gulp it all down in one, savouring the saltiness on her tongue. 'So tell me how you ended up here,' she said, as Kyle poured the rest of the water into a second glass.

'We were all working way down in the south in Dhi Qar Province as part of a project run by an international aid organization.'

'Ortus,' Liv said.

'That's right. How did you –'

'– I recognized the logo on the side of your jeep. I know one of the people who runs it, Gabriel Mann.'

Kyle smiled in a way that suggested he both knew and liked him. 'You know Gabriel?'

She nodded.

'Ah, he's a good bloke. When we first set up the project here he came and helped us out a lot. I heard he was in some kind of trouble with the law.'

'He was. He is.'

'Well I hope he's OK.'

'So do I . . . You said you were working down south.'

'Yeah, way down in the southeast the other side of Baghdad in the Mesopotamian marshlands, or what's left of them. The people there were pretty badly persecuted by Saddam and his mob after they rebelled against him in '91. As part of his system of punishment he built huge canals to redirect the Tigris and Euphrates away from the marshes to drive the tribes out. He was pretty successful too. There's only about ten per cent of them left. Then the war came. As soon as Saddam started losing, the locals blew holes in the dams and dykes and let the water flow back in again. We were sent to help monitor the water quality and manage the restocking of the wetlands with reed beds. There were sixteen of us.'

'What happened to the others?'

'Gone.' He took a drink then carefully placed the glass down on the counter. 'We'd been working together for six months. It was good work. The people were returning, the reeds were growing, we were even seeing some of the wildlife coming back. The marshes used to be a major staging post for millions of migratory birds until Saddam buggered it all up. Every day more life returned – both man and bird. Then all of a sudden the plug got pulled on us. It had something to do with what happened to Gabriel. Our headquarters are in Ruin and he was arrested on suspicion of being a terrorist or something, trying to blow up the Citadel using Ortus resources. The upshot was that all of Ortus's bank accounts were frozen while the charges were being investigated. Which meant we could no longer pay for anything and weren't getting paid ourselves.

'We kept going as long as we could, hoping the money would get unfrozen but pretty soon we started running out of food, fuel, you name it. So we pulled out and headed back towards the border.' He rolled the water around in the glass, staring at the liquid, deep in thought.

'So how come you ended up here? Did you get lost?'

'No, nothing like that.' He continued to stare at the glass, as if the answer might lie in it somewhere. 'I'm still not really a hundred per cent sure what happened. We were travelling north, heading for the Turkish border in a four-vehicle convoy, which is the only safe way to travel on these roads. We were making pretty good time, considering all the roadblocks on Highway 8, had made it as far as Al-Hillah and we were getting ready to push on as far as Baghdad when I got a feeling that we were going in

330

the wrong direction. I can't really explain it. It was like I knew that the maps, the GPS were wrong. I wasn't alone, Eric and Mike felt it too.

'The rest of the guys thought we'd gone mad. They told us to shut up and keep driving but we couldn't do it, none of us could. It was such a strong feeling. For me it was like a magnet pulling at some kind of metal core inside me.' He looked up and smiled. 'I've always been a bit of a nomad, never really stayed in one place for too long. No matter where I ended up and how good a time I was having there would always come a morning when I'd wake up with an overwhelming urge to be somewhere else. And this was exactly like that, only instead of wanting to head off into the unknown it felt like I was returning somewhere. Like I was coming home.

'It's like – for the last six months or so, ever since I've been working on the marshes, I've been watching the birds: flamingos, pelicans, hooded crows, teals. Some of these guys fly halfway round the world from as far north as the Arctic Circle and as far south as Africa and India to end up in the exact same place where they hatched. They've been doing it for thousands of years, hundreds of thousands probably, and we still don't really know how they do it. It's just an instinct in them, a natural urge. Then a few years back the marshes vanished, I mean there was nothing there at all but cracked earth and the odd abandoned boat. But as soon as the water came back, they knew. Somehow they just knew that's where they needed to be. That's what it felt like for me. I felt such a

331

strong pull to be here, though I didn't know what this place was, or even if it was here. I've never been here before in my life, but I felt like I was coming home. Explain that.'

Liv shook her head. 'I can't,' she said. But I felt something like it too.'

Behind her the door opened and she smiled when she saw Tariq standing there looking better than she'd seen him for a while. Her smile faded quickly when she saw the look of concern on his face. 'What is it?' she asked.

'You better come see for yourself.'

CHAPTER 57

Liv saw why Tariq had fetched her the moment she stepped out of the main building. A thick column of dust was rising in the eastern sky heralding new arrivals.

'Soldiers,' a voice shouted down from the guard tower.

'How many?' Tariq called back.

'Difficult to tell. There's one Humvee and one truck. The truck could be empty or it could have twenty men inside.'

Tariq looked over beyond the perimeter fence to where a group of workers were hurrying back to the compound. He waited until the last of the grave-digging detail had slipped through then shouted, 'Close the gate and man the guns.'

'No,' Liv said. 'We've been through this. We cannot meet everyone who comes here with suspicion and loaded weapons.'

'We tried it your way last time,' Tariq replied. 'First we talk, then we let them in. I cannot risk all our lives again.' Then he walked away before she had time to argue.

The Humvee and the truck pulled to a halt about

fifty metres short of the gate and sat there for a while, engines running, shrouded in a cloud of their own dust.

'American,' Tariq said, reading the markings on the side of the vehicles.

Liv was standing next to him, inside the perimeter gate waiting to greet them. 'What are they doing?' she asked.

'They are being cautious,' Tariq replied, his eyes never leaving the lead vehicle.

'Can you blame them.' She glanced up at the .50-cal gun in the guard tower, a man standing behind it, poised and ready.

She noticed Tariq's hand tighten on the grip of the AK47 slung across his back and wondered for a fleeting moment if he wasn't spoiling for a fight. This was the problem with letting men do the negotiating. Sooner or later their hormones took over and it usually ended in battle. 'HEY,' she shouted at the Humvee, 'OVER HERE.' She waved her hands over her head and jumped up and down to get their attention.

'What are you doing?' Tariq looked at her as if she had gone insane.

'You said we should talk first so I'm talking. HEY. I'M AN AMERICAN.' She pulled a keffiyeh from round her neck and started waving it in the air. 'USA. HELLO.'

'You can stop now,' Tariq said. 'I think they heard you.'

The Humvee started to creep forward along the

tracks in the dirt leading to the gate. It was impossible to see who was inside because of the sun on the windscreen, a bright slash of light that shimmered as the hard wheels crept over the rough ground.

'Can you do me a favour?' Liv said out of the corner of a fixed smile, 'take your hand off your rifle strap.'

Tariq reluctantly obeyed just as the Humvee crunched to a stop ten feet short of them. The door popped open and a rangy corporal got out. Liv felt Tariq stiffen beside her as he saw the M-4 the soldier was cradling in his arms, eyes shielded by the standard-issue Oakleys most of the soldiers seemed to favour. He stood by the vehicle saying nothing. By the slight tilt of his head Liv could tell he was scoping out the guard tower and the .50-cal cannon that had tracked the Hummer all the way to where it now stood.

'Hi,' Liv said, smiling through the tension. 'I'm Liv Adamsen. I'm an American. Who are you?'

A hand let go of the M-4 and pointed at the name badge stitched to the left breast of his desert fatigues. Liv squinted against the glare coming off the Humvee's windscreen and read the name. 'Williamson. You got a first name?'

He nodded. Liv's smile was starting to hurt now. 'Want to give it to me?'

The soldier ignored the question, looking straight past her at the fountain of water shooting up from the spire of the drill in the centre of the compound. 'What is this place?' His voice was soft, almost childlike and totally at odds with the hardened image the rest of him radiated.

'It's . . .' Liv paused as she realized she did not have a ready word to describe it.

'It's beautiful,' the soldier whispered, his shaded eyes taking in the lines of the rivers snaking away across the dust. Behind him the truck's engine fell silent. It rocked on its springs and other men emerged, dropping down one by one to the ground, six of them, all wearing the coffee-stain camouflage of the US military. Liv was reminded of the welcoming committee she and Gabriel had encountered crossing the border from Turkey what seemed like a lifetime ago. Three more uniformed men climbed out of the Humvee. And though they were wearing uniforms and carrying weapons, there was nothing threatening or hostile about them. They just seemed like a bunch of cautious guys edging their way into a party they weren't sure they were invited to. Tariq must have sensed it too. He raised his hand to the man in the guard tower and the .50-cal cannon swung away as the man stepped back.

'Where you from?' The soft-spoken corporal removed his shades and squinted at Liv with pale blue eyes that looked like they should be peering out at a wheat field from beneath a faded starter cap.

'I'm from New Jersey,' she said. 'You?'

He shrugged. 'I'm from all over, I guess. Illinois originally but I wouldn't exactly call it home.' He looked back at the spout of water shooting up from the ground, like a kid watching a firework. Then he smiled. 'Did you feel it too?'

Liv frowned. 'Feel what?'

'The pull to this place. We all felt it. We all volunteered to stay behind when orders to ship out came through – the rest of the men were off like rabbits, they been pining for home for weeks, never seen homesickness like it. But none of us have any real homes to go to . . .' His hand clenched into a fist and tapped on his chest above his heart. 'But then we felt the pull to come here. So we came.'

Liv looked up at Tariq. 'Why don't you come on in,' she said.

Tariq glanced down at her then back at the row of soldiers. 'How many are you?'

The Corporal shrugged. 'Just what you see here.'

'The vehicles stay outside the fence,' Tariq said, 'and you need to hand over your weapons. We'll keep them over there, locked in the armoury,' he pointed to the nearest guard tower. 'If you want to leave you can have them back again, no arguments, but no one walks around with a weapon inside the compound, understood?'

The Corporal stared hard at Tariq for a few long moments. Asking a soldier to hand over his weapon was like asking him to surrender. 'How come you get to keep your AK?' he said.

'I don't,' he replied. 'You lock up your weapons, I lock up mine. Everyone's the same.'

'But who gets the key?'

Tariq nodded at Liv. 'She does.'

The Corporal smiled. 'Well in that case it's a deal breaker. In my experience you can never trust a Jersey girl with something of value.' His face broke into a laugh and she saw the boy in him again. 'I'm only kidding.' In a few well-practised moves he made his M-4 safe and held it out to Tariq. 'Hey man, no problem – your house, your rules, though you might want to reconsider letting the vehicles in, or the truck leastways.' He turned to it as one of the other men climbed up and raised the canvas siding to reveal the truck was full of boxes and crates of food. 'We just got a re-order in at the same time as all the other guys were shipping out. There's K-rations in there and enough food to feed a battalion for about a month. We thought we'd bring it along, seeing as we had no idea where we were headed. The only thing we don't got much of is water, but I see you pretty much got that covered.'

Tariq nodded. 'OK,' he said. 'You can bring the truck in, but the Hummer stays outside.' The gate clanged like a bell as it was unlocked and then swung open to let the new arrivals inside. They filed in quietly, handing over their weapons to Tariq as if they were just checking in coats at a nightclub and Liv watched them closely, sizing them up. They were foot soldiers, enlisted men who more often than not joined up to escape jail or the crushing boredom of a dead-end life with no job and no prospects. Back home they joined gangs and fought to create the families they'd never really had. In the army they did pretty much the same. They were nomads, homeless, just like the guys from Ortus. Just like she was.

'Where were you stationed?'

'East of Baghdad,' Williamson said, still staring up at the water fountain.

Liv nodded and walked over to Tariq who was checking weapons and making them safe.

'It's spreading,' she said.

'What is?'

'The pull of this place – it's spreading. The guys from Ortus felt it yesterday at Al-Hillah, these guys felt it today in Baghdad.' She looked up and scanned the horizon all around, thinking of the whole world that lay beyond it. 'We should get ready for more people,' she said. 'Lots more.'

CHAPTER 58

It was early afternoon by the time Franklin and Shepherd finally eased onto the I-26 going northwest into a flurry of fine snow that drifted out of a light fog. The traffic was solid heading into Charleston, a three-lane parking lot, inching its way into the city. The outbound lanes were almost empty.

Franklin drove. Shepherd sat in the passenger seat, studying a series of maps he'd borrowed from the highway patrolman who'd 'loaned' them his Dodge Durango with about as much grace as someone handing over a personal credit card, pointing to a mall and saying 'Knock yourself out'. For the first twenty minutes or so the only sound was the rumbling of thick wheels on blacktop, and the occasional rustle of paper as Shepherd unfolded the maps one by one and studied them. They were topographical maps showing the border region between South Carolina and North Carolina, with the Smoky Mountains rising up in the west. His finger traced each winding track, searching for a road he had only travelled once before, nearly twenty years previously.

'Find what you were looking for?' Franklin asked from the driver's seat.

Shepherd stared out at the whiteness, the road disappearing into the fog within fifty metres either way so that it felt like they were moving but not going anywhere. 'Hard to tell from these maps,' he said. 'Guess I need to be there and see what looks familiar.'

'You won't be seeing much if this fog doesn't lift. The snow will make everything look different too.'

Shepherd wondered if this was all a waste of time. 'We could always turn around and head back, follow one of our many other leads,' he said.

Franklin chuckled. 'Man you sure got cynical awful quick – normally takes a couple of years in a field office to wear the shine off a new agent.'

Shepherd said nothing. He kept thinking about the photograph of the dead woman and imagining how he would have felt if it had been his Melisa lying there instead. He could almost feel the pull of the laptop in the footwell behind his seat, taunting him with the knowledge it contained. It was the danger that came with allowing something to become the single pulse of your life: it drove you, gave you focus and purpose, but it could also derail you the moment it was no longer there. Melisa had been the light that lured him out of the darkness. He closed his eyes, and found himself back in the women's shelter attached to the place he had washed up. Melisa was doing

341

her thing, helping some poor woman who was not much more than a kid herself deliver a baby. The woman was Chinese and when the baby was finally born, wriggling and mewling into the world, Melisa whispered something to him: 'Do you see them?'

She often did that: asked a question that made you ask one back.

'See what?'

'The threads. The Chinese believe that when a baby is born, invisible red threads shoot out and find their way to all the people they will connect with in their life. And no matter how tangled up they get as they grow, those threads never break so they will always end up finding their way to the people they were destined to meet.'

He imagined those threads now, connecting him to Melisa, twisting through the air and pulsing like veins.

'That thing you said back there,' Franklin's voice rumbled like the tyres, low and serious, 'the thing about something heading towards Earth, you think that's a possibility?'

Shepherd opened his eyes and realized he must have been dozing. They were in flat country now, hardly any buildings, hardly any sign of life apart from the odd car heading in the other direction towards Charleston. 'Statistically speaking it's possible.'

'So how come other telescopes haven't seen it?'

'Hubble can see further than anything on earth.'

'OK, but presumably anything far enough out that only Hubble could see would take millions of years to get here.'

'Not necessarily. There are a lot of theoretical objects in space, physics-defying things that we can imagine but have not been able to find or measure. One of them is known as a Dark Star. It has huge mass and travels at or near the speed of light. If one of these things was coming straight at us then the light from it would only just outrun the object. We wouldn't know anything about it beforehand, not until it was about to hit because the object would arrive at almost the same time as the light, like it had just appeared out of nowhere.'

Franklin stared ahead at the road. 'OK, say, for argument's sake, one of these Dark Stars is heading our way, would that explain all this stuff that's going on: the ships, the soldiers, the people heading home?'

'It's possible. We can see the effect the moon has on the sea and humans are sixty per cent water, our brains are nearer seventy-five per cent, so it stands to reason the moon must have some effect on us too.'

'That's for sure. If you ever work a midnight shift at a hospital or a police precinct during a full moon you'll know it's true. Everyone goes nuts.'

'And the moon is only one tiny object. Imagine what effect a massive star would have on us all. We're all related to each other on an atomic level – you, me the car, the stars – we're all made of the same stuff.'

'What do you mean?'

'I mean the atomic building blocks that make up you and me are the same ones that burn at the heart of stars, and all of it came from the same place. Around fourteen billion years ago the universe was born. It started out as something called the point of singularity, smaller than a sub-atomic particle, incredibly dense and incredibly hot. Every single thing that is now in the universe exploded out from it and began to cool as it expanded, forming the protons, neutrons and electrons that, over time, became atoms and eventually elements. The first element was hydrogen. Most of the atoms in the human body are hydrogen. These elements then started to coalesce into huge clouds that slowly condensed to form stars and galaxies. Then heavier elements began to be synthesized inside stars and in supernovae when they died. One of these was carbon, the essential building block of all organic life forms. And this process is still happening throughout the still-expanding universe. Things are born. Things get torn apart. And the elements of those dead things become something else. Nothing lasts for ever, but nothing ever entirely disappears either. It just becomes something else.'

The sound of the tyres rumbled through the silence that followed. Outside the white, frozen countryside continued to slip by. The Interstate was practically empty now. From time to time a building or sign would loom out of the fog giving variation to the otherwise flat white landscape, but most of the time they might just as well have been driving along in a huge hamster wheel – always moving but getting nowhere. It was a fair visual representation of the limbo Shepherd was feeling, halfway between something and nothing, with no real concept of either. Maybe the world had already ended and this was purgatory, driving through the fog for ever with Franklin at the wheel, never knowing what had happened or whether they could have done anything to stop it.

A ticking sound punctuated the silence as Franklin hit the indicators and started to ease off the highway onto a side road. 'Just taking a little shortcut,' he said. 'We need some gas and a bite. There's a town up here.'

Shepherd looked down at the map, following the line of the road they had just taken until it stopped at a dot of a town called St Matthews. 'We could have got gas and food on the Interstate. This is going out of our way.'

Franklin reached into his pocket, took out a cigarette and popped it between his lips. He stared ahead, his fingers tapping on the wheel, the cigarette hanging unlit in his mouth.

'Sorry,' he said.

Shepherd thought back through all the wrong notes he'd picked up over the last few hours: the way Franklin had ushered the cop who had clearly known him out of the room back at the station; the way he had insisted on driving rather than flying up to Cherokee; even his suggestion to come to Charleston in the first place to interview Cooper rather than hand it over to other agents. 'Sorry for what?'

Franklin wound down his window a little then lit the cigarette, blowing smoke out into the cold. 'You'll see,' he said.

CHAPTER 59

The soldiers immediately made themselves at home.

As well as the food and fresh fuel supplies – which they offloaded from the lorry with impressive and well-drilled speed – they volunteered to take over the grave-digging detail their arrival had disrupted. They also brought something far more valuable than any of these – they brought a laptop.

All the communications and technology in the compound had either been destroyed or looted, effectively cutting it off from the wider world. So while everyone else was out beyond the perimeter fence Liv traced cables from the dish on the roof of the main building and hot-wired the laptop into the compound's satellite link.

Like any journalist Liv was a total information junkie and she'd been cold-turkey for days now so the first thing she did when she fired up the laptop and got online was call up some news sites. She scanned the headlines feeling the buzz of an addict getting a fresh hit. Since her brother had fallen to his death from the summit of the Citadel, Ruin and the story that had unfolded in the wake of his

347

sacrifice had never been far from the news. It was her story too – and also Gabriel's. She did a News search on Google with GABRIEL in the subject line. Pages of results came back, all several days old and just retelling stories she already knew: his arrest at the hospital for suspected terrorist acts and homicide; his subsequent escape from custody; the manhunt that ensued with her picture and name next to his. After that there was nothing. The only more recent stories relating to Ruin were medical ones concerning an outbreak of what some of the more tabloidy sites were calling 'a plague'.

Liv clicked on the top result, her heart racing at the implications of this. She remembered the symbol she had seen on the Starmap, the circle with the cross through it that made her think of disease and suffering. Was this what it predicted – the event that would result in the end of days?

The article opened and she speed-read it, her mind pulling out the facts as her eyes skimmed the words: outbreak centred around the Citadel – eighteen dead, eighty-six in isolation – the whole city of Ruin in quarantine and under police control.

She opened another window and searched for RUIN POLICE. Skype was already installed on the desktop and she opened this too, logging in through her own account that thankfully still had some credit on it. She copied the number of the switchboard into the keypad, adding the international dialling codes for Turkey then hit the key to boost the speakers as the number dialled and started to ring.

It rang for a long time, long enough for her to read another article about how the infected had been transferred from the Public Church into the Citadel itself. There was a link to a news clip but someone answered before she could play it.

'Ruin Police,' a voice said, with chaos sounding in the background.

'Hi,' Liv said in fluent Turkish, 'could you connect me to Inspector Arkadian?'

'Name please?'

'Liv Adamsen.'

'One moment.'

The line switched to musak and Liv flipped back to the news site, scrolling through another article about the outbreak. It featured apocalyptic photos of empty streets and people standing by the public gate to the Old Town wearing full contamination suits. The Citadel soared up in the background, so terrible and familiar. Seeing it in this context made something click in Liv's head and she pulled the folded piece of paper from her pocket and smoothed it flat on the desk while the tinny hold tune continued to play. She scanned the symbols again, her eyes settling on the beginning of the second line.

The symbol for disease followed by . . .

She looked back at the photo on the screen, the

man in the contagion suit with the sharp outline of the mountain behind him.

. . . of course . . .

The second symbol represented the Citadel and the disease had started there and was now spreading. The next part of the prophecy was coming to pass.

The musak cut out.

'Liv?'

'Arkadian.' More noise in the background, like he was on a street full of children. 'Are you OK? I just saw the news about the outbreak.'

'It's chaos here. People are scared. I'm scared. We're evacuating the children from the city. Where are you?'

She looked out of the window at the distant movement of people working on the hill as they dug the new grave. 'Still in the desert,' she said. 'We found it.'

'I know. Gabriel told me.'

Liv felt the world shift. 'Gabriel! You spoke to him?'

'Yes.' Another pause filled with the babble of children. 'Just before he was taken into the Citadel.'

Liv felt like all the air had been sucked from the room.

'He was sick, Liv, he had the virus – but he was not as sick as the others.' She gripped the sides of her chair and reminded herself to breathe. 'Most of them go mad when the disease takes them, but not Gabriel. He rode all the way back here because he knew he had it. He didn't want it to spread. It was

Gabriel who insisted the disease be contained inside the Citadel. He wanted to take it back where it came from. He wanted to beat it. And if anyone can do it, it's him.'

Liv tried to speak but couldn't. In her ear she could hear Arkadian still speaking but she didn't hear his words. Her eyes dropped down to the red stained piece of paper and scanned the second line again, a terrible new meaning emerging from it in the light of Arkadian's revelation.

$$\varnothing \quad \overline{\wedge} \quad \overset{\perp}{\mathbf{\wedge}}$$

Disease
Citadel
A knight on horseback – Gabriel

She remembered the words on the note he had left her, telling her that leaving her was the hardest thing he had ever done. And now she knew why. He must have known he was infected. He'd known that and had still ridden all the way back to the Citadel, just to protect her.

She looked at the remaining symbols on the second line of the prophecy, hoping she might find something hopeful in them, but all she saw was more misery.

She knew what it meant now. The T was her, the circle confinement and the moon and chevron told her how long it would all last.

Nine moons – Eight months.

She clicked on the video clip embedded in the news article. It had been filmed from a news helicopter at night so the quality wasn't great. A bright searchlight picked out a procession of patients strapped to stretchers and being carried to the mountain. She studied the faces, all looking straight up into the sky. Even through the grainy images she could see the masks of pain their faces had become. Tears started to run down her cheeks then the light swung away, settling again on the last stretcher to emerge from the church. She hit the space bar to pause it just as Gabriel looked straight up at the camera. It was like he was staring straight at her, like he was saying goodbye. Her love. Her life – being carried away on a stretcher, and into the heart of the hateful mountain.

CHAPTER 60

Franklin finished his cigarette and flicked it out of the window. 'You ever been married, Shepherd?'

'No.'

'And you don't have kids, do you?'

'No, I don't.'

They were on the outskirts of the town now with widely spaced houses emerging from the trees, a general store with lights burning in the windows and a sign outside saying *St Matthews Piggly Wiggly*. There was a gas station on the other side of the road, also open for business. Franklin drove past them both, all pretence of getting food and gas now abandoned.

'When you have kids, everything changes. It's like taking your heart out of your chest and watching it walk around. You'd do anything for them, anything at all. And if you have a daughter,' he shook his head, 'well that's a whole other ball game. The world suddenly seems ten times more dangerous than it did before, a hundred times, and she is so vulnerable and fragile in it.'

He slowed down and took a right into a one-lane

street lined with neat, single-storey houses with wooden porches and brick chimneys, their front lawns all blanketed in white.

'So you work your ass off to put a roof over her head, give her a good life, protect her from all the crap that you know is out there, the stuff that you see every day. Everything you do takes on new meaning, every bad guy I ever put away was dedicated in some way to my daughter. I did it for her, to make the world a safer place for her, and for her mother.'

He took another left onto a road lined with bigger houses, some with four-car drives.

'And you try so hard to shut off the darkness you have to deal with but it's always there, like a stain. So you keep it from your kids by keeping yourself from them, because, in a way, you are the thing you want to protect them from.'

He brought the car to a halt outside a house with a long sloping roof like a ski jump. Franklin fixed his eyes on it and killed the engine.

'Then one day you realize you don't know who they are any more, either of them. You've spent so long working to give your family a better life that you're no longer a part of it. You've become a stranger in your own home. You can't talk to them, you can't understand them, you're only aware of the distance between you where once there was no gap at all.' He looked away and Shepherd wondered if the tough old bastard was actually crying.

'I'm sorry I dragged you all the way out here,' Franklin said, turning back and looking him square in the eye. 'I kind of convinced myself it was all about the investigation but in the end it looks like it's all about me.' He nodded at the sideways house. 'And you were right about the homing instinct.'

'You don't have to explain it.'

Franklin turned to him. 'You said you didn't have a home.'

'I don't, at least not like this. But home means different things to different people.' He took a breath ready to tell him . . . about Melisa, about his missing two years, even about how he was using the MPD files to try and find her again. But just then the door of the house opened and a girl of about twenty stepped out.

Cold air flooded in as Franklin got out of the car. Shepherd watched him walk up the drive towards her, like he was being pulled by an invisible thread. He stopped a few feet short of her and they stared at each other. Then she stepped forward and wrapped her slender arms round his neck and buried her face in his chest. Behind them another woman, an older version of the girl, stepped onto the porch and stared at them for a moment. Then she too came forward, a smile breaking on her face like a sunrise, and Shepherd looked away, feeling uncomfortable about sharing such a private moment even from a distance.

He stared down the street at the other houses. Some were empty and dark, the drives showing the fading tyre tracks of cars no longer there. Other houses glowed, their festive decorations lighting up the snow like Christmas cards.

Witnessing the power of the homing instinct and its effect even on someone like Franklin made him realize that the pull to find Melisa and the reckless things it was making him do was simply the same thing working in him.

The rap of a knuckle on his window snapped him back to the present.

Franklin was standing outside the car. Shepherd got out, snow crunching beneath his shoes and cold air on his skin.

'You want to come in, grab some lunch?'

Shepherd looked over at the porch where the two women were standing watching them. 'I don't think so. I'd just be in the way.'

Franklin nodded. 'Listen,' he said. 'When I drove here I thought . . . well, I don't know what I thought, but now I'm here I don't think I can leave again, not for a while at least.'

'It's OK, I understand. I'll go on to Cherokee alone, see if I can find Douglas's place. It's probably a waste of time anyway, I only ever went there once.'

'Don't do anything stupid,' Franklin said, his brow creasing with the difficulty of what he was doing. 'And if you do find him, don't approach him on your own. Call me first, OK?'

'He's my old teacher – what's he going to do, give me a tough assignment?'

'He's a wanted terrorist who nearly got you killed in an explosion this morning. Don't forget that.'

'OK, if I find him I'll call – I promise. Now get inside that house, Agent Franklin, and spend some time with your family.'

'Ben.'

'What?'

'Name's Ben, short for Benjamin: it's not my bureau name, it's my real one. My old man won a hundred-dollar bill for calling me it when I was born, asshole that he was. He'd probably have called me George if our name had been Washington, just to win a dollar.'

'It's a fine name, Ben. You wear it well.' Shepherd held out his hand.

And Franklin shook it.

CHAPTER 61

Rosie Andrews crunched through the snow towards the ATM. It was out of service, just like all the others. Nothing was working. Everything was falling apart. She felt tears bubbling up through her growing panic. She had about fifteen dollars in her purse, two maxed-out credit cards, a quarter of a tank of gas and at least a three-hour journey ahead of her. The gas would get her maybe fifty miles out of Asheville, about a third of the way down to her mom's in Atlanta, maybe even less the way her station wagon was loaded up.

From somewhere across the parking lot she heard glass shatter followed by a roar of voices that made the hairs bristle on the back of her neck. She turned and hurried back to where she had left the car, parked behind a dumpster on the far side of the lot, away from the large angry-looking crowd she had seen outside the big Petro Express when she had driven in. It all added to the sick feeling that had been growing inside her that made her feel something was terribly wrong. The crowd had been arguing with security staff who were allowing only a few people in at a time to control numbers.

There was another crash and the roar got louder.

Sounded like the security guys had lost the argument.

The noise frightened her. It was the sound of violence and chaos and it made her feel small and vulnerable. She just wanted to get some money and get out of here. She just wanted to get home.

She rounded the edge of the dumpster, fretting in her pocket for her keys, and saw the man leaning down by the side of the car, his face pressed against the rear window. Rosie felt blood singing in her ears and her vision started to tunnel.

'What are you . . . you get away from there.'

The man looked up but didn't move – he just kept looking at her in a way she didn't like.

Another crash of glass behind her. Another roar.

She pulled her hand from her coat and pointed it at him. 'You step away from the car, you hear me?'

The man looked down and registered the gun she was holding, but still he didn't move.

'Is this man bothering you, sweetie?'

The voice made her jump. Rosie's head jerked round to discover a birdlike woman standing next to her, so small she was almost like a child. She was looking up at her, her blue eyes cold against the snow. In her peripheral vision she saw movement, the man moving forward, using the distraction to close the gap between them.

She stepped backwards, slipping on the ice a little but holding the gun steady in a good grip like she'd practised on the range. She was going to shoot him. If he took one step closer she would fire without hesitation. She had often wondered if she would be able to do it if she found herself in a situation like this but now there was no question in her mind that she could. It was a nature thing. A primal instinct to protect what was yours. She took another step back, opened her mouth to warn the man one last time, then an object banged against her side.

The movement was so fast she didn't even feel the pain until the blade was sliding back out from between her ribs, so sharp and sudden that it snatched the breath from her mouth as quickly as the man took the gun from her hand.

She felt confused, like everything was happening to someone else and she was just watching. Warmth spread out from the burning pain in her side and she looked down at the red bloom spreading over the white of her coat.

Blood. Her blood.

The sight of it shocked some sense back into her and she took a ragged breath ready to scream but a strong hand clamped over her mouth and dragged her further back into the shadows behind the dumpster.

Carrie watched Eli holding the woman tightly, making sure her blood spilled away from him and onto the snow and not his boots. When her body went limp he laid her gently on the ground and patted down her pockets until he found the keys.

'Shame,' he said, standing up and moving over to the car.

'Just bad timing I guess,' Carrie said, inspecting the blade of her knife and wiping it with a handful of snow.

'I didn't mean her,' Eli pressed the button on the keyfob and the car *thunked* as the central locking disengaged. He opened the back door and nodded towards the interior. 'I meant her.'

The backseat was crammed with boxes of groceries, rolls of bedding and a couple of laundry bags overflowing with baby-girl clothes. The owner of the clothes was wrapped up tight in a quilted snowsuit and strapped into a kiddie car-seat, asleep, a single strand of blonde hair escaping from beneath a hand-knitted woollen hat.

Carrie moved over and watched the tiny chest rise and fall, eyes moving beneath the lids as she dreamed her little-girl dreams. Carrie's hand found Eli's and she wrapped all of her fingers round one of his but he pulled away, reaching across the tiny sleeping form to pick up a pillow from the pile of bedding. 'Look away, honey,' he said, 'you don't need to see this.'

She opened her mouth to speak but then thought better of it. Eli was right. This was no world for a little girl to go through without a mother by her side, she knew that much herself, and this little poppet was sweet and innocent enough to pass straight into heaven, no questions asked. Eli was doing her a favour, a great favour, by doing this thing for her. He was so kind and strong where it really counted, in the heart – and that was why she loved him.

'Suffer the little children to come unto me,' she said, reaching out to gently tuck the lock of hair back under the woollen hat. Then she kissed Eli on the cheek and turned away.

PART V

And the kings of the earth, and the great men, and the rich men, and the chief captains and the mighty men . . . hid themselves.
For the great day of His wrath is come; and who shall be able to stand?

Revelation 6:15–17

CHAPTER 62

Gabriel drifted in and out of consciousness. At times he raved, howling and bucking against the bindings, other times he was calm enough to converse with the doctors for minutes at a time, giving them insights into how the infection felt, like a drowning man describing the experience in snatched breaths to someone in a nearby boat before another wave engulfed him and dragged him back under. He fought, he screamed, he scratched and he cried – but he did not die.

Athanasius watched it all from a seat by the bed. He was there at night when the flicker of candles and flambeaux cast ghoulish light across Gabriel's face, and in the day when the sunlight streamed through the huge rose window, dappling the damned with colour. The beds surrounding them emptied and filled, over and over as the tide of sickness ebbed and flowed, and more and more people entered the mountain. First it was those who had rested in quarantine in the Seminary. Then new faces began appearing, steady in number, their brief stay always numbering a day or two at most and always following the same journey: carried in writhing and screaming, carried out silent and still to the centre of the mountain and the firestone where the pyre always burned.

Then, on the second day of the fourth week after the Citadel had opened its doors to the sick, Gabriel opened his eyes and they stayed open. It was the middle of the afternoon after the doctors had finished their rounds and Athanasius was away attending to the organization of what was left of his flock. He lay there, staring up at the soot-blackened stalactites high above him, listening to the drugged moans of the infected and the creak of their bindings as their bodies clenched and twisted all around him. He lay there a long time, bracing himself for the moment when the fever would drag him back down again, as it always had before. But this time it did not.

'Hello,' he called out, his voice raw and unfamiliar. Murmurings rose from the beds surrounding him, the sick roused from their drugged slumber.

'HELLO,' he called again, loud enough to hurt his throat and bring footsteps hurrying. A face appeared above his bed, brow furrowed, eyes ringed with the shadows of deep fatigue. Gabriel didn't know him but he recognized the contamination suit he was wearing – and he also noticed the loaded syringe.

'No,' he said. 'You don't need to do that. I feel better.'

It was as if the doctor hadn't heard him, his sleep-starved brain running through the well-worn routines of patient sedation. Gabriel felt the cold alcohol swipe of an antiseptic swab on his arm. He tried to twist away but the bindings held him fast.

'WAKE UP!' he shouted, as much to the doctor as to those surrounding him. 'WAKE UP!'

The effect was instant, the faint murmurings erupting into howls as the sleeping sick were shocked into wailing wakefulness. The doctor looked up at the chaos now surrounding him, every patient around him now bucking and thrashing against their bindings as they howled in torment. He looked back down at Gabriel, his eyes shining with annoyance at the trouble he'd caused, he held up the syringe and readied the shot.

'What are you doing?' Gabriel growled, his throat raw from his shouting. 'I do not need sedating. See to the others first. Their need is clearly greater.'

The doctor hesitated, looked like he was still going to spike him, then a shadow passed over Gabriel's face and he glanced across to see the smooth-headed figure of a monk standing on the other side of his bed. 'It's OK,' Athanasius said to the doctor, 'I shall sit with him. You see to these other poor souls.'

The doctor blinked as though a spell had been broken, then turned away to start dealing with the others.

Athanasius pulled the stool out from beneath Gabriel's bed and settled on it. His eyes were bloodshot and sunken and he smelled of wood smoke. Gabriel breathed it in, relishing the smell. It was the first time in a long while he had smelt anything other than the strange and permanent odour of oranges. And there was something else. He was cold and his sweat-soaked bindings felt wet and unpleasant against his skin.

'The fever,' he whispered in realization of what this meant. 'It's gone.'

Athanasius laid a warm hand on Gabriel's forehead and straightened in his chair. 'Thank God,' he said.

Another figure appeared by the bed and held a thermometer in his ear. It beeped and he checked the reading. He reset it and did it again.

'Ninety-eight point six,' he said, the hint of a smile on his weary face. 'You're probably a few points cooler than I am.'

'Dr Kaplan, allow me to introduce Gabriel Mann,' Athanasius said.

Gabriel nodded a greeting. 'I'd shake your hand but someone tied me to this bed.' Kaplan smiled again. 'Tell me. Did the quarantine work. Has the disease been contained?'

He knew the answer before either of them spoke. He heard it in the pause and saw it in the flick of their eyes as they looked away from him.

'There have been new cases,' the doctor replied, 'ones that have originated beyond the line of the original quarantine in the metropolitan districts of the city. We have continued to remove the infected and quarantine those at risk but we have so far been unable to contain it. As of last week a state of martial law has been in place in the greater city of Ruin to try and prevent the further spread of the disease. The army and the police have set up roadblocks on the road leading out of the mountains. No one is allowed in, no one is allowed out. But we have made significant steps since moving here. And you may hold the key to all of our salvation. No one has fought the disease as long as you have, and no one has recovered – until now. But it's still early days and you may yet relapse.'

He looked up at Athanasius. 'We need to move him somewhere isolated.'

'No,' Gabriel said, 'I'll stay here, I don't need special treatment.'

'You don't understand,' Kaplan said. 'You *need* to be in isolation, not just for your own comfort but for the safety of others. Your body may have defeated the infection but there is another possibility. Sometimes the body's natural defences do not entirely vanquish a hostile agent. Sometimes a kind of truce is arrived at where the disease is kept in check and the symptoms disappear. If this has happened then you may now be an asymptomatic carrier of the disease, immune yourself but deadly to anyone who comes into contact with you. There is also the possibility that the infection has mutated inside you and formed a new strain, one that your body is immune to because it helped create it but one that is every bit as deadly as the first strain – maybe even more so.'

Gabriel stared up at him. He hadn't given conscious thought to his hopes until now. The one thing that had kept him going throughout his suffering and delirium was the thought of Liv. She was the one he had fought death for. He had left her in the desert in the hope that he carried the disease away with him. He had travelled all the way back to Ruin in the hope it may not have spread. He had insisted on being taken inside the Citadel where the blight had first come from and then refused to die in the hope that he might finally be reunited with her. Now he was told that he must stay here, isolated even within this place of isolation. There were many words to describe the pain that filled him, but only one that completely summed up the way he felt.

Cursed.

Athanasius read the pain on his face. 'I know a place where we can move him,' he said.

CHAPTER 63

Following her conversation with Arkadian, Liv scoured every news site and story relating to the contagion in Ruin until the laptop's battery ran out.

She sat alone for a while in the sweltering heat of the building feeling like she had just experienced a bereavement. She closed her eyes and remembered the last time she and Gabriel had been alone together, sheltering from the dust storm in the cave out in the desert. She had thought then that her life was slipping away, that the Sacrament she carried inside her would die without finding its way back to the home it had lost, and drag her down to death with it. She had clung to him then like she was clinging to life. She remembered the feel of him, the salty taste of his skin as they had kissed when they had given themselves to the moment and each other in case it turned out to be the only night they ever had.

It was strange that someone she had spent hardly any time with and whom she knew so little about could have such a strong effect on her. There was something about Gabriel that calmed her soul when she was near him and made it ache whenever he was away – like it ached now.

She stood abruptly, angry at the world, the scrape of the chair legs cutting through the silence, and headed out through the dining hall into the bright sunlight. The thought of hard physical work seemed infinitely appealing in the wake of the emotional battering she had just experienced. She grabbed a pick, fell in line and happily took orders from Corporal Williamson, losing herself in work as they dug a pit big enough to bury all those who had drunk the poisoned water.

It took all day and when all the dead lay buried beneath the dry ground, the group collected by the water's edge to wash and drink and relax. You could see in their easy conversation and open gestures that a new bond had been formed, one forged by hard work and collective endeavour. It was a testament to the human spirit that they had met that morning in a circumstance of mistrust and suspicion, one group inside the compound and one without, and in less than a day those divisions had been removed entirely. It reminded Liv that, despite all the darkness that had swamped her recently, there was so much goodness in the world, and so much good in people. It made her hopeful that, whatever had been started here, whatever ancient spark had been re-ignited by the Sacrament's return, it might just have a chance to succeed and grow into something wonderful and free, the exact opposite of the Citadel in fact.

Something about this thought struck her and made her pull the folded paper from her pocket and study the symbols anew. Her eyes flicked between the upwards arrow symbol for the Citadel on the second line and another on the third which was its exact opposite.

She looked over at the fountain of water in the centre of the pool, forming an elongated 'V' in the air. The symbol was the fountain. The symbol was this place.

She looked back at the second and third lines again, searching for other points of comparison.

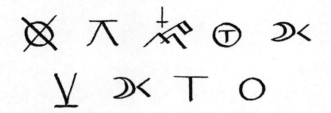

The moon sign appeared in both, linking them to the same time frame, and the T was there too, encircled in the first line and beside a circle in the other. She looked down at the perimeter fence surrounding the compound below her and understood now why she felt so strongly about not locking the gate. This place was meant to be somewhere the Sacrament was free, outside the circle not in. It had to welcome everyone and spread as far as the horizon if it needed to. The water had already begun this process, flowing out through the links in the fence and bringing the land back to life.

'Not a fortress but a haven,' she whispered.

'What was that?'

Liv looked up and saw Tariq standing nearby.

'Nothing,' she said, aware that everyone was tired and the plan she had just hatched would keep. 'I'll tell you tomorrow.'

CHAPTER 64

Gabriel was wheeled into the Abbot's private quarters at the head of a procession of equipment and medical personnel. The rooms had been left largely unused since the Abbot's sudden death and the subsequent spread of the blight. Elections had been planned but the disease had ravaged the electorate before they could be held and since then, in a dark twist of irony, the only thing truly running the mountain was the very thing that had derailed the electoral process in the first place.

'This is the main living room and office,' Athanasius said, moving across the large space. 'There is also a bed chamber through here that could be turned into a laboratory.' He opened a thick, metal-studded door onto another cave containing a wooden bed, an ottoman and several smaller pieces of furniture. 'And in here is a washroom giving you all the running water you should need.'

Gabriel surveyed what he could of the new surroundings from the fixed viewpoint of his bed while everyone else started to unpack. His mattress had been raised at one end to render him upright and the bindings that had held him so tightly and for so long had now been loosened, but not removed. Dr Kaplan had advised that they stay in place for the time being until they were sure he wasn't going to suffer a relapse. He wasn't allowed to walk either, which was fine with Gabriel. He was so weak that even keeping his eyes open was an effort.

He took in the room, this comfortable prison that would be his home for who knew how long. There was a huge fireplace as tall as a man that dominated one wall and a stained-glass window set into the rock, its ancient, hand-blown panes of blue and green glass forming a peacock motif that distorted the world beyond.

'How are you feeling?' Athanasius pulled a chair over and sat down as behind him the room began to be shifted around and dismantled.

'Like a condemned man.'

Athanasius smiled and ran his hand over the smooth dome of his head. 'I think we all feel that way to some degree, though I know you have suffered more than most.' He leaned in closer and lowered his voice so only Gabriel could hear. 'I sometimes wonder whether all this could have been averted – that if we had just left things as they were, left the Sacrament in place and not challenged the old traditions, all this pain and suffering, all this death would not have come to pass.'

'You really think that?'

'I have considered it. One does what one thinks is right, but sometimes we do the wrong thing for the right reasons.'

Gabriel closed his eyes and let his head fall back on the bed. He had been plagued with similar thoughts. He had lost so much as a result of the sequence of events he had helped set in motion. 'Setting the Sacrament free was the only right thing to do,' he said.

'So you are happy with the apparent consequences of our actions?'

He shook his head, 'Of course not. I feel personally responsible for every single person who has died from this blight or is still suffering now. I feel guilty that I may have helped spread it beyond these walls by leaving here, guilty that my mother is dead and my father too, but most of all I feel guilty that I abandoned Liv and left her alone in the desert. I was forced to, I was infected. I left her for all the right reasons, but it did not bring me happiness. And despite all of that I would rather never see her again than risk harming her.'

Athanasius nodded. 'I just wish, when I see how you have suffered, that I could do more myself.'

'Maybe you can. When I last came here I was searching for something.'

'The Starmap.'

Gabriel nodded. 'I thought it was the only thing that could lead us to Eden in order that the Sacrament could finally be returned to its rightful place. But in the end we found it another way – and we discovered the Starmap was already there. It had directions carved into it that used the stars as a guide. But it had something else carved on the reverse, another part of the prophecy.'

'And what did it say?'

'I don't know. It was written in a language I didn't recognize. But from what we already know doesn't it strike you that everything that has happened was predicted – Brother Samuel climbing to the top of the Citadel and making the sign of the Tau with his body; the release of the Sacrament and its restoration to its original home. It was outlined in a series of prophecies, first in the Heretic Bible and then on the Starmap. When we first started looking for it we only had my grandfather's notebook to go on and a photograph my father had sent him. But the photograph only showed one side of the stone. When I found it and saw it for myself I realized there was much more on the other side. If we could read it now, in the light of all that has happened, we might discover that all of this was predicted too. We might even learn how it could end or what we might do to influence it. There must be more experts in ancient languages here in the Citadel than anywhere else in the world. If the stone can be deciphered anywhere, it's here.'

'There are, or at least there were. Many of the scholars have succumbed to the blight, though there are still a few remaining. I myself have studied many of the lost languages. If the text on the stone is written in one I am familiar with then it should be easy to translate. But how could we get to see it?'

Gabriel smiled. 'I took photographs and sent copies to a police inspector in Ruin.'

Athanasius sat up in his chair, his eyes alive. 'Give me his name and I shall send a message immediately.'

378

'His name is Arkadian. And if you find me a cell phone I can call him and get him to message us a copy right away.'

Athanasius frowned. 'All communications devices are forbidden inside the mountain.'

'So are civilians, and yet here I am. I'm sure one of the medics will have brought a phone along with them.'

Athanasius shook his head. 'It was a condition of granting access to the sick that those admitted must abide by the rules of the mountain. Everyone had to surrender their phones before entering. You will not find one in here.'

Gabriel went quiet, his mind thinking his way around the problem.

'What about the phone I gave you when I was last here?'

'It no longer works, the battery is empty and you did not leave a charger – although . . .' He glanced across the room at a small writing desk positioned beneath the peacock window. He rose and moved towards it, weaving between the medical staff and the stacks of equipment they were setting up. Gabriel watched until his view was blocked by a man in a contamination suit. 'You OK?' Dr Kaplan asked in a bedside voice that instantly made Gabriel feel nervous.

'Just peachy,' he replied, catching a glimpse of Athanasius over the doctor's shoulder as he opened the desk and retrieved something from inside.

'We're nearly ready to start the first bank of tests.' Kaplan stepped across and blocked his view again.

'Which means we're going to have to take a little blood, I'm afraid. Normally when someone has been through what you have, I would be very reluctant to take more than a few millilitres at a time to give the white cells time to recover. But the more we take now, the more parallel tests we can run and the quicker we can process the results, so I'm inclined to be slightly more aggressive – if you are willing.'

Gabriel took a deep breath. 'Help yourself,' he replied. 'I'm not going anywhere, just try not to kill me.'

Kaplan smiled and nodded at a medic who stepped forward and fitted a syringe to the cannula already sticking out of Gabriel's arm. He twisted the valve and watched dark, wine-coloured fluid fill the first of several blood-collection tubes. 'This might make you feel a little drowsy,' Kaplan added, 'so feel free to close your eyes and rest if you want.'

Gabriel did as he was told and tried to relax.

'What about this, would this work?'

He opened his eyes and saw Athanasius standing over him holding a laptop in his hand with a charger dangling from it. 'Maybe. Can you send email from it?'

'No. But I thought maybe this charger could be adapted to work with the phone.' He placed the laptop on the bed, the charger coiled on top of it in a tangle. Gabriel unplugged the lead and examined the jack. It was entirely different from the socket on the bottom of the phone he had left. Next, he opened the laptop. It was a relatively new model and started up quickly, the desktop filling with hardly any icons. He searched the main directory for wi-fi hardware and software or anything that could send a message or an email.

Nothing.

Athanasius was right.

He glanced at the battery status and saw it was full, so at least the charger was working. But even if he managed somehow to customize the connectors to fit, the ampage would be too strong and would most likely fry the phone. Then something struck him. He span the computer round and smiled when he spotted the USB port. 'We can use the laptop to charge the phone,' he said, pointing at the square socket. 'We can plug in the laptop and then hardwire the phone to the computer through one of these ports. It will act as a transformer and send a weaker trickle charge to the phone's battery.'

'Can you do it?'

'Yes.' Gabriel leaned back against the pillow. 'But I'll need some tools and both my hands.' He could feel what little energy he had leaking out of him with every drop of blood. 'I'll need some raw wire, something like needle-nosed pliers –' He closed his eyes and instantly regretted it as the room started to spin. 'Hey,' he said, glancing over at the medic by the bed who was still diligently taking his blood. 'I think you should . . .'

Heat rose up in him like steam in a geyser, so sudden that it overwhelmed him before he could even finish his sentence. His body started to shake and he felt urgent hands clamp down on him and pin him to the bed.

'Sweet Jesus,' he thought as his eyes rolled back in his head and darkness washed over him. 'Not again.'

CHAPTER 65

Inspector Arkadian was standing in a car park just outside the city limits, supervising the disembarkation of a busload of children when he became aware of eyes upon him. He looked down at a terrified and tearful-looking girl of about eight. He crouched down, bringing his head level with hers, fully aware of how frightening he must seem after all she had already been through, towering over her in the contamination suit that had become his second skin since the outbreak.

'What's your name?' he asked, brushing her wavy brown hair away from her face with a gloved hand.

'Hevva.'

'Well, Hevva, there's chocolate and cola inside.' He pointed to the backpackers' hostel that had been commandeered as a temporary orphanage.

'Are we going to be taken into the mountain to die, like Mummy?' she asked, wiping her eyes with the back of her hand.

He felt something break inside him. 'No. You'll be safe here – I promise.'

She stared at him for a moment with the clear and

searching expression only a child can manage, then slowly turned and rejoined the others.

The quarantine had been swift and had been put in place the moment the first infection occurred outside the Old City walls – a local teacher who had already infected the rest of the teachers in her school and many of the parents by the time her symptoms manifested. Arkadian's blood had run cold when he first heard this news. Madalina, his wife, worked at a school, not the one that had been infected, but it was still a chilling reminder of how vulnerable everyone was in the face of this thing. Madalina was now in semi-quarantine in St Mark's church near their house. All public workers who'd had extended contact with other people had been moved to large civic buildings for observation and she had been one of them. But these internal precautions were only part of the overall plan.

The last thing the national and international community wanted was a new killer disease to escape into the wider world. Ruin's natural isolation, surrounded by the high, unpopulated foothills of the Taurus mountains, made it uniquely suited to be placed in its own self-contained quarantine. The rapid evacuation of the Old Town after the first outbreak had been effective enough to hold back the spread of the disease for the first month and so the policy was now extended to the city as a whole. There was only one road leading into Ruin and it was now blocked with no access in or out save for the daily food and medical supplies delivered by truck to the outer barrier, and only collected and transported into the city once the trucks had driven away again.

Inside the city there were further divisions. Ruin was naturally split into quarters by four great, straight boulevards that radiated out from the Citadel at the centre. Each quarter was now a self-contained borough, with the boulevards between them acting as a no-man's-land no one was allowed to cross. There had been near riots as people tried to flee one part of the city and relocate in another following a rumour in the first few days of the quarantine that all new cases of the blight were in the Lost Quarter and that the neighbouring three boroughs were disease free. The unsteady peace that had eventually been re-established was now maintained by constant armed patrols. The only movement of any kind had been the transportation of the infected down the empty boulevards towards the Old Town and the Citadel, and the evacuation of children in the other direction.

Arkadian stepped into the hostel and was hit by the sound of activity and children's voices. There were about a hundred kids here, some of them orphans of the disease, but many of them not. Most parents, once news spread that the young were immune from the disease, had elected to send their children out of the city, preferring that they were away from the newly formed ghettoes where fear and violence bubbled beneath the quiet surface of a city held together by little more than tension and

385

hope that the work of the doctors inside the Citadel would soon bear fruit.

He saw the girl with the wavy brown hair over by a table. She was clasping a locket round her neck tightly in her hand but now held a bottle in the other with a straw sticking out of it. Behind her a movement caught his attention and he looked up into the grim face of Bulut Gül staring out from behind the visor of his contamination suit, his face set in the grim way he had seen before when he had bad news to impart.

'Did you get the message?' Bulut said, his voice muffled and sounding like it was coming from a long way away.

'What message?'

'You need to get over to St Mark's quickly. It's your wife. It's Madalina.'

CHAPTER 66

Cherokee hadn't changed much in the near twenty years since Shepherd had last driven through it: rows of tacky souvenir shops still sold rugs, stone axes, arrowheads, feather and bead head-dresses that owed more to Hollywood than to history. The one big change was the number of motels and fast-food joints that had sprung up along the only road through the middle of town. They spoke of prosperity but of a particular and transient form. The casino had not been open long the last time he was here but its influence had clearly spread wide in the intervening years. The whole town had a soulless quality, of the kind only gambling money could buy. It also seemed deserted, every hotel and motel had vacancy signs outside and the huge parking lot surrounding the glass tower of the main Harrah Casino contained lots of virgin snow and hardly any cars. The homing instinct that was taking hold of the world was clearly not being kind to Cherokee. Clearly there were not many that called this place 'home'.

Shepherd parked up outside the Tribal Grounds

Coffee Shop, drawn by a sign in the window inviting him to *'Come in and enjoy our world famous Elk latte and free wi-fi'*. He kept the engine running and the heater on, opened up the laptop and hooked on to the internet. A new window opened, asking for his security clearance codes. He punched them in and the saved search reappeared on the desk top. The processor crunched. The windscreen wipers swiped back and forth and a ping rang out as the new search results loaded.

There were seven of them now.

He opened the first and scrolled straight to the PDF file attached to the bottom of the document. He clicked on it, holding his breath as he waited for it to open. A depressing parade of images appeared on the screen, similar to the ones he'd seen before, charting a blighted life then an early death. But it wasn't her.

He closed the file and moved on, keeping the momentum going before his nerve failed him. The next result opened, a solid block of text cascading down the screen. He found the attached file at the bottom and clicked it open, bracing himself for the photographs.

They were different to the first photos but none the less tragic. A well-scrubbed, bright-eyed woman smiling from a picture that had been taken at a dressy function, the flashbulb capturing a moment of pure happiness and hope. The picture below showed the same face, the eyes now closed and bruised, her clear skin lacerated by the windshield she had passed through after her car had left the road and hit a streetlamp. A brief note beneath the photo read:

Melisa Erroll – Junior attorney at law
Fatal RTA. 02.34 Feb 16th.
BAC negligible. No suspects sought.

The time of her death, the minimal Blood Alcohol Concentration and lack of suspects told the whole story. She was probably just working late, fired by youthful ambition and a desire to one day make partner, and fell asleep at the wheel on her way home, never to wake again.

He closed the window and continued to work his way down the strange roll call of the dead, experiencing the see-sawing of emotion between tragedy and relief. He reached the last result and clicked it open. And there she was.

He felt like someone had punched him in the gut. He couldn't breathe, his vision swam as eight years of hope evaporated in an instant and tears welled in his eyes. She looked exactly the same as he remembered, more beautiful even, her huge dark eyes staring out from a passport photograph. He wiped his eyes with the back of his hand and took a shuddering breath. 'Oh Jesus.'

The blood drained from his face, and his breathing started to race. He forced himself to calm down, breathe more deeply, more slowly. His eyes darted over the file, trying to take in all the details at once. It was too much. Words and figures tumbled through his mind, disjointed fragments, missing pieces of someone he hadn't seen in eight years. His brain re-engaged and his focus returned. The top document was a visa application. She had applied for an extension to her F-1 student visa around the time she had disappeared. It had been denied. Had this been the reason she had gone, something as mundane as this? It can't have been, they were going to get married; she wouldn't have needed a visa if she was married to a US citizen. It had to be something else.

His eyes shifted over the facsimile of her application form. There were details here he had never known. Her date of birth – she was two years older than he had guessed; her middle name – Ana; her place of birth – Ruin, in southern Turkey.

Ruin again.

His eyes flicked back to the photograph, her sharp-cheeked, almond-eyed face framed by long dark silky hair with a kink in it like ripples over dark water. He could see by the side of the file that there was another photograph further down, just a scroll and mouse click away.

He thought of all the other final images he'd seen, all tragic in their own way but nothing compared to what this would be. There would be an autopsy report too most likely, depending on how she had died. He wasn't sure he could face either. But he had to. He had to know.

He clicked on the scroll button to bring up the final photograph.

Shepherd had been so prepared and braced for

something else that it took him a few moments to register what he was looking at. It was a picture of Melisa smiling, her personality fully evident here in a way it had not been within the stiff pose of the passport photograph. It was attached to a scanned copy of a medical registration document showing that Melisa Ana Erroll had qualified as a midwife and was licensed to practice for an international aid organization called Ortus. The document was simply to register the fact in the United States and qualify her for the company insurance.

He clicked on the scroll bar again but there were no more pictures. He switched back to the file and flicked through to the last page where the autopsy report or death certificate would have been. Nothing – just the insurance paperwork that corresponded with the photograph.

He laughed and cried at the same time, a sob of pure relief as he realized what had happened. The MPD search must have finished trawling through the death registers and moved on to the live files linked to the database. And then it had found her.

His Melisa.

Alive.

CHAPTER 67

Gabriel woke slowly as though rising up through thick, warm liquid.

He became aware of the sounds of the room, the blip of the monitors, the chink of glass on glass, the shuffle of booted feet across the stone floor. He lay still for a while, feeling he was gradually materializing in the room, atom by atom. He opened his eyes and saw a bluish green light washing over the arched ceiling of the cave. He turned his head and saw the peacock window, the low evening sun lighting it up from behind.

'Ah, welcome back.' Athanasius moved across his field of vision, blocking the light from the window. Gabriel tried to sit up but found that he could not. 'I'm afraid the doctor thought it best to restrain you again, for your own protection. That's the bad news. The good news is –' He carefully held up the smartphone Gabriel had left him. There were two wires sticking out of the bottom, stripped from the end of a USB cable that wound down to the laptop which was resting on a table by Gabriel's bed. Athanasius touched the screen of the phone and it lit up.

Gabriel smiled. 'You did that?'

'I did.' Another man stepped into view from the end of the bed. He was clean-shaven beneath his surgical mask, and wore the dark surplice of a priest.

'This is Father Thomas,' Athanasius explained, 'chief architect of all the modern improvements within the mountain and someone who knows more about electronics than I could ever hope to.'

'It was quite simple really,' Thomas said, taking the phone from Athanasius. 'Just a question of reverse engineering the phone and working out which of the contacts in the docking slot connected to the battery. It's been on charge for almost an hour now.'

'How long have I been out?'

'About three hours,' Athanasius replied. 'Dr Kaplan said it was a natural reaction after what your body's been through. They got enough blood though, so they've been running tests all the while you've been asleep.'

'Great. Do you want to loosen my bindings so I can send a message?'

Athanasius and Father Thomas exchanged a look. 'I'm afraid Dr Kaplan advised that you remain restrained, just for the time being. You are obviously still at risk from fits, which might be a danger both to you and others. If you tell me, or rather Father Thomas what to do then we can send the message for you.'

Gabriel closed his eyes and felt tears of frustration pricking the backs of them. He hated feeling like this, so powerless and weak.

'Find the menu,' he said, 'then scroll through the call log until you find one from an Inspector Arkadian.'

'Got it,' Thomas said.

'OK, create a new message and then put –' he paused as he considered what to say. So much time had passed since he'd last seen Arkadian at the base of the Citadel, so much had happened it was hard to know where to start.

'Just put "Surprise! I'm not dead. I need the photos I sent you of the Starmap. Hope to see you very soon. Gabriel."' Thomas typed it then read it back. 'You have a signal?'

'Yes.'

'Then press "Send" and let's hope to God he's got his phone with him.'

CHAPTER 68

The phone buzzed in Arkadian's pocket but he barely noticed it. He was walking fast, the effort of it making him hot inside his contamination suit. St Mark's was up ahead, the quarantine signs fixed on the outside of the windows, the suited armed guards outside. The churches were being used as general clearing-houses for the infected in all four quarters. Any new cases were brought here to be transported into the Old Town and ultimately the Citadel but they were mainly being used as isolation areas for the observation of high-risk individuals, people whose jobs had brought them into contact with others – which is why Madalina had been brought here.

He pointed to his badge as he reached the main door and the guard stepped aside. He had prayed on the way over that his sudden summons would prove to be nothing, just a scare or a misunderstanding. But now he was here he knew it was as bad as he had feared. He could hear the noise already coming from inside the building: the sound of suffering, the howl of the Lamentation.

He pulled on the heavy door and the noise spilled

out onto the street like a physical thing. It was inhuman, terrifying, and all the more so because he knew his wife was in here somewhere. He looked for her in the crowd of frightened faces that turned his way as he entered but she was not among them. There was a separate area to one side of the altar, a private chapel with a lock on its door. This was where the noise was coming from. He moved through the parting crowd and through the door – and there she was.

She looked like she was sleeping but he knew she would have been sedated. Her skin shone with fever and her eyes moved behind lids that were already showing the first blisters. And she was tied fast to the bed. He could see her hands moving rhythmically, despite her drugged state, her finger-nails scratching at the one piece of flesh they could reach.

A doctor turned to him, his eyes dropping to the ID badge fixed to the front of his suit. He stepped back from the bed, realizing who he was, and Arkadian took his place by his wife's bed. He laid his hand on hers but the mechanical scratching carried on.

'We're just preparing them for transfer to the Citadel,' the doctor said.

'I can look after her,' he said, 'I can take her home.' He had spoken to her only a few hours ago. This couldn't be happening.

'All new cases have to move to the Citadel,' the doctor said, 'you know that.'

Arkadian had had so many of these conversations

with husbands, wives, sons and daughters that it was odd being on the other end of one. It all felt wrong. He had always felt great sympathy for the people he'd had to comfort but now he had become one of them he realized he hadn't understood how they'd felt at all. All words about how they would be better cared for in the mountain meant nothing when you were saying goodbye. And that's what this was. No one had come out of the mountain yet – people only ever went in. And now his wife was about to become one of them.

The next half an hour unfolded in a nightmarish blur. First they moved her to one of the ambulances parked outside the church and he sat by her side, holding her hand and talking softly to her as they bumped along the cobbled, serpentine streets of the Old Town and up to the embankment where the ascension platform waited. Usually the relatives had to say their goodbyes at the Old Town wall but a combination of his rank and his calm demeanour convinced the orderlies to let him travel with her right to the foot of the Citadel where he helped them move her stretchered bed out onto the platform and fix it in place next to the others ready to be hoisted into the mountain. But then his nerve gave out. In the end it took three men to pull him off the platform and they held him fast until the platform had risen up too far for him to reach it.

He sat on the floor and wept as he watched it rise higher, carrying his love away from him while in his pocket the phone continued to buzz. It occurred to him that all the messages he had ignored all morning because of the difficulty of extracting the phone from the suit might contain one from her. He slid his finger under the sealed flap in the seam of the suit and unzipped the side opening. His phone was warm from its long confinement and he felt like someone had ripped his heart out when he read the first message.

Come back. I can smell oranges. I'm scared. Mx

His wife had slipped into a fever alone while he'd been on the other side of the city. He blinked the tears away to stop his vision swimming and looked at the other messages. There were no more from her. The infection must have taken hold quickly, as it did with some people. The rest of the messages were from colleagues who had heard the news before he had and were trying to get hold of him. Then he saw the last one, a message from a ghost.

When he had said goodbye to Gabriel he had firmly believed he would see him again. But as the days and then weeks passed by, and the disease continued to spread into the wider city, and the steady flow of the infected continued into the mountain with no sign of anyone coming out, he had finally let go of that hope. He re-checked the message. Whoever had sent it was asking for the picture Gabriel had sent from the desert. Who else would know about that? It had to be him.

Arkadian fumbled with the phone, his hands shaking as he went through his old messages, looking for the picture file from over a month ago. Gabriel was alive, and so was Arkadian's hope. Because if one person could survive then others could. It meant the infection could be beaten and he might just see his Madalina again.

CHAPTER 69

Shepherd felt the rise in the road out of Cherokee, heading north towards the Tennessee border. He was riding high on his discovery that Melisa was alive and buzzing on the coffee he had ordered from the Tribal Grounds Coffee Shop in grateful thanks for the wi-fi that had brought him the news. Before leaving he had refined the search, inputting some of the new data and set it searching for recent passport information, visa applications, anything that might point him in the direction of where she was now. He had set it running and driven away, the mission to find Professor Douglas almost an afterthought something to get out of the way so he could carry on with the real business of following the red threads of his lost love.

The weather had eased slightly, though powdery snow continued to fall from the low cloud that clung to the mountains rising ahead of him. There was maybe an hour of daylight left, possibly less. He knew he should have started this search earlier, but he didn't regret the time he had taken to check the MPD results. Everything was different now, the rock he had been pushing up hill for the last eight years had finally tipped over the summit and started to roll down the other side. He was ready for anything and his eyes in the rear-view mirror glowed and glittered back at him as though he'd just woken from a long, long sleep.

The road was deserted and the thin dusting of snow on the blacktop had few tyre marks in it. Shepherd kept his foot steady on the gas pedal, his eyes scanning the way ahead, trying to match what he was seeing with the faded memory of twenty years ago. Franklin had been right: the snow did make everything look different, but he still had a few solid things to go on.

First, there was only one main road that headed north out of Cherokee towards the Tennessee border – Tsali Boulevard, named after a Cherokee prophet. Second, he remembered the road had run alongside a river for several miles before meandering up into the hills, and he could see the white frozen ribbon of the Oconaluftee River out of his passenger window. Finally, he knew Douglas's cabin had been high up on the side of a ridge, with elevated views all around that had enabled them to see over all the other ridges and peaks, giving them the whole sky to look at. He had studied the topographical maps and located a section of the highway, close to the Tennessee border, that rose to nearly five thousand feet. It was right in the mountains, miles from the nearest town, and he also remembered how dark it had been at the cabin, well away from any sources of light pollution, making it perfect for stargazing. He felt sure, or as sure as he could be, that Douglas's cabin was somewhere here in this part of the mountains. All he had to do now was find it.

He'd been driving for about ten miles when the road began to rise more steeply. His eyes flicked to the sat nav display in the central stack of the dashboard. He'd found an option in the menu that displayed the car's height above sea level and he watched it creep steadily up, ten feet at a time, past three thousand feet and still rising. After another mile the river thinned out to little more than a mountain stream, fringed with ice, a steady babble of black water running through the middle on its way down to the main river. There was a break in the trees up ahead and he slowed as he approached it.

A forest track snaked up and away from the main road, the mud rutted and frozen and clogged with snow. A similar track had led up to Professor Douglas's cabin. It had been rough, like this one, but this was not it. A quick glance at the Sat-Nav confirmed that they were not high enough.

He carried on climbing, one eye on the altimeter as it continued its steady rise, checking each break in the trees and every track that wound its way up the side of the valley. He was edging close to the four thousand feet mark now and he noticed the temperature gauge on the dashboard was dropping. It was a few points below zero outside and the ground was starting to fall away sharply to his right. He eased his foot off the gas and tried to keep the car in the thin tracks of the few other vehicles that had come this way before him.

He rounded a corner and saw something tucked into a rest stop ahead – a car, the first one he'd seen since branching away from the main river and starting his climb. It was a big old station wagon and he slowed almost to a stop as he drew close to it, but there was no sign of the driver. There was a dusting of snow on it, including the hood, suggesting the engine was cold and it had been there a while. He noticed a baby seat in the back, probably just someone with car trouble who must have called a friend to come pick them up. He put his foot on the gas as gently as he could but the wheels still spun a little before they got a grip on the frozen surface.

The road continued to curve upwards and the car disappeared behind him, swallowed by the tree-line. After a couple of hundred metres the altimeter stopped climbing, hovering steady around the 4,600 feet mark as the road started to level off. He had to be close. He glanced up at the strip of sky visible between the trees. It was darkening fast as the day drew to a close. The temperature was now minus five and still falling. If he didn't find the track soon he might be forced to head back and try again at first light, provided the weather didn't worsen in the night and shut down the mountain roads all together.

The curve of the road became sharper as it hair-pinned back on itself, following the contours of the valley. Trees loomed overhead, laden with heavy snow and throwing deep shadows onto the road, making it hard to see very far ahead. Shepherd flicked the headlamps on full beam, which picked out the falling snow and the shallow shadow of another break in the treeline ahead. He drew closer, touching the brakes and feeling the slippery road through the steering wheel. His heart pounded and his hands gripped tight as he willed it to be the turning he was looking for. He drew level and slumped in his seat as he saw that it was barely a track at all. It ended just a few feet back from the road in a wall of tangled branches.

He checked the altimeter again – still steady at 4,600 – then turned his attention to the road again. With the curve it was impossible to see too far ahead. He couldn't see any more breaks in the trees, but he could see the road starting to fall away. The altimeter dropped by ten feet, confirming he was beginning to descend. Then something struck him.

He took his foot off the pedal and glanced in the rear-view mirror at the track he had just passed. The road here was too narrow and treacherous to try to turn the car round so he braked as carefully as he could to slow the car to a stop. He put on the handbrake and the hazard warning lights then opened the door and stepped out into the cold, leaving the engine running.

The road was more slippery than he had thought, and he skated across it, holding his arms out for balance, heading back to the break in the trees. The wall of branches seemed bigger up close with dense twigs and dry, dead leaves bulking it out, making it seem impenetrable. But whereas the ground and the trees surrounding it were weighed down with snow, the branches had hardly any on them at all and there were drag marks in the snow either side showing where they had been pulled across the track. There were footprints too, softened a little by the recent snowfall, but footprints none-theless – just one person by the looks of things, though he couldn't be sure. They clumped together in groups around the branches then split off and headed up the track, ending at a spot where deep tyre marks chewed up the snow and ice and drew two lines straight up towards the summit of the mountain. And there was something else. Something that carried on the breeze sifting down through the rapidly darkening woods triggering a memory of the last time he had been here. It was wood smoke, coming no doubt from the potbellied stove that warmed the cabin and brewed the coffee.

Shepherd smiled. 'Hello, Professor,' he murmured under his breath. 'Remember me?'

CHAPTER 70

Dawn rose fast in the desert, rapidly warming the land and the buildings of the compound. The soldiers were the first to appear, rising with the sun, their bodies conditioned to early starts by military life. They stretched and scratched as they emerged from the main building, their eyes screwed almost shut against the brightening sky then abruptly stopped as they saw the swathed figures hunkered down by the water and filling their canteens.

Williamson instinctively held his hand up to halt his men and a crackle of adrenalin passed through each of them as they saw what had prompted it. They were nomadic goat herders, their faces whitened by desert dust and still partly wrapped in keffiyeh. Williamson glanced over to the guard tower where their weapons were stashed and noticed the gate next to it, rolled all the way back, a team of goats drinking from one of the streams in the desert beyond it.

'Who the hell are these guys?' he muttered.

'They arrived about an hour ago.' Liv and Tariq appeared behind him, dragging a crate out of the transport hanger. 'They are welcome here,' Liv said, 'just as you are.'

406

'How do we know they can be trusted?'

'I don't, not fully, any more than I knew you could be trusted. What I do know is they are here because they felt the same pull as you, which means others will undoubtedly be coming here too. We can either choose to meet them with closed gates, suspicion and loaded guns, or welcome them, as we did you.'

Williamson continued to stare at the newcomers. 'The way I remember it, the gate was closed when we arrived. Seems pretty sensible to me.'

Liv shot Tariq a look. 'That was not my idea. But letting you in was.'

Williamson tipped his head. 'Much obliged.'

Others had started to drift out of the compound buildings, roused by the heat and raised voices. Liv had intended to talk to everyone individually, quietly sowing the seeds of her plan rather than risking a public debate that she might well end up losing. Now she had no choice.

'Tell me, what would you have done if we hadn't let you in? What if we had kept the gate shut, turned the big guns in the guard tower on you and told you to leave, would you have just turned around and gone away, after travelling so far to find this place?' Williamson said nothing. 'Or would you have camped out in the desert, sticking close to one of the rivers so you had plenty of water, maybe far enough to be out of range of the cannons but still close enough to watch us and assess our strengths and weaknesses? Perhaps you would have decided eventually that you could take us. You might even have managed it, stormed this fortress in the middle of the night and taken control. Then what? What would you have done with us – killed us, kept us prisoner, banished us to the desert? And what about all the other people who are on their way here now, answering the same call you did, the same one they did?' She pointed to the goat herders who had stopped drinking and were now listening too. 'Would you try and keep them out, keep the gate locked and defend this scrap of desert with your last bullet, or until a stronger force arrived and took it from you so the whole thing could start all over again? Would you do that – for a bunch of buildings and a pool of water?'

Williamson continued to stare at her, though she sensed the challenge in his eyes had slipped a little. She shook her head. 'This has been the pattern throughout human history: men possessing things, others seeking to take those things away by force. And what good has any of it done? Few things can truly be possessed.' She pointed to one of the holding pits where the water had broken the banks and flowed freely through the links of the perimeter fence. 'And some things cannot be contained. And whatever this place is, whatever it represents to the people drawn here, it is not something to be owned or fought over. It is simply something to be shared. A place where people can come together and not be divided or driven apart. A place of safety. A kind of home.'

She moved over to the crate and levered the lid off with her foot to reveal its contents. Williamson and his men gathered round. The nomads by the waterline moved closer too. It was full of tools: crow-bars, wire-cutters, shovels still coated in dust from the graves they had recently dug. 'We should take down the fences,' Liv said. 'They have no place here.'

Silence surged back in on the heels of her words but nobody moved. Liv surveyed the line of faces. They were looking at the tools, the fence, each other – but not at her. She was done talking and didn't know what else she could say.

'Dust cloud!'

The shout snagged everyone's attention. All heads turned to the horizon. A new column of dust was rising up in the east, backlit by the sun now clawing its way up into the white sky. The timing could not have been worse. Liv felt sure that no one would want to start dismantling the perimeter fence with more strangers on the way. They would wait and see who it was first, and then the moment would be lost and she would have to try and persuade them all over again.

A movement to her right caught her eye. Williamson had stepped forward and reached down to pick up the lid of the crate. He fitted it back on top, sealing the tools inside in a wordless, symbolic full stop on the whole argument. Then he did a curious thing, he turned towards the nomads and waved them over. They hesitated at first then slowly responded, walking over to join the main group.

Corporal Williamson smiled a greeting then turned to his fellow soldiers. 'Why don't y'all go find what other tools they got in the transport bay, maybe see if they got a winch back there, or some kind of a towline we can hook up to the truck.' He turned to the nomads, smiled again and ambled to one end of the crate. 'Williamson.' He patted his chest with the flat of his hand then pointed back at the man. 'What's your name? Asmuk?'

'Yasin,' the man replied.

Williamson squatted down and grabbed the side handle of the crate. 'Wanna help me with this, Yasin?'

Tariq translated the request and the goat herder's face exploded into a smile. He squatted down, grabbed the other handle and heaved the crate up so enthusiastically Williamson was nearly knocked over. 'Whoah there, tiger,' he said, lifting his end and steadying himself until they were carrying the burden equally. 'Why don't we start at the gate,' he said, leading the way. 'See if we can't get that sucker down before the new guys arrive.'

CHAPTER 71

The unaccustomed sound of plastic on plastic buzzed through the Abbot's private chambers as the phone shivered and shimmied across the keyboard of the open laptop, drawing all eyes to it. Thomas walked across from the huge fireplace, picked it up and opened the message.

'Well?' Athanasius appeared too, crowding over the phone to try and see what message it had brought. Gabriel lay on the bed, still strapped down. Thomas angled the phone so they could both see the screen as a photograph of the dark stone appeared on it. Another downloaded, this time showing the reverse side.

'The Starmap,' Athanasius whispered, a smile curling the edges of his mouth. The smile faltered. 'It's too small,' he said, moving his head back and forth to try and focus on it.

'Give me a second,' Thomas said, 'I thought this might be a problem.'

He opened an application on the laptop then selected a different stripped wire from the doctored USB cable and touched it to a contact point at the base of the phone. After a few seconds the mouse arrow on the laptop screen turned into a spinning wheel and a command box opened asking if he wanted to IMPORT ALL IMAGES?

'Could you hit Enter please,' Thomas said, looking up at Athanasius. 'My hands are somewhat occupied.'

Athanasius did as he was asked and a progress bar tracked the slow transfer of data from the phone to the laptop. No one breathed or moved, least of all Thomas who was literally holding it all together. The progress bar vanished and two new icons appeared on the desktop. Thomas let go of the phone, clicked them open and two images of the Starmap appeared on the screen. He enlarged them and arranged them so both were visible next to each other.

'That's Malan,' Athanasius said, pointing at the image with the block of text forming the inverted shape of the Tau. He translated as he read:

The Key unlocks the Sacrament
The Sacrament becomes the Key
And all the Earth shalt tremble
The Key must follow the Starmap Home
There to quench the fire of the dragon within
the full phase of a moon
Lest the Earth shalt splinter and a blight shalt
prosper marking the end of all days

'That's the second prophecy, the one that led us out into the desert — where the prophecy was fulfilled. Only the last line doesn't make sense in the light of what actually happened.'

412

'What did happen?' Athanasius asked, leaning forward and studying the screen.

A jumble of images flashed through Gabriel's mind. Liv falling to the ground, the flame pouring from the drill tower and turning to steam as the oil turned to water. 'We did return the Sacrament within the full phase of the moon. And the fire was quenched. So I can't understand why the blight still prospers. We need to know what else it says on the stone.'

Athanasius studied the second image, tracing the constellations of Draco, Taurus, and the Plough.

'There's more than one language here,' he said, 'and they're not Malan. This little block of text next to Taurus is some kind of proto-cuneiform. Perhaps it relates directly to this extra star drawn in the constellation of Taurus, just there, between the bull's horns. It says something like "The Sacrament reaches home, a new star is created and a new king or ruler reigns or rules over the end of days".'

He scanned the rest of the symbols and ran his hand over his head. 'There are pictograms or possibly ideograms here that could be from different sources. They represent concepts and ideas rather than individual words and must be interpreted rather than read. But to understand them properly one would need to know the context and time in which they were written. There is a bird here for example that could be an eagle. In Egyptian hieroglyphs the eagle represents the letter "A", but in Aztec it means the sun. So you see how easy it would be to misinterpret this message.'

'We can safely assume the tablet originated in ancient Mesopotamia,' Gabriel suggested. 'That's where we found Eden and that's where all the other references to the Sacrament point.'

'Indeed, but without knowing exactly what era and in what region it was written I would only be guessing at its meaning. However there is one person in the Citadel who has spent his life studying pictograms like these. I feel sure he would not only be able to tell us exactly where and when this was made just by looking at it, he would also be able to translate it.' He glanced at Father Thomas and they exchanged a troubled look. 'Unfortunately he is not a man who is likely to want to help us. He's the chief Librarian – Father Malachi.'

CHAPTER 72

Dragging the branches away from the track proved much harder than Shepherd had anticipated. The drop in temperature had frozen them to the ground and he had to tug hard to get them free before he could haul them away. On top of this his shoes were made for city streets, not trudging through thick snow and they gave him little grip or insulation as he slipped and stumbled through the snow, until he was sweating despite the cold.

It took him nearly twenty minutes to create a gap in the tangle of branches wide enough for the Durango to pass through, stopping only once when he heard a knocking sound coming from somewhere above, like someone hammering nails into wood. After a pause it came again, three distant bangs that echoed in the woods before the silence flooded back. By the time he had finished, night had bled into the forest and it had mercifully stopped snowing. The moon had risen too, shining bright behind thinning clouds and casting a silver light over the forest. Shepherd could no longer feel his feet or the ends of his fingers and could almost hear the tinkle of ice forming in the air he breathed out then falling to the ground.

He made it back to the car and whacked the heater on full, stamping his feet and holding his hands in front of the vent, not caring about the pain as his veins opened up and the blood flowed through his flesh again. The read-out on the dash said the temperature was now minus eight and he could well believe it. He had intended to defrost himself a little then hike up to the cabin but the job of clearing the branches had proved how ill-equipped he was to spend much time out in the cold. He also remembered that Douglas's cabin had been a fair trek up the track, much too far to attempt in his city shoes. He could leave it until tomorrow, maybe get some better boots from somewhere in Cherokee, but who knew what the weather was going to do in the night and whether he'd even be able to get here again. It would also mean going out and dragging the branches back into position so no one would know he had been there. There was a third option but the ghost of Franklin rose up in his head to repeat the last words he'd said to him:

Just check it out – he'd said – *don't make a move on your own.*

But he was here now and had seen the footprints in the snow. What was the harm in a student looking up his old professor?

He waited until he had some feeling back in his feet then slipped the car back in gear and slowly reversed back up the road. The tyres crunched through a crust of ice as he eased the car off the road and onto the track. Dry branches reached out and raked the side of the vehicle like witches' fingers as he squeezed through the gap that wasn't quite as wide as he'd hoped.

Whoever was up in the cabin would be able to hear his engine rumbling its way up the track but there was little he could do about it. To compromise, he cut the lights, plunging himself into a bluish darkness that was still bright enough to drive by and would preserve his night vision, just in case he needed it when he got there.

The tyres found better grip on the broken and frozen ground than they had on the flat, icy road and he bounced and lurched his way up the track and between the trees. After a while he could see a light, high above him, warm and orange like a lantern winking through gaps in the thick woods. As he got higher the trees started to thin out a little until he could see the outline of the log cabin, lights on inside and smoke leaking from the chimney and drifting away in the cold, clear night. He let the car crunch to a stop just short of the end of the track where there was still a little tree cover, then killed the engine. He slipped out of the driver's seat and closed the door quietly, keeping the car between him and the cabin while he listened to the night and studied the cabin.

It had changed a lot since he'd last been here. There was a woodshed that hadn't been there before and the basic hunter's hide on the rocky ledge above the cabin had been extensively modified so it now looked like a second home. A wide pathway had been cut through the trees leading up to it and there was now a proper roof on top with solar panels fixed either side of a large open hatch, suggesting it was still being used as an observatory. The rope they'd used to scramble up the side of the rock had now been replaced by a solid set of wooden stairs.

He scanned the periphery of trees, trying to work out the best way to approach the cabin. He reached into his jacket. This was the third time he'd held a gun in his hand in less than twenty-four hours. He stepped round the back of the car, his pulse pounding in his ears and sweat prickling beneath his shirt despite the cold. He made his way carefully through the trees, working his way round to the side of the cabin, trying not to make any sound as he headed for the woodshed. It would provide cover between him and the cabin when he stepped out of the trees. There was no reason to believe Douglas would be hostile, but he had blown up several hundred million dollars' worth of government facility earlier that day, so there was always a chance.

He kept his eyes on the cabin and the observatory, looking and listening for any movement inside. The storm shutters were open on the cabin and the curtains pulled back so he caught glimpses inside, the warm orange glow making him feel even colder. His feet were numb inside the wet thin leather of his shoes. As he picked his way through the tree trunks and low branches, the crunch of snow far too loud in the still of the night, a parked car came into view behind the woodshed, a newer model of the same sort of jeep Douglas had driven all those years ago. Footprints in the snow spread out from it, heading to the woodshed and the cabin. More footsteps went back into the forest. They looked pretty fresh. Whoever was inside had been out here fairly recently, maybe just to get fuel for the fire, or maybe for another reason. He glanced back into the dark of the woods, wondering he should maybe check things out in that direction first, make sure it was clear and cover his back, seeing as there was no one else out here to cover it for him.

Carrie watched him through the night-sight, her eye pressed against the rubber cup to stop the green phosphorescent light leaking out and giving away her position. Even on the lowest magnification he filled her vision, his outline solid and dark against the bright glow coming from the buildings behind him. She could see his face, right in the centre of the cross-hairs, his eyes scanning the dark, looking straight at her from time to time but always moving on. If he chose to follow the tracks into the woods he would find them easily enough.

Her finger tightened a little on the trigger, ready to squeeze if he took so much as one step forward. A knife would be quieter but he was a trained federal agent and it wasn't worth the risk letting him get close enough to use his weapon.

The cross-hairs remained steady on the centre of his head.

Just one step.

Shepherd scanned the woods, listening out through the muffled silence to the crack of ice and the sound of his own breathing. He felt sure he was being watched, but then he always did when he stared into woods at night. There was bound to be all sorts of wildlife checking him out, ready to bolt or take flight the moment he got too close. He shivered at the thought of all the potential eyes upon him. He needed to get out of the cold and into the warm before he got frostbite and his toes started falling off.

Franklin would tell him to head back to the car right now and warm up on his way back to Cherokee – come back again in the morning with some backup. But Franklin wasn't here. Shepherd turned back towards the cabin. It looked warm in there. He took a deep breath to steady his shivers, then stepped out of the trees towards it.

The sound changed the moment he moved forward, opening out as the baffling effect of the trees was left behind, making him feel very exposed. He made it to the jeep and felt the side panel by the engine with his free hand. Stone cold. He moved round, stopping a foot short of the wood-shed wall, his gun held in front of him, always pointing where he was looking. He had to make a choice now, head to the cabin and risk being spotted from the observatory, or check out the observatory first. He studied the tracks in the snow, but there were too many to give him any clues. He made a choice and headed for the porch of the cabin, figuring that walking up the wooden steps to the observatory before he'd checked the cabin would be too dangerous.

The deck creaked as he stepped onto it and made his way over to a window. He wondered, standing here now, if he should knock and give whoever was inside the chance to reveal themselves before he burst in with a gun in his hand. But silence and surprise were just about the only things he had on his side and he wasn't about to give them up lightly.

He eased his head round the edge of the window frame and took in the room. The stove was lit and loaded with logs, the fire throwing enough shifting orange light into the room to show him that no one was there. He moved over to the door and tried the handle, it creaked, not much but loud enough in the tense silence, then opened.

The trapped warmth of the room was like stepping into a bath. Blood rushed to his face and feeling began to return painfully to his fingers and feet. He moved quickly across the room, keeping low and away from the windows. The bedroom was behind a partition at one end of the cabin, a thin wooden wall defining a space just big enough for a bed.

There was no one here.

He moved over to the back door and looked up

at the observatory, the glow from the open roof hatch making it stand out against the night. He should have known Douglas would be stargazing on a clear night like this. He twisted the handle and slowly opened the door then stepped out into the frozen night again.

He moved across the snow between the cabin and the wooden steps leading up to the observatory, feeling both excited and nervous about the imminent reunion with his former mentor. He suddenly felt vaguely ridiculous and ashamed that he had his gun in his hand. Professor Douglas wouldn't know that his old student was an FBI agent now. His best approach would surely be as a friend and colleague. He reached the foot of the steps and slid the gun back into its holster.

'Professor Douglas?' he called up, his voice a little high and much too loud in the muted silence. 'It's Joseph Shepherd. Remember me? You brought me here once when I was a grad student.' His words echoed back from the surrounding trees then faded away. He listened for a response, a movement.

Nothing.

'I'm going to come up now, OK?' He took a step, making it a heavy one so it could be heard. 'I just want to talk.' He continued upwards, stamping the snow from his shoes as he went, his eyes fixed on the closed door at the top of the stairway. He could hear something now, low music from inside the shack and Shepherd smiled as he recognized it. It was from the Planet Suite by

Holst. The professor had played it that long ago summer, switching tracks depending on which planet they were observing. The track playing now was the final piece: 'Neptune, the mystic' – slow and mysterious, the tinkling harp and shivering violins a perfect soundtrack to the frigid night.

He reached the top of the stairs and stepped onto solid stone that was slick with ice. A breeze was blowing the snow from it and singing in the steel cables that anchored the corners of the cabin to the rock. It was on odd place to build a cabin, high and exposed like this, but the rock provided the perfect, solid platform for stargazing. Even ground vibration was hugely magnified by a telescope so with the windbreak of the cabin and the high elevation and solid base of the rock, Douglas had created the perfect backyard observatory.

Shepherd moved carefully across the stone, the music getting louder with each step and building towards the climax, the eerie voices mixing with the instruments like a spectral choir. It was loud enough to explain why the Professor might not have heard him approach.

'Professor.' He rapped a knuckle on the door. 'It's Joseph Shepherd, remember me?'

The ethereal voices were his only response, chilling him along with the cold then melting away as the track ended, leaving him alone with the whisper of the wind and his pounding heart. He leaned in close to the door, listening through it, willing it to open or a familiar voice to invite him in from the other side. He jumped as the music started again, loud and urgent, the ominous stabbing strings of 'Mars' the Bringer of War suggesting that whatever the music was playing on was set to repeat.

Shepherd reached out, twisted the handle and opened the door.

A large telescope dominated the space inside. It was sat on a heavy-duty tripod with electric motors hooked to a laptop on a table beside it, the screen displaying the piece of sky it was currently pointing at. A cell phone was plugged into it as well as some small speakers from which the Planet Suite was booming out. He took a step inside and the door started swinging shut behind him. Then he saw the figure from the corner of his eye.

He spun round. Douglas was in the shadows, his arms stretching out, his head hanging forward. Shepherd gasped and stumbled backwards, reaching for his gun as his eyes adjusted and the shadows took form. Professor Douglas didn't move. He couldn't. His hands were pinned to the wooden walls, blood running thick from spikes in his hands and a deep gash in his neck, mouth bound, eyes open and staring at the floor. Shepherd hit the back wall with a sound that recalled the one he had heard from the road – like someone hammering nails into wood. Then he saw the writing scrawled in blood on the wall.

HERETIC

CHAPTER 73

Shepherd fumbled for his phone, gun pointing at Douglas, 'Mars' the Bringer of War still booming from the speakers. Eyes wide, his adrenaline-sharpened senses sucked everything in: the curtains of blood from the hands and throat – *so much blood* – the slash and spatter of the writing on the wall, the slump of Douglas's body, the way the weight of it pulled grotesquely at the flesh where the spikes had been driven in . . . steam rising up from the dark pool on the stone floor.

His numbed fingers closed around the phone in his pocket and he raised it to his face, not wanting to risk dropping his sight or the gun. His eyes flicked to the screen, found Franklin's cell phone number and dialled. He held the phone to his ear, his breathing rapid, eyes scoping the rest of the cabin from over the top of his gun.

Nothing was disturbed, there had been no struggle. The kill must have been fast and deliberate, efficient even.

He stared at the body, almost disbelieving the violence it spoke of.

The phone connected.

'It's Shepherd.'

'You find him?'

'He's dead. Throat cut. Nailed to the wall.'

'Jesus. What's your situation?'

'Scared shitless.'

'Good. You in cover?'

'Yes. I think it only just happened.'

'Why?'

'The blood. There's steam coming off it. I saw tracks in the snow. Thought they were his. Tracks leading into the forest. There was a car too. Parked on the road.'

'Did you get the plate?'

'No. I didn't think it was anything. Just someone broken down.'

'What about make and model?'

'It was a station wagon, nothing fancy, an old Volvo, I think. It had a baby seat in the back.'

'Colour?'

'Yellow, white. Hard to tell in the light.'

'OK, that's good. Don't do anything. Stay in cover, do not try and be a hero. Hunker down, sit tight and I'll send the local cops to you. Keep your phone on so they can follow the locator, OK?'

It clicked in his ear and Franklin was gone before Shepherd could reply.

He felt alone and scared, the loud and ominous strains of Mars not helping at all. He was shivering from cold and adrenalin, the open hatch in the roof letting the cold of the night pour in on top of him.

He stared at the body, forcing himself to breathe more steadily and see it through the eyes of a professional assessing a crime scene.

There was something very deliberate about it all. The spikes in the hands were large, not the sort of thing you would find lying around, the killer must have brought them with him.

Shepherd tried to picture him coming here through the snow, nails and a hammer jingling in a bag, knowing he was going to do this.

He was already building a profile. Had to be a man because of the strength required. Douglas wasn't a big guy but he was big enough. And it looked like his throat had been cut last, while he was already pinned to the wall, the arterial spray and blood flow all centred on his current position. How much strength would you need to do that – nail a struggling guy to a wall? Too much for one person. Two people then, maybe more.

Shepherd squatted low and moved closer, heading for the middle of the floor where the telescope stood. Anyone out there watching would have seen his head pass by the window as he recoiled from his initial sight of Douglas. The thin wooden walls of the shack wouldn't stop a bullet if one came so he kept low and out of sight.

The music was frightening and oppressive now and he glanced at the laptop. He wanted to turn it off so he could listen for exterior sounds but knew if it suddenly cut out then anyone out there would know exactly where he was. He should wait for the track to end at least, then it wouldn't be so obvious.

He searched the laptop screen, looking for the application controlling the music. Most of it was filled with the video feed from the telescope. It was pointing towards the eastern sky, the computer-controlled motors adjusting it imperceptibly, keeping it fixed on a single bright star. Shepherd looked up and followed the line of the telescope. The constellation of Taurus was perfectly framed in the open hatch showing that the bright star was Aldebaran, right eye of the charging bull.

Thoughts tumbled through Shepherd's head. The telescope was pointing at exactly the same part of the sky Hubble had been probing before it was turned round and put out of action. He stared at the rectangle of night, half expecting to see something new there, growing larger and brighter as it hurtled towards Earth. All he saw was a wisp of cloud and the usual stars twinkling in the black.

He looked back at the screen, Aldebaran burning bright in the centre of the video feed. Below it was a small iTunes controller, the scrub bar showing that the track currently playing had almost finished. Shepherd used the knuckle of his little finger on the trackpad to drag the arrow over to the *Play* button so as not to leave fingerprints. The final stab of horns and strings bounced off the thin walls then faded away. He clicked the pause button and let out a long breath that sounded loud in the sudden silence.

He quit the application to make sure the music wouldn't come back on and studied the screen. There was an email inbox with some recent messages, the video feed from the telescope, and another window filled with a sequence of changing numbers he assumed must be something to do with the telescope, though it didn't look like any control program he'd seen before. Normally they displayed a sequence of co-ordinates, which changed by tiny degrees as the program tracked a designated object. This looked more like a measurement, though one that was getting smaller all the time. The phone buzzed in his hand, and he stabbed the button to silence it.

'Yes?'

'The local sheriff is on his way to you now, name of Brodie. He's bringing everyone with a gun he can lay his hands on. They're also going to keep their eyes open for that vehicle. You got anything else?'

'They're looking for more than one person.'

'OK good, you know this how?'

'By the way he was killed. They nailed him to the wall and wrote "Heretic" next to him in his own blood, so I'm guessing the religious angle just got a little more weight to it.'

'Jesus. Listen, Shepherd, I'm sorry about this.

You shouldn't be there on your own. It was . . . I should have –'

'It's OK, really. There's something else. You remember the countdown Merriweather told us about at Goddard. The one he saw on Dr Kinderman's computer just before the virus took Hubble out? It's here too. It's hooked up to a telescope pointing to the same piece of sky Hubble was exploring. Only the huge number he talked about isn't so huge any more. Whatever it is, whatever's coming – I don't think we don't have long left.'

CHAPTER 74

The heater was on full, filling the station wagon with dry air and noise. Carrie was at the wheel, Eli sitting next to her. He was quiet and she didn't like the character of it. Part of her gift was that she could read the stillness in people the same way others could detect a strain in someone's voice when they were lying. She was used to silence, had known a lot of it when she was growing up, so she could see things in it others could not.

The mission had gone as smoothly as she could have hoped. They had found the target exactly where Archangel said they would. He'd been alone, passive, almost resigned, like he'd been expecting them. He barely showed surprise when they walked through the door of the cabin and caught him staring up to heaven, looking in vain for God. He was surprised when Eli punched him in the solar plexus to squeeze the air from his lungs though. He was more surprised when she slapped the Duct tape on his mouth and Eli drove the first rail spike through his hand.

Make an example – Archangel had said – *Send a clear message.*

Well, they'd certainly done that, though now in the shadow of Eli's silence, she wished it could have been her who had carried out the kill. She was better at handling the consequences of death than Eli was, though he was much better at dealing it out. He was an artist when it came to that, she had seen it with the dog, with the woman and her sleeping little girl, and now back there in the cabin. It was as if all the self-doubt and awkwardness simply fell off him when he was doing what he did best, what he was born to do – God's work. She didn't think she could love him any more than she already did, but watching him like that, so confident and strong, had been awe-inspiring, like watching God's terrible beauty in motion. An avenging angel. An artist.

The car slipped a little on the road and she corrected the steering, easing her foot off the gas. She had been speeding up a little without realizing it, the engine racing in time with her humming heart.

A sign by the side of the road said SPEED LIMIT 25 as they approached a curve. She checked and they were barely doing fifteen. She could feel the tyres sliding over the freezing road, the back threatening to drift sideways if she was too heavy on the steering or the brakes. They couldn't afford any accidents now, not after everything had gone so perfectly; they just needed a clean ex-filtration with no drama.

There could be no dogs this time. No sleeping little surprises in the back of a car. No mistakes.

CHAPTER 75

Shepherd heard the engines first, growling low and distant through the forest as thick snow tyres gnawed at the ground.

He was crouched over Douglas's computer, using a pen to type his private email address into an email message. As soon as the cops arrived everything in the cabin would become part of a crime scene, something to be tagged and bagged and ultimately shipped back to Quantico for Agent Smith to crack open and explore. Anything useful would be fed back to him through the ghost file – assuming he was still part of the investigation – but he wanted to keep his eye on the countdown and had found the application file that was running it. He had also found something else potentially even more interesting, an email message, sent less than an hour previously from a Hotmail account assigned to Mala210. There was nothing obvious to indicate who Mala210 might be except that Shepherd remembered 210 had been Kinderman's network address at NASA. The message also got Shepherd's antennae twitching:

The Mala star is almost in position. See
you very soon.

Outside, the engine noise grew louder and the
first hint of headlights flickered briefly on the wall
above his head.

He finished typing, attached the countdown
application to the Hotmail message then pressed
Send. He watched the activity wheel spin as the
computer began slowly transmitting bits of data
through the attached phone. The application was
a decent-sized file so it wasn't going to be fast.
He was sending it to an address linked to his
phone so he would be able to check it had gone
through.

He moved over to the window and peered round
the edge of the frame. He could see the bounce
and wash of headlamps angling up through the
woods as vehicles made their way up the track,
throwing shifting, tortured shadows through the
frozen trees. He figured he had maybe a minute
before they arrived.

On the screen the wheel was still spinning, the
progress bar creeping towards 100%. He watched
the last piece of the message leave the laptop and
his phone shivered in his hand as it arrived. He
got to work, quickly erasing the message from
the *Sent* log on the computer. It would still be
in the hidden memory cache but it would be a
while before Smith found it and he'd cross that
bridge when he came to it.

He stashed his phone in his pocket and dug out his ID. The last thing he wanted now was for some hyped-up local cop with a heavy trigger finger taking a shot at him. He took one last look at the charnel house of the hut then opened the door and stepped out into the night with his hands raised, just as the headlights bounced to a halt behind his own parked car.

Two figures in heavy parkas emerged from the car, guns drawn and pointing right at him. 'FBI,' he called out, holding his badge high above his head. My partner called this in – Agent Franklin. I'm Agent Shepherd. I got a body back here and tracks leading into the woods. Did you intercept the car?'

'We didn't see no car,' a voice called back.

'Which way did you come?'

'From Cherokee.'

'What's in the other direction?'

'Tennessee,' the same voice replied. 'Gatlinburg's first big place you come to.'

'Do they know what's happened here?'

'Not that I know of, it's across the state line.'

Different state, not their responsibility – goddamn local cops, no wonder Franklin had no time for them. 'Call it in,' Shepherd shouted, moving down the wooden stairs. 'Give them the description and tell them to arrest anyone driving a white or yellow station wagon. And tell them to approach with caution. There are at least two suspects and they're fleeing a murder scene.'

435

One of the cops ducked back inside the car and got on the radio. The other started walking towards him, gun still out and still pointing in his general direction.

'Walk through the fresh snow,' Shepherd pointed at a pristine patch between him and the cop, 'that way we'll know we're not trampling over any evidence.' The cop complied, veering off from his intended route and trudging through the snow towards him. 'And put your damn gun away.'

Shepherd looked away and through the trees to where he imagined the road continued. It was too dark to see much but as he scanned the wall of trees he caught a flash of light, distant and soft, moving along the road towards the border.

CHAPTER 76

Carrie eased her speed down even more as the tyres continued to slip. They were now crawling along at barely more than ten miles an hour, good for keeping on the road, not so great for getting away. The station wagon was old and heavy and only had two-wheel drive. This was taking too long. The man she had tracked through the trees with her night scope must have found the body by now and called the cops or be driving back to town to tell them what he'd found.

It would be all over the news by morning, a warning to all of the consequences of sin and blasphemy. The cops would probably play down the nature of the death, keep the bloody details out of the public eye but it wouldn't do any good, she had taken some pictures of her own that could be leaked onto the internet to make sure it was seen by everyone. Archangel would be pleased with them – which meant they were one step closer to being together, one step closer to driving a car like this of their own, maybe with their own baby seat in the back. She felt both happy and sad at the thought of it. They would be married for sure, but the judgement was coming too soon for them to be able to have a child of their own.

Unless.

Maybe the work they were doing now, these blood sacrifices they were making would be enough to stop it from happening. Maybe God would stay his hand and spare the judgement because he would see there were still those like her and Eli prepared to serve him and honour His name.

'Hey baby, you want to make the call? Archangel's gonna be real happy with us.'

Eli remained silent.

'It's OK, honey,' she said, reading his mood. 'I know how you said th'other night, how you wished you didn't like killing so much, but it's the Lord's work you're doing here, don't you forget that – and there ain't never no sin in that.'

Eli took a breath and blew it out, fogging the inside of the windshield. 'Dog ain't got no immortal soul,' he said in the small guarded voice she didn't like, 'but a man do. And so does a little girl and her mom.'

She reached out and placed her hand on his cheek, risking the slippery road and feeling the jaw muscle working beneath his skin. 'But if they were all good and righteous people, then their souls will be up in heaven right now. And if not, well then you done rid the earth of some sinners and you shouldn't be ashamed of either thing. Why, I reckon you should be proud.'

He turned to her and she risked looking away

from the road for just a second. 'You always know the right words to say,' he said, digging a phone from his pocket, 'you always shine a light through my darkness in a way that no one else ever can.'

The screen lit up his face as he dialled the number and switched the phone to loudspeaker. Carrie leaned forward and turned the heater down so she could hear better, her eyes never leaving the road. Ahead of them she could see the glow of headlights sweeping across the night, picking out the trees and getting brighter as a car came towards them. It burst round the curve, full beams blazing, going far too fast for the road conditions.

'Yes?' Cooper's voice rose out of the phone.

'The Professor is dead,' Eli said.

'Where are you now?'

'Driving,' Eli looked up into the glare of the oncoming lights.

'Anyone see you?'

'I don't think so.'

The headlights were almost upon them now, so bright it looked like the car was in their lane. Carrie eased further over, slowing almost to a stop as a red pick-up flew past them, the snow chains on the tyres throwing grit and ice over the side of their car. Carrie blinked away her blindness and saw a sign right in front of them saying WELCOME TO TENNESSEE with two arrows beneath it pointing back to Cherokee and on to Gatlinburg.

'There was someone else there but they didn't see us,' Carrie said, picking up speed again now she could see the way ahead. 'I left him to find the body. Maybe he saw our car.'

'Will that be a problem?'

There was a left turn ahead and another sign for Clingman's Dome Road.

'No,' she said, turning onto the road, carefully following the tyre tracks they'd made earlier, fighting the car up the gentle incline and round a shallow bend.

'Did you take pictures?'

'Yeah, we got pictures.' Ahead of them, the headlights picked up the back of the black Ford Escape they'd driven all the way from Charleston.

'Good,' Cooper said. 'Call me again when you're clear. I have news. God has smiled on our mission once more.' Carrie eased the station wagon to a halt then cut the engine. 'Check your emails. I have sent you instructions of where you should go next. I just found out where Dr Kinderman is.'

CHAPTER 77

Neither Athanasius nor Father Thomas had seen Father Malachi since he had opposed their plans to help the infected of Ruin. Since then Malachi had removed himself and the rest of his guild entirely behind locked doors. There were now two distinct societies within the mountain, those fighting the blight and caring for those who had it, and the black cloaks in the library.

They knew they were still there only because the supplies that were delivered weekly to the airlock were always collected, and because whenever one of the black cloaks became infected they were left outside the door, tied to a board to stop them from tearing themselves to pieces, their howls serving as an alarm to bring someone running. Athanasius found this inhuman and un-Christian and it made him furious whenever he thought of it. But now was not the time to pick that particular fight. They were here because they needed Malachi's help.

He had agreed to talk with them at Vespers and the bell rang now, echoing six times through the tunnels of the mountain, showing that the appointed hour had arrived.

441

'Do you think he'll come?' Thomas whispered, studying the still darkness of the library through the window of the airlock.

'He'll come,' Athanasius replied. 'I dropped hints in my note that we had acquired a document that may have some bearing on our current plight. There's no way he could resist taking a look at something like that. However I'm sure he will first make us wait.'

Athanasius was right. They stood there for nearly ten minutes before a light finally appeared in the distant dark, flickering as it moved towards them.

'There's something wrong with the lights,' Thomas whispered.

Athanasius peered at the still distant figure and realized he was right. Instead of the usual follow light, Malachi's journey towards them was illuminated solely by a candle lamp. He held a hand in front to shield it and walked slowly to stop the flame from snuffing out. Thomas and Athanasius watched his steady progress, realizing as he drew nearer that the month of isolation inside the library had not been kind to Malachi. His pale skin, pallid and translucent from a near lifetime spent out of the sun, was flaking around his nose and mouth and his eyes were circled with red as though he had hardly slept.

'Thank you for agreeing to speak with us,' Athanasius said the moment Malachi stopped the other side of the locked door, huffing and perspiring from his long walk. 'Is there some problem with the lighting?'

'No,' Malachi replied. 'I have simply turned it off. Those of us who still cling to the sanctity of the old ways have agreed to shun the corrupting influence of modernity, in all its forms.'

Athanasius nodded as if this was a perfectly reasonable response. 'And how are things with you and the others of your guild?' he asked, before Thomas could lose his temper.

'We are dying, thank you – slowly but steadily.'

Yes – Athanasius thought – we hear them screaming each time you abandon them, and then burn them for you once they are dead.

'What about you,' Malachi countered, 'did your little coup achieve anything? Has the bringing of civilians into the Citadel and trampling on thousands of years of venerated tradition been rewarded with the discovery of a miracle cure?'

'Not yet – but we are making progress.'

Malachi's eyes brightened. 'Really? What sort of progress?'

'One of the infected has been successfully nursed back from the brink of death, a civilian. He seems to have developed a form of natural immunity to the disease. The doctors are now working to try and extract a vaccine from his blood.'

'Really – a vaccine? And is he fully recovered, this – civilian?' He said this last word as he might utter the word 'snake'.

'Not fully recovered, he is improving but still weak. He has been removed to the Abbot's private quarters to rest and allow the doctors to conduct further tests.

It is a vital period in their search for a vaccine, they must try to understand the reason for his recovery. At the same time, in our own way, we too are desperately trying to understand the blight better. I mentioned in my note that a certain document has come into our possession, a prophecy that was originally carved on a stone long ago.'

'Yes, do you have it with you?'

'Not exactly. We have a facsimile of it. A detailed photograph showing both sides of the stone.'

Malachi's eyes grew larger behind the pebbles of his glasses. 'Show it to me.'

'I was hoping you might allow us into the library, so we can study it together and utilize the huge wealth of resources and reference material to try and decipher its meaning.'

The magnified eyes clouded with suspicion and flitted between the two of them as if he suspected some kind of trap. 'Why don't you give the document to me and I will see what I can make of it? You know I am familiar with all the ancient languages collected here. I have studied them and decoded many. If this stone is written in any of these then I will be able to recognize and translate it without need for further study or research. I might be able to tell you what it says right now – if you show it to me.'

Father Thomas and Athanasius exchanged a glance. They had expected this and, though neither of them liked it, they had little choice but to agree. Time was too pressing.

'If we show it to you, you must share what you see in it.'

'Of course.'

'Whatever it contains affects us all.'

'Indeed.' Malachi was fidgety, the candle shaking in his hand with anticipation.

Thomas opened his jacket where the laptop was secreted. He opened it and held the screen towards Malachi. Cold blue light lit up the librarian's face, turning it into a grotesque, glowing mask that appeared to float beyond the window in the door, the eyes pecking information from the screen like hungry birds. 'It's Malan,' he said, studying the first image.

'That's what we thought,' Athanasius replied, sensing Malachi's deliberate evasion but choosing not to challenge him on it. 'What about the second image?'

Malachi's eyes flitted across the screen but he said nothing. Thomas closed the laptop abruptly, prompting Malachi to look up as though he had been slapped.

'You promised to share your thoughts. If you do not honour your side of the bargain then we will not honour ours.'

'Of course, my apologies, I was just trying to – to get a sense of it. It's written in two different languages – three if you consider the constellations might also be telling part of the story.' Athanasius nodded, he had not considered this, but it made sense. The proto-cuneiform section he had been able to partly

445

understand was linked by a line as well as by meaning to the extra star marked in the constellation of Taurus. 'Can you decipher any of it?'

'I'm sure I can – but I will need to see it again and study it a little longer.'

Athanasius paused. Malachi was a slippery, self-interested character at the best of times. 'Very well,' he said, 'but the moment I think you are holding something back from us, we shut it again and walk away. Understood?'

Malachi nodded and attempted a smile that looked monstrous in the wavering light of his candle. Thomas opened the laptop again and turned it to face the window in the door. Malachi's eyes crawled over it hungrily. 'It's very old, reminiscent of proto-elemaic but not the same. There is a symbol here for the Citadel, also one for death and another that refers to disease or a plague . . .'

Athanasius glanced at Father Thomas. They had been right. The stone did predict what was happening here. 'What else?'

Malachi shook his head. 'It is hard to render it into a formal sentence. It is impressionistic rather than narrative.' His eyes continued to scan the symbols. 'Maybe if you leave it with me I can cross reference it with some of the other elemite documents in the library from the same period and arrive at a clearer meaning.'

'No. If we need to use other resource material to decode it then you must let us into the library so we can work on it together.' Malachi didn't respond, his

446

hungry eyes wide and unblinking as they slipped down the text. He reached the bottom and visibly flinched as if he had been struck.

'What is it?'

'The man who came back from the dead, did he ride here on a horse? Did he ride out of the wilderness?'

Athanasius recalled conversations he'd had with Gabriel about his long journey back to the Citadel. 'Yes.'

'And what is this man's name?'

Athanasius frowned. 'His name is Gabriel. Now tell us what it says on the stone.'

Malachi shook his head. 'It's . . . I'm not sure . . . I'll need to –' He started to back away, eyes wide and fixed on the laptop.

'Tell us what it says.'

He looked up at them, his eyes full of fear. 'I need to check some things,' he said, still backing away. 'I need to be sure, before I –'

'Malachi!' Thomas closed the laptop, but all it did was release Malachi from the spell of it. He turned and started moving away.

'MALACHI!' Athanasius called after him. But it was too late, he was already gone, almost running into the solid blackness until his flickering candle disappeared entirely.

CHAPTER 78

Corporal Williamson and his crew made impressively short work of the gates. They had found some chains and dragged them to their truck outside the fence. The chains were fixed by one end to the tow bar and the other to the main support posts while everyone else dug away at the foundations with shovels, picks and whatever else they could swing. When Williamson figured they'd dug far enough he fired up the engine and eased it over to where the earth fell away and used gravity and the weight of the truck to rock the posts clean out of the ground. Then they got to work on the rest.

Williamson took command, tasking some of his men to decommission the cannons up in the towers and the rest he split into teams to coordinate the demolition effort. Using a series of interpreters relaying Williamson's orders they got everybody working together, some digging at the post foundations, others cutting the wire and rolling it into bundles. Liv had been stationed at one of the posts and was snipping away at the ties with an industrial-sized set of wire cutters. She felt deep satisfaction at how quickly the different groups had gelled into one unit, everyone working together, everyone suffused with a sense of urgency by the column of dust growing steadily in the east, marking the approach of the newcomers.

'Those soldiers, they're very good at this,' she remarked to Tariq who was hacking away with a pickaxe at the concrete foot of the post she was working at.

He leaned on the axe handle and wiped the sweat from his face. 'They should be,' he said, 'they're USACE – United States Army Corps of Engineers. These guys are used to taking things down and building them up again. It's what they're trained for.'

Liv frowned as a thought began to form in her head. 'Don't you think it's odd that exactly the right people seem to arrive here just when they're needed? When the water was poisoned some water experts turned up out of nowhere with all the right equipment to test it. Then these guys show up just when the need to dismantle this place suggests itself.'

'The goat herders too,' Tariq nodded over at the nomads who were now quite happily being ordered about by the soldiers.

'How do they fit in?'

'We have plenty of dried food but hardly anything fresh. In the desert the goat is the best source of fresh milk and meat. Those goats are as important for the sustainability of this place as the water.' He frowned as something occurred to him. 'What about Azra'iel and his riders, how do they fit into your theory?'

Liv contemplated this for a moment then shook her head. 'They were not drawn here by the call of this place like the rest, they were led here by Malik. They shouldn't have been here. And they died.'

Tariq turned back to the column of dust in the east, close enough now to make out three white trucks at the base of it, their outlines shimmering and breaking up in the heat haze. 'So who is coming now?' he asked, more to himself than anyone else. 'What do we need here that we haven't got already?'

Liv followed his gaze. 'Whoever it is they will be met with a welcome and not a closed gate,' she said.

She continued to watch the shimmering vehicles drawing closer, emerging from the liquid air until they crunched to a halt in a cloud of fine dust. The driver's door of the lead vehicle opened and a man got out. He was tall and olive-skinned, but not Arabic looking. Gentle eyes surveyed the ring of welcoming faces then looked past them through the ruins of the gate to the compound beyond and the fountain of water. 'What is this place?' he asked in accented English that placed him as Italian or maybe Spanish.

Liv stepped forward, fixing a smile on her face 'We're not quite sure what this place is really, we're kind of making it up as we go along, but there's plenty of room and plenty of water and you're very welcome to stay.'

More doors opened and others stepped out into the desert, a mixture of Arabic, European, mature and young, six of them in all, two to a vehicle. Then

Liv spotted something on one of their sleeves, a logo that looked familiar but she couldn't quite place. 'What is it that you all do?' she asked.

The driver of the lead vehicle turned his gentle eyes on her and smiled. 'We work for Médecins Sans Frontières,' he said. 'We're doctors.'

CHAPTER 79

Franklin saw something harden in his wife's face the moment his phone rang for the second time.

They were sitting in the kitchen – Marie, Sinead and him – the remains of a home-cooked meal on the table, talking like they hadn't talked together in God knows how long. It was as if all the bad history and all the distance that had formed between them had been swept away by the same force that had pulled them home.

'I got to take this,' he said. Marie nodded, a quick twitch of her chin, then slipped out of her chair, picked up some plates and headed over to the sink. How many times had he seen her do that? Too many. He looked at Sinead, so like her mother, and caught the same disappointment in her eyes – not as hard or as cold as her mother yet, but the seed was there.

He took the phone from his pocket and checked the number.

Shepherd again.

He knew he should turn the damn thing off and go over to Marie, tell her he loved her, that the old days of work first and everything else a poor second were gone. But they weren't. Not yet.

He pictured Shepherd, exhausted from the day he'd had, standing out there alone in the freezing night with a fresh corpse for company and no one watching his back. 'I got to take it,' he repeated standing and walking from the room, hating himself with every step. He moved into the hallway and snapped the phone to his ear. 'Franklin.'

'It's Shepherd.'

'I know.' He walked towards the front door but changed his mind and sat on the stairs instead. It was too cold outside and he couldn't face leaving the house.

'The cops are here. They didn't see the car on their way in and didn't intercept anyone. I think the killers must be heading north into Tennessee.'

'I'll make some calls. Spread the net.'

'I already got the local cops to call it through.'

'Well I'll fire a rocket down from Quantico too, make sure it sticks.' The loud and angry chink of dishes being rinsed in the sink sounded only a few feet away. He covered his ear with his free hand and felt his mind automatically snick back into the well-worn grooves of a moving investigation. 'OK, this is what's going to happen. They won't have the right resources locally to process the scene properly so I'm going to send a team out to you from Charlotte. You need to stay put until they get there, make sure those down home cops don't get all excited and contaminate the scene with cigarette butts and good intentions. They're going to take a while to reach you so you'll need to take charge until they do. I already put in an urgent search for any of Dr Kinderman's previous known addresses and got a hit on two that might be considered "home". There are armed units heading to both of them now. If Kinderman's there we'll get him.'

'Always assuming whoever killed Professor Douglas hasn't got there first.'

'I doubt it. Both addresses are way up north and so far everything has taken place south of Washington. This feels like a very contained operation, one mobile unit and someone controlling them centrally. What's the cell phone coverage like where you are?'

'I'm on top of a mountain, I got five bars, but I don't know about the rest of the area – why?'

Franklin stared at his daughter's snow boots, lined up by the door where she had stepped out of them; one had toppled over. He had a flash of a smaller pair abandoned in exactly the same way maybe fifteen years earlier. He closed his eyes. The memories were too distracting. 'You remember our little talk with the good Reverend?'

'Unfortunately, yes.'

'You remember what I did just before we interviewed him?'

There was a pause on the line. Franklin could hear the wind through the trees where Shepherd was. It sounded cold. 'You asked him to put his phone down on the table.'

'Then what?'

'You asked if you could smoke.'

'And when he said "no" I put my cigarettes down on the table next to his phone. There's a little piece of kit not covered in class called an Eavesdropper. It's a new-generation bug that can read and duplicate a SIM card without the need to tamper with a phone. All you have to do is place it close enough to a target unit and leave it there for about a minute so it can pick up the Mobile Identification Number when it checks in with the nearest cell mast. It then mirrors the phone activity and makes voice recordings of any calls. It's got a four gigabyte chip built in so it can store around fifty hours of audio. The one drawback is that it only works in close physical proximity to the target phone.'

'Which is why you stashed your pack of cigarettes in that crack in the wall.'

'Exactly. So I'm thinking if there's good phone reception where you are the killers may already have called in a status update to their controller. You hang tight, Shepherd. I'll let you know how it shakes out.'

He hung up and hit the zero key to speed-dial Quantico. From the kitchen all he could hear now was silence. He pictured Marie and Sinead sitting at the breakfast bar, listening to him talk in the hallway. It made him feel crummy. But he couldn't leave Shepherd hanging in the wind. He was the only reason he was here at all. He'd explain that to them, as soon as he finished this call.

The phone connected and Franklin navigated his way through the various departments: authorizing and mobilizing a crime-scene detail to hit the road and head to Cherokee; issuing an urgent look out for a yellow or white station wagon with police departments in three states; and ultimately getting patched through to the surveillance control room where, after confirmation of his agent ID number and the investigation code, he was told by the operator that the Eavesdropper unit assigned to him had logged its last call six minutes earlier. Franklin listened to the crackle of the line and the solid silence in his house while the operator sent a code that bounced off a communications satellite in space and beamed a signal back through the snow clouds and down to the Eavesdropper wedged between the mailbox and the outside wall of the Church of Christ's Salvation in Charleston.

The circuit responded to the code and switched from a receiver to a transmitter, using the cell-phone network to send an encoded stream of information back to the operator who then decoded it and fed it straight down the line to Franklin.

Franklin kept his eyes closed as he listened to the last recorded conversation the device had picked up. It was between Cooper and two unidentified voices – a man and a woman. He registered the key phrases in the short exchange:

. . . The Professor is dead . . . just passed into Tennessee . . . Yeah, we got pictures . . .

Then Cooper ended the call with words that hammered the lid shut on his own coffin.

. . . I just found out where Dr Kinderman is . . .

Franklin cut the connection and stared down at his daughter's empty boots. Whatever hope he had been clinging to that he might still be able to deal with this by phone had just flown. Cooper needed to be taken down quickly and he couldn't leave it to Charleston's finest.

He dug around in his pocket, found the card Jackson had given him in the police station and started punching his number into his phone. He hit the dial button and became aware of Marie and Sinead framed in the kitchen door. They were both looking at him, their arms folded across their fronts, each a mirror of the other's disapproval.

'I've got to do this one thing,' he said, holding up his phone, 'just this one thing in Charleston then I'll be back, I promise.' He heard the phone connect and start ringing. By the look on Marie's face she heard it too.

'It's always just one more thing,' she said. Then she turned and walked into the kitchen.

Sinead stayed where she was. 'Just one thing?' she said.

'Literally this one thing, I promise you hand on heart.'

She nodded but didn't smile, then turned and followed her mother into the kitchen as Jackson

457

answered. Franklin clamped the phone to his ear, closing his eyes to shut out all the things he didn't want to leave. 'I need your help,' he said keeping his voice low. 'But first I need to get into Charleston as fast as possible, preferably avoiding the parking lot that is the I-26.'

CHAPTER 80

'He asked about me?' Gabriel was propped up in bed looking at Athanasius and Thomas, their faces serious after their strange meeting with Malachi.

'Yes, and his questions appeared to have been prompted by whatever he had just read on the Starmap. He asked if you had ridden to the Citadel out of the wilderness.'

'You think he knows what the symbols mean?'

'Undoubtedly,' Thomas replied. 'Malachi knows more about early writing than any man alive. If there is anything in the library that will help decipher this text then it will already be in his head. He knows exactly what it says.'

'So how do we get him to tell us?'

'We don't,' Athanasius replied. 'Malachi has never been a man who could be swayed. And he hates me. He thinks I have betrayed the brotherhood. There is no way he is going to share what he learned with us. I should have known better than to trust him, but I wasn't counting on him being so – unhinged.'

'Yes,' Thomas agreed, 'there was something

desperate about him. He's not going to help us. I fear he is already lost.'

'So it seems we must take matters into our own hands,' Athanasius said, rubbing his hands together as if, on some level, he was enjoying all this. 'If we are going to interpret the rest of the stone we need to gain access to the ancient records. You helped me break into the library once before.'

Thomas smiled. 'And that was when the lights were still working, the security protocols were in place, armed guards were on constant patrol and unauthorized access was punishable by death. This should be relatively easy in comparison.'

'Can you do it tonight?'

'I'll need to hook into the library systems to see what is still running and what has been disabled, I don't want you walking into a trap or tripping any alarms. The absence of the lights will be a big help, and I don't suppose they're availing themselves of the night-vision goggles, what with "the corrupting influence of modernity", which means we can use them. They are kept in the control room by the main entrance.'

'Could we gain access via the reading rooms? We could go via the restricted section to the one used by the Sancti?'

'What's that?' Gabriel asked.

'The Sanctus monks were kept strictly segregated from the rest of the population to preserve the secrets they kept. However they still had access to the library at certain times when no one else was there, and they had their own reading room. It's reached by a staircase from the upper section of the mountain. There are other stairways too, one in the prelate's quarters, one close to the cathedral cave and one just through there.' He pointed to the door leading to the Abbot's bed chamber. 'They enabled the trusted senior members of the mountain to meet with the Sancti and partake in their ceremonies. Since there are no longer any of them left, the stairways and Sancti's reading room have been unused.' He looked back at the door leading to the bedchamber. 'I have the Abbot's key for that door. But not one for the door leading into the reading room. We'd have to force it.'

Father Thomas shook his head. 'We would make far too much noise. It's a heavy door with a solid lock and the reading rooms where Malachi and the black cloaks are residing is right next door. I'd rather break in using my own systems than bludgeon my way through a door. Once we are inside and have acquired the night-vision goggles it should be easy. We can find our way to the ancient texts and read anything we like in total darkness. Give me a couple of hours and I'll have worked out how to get us in. That should also give everyone time to go to sleep. Shall we say midnight?'

Athanasius nodded. 'Between Matins and Lauds.'

'Can I come with you?' Gabriel said, clearly meaning it.

'You're not going anywhere.' Dr Kaplan appeared behind Thomas with something in his hand and a

461

serious expression on his face. 'You're far too weak to do anything other than lie here and rest. However, if you really want to help . . .'

He opened his hand and Gabriel felt his stomach flip when he saw several empty test tubes lying in his palm. 'This is the situation. So far we've taken eight hundred mils of your blood which would take your body about five weeks to fully replace. The plasma gets replaced in a day or two. The blood cells take much longer. In the study of disease it is these cells that give us the most information. They're the things that have battled the disease and, in your case, won. At the moment your body will only just have started replacing the plasma and your white cell count per litre will still be relatively high. As far as virology and toxicology is concerned this is the good stuff, packed full of all the information we need. It would really speed things up if we could take some more of this rich blood now.'

'How much?'

'Another five hundred mils.'

'And how much would that leave me with?'

'Enough, you'd still have seventy-five to eighty-five per cent of your usual amount, which is in the safe zone for a healthy patient. My concern is that the last time we took blood it triggered some kind of mild relapse, though you recovered quickly and seem fine now.' He looked at the ECG monitor connected to Gabriel's finger by a clip. 'Your vital signs are all strong and there's no obvious reason for concern. But ultimately it's your decision.'

Gabriel looked at the stained-glass window, the peacock motif hardly visible now as evening darkened the sky behind it. 'What the hell,' he said. 'I'm not going anywhere. But if I do pass out please don't wake me until morning.' An assistant appeared from nowhere and started to tighten Gabriel's bindings.

'Just a precaution,' Kaplan said. 'In case you do have another fit.'

Gabriel turned to Athanasius. 'Good luck,' he said. 'And I sincerely hope you have a better night than I'm about to.'

CHAPTER 81

Malachi's candle lit up the words carved into the inside of the upper curve of an archway as he passed through it: CRYPTA REVELATIO – Vault of the Revelation.

Most of the library was organized according to date and origin, with the newest items nearest the entrance. But the contents of the Crypta Revelatio were drawn from every culture, every century and every part of the world. It was a collection with one unique subject in common: all of the texts and references gathered there contained prophetic accounts of the end of the world.

He made his way over to the far side of the vault and held his dying candle to a fresh one until the new wick caught and wavering orange light rippled across a desk entirely buried beneath books and sheets of paper filled with Malachi's dense handwriting. Collapsing in the seat at his desk, he grabbed a fresh sheet of paper and took up his pen. His hand shook as he wrote, his lips moving as he recalled the symbols he had seen. He had not been able to memorize them all in the short time, but he had seen enough. He drew the symbols from memory, writing his interpretation of each next to it so he could capture as much of it as he could remember: one sign for a rider – a warrior on horseback; one sign for the Citadel, which occurred more than once; and at the very end of the prophecy the symbol of a skull – meaning death or an end – followed by the moon in the sun, representing a day.

End of Days.

He pulled the candle over and his magnified eyes moved behind the lenses of his spectacles, his skittish hands extensions of his tumbling thoughts as they searched through the accumulated mass of doom that spilled across the table top and down to the floor, looking for one item in particular. He had read and re-read the documents so many times that the terrible imagery and predictions they contained bled into his dreams as he slept here each night in his nest of prophesies.

He found what he was looking for buried beneath the handwritten, original manuscript of the **Poetic Edda** and a first edition of **Les Propheties** by Michel de Nostredame. The text was written on papyrus in Ancient Greek and bound into a codex with thin strips of leather. Such binding was usually reserved for pristine texts but these pages were filled with crossings out and additions crammed in the borders and between every line.

Malachi turned the pages, his hands touching only the edge of each page in recognition of the great delicacy of the book. It had arrived in the Citadel barely a hundred years after the death of Christ, shortly after it was written on the island of Patmos. Any Christian scholar with a passing knowledge of Greek would have instantly recognized the apocalyptic imagery of dragons and lambs that whispered up from the dry pages. It was the Book of Revelation of Saint John the Divine, the last book of the Holy Bible, written in the saint's own hand.

The first copies of the Bible had been compiled and written in this very library, using the original texts as reference. But not everything had been copied into the official, public version everyone now knew. Under the supervision of the earliest scholars whole books had been omitted in order to help clarify God's meanings. And anything that alluded too closely to the Citadel or the Sacrament was also omitted so the secrets would remain so. But the complete visions and prophecies of Saint John had been preserved in this, the one remaining copy of the original work. Malachi found the page he was looking for and scanned the confusion of crossings out and notes until he found the seventh verse:

And when he had opened the fourth seal,
I heard the voice of the fourth beast say,
Come and see.
And I looked, and behold a pale horse:
and his name that sat on him was Death,
and Hell followed with him.

The same version was written in every Bible on the face of the earth. But in this Codex there was an additional part that had been marked for exclusion by one of the fathers of the Church because of the direct reference to the Citadel.

And he did ride forth from the wilderness
A demon disguised as an angel
And the keepers of the flame within the great
  tower, which had
stood and held the secret
of God since Adam's time,
Were fooled and they did let him inside
And there he did remove the light,
But the pure of heart were fooled not
And God did give them a white fire to burn
  away all corruption
and carry the false one away unto death.
And God did smile upon those who had done
  His work,
And they did take their place by His side.
Blessed among the blessed.

And what had Athanasius – that fool – told him about the man who had cheated death and recovered from the blight? That he had ridden to the Citadel on a horse, and that his name was Gabriel.

What had they done?

The Revelation of St John the Divine and the prophecy etched on the stone both predicted the end of days – and Athanasius had made it all happen. He had lit the fuse to something that would blow everything apart.

Malachi closed his eyes and tried to think. There had been constellations etched onto the stone too and moon symbols denoting a time frame. Maybe the end was not here yet, Maybe it could be avoided. He re-read the words of the Saint, looking for fresh meaning in them, his eyes drawn to one phrase in particular:

But the pure of heart were fooled not
And God did give them a white fire to
burn away all corruption and carry the
false one away unto death.

What had Athanasius said about the demon, the one who called itself Gabriel? That it was recovering from the blight, and that they had taken it to the Abbot's private chambers to recover while they conducted their tests and pandered to it, slaves already without even knowing it – the fools. But Athanasius had also said something else – that it was still weak, not fully recovered. And he knew a way to the Abbot's private chambers through the stairways and corridors leading up from the locked reading room of the Sancti. And Malachi had the key. There was yet time to vanquish it, but he would have to strike quickly, before it grew too strong.

CHAPTER 82

Franklin drove back into Charleston the same way he'd driven out. He had borrowed Sinead's car, preferring the indignity of turning up to an arrest in a Hyundai Elantra to the pain and probable rejection of asking Marie if he could borrow her Chevy Malibu.

Jackson met him with two other uniforms as arranged at a gas station twenty miles outside the city limits. They drove back into town the wrong way on the empty lanes of the outbound interstate, lights flashing and sirens blaring in case they met anything coming the other way. The traffic on the inbound lane was as bad as it had been before and they drew envious glances as they blew past from all the people behind wheels, still waiting patiently in line and inching their way back home.

They killed the sirens and lights when they made it downtown and the traffic started to thin again. They weaved through the snow-softened streets and parked round the corner from Cooper's church where Franklin went through his strategy for the take-down, the layout of the building, the number of people likely to be inside. He even called up a picture of Cooper on his phone to show them. The cops barely looked at it. Everybody knew who Fulton Cooper was.

They checked their weapons and put on body armour vests. Due to some mess-up they had only brought three so Franklin decided to do without. He couldn't imagine Cooper was going to put up any kind of a fight. They went through it all one last time then split up, the two uniforms heading round the back to cover the rear entrance just in case the good Reverend lost his faith in the Lord and decided to make a run for it.

Franklin and Jackson took the front. Franklin yanked hard on the bell pull and heard it ring somewhere inside the building. There were lights on and the most recent update from the Eavesdropper log suggested that Cooper, or his phone at least, had still been in the building as of ten minutes ago. Franklin reached into the gap between the mailbox and the wall to retrieve the crumpled pack of cigarettes with the bug inside.

Snow fell. They waited.

A light came on above them, lifting them from the dark and throwing their shadows out onto the blank whiteness of the road. Miss Boerman appeared in the doorway and regarded them with a look as cold as the ground they stood upon. 'Yes?'

'Is the Reverend in?' Franklin asked.

'Can't this – whatever it is – wait until tomorrow?'

'No.' Franklin noticed her shirt was unbuttoned at the neck, a small thing but on her it seemed as though he'd caught her half-dressed. Her hand rose to her shirt collar and her face hardened. 'I'm afraid he's unavailable.' The fine scar on her face wrinkled as she spoke. Franklin wondered if it was the reason she never smiled.

'Mind if we come in and see for ourselves?'

'Do you have a warrant?'

'What, you mean like this?'

Jackson held up the signed paperwork he had managed to hustle out of the one judge who was still in town and answering his phone and Franklin enjoyed the surprise that registered on the blank mask of her face. She looked up, still making no further move to unlock the gate.

'OK, I'll tell you what I'll do.' Franklin opened his hands in his I'm-being-reasonable-here manner. 'You have exactly three seconds to open this gate or I'm going to shoot the lock off and arrest you for obstruction of justice, sound fair?'

He held up three fingers.

Then two.

He reached into his jacket for his gun.

She stepped forward and jabbed a key into the lock, twisting it open and standing aside to let them in.

'Where is he?'

'I'm not sure.'

'Well take a guess and make it a good one.'

'He's probably at prayer, in the chapel.'

'You think so or you know so?'

Her hand went to her collar again. 'He's there.'

'Where is it?'

'In the basement, down the side stairs you went up earlier.'

'Is he alone?'

'Yes.'

'Anyone else in the building I should know about?'

'The church is closed.'

'That's not what I asked.'

'No. There's no one here but Fulton and myself.'

Franklin smiled. 'Thank you, miss. You have been most helpful. Why don't you wait here until we're done.'

He pushed through the front door and into the warmth of the entrance hall with Jackson following close behind. The phone room was empty and so was the post room. They continued through to the narrow stairs and headed down, Franklin's steps loud on the bare boards, announcing his approach to whoever might be listening in the basement. He reached the bottom and waited for Jackson to join him. 'You set?'

A short nod.

'OK, let's do it.'

They moved together through the gloom towards a solid wooden door that swung open easily on well-oiled hinges to reveal a small chapel beyond lit by sunlight miraculously pouring through a large stained-glass window. Cooper was on his knees in front of it, head bowed, hands in front of him where they couldn't be seen.

'Hello, Reverend,' Franklin said, moving to the

centre of the room. 'Sorry to burst in on you like this but I was just dying to introduce you to a friend of mine. Detective Jackson of the Charleston PD, meet the man we're here to arrest for conspiracy to murder.'

Cooper didn't move. Franklin glanced over at Jackson. 'You want to Mirandize him while he's saying his goodbyes to the Lord?'

Franklin sat down on one of the benches while Jackson read Cooper his rights. He felt suddenly tired from the long and event-filled day. Driving away from Marie and Sinead had taken more out of him than he thought. At least Cooper wasn't kicking and screaming. He watched the Reverend lower his hands and look up at the cross built into the design of the window. 'Might I ask on what evidence you are arresting me?'

'You might.' Franklin produced his phone and played the intercepted phone message, Cooper's voice sounding thin and tinny on the small speaker. He switched it off before it got to the end.

'You really have no idea what all of us are facing here, do you?' Cooper said.

Franklin smiled. 'Feel free to enlighten me,' he said wearily, 'though you would be advised to keep it short as everything you now say constitutes evidence that can be used against you in a court of law.'

'Whose law – the law of man? The law of governments? What fear I of such flawed and inadequate things?'

'Well now, let's see, they still have the death

penalty in this state, so that's one thing. Then there's the lengthy custodial sentence you'll get either way where you may well be stuck in a tiny jail cell with a huge, horny dude by the name of Bubba or somesuch, that would certainly put the fear of God into me.'

'There is only one law I answer to, and that is the law of Jesus Christ the Saviour, and He is close at hand. He knows who serves Him and who does not. And He will gather the righteous to His side when the time comes.'

The suddenness and speed of Cooper's movement took Franklin totally by surprise. One moment he was kneeling on the floor, the next he was across the floor and behind the solid wooden lectern. Franklin automatically dropped down, snatching his gun from his shoulder holster and using the bench as cover. Out of his peripheral vision he saw Jackson break right and do the same.

'We know about the rear exit, Cooper, and it's covered, 'Franklin shouted. 'There's no way out of this.'

'That, my friend, is where you are wrong.' Cooper rose from behind the lectern, a gun in his hand, pointing straight at Franklin.

Instincts honed over a lifetime of service flooded Franklin's brain, producing the slow, hyper-sensory state that existed in the middle of a live gunfight.

He saw Cooper's knuckle glow white as it tightened on the trigger.

Vest. He wasn't wearing a vest.

He heard his own breathing, loud and slow as he took a breath and held it. Felt the re-coil jolt his arm, saw the flash of his gun firing, then again, along with the slow, deep boom of both shots as they echoed in the chapel. He watched through the smoke as Cooper spun away and fell, his gun falling from his hand as he hit the stone floor. Franklin was already moving, driven forward by muscle memory, leading with his gun to make sure Cooper was properly down while part of his brain checked for any signs that he had been hit.

Had Cooper got off a shot? Hard to tell.

He'd seen agents sprint up flights of stairs with serious wounds they hadn't even known about because of adrenalin and delayed shock. And he had promised Marie he would come back.

He reached Cooper's body and assessed him from behind his gun. He was still breathing but only just, his eyes looking up at the window, a pool of blood spreading beneath him too fast to be minor. Both shots had caught him centre mass. Major organ damage, possibly arterial too. He could hear the rattle in his breath as his lungs filled with blood. He would drown before he bled out and there was nothing he could do but watch.

Franklin bent down on one knee, placing his hand on Cooper's shoulder so he knew he was there. 'You've been hit pretty bad but you'll be OK,' he lied. 'There's an ambulance on its way. Why don't you tell me where Kinderman is?'

Cooper opened his mouth, still staring up at the

cross. Franklin dropped down lower so he could hear him. Heard the whisper of a voice broken by shallow breaths. 'He's on his way . . . to hell.'

Footsteps echoed outside as Miss Boerman clattered down the stairs in response to the gunshots. Jackson headed over to intercept her. No point her seeing any of this. Through the noise Franklin became aware that Cooper was saying something else. He leaned down lower, his ear so close he could feel the snatched breaths.

'Thank you . . .' Cooper whispered, 'for . . . helping me . . . leave.' The last word came out as a long sigh that ended in a rattle he had heard too many times before. It was over. Cooper was dead.

Behind him he could hear voices now, Jackson low and calm, Miss Boerman angry and hysterical. He could hear more footsteps too as the other two uniforms also responded to the gunfire.

Too late. Nothing to see.

He moved across to where Cooper's gun was lying on the stone floor, holstering his own and slipping a pair of Nitrile gloves over his hands. He picked up the discarded weapon and instantly knew from the weight and balance of it that it was empty. He checked to make sure – no magazine in the clip, no bullet in the chamber – and realized what Cooper had meant with his dying words. He wouldn't have been able to face his Lord if he had taken his own life. Suicide was a mortal sin. So he had got Franklin to do it for him.

Suicide by cop.

CHAPTER 83

Shepherd was standing on the porch of Douglas's observatory watching the FBI tech team trample all over the local cops when his phone buzzed in his pocket.

'Cooper is dead,' Franklin said the moment he answered.

'Jesus.'

'He pulled a gun so I had to put him down. He was involved in the hit on Douglas, no question. I've got an intercepted phone call of him discussing it and I'm currently standing in his studio looking at some particularly nasty phone images of the professor taken post-mortem. They were being edited into a video package that was no doubt going to be the cornerstone of the late Reverend's next sermon: God's retribution on the blasphemers, behold his mighty wrath – you can imagine.

'Bad news is these same pictures are already on the internet, leaked anonymously, and now popping up on all the nuttier religious conspiracy sites presumably so they could hide the source of them for their news piece. We'll take them down as fast as we can but they're starting to get picked up by some of the news outlets and spread around on Twitter. We can't keep this genie in the bottle, which means we have to find Kinderman fast before he really goes to ground or Cooper's angels of death get to him.'

'I could use the email I found on Douglas's laptop, tell Kinderman what's happened here and offer the hand of friendship and protection.'

'The tech guys arrive there yet?'

'Yeah, they're currently making friends with the local folk.'

'I bet. They're not going to like you walking all over "their" crime scene but a man's life is at stake here. Use the laptop and wear gloves. If they complain about it in their report I'll say I ordered you to do it.'

'OK. I'll let you know if he bites. You want me to head back to Charleston after I'm done here?'

There was a silence on the line and somewhere in the background Shepherd could hear Cooper's voice still ranting away. 'You still there?'

'Yeah, I'm here,' Franklin sounded distracted. 'You should get some rest then drive to Charlotte, it's nearer than here. I'll warn them you're coming.'

'What about you?'

'Call me if you get anything from Kinderman.' The phone clicked before Shepherd could respond and the line went dead.

By insisting that he needed to use Douglas's laptop Shepherd succeeded in annoying both the FBI tech guys and the local PD. He ignored their looks and whispers as they worked together to photograph and remove Douglas's body from the wall while he crouched over the keyboard, figuring at least he'd done his bit to get them co-operating with each other. They were united now in thinking he was an asshole.

He opened Kinderman's last message using pens to tap the keys, hit *Reply* and then paused. He would only have one shot at this. Get it wrong and Kinderman would shut down the email account and vanish again. His eyes flicked to the countdown, getting smaller all the time.

He could try and draw him out by pretending he was Douglas but he didn't know enough about their shared history to do it convincingly. Also, according to Franklin, the pictures of Douglas's murder were already on the net and starting to garner press interest. If Dr Kinderman had already seen them then a voice from beyond the grave was hardly likely to win his trust. On the other hand if he had seen them, fear was a useful tool.

Shepherd tapped on a browser icon and started hunting for the pictures. It didn't take him long. A couple of clicks away from Cooper's own website he found a page dedicated to the coming revelation. It was a thoroughly nasty piece of work, full of hate and damnation, with a whole section dedicated to what it called 'The Great Blasphemy of the New Tower of Babel'. There were pictures of Hubble as well as Kinderman and Douglas with captions beneath identifying them as the architects of the great offence. There were also headlines and links to various unfolding news stories telling of the sabotage and explosions, then – at the bottom of the screen – Shepherd found a grainy version of the room he was now standing in, a quote from Ezekiel emblazoned beneath it:

Then they will know that I am the Lord,
when I lay my vengeance upon them.

The quote was typed in letters the same colour as Douglas's blood. Shepherd imagined someone in a basement, lit by the glow from his screen and the demented fire that burned within him, matching the colour from the photograph then hitting the *Publish* button, pleased with his little design flourish. He hoped the FBI would hit him hard when they eventually caught up with him. He copied the link and posted it in the email.

He then found the link on Cooper's site to the clip of him and Franklin being quizzed about the explosion at Marshall and the sabotage of Hubble. He pasted that in too and started to type:

Dr Kinderman,
I hope this is you. If so, my apologies for contacting you in this way. I am a former

480

student of Professor Douglas now working for the FBI. I'm very sorry to inform you that the professor is dead – murdered – and that your life is also in danger. The same people who tracked him down to his mountain lodge are now looking for you. We know you received the same warnings as he did and that you both saw something in the missing data from Hubble. Let me help you, either in my capacity as a Federal agent or as an old friend of the Professor's. Either way, I want to help. Please let me.
Yours,
Joseph Shepherd

He re-read it and was surprised to discover tears in his eyes. He turned away from everyone and wiped them away. He had been so carried along by the speed of events that he had kept the brutal shock of finding the professor's body at arm's length – until now. Writing the message to Dr Kinderman had opened a window straight into something raw and painful. He hadn't been looking for the professor for very long, barely more than a day, but there was something ominous about the tragic way this search had ended that made him think about the other one, the one he had been on for eight long years. And it made him afraid.

He copied the message to his own email account so he could monitor any response, then hit *Send*

481

and let out a breath that he hadn't even known he'd been holding.

'OK,' he said, 'it's all yours.' And turned to the others just as they were zipping Professor Douglas into a body bag.

CHAPTER 84

Liv felt the tickle of sweat running down her back, her neck – everywhere. She had chosen to stay outside and lead by example. It also gave her the chance to think, the quiet monotony of her task helping to clear her mind as she tried to evaluate the significance of the new arrivals.

The doctors were now inside the compound building. Eric was immensely relieved that he was no longer the only medically trained member of the growing desert community. Liv, on the other hand, felt that there was something ominous and unsettling about the sudden arrival of so many doctors. With the last of the victims of the poisoning now dead and buried it suggested that some other medical emergency was about to manifest itself.

The convoy of 4×4s they had arrived in had also contained boxes and boxes of much-needed supplies and medical equipment. Most of the existing stock from the sick bay had been used up so Liv had tried to rationalize this as being the reason they'd been drawn here. But at the core of her finely tuned instincts she knew it could not be as simple as that.

She thought about the circle with a cross through

the centre – the symbol of disease and destruction. It was positioned between the upward arrow of the mountain and the downward one of here. When she had first studied it she had assumed and hoped it referred to the Citadel. But now she felt the meaning was ambiguous. Its position suggested that whatever disease the symbol represented might either link the two places or separate them in some way.

She leaned against the fence post, grateful for its sturdy support, and felt the weight of everything closing down on her. The blinding light and heat were making her faint and light-headed and she felt a lurch in her stomach like she'd eaten something bad. She shivered, genuinely cold despite the enveloping heat and the sweat still running off her. Her heart thrummed in her chest making her vision throb. Maybe she needed to get out of the sun for a bit, have one of Kyle's re-hydration cocktails, and lie down and rest for a while.

She started to walk back towards the compound, focusing on the nearest building. If she could just get out of the sun she would be fine. She concentrated on her breathing, in through the nose and out through the mouth, placing one foot in front of the other to close the distance to the nearest door. She had made it about half way when the earth started to shift beneath her feet. She fixed her eyes on the dark rectangle of the door but it seemed to be getting further away.

She was stumbling now, the ground moving in waves beneath her feet, something close to panic rising inside her. Everything was mixing together, the heat, her exhaustion, the half-glimpsed truths and fragments of ancient warnings that led her to the edge of knowing what was to come without ever revealing what it was. And then there was Gabriel, always Gabriel – gone with hardly a word save for the note she carried with her like a spell.

. . . Nothing is easy, but leaving you is the
hardest thing I have ever done . . .
. . . keep yourself safe – until
I find you again . . .

But when would he return so she could finally rest? Clinging to the memory of him like this, was a form of grief.

At last her hand touched the metal skin of the door and the burning heat of it shocked her back to her senses. She caught a whiff of something acrid, citrus, while her head thumped, the blood continued to drain and her mind pulsed through the percussive beat of repeated thoughts:

Gabriel

The Citadel

The symbol for Contagion

The arrival of the doctors

The door gave and she almost fell to the floor as it opened. A wave of warm air billowed out, the air-conditioning not yet turned on because everyone was working outside and fuel was too valuable to waste. It carried the same smell of lemons with it, thick and sweet, making her feel nauseous again. She leaned against the wall, sliding forward and along it, using it for support as the ground beneath her continued to shift and roll. She just needed to find a bed and lie down for a while until the world stopped spinning.

Another door opened at the end of the corridor and Eric appeared, leading the doctors on a tour through the building. They looked up at her and she saw concern cloud their faces. Then her knees gave way and she crumpled to the ground. She was unconscious before she hit the floor.

CHAPTER 85

Shepherd finally got away from the crime scene shortly after midnight. He headed north along the same road the killers had escaped on and then east towards Charlotte. When he started the drive he was convinced that he was heading to the nearest field office to report in and await new orders, but at the back of his mind he knew there was something else in Charlotte that would offer him a different choice.

Exhaustion hit him hard after a couple of hours. Conditions had been pretty bad most of the way, snow and ice and dark unfamiliar roads. Once he'd dropped down from the higher ground the weather improved, or at least became good enough that he wasn't scared of getting snowed in, he pulled into a rest stop and closed his eyes for a few minutes. He awoke with a start when his phone buzzed in his pocket. He checked the time and realized he'd been asleep for nearly three hours. The car had turned into an icebox with frost on the inside of the windows where moisture from his breath had frozen. He dug his phone from his pocket and discovered he had mail. He opened the app and the temperature dropped a little more. It was from Kinderman.

> You seem to know a lot, Agent Shepherd, and I appreciate your concern.
> If you are truly knowledgeable then you will know where to find me. I'm just standing on a hill looking to the east for new stars in old friends, as those like us have done since the beginning of time.

Shepherd stared at the message, trying to make sense of it through the fog of his sleepy brain. He re-read it, his fatigue making him irritable that he was having to deal with this riddle in the middle of the frozen night. Why couldn't Kinderman just tell him where he was?

Twice he hit reply and started composing a message to that effect, but both times he deleted it, instinctively knowing that he would not get another response. In the end, he slipped the phone back in his pocket and drove the rest of the way to Charlotte thinking it over with the heater on full, sipping black coffee from a Big Gulp he'd bought at a truck stop.

It was almost six in the morning when he hit the outskirts of Charlotte and parked next to a McDonalds, retrieved the Bureau laptop from the passenger footwell and hooked onto the free Wi-Fi that was thankfully still working. From where he sat he could see downtown lying dark before him, the result of a power outage that had sunk half the city into blackness. The only light was coming from a few cars that sketched the lines of unseen streets and a few flickering orange patches where fires burned. It was terrifying how quickly the ordered world had started to unravel. Maybe this would be how it ended, not with some cosmic collision or the wrath of some vengeful god but with society quietly imploding on itself as everyone just headed home and stayed there, all deliveries ending, all crops lying ungathered in fields, the major utilities switching themselves off one by one as no one turned up to work any more. Maybe no one would actually care, or even remember how things used to be.

He opened the laptop to check in on whatever Agent Smith had dredged up in the night and was greeted by the pinging sound that made his heart tumble in his chest and he was rapidly growing to hate. The new search he had put in place for Melisa had come back with two results.

The first hit was her name on an old passenger manifest out of Dulles Airport in Washington. She had flown out of the country eight years ago on a Cyprus-Turkish airliner heading for a place called Gaziantep. He opened a browser and looked it up. The Wikipedia entry told him it was a city in southeast Turkey. He clicked on the map embedded in the article. Just to the north-west of Gaziantep, in the foothills of the Taurus

489

mountains, was another city, marked by a T shaped-cross: Ruin – the place Melisa had listed as her birthplace. She had been going home.

The second result was more recent. It was an application for a temporary work visa dated only a year ago. She had been trying to come back to the States but her application had been denied. He noticed the name on the form was Erroll. Maybe she never married, or maybe had but had kept her name.

He looked at the two results, two more precious pieces of evidence of her continued existence, and felt an almost physical yearning to be with her. He pulled his phone from his pocket. The count-down application was now installed on it and running as his wallpaper. He watched the numbers steadily declining towards zero.

All the time he had lost. How much time left?

Kinderman's message was still open and he re-read it, hating him now for playing games when so much was at stake. It was like a taunt – 'If you're smart enough then come and get me' – a clever test to find out what he knew. Well, Professor Douglas had been standing on a hill, staring up at the stars and look where that got him. Maybe Kinderman had a similar place and that's where he was now, drawn there by the homing instinct. But Franklin had run checks on Kinderman's background and nothing like that had shown up.

. . . standing on a hill looking to the east for new stars in old friends, as those like us have done since the beginning of time.

What the hell did that mean? It wasn't enough to go on. He didn't have time to look up every old observatory in the world and then go and check them out on the off-chance Kinderman might be there when all he really wanted to do was get on a plane and fly to southern Turkey.

He froze as a thought struck him.

He clicked on the ghost icon and scrolled quickly through the document looking for the second lot of CARBON results. There they were:

GOBEKLI TEPE

HOME

There was a link next to the first one and he clicked it open to remind himself what it said.

Göbekli Tepe Turkish: [gøbɛkli tɛpɛ] [2] ("Potbelly Hill"[3]) is a Neolithic (stone-age) hilltop sanctuary erected at the top of a mountain ridge in the southeastern Anatolia Region of Turkey. It is the oldest known wholly human-made religious structure and also the oldest observatory, believed to have been constructed by the proto-religious tribe known as the Mala [1][4]

He clicked back to the map still open from earlier and typed *Gobekli Tepe* into the *Get Directions* field.

491

The map widened a little and marked a route there from Gaziantep. It was just over an hour's drive east. Ruin was a half hour's drive northwest. Shepherd closed the laptop and started the engine, his mind made up and his destination set. He could decide which way to go when he got there.

CHAPTER 86

The phone buzzed.

The Novus Sancti rose from his chair and quickly walked out of the building, answering it as he passed through a door and into the chill of the day.

'Yes?'

'Archangel is dead.'

Miss Boerman's voice sounded tense and stretched thin. Behind her he could hear the clamour of people.

'Where are you?'

'At the police station. They gave me my phone call so I called you.'

The Sanctus nodded, his mind working through the ramifications of this news, moving the various pieces in play around in his head like he was re-setting a chessboard. 'Archangel has served the Lord well, and so have you. Say nothing and the Lord will provide for you, both in spirit and of course in the more earthly matter of legal counsel.'

He hung up, uncomfortable about talking on an open line coming from inside a police station. He powered the phone down, prised the back off, removed the SIM card then crushed it under his boot.

Back inside the building he settled behind his desk, his face lit by the glow of a computer screen. He tapped a code to unlock it and an email program opened up. It was an online account operating behind a daisy chain of virtual networks, so anything sent to or from it was totally untraceable. He re-read the message he had been composing, his lips moving slightly as if uttering a silent prayer:

This is a warning.

Attached to this message is a countdown clock, discovered in the files of Dr Kinderman and Professor Douglas, two eminent astronomers who have gone missing.

The world knows something is coming. The armies are refusing to fight, snow falls in deserts and we are all feeling the spirit of God moving through us, sending us back to our homes so we might be ready for His arrival.

Judgement Day is upon us. You still have time but this countdown shows that time is measured in days not weeks. Show Him we still have faith and be ready for what is coming.

Repent and return to God while you still have time.

A friend

Novus Sancti

He checked the addresses against a list he had spent months compiling. It contained direct contacts for every major news outlet across the globe as well as the press offices of most major Western governments. He re-checked the various attachments: the countdown application found on Douglas's laptop; copies of the latest FBI and police reports regarding the events at Goddard and Marshall so they would take the message seriously. When he was satisfied everything was in order he typed three words into the subject line: *REVELATION OR DEVASTATION?*

Then pressed *Send* and watched his message fly.

CHAPTER 87

Liv came to with a start. The citrus smell was stronger now and mixed with something acrid and dry that burned the back of her throat. Someone was standing over her, holding a bottle under her nose and she turned, raising her hand at the same time to bat it away.

'Hey, take it easy. You're OK. It's just smelling salts.'

She blinked and looked back into the gentle eyes of the Italian doctor.

'What happened?' she asked.

'You passed out.'

Liv tried to get up but he laid a hand on her shoulder and firmly eased her back down. 'You should stay here for a while, get some rest. I've put you on a saline drip to get some fluids into you and there's some Perfalgan in there too to get your temperature down: you were up at forty degrees – not good. I also took the liberty of stealing a little blood.' He pointed at a small plaster in the crook of her arm.

'What's your name?' she asked.

'Giorgio Giambanco – hell of a mouthful, no? You can call me George if you like. What's yours?'

'Liv – Adamsen,' she added, defaulting to formality in the face of a medical professional.

'OK, Miss Adamsen, talk me through your fainting episode, was it sudden or did it come on gradually?'

'It was the heat I think. I started to feel feverish so I headed inside.'

He tilted her head up, checking the glands in her neck with his fingertips. 'Any nausea?'

'Yes, a little, and the ground felt like it was moving. I started getting tunnel vision. There was a smell too, like lemons.'

He frowned, checking her blood-pressure readings from a cuff. 'When did you notice the smell?'

'When I was still outside, though it was stronger inside the building. In fact I can still smell it.'

He was about to respond when one of the new people stepped into the room and placed a small tray on the countertop. It contained two small vials filled with blood and a piece of paper with various results written on it by hand. The new doctor shot her a smile that was hard to read then was gone. George ripped the Velcro of the pressure cuff from her arm. 'Sounds like heat exhaustion,' he said, turning to the blood results and picking up the piece of paper. 'You need to rehydrate and take it easy. No more demolition work in the midday sun for you.' He studied the results and frowned. 'You said you experienced nausea?' He looked up at her in a way that made her feel vaguely nervous.

'Yes.'

'Have you vomited at all?'

She shook her head.

'And you said you smelt the lemons while you were still outside the building.'

'Yes, I can still smell them.'

'And does the smell also make you feel a little sick?'

'A little.' She felt panicky. 'What is it? Am I having a brain haemorrhage or something? I read somewhere that people smell things before having a stroke.'

'No, no – it's nothing like that. What you're smelling is just some disinfectant we brought with us that they're now using to swab out the canteen. It's got some lemon scent in it, not much – I can't really smell it at all. But you smelled it way off when you were still outside the building.'

Liv's heart continued to race at the prospect of whatever was wrong with her.

'There are many things that can cause hyperosmia,' he said in a gentle way that wasn't helping. 'That's just a fancy word for an enhanced sense of smell. And your blood tests confirm that the reason for yours is very common.'

Liv relaxed a fraction. At least whatever she had wasn't exotic and therefore more likely to be treatable. 'What do I have?'

He smiled and the skin crinkled around his eyes. 'It's not so much what you have as what you're going to have. You're pregnant, Miss Adamsen. You're going to have a baby.'

PART VI

And I heard, but I understood not: then said I, O my Lord, what shall be the end of these things?

Daniel 12:8

CHAPTER 88

Shepherd parked the Durango in long-term parking and headed for the ticket office.

Charlotte/Douglas International Airport was the usual cavernous barn of a building and was in total chaos when Shepherd stepped through the door. There were long queues snaking away from every ticket desk and the whole building vibrated with noise and stress. A lot of it was coming from the large crowds of people gathered round the TV sets dotted around the waiting lounges and Shepherd felt sick when he saw what was on them.

It was the countdown Shepherd had seen in Douglas's cabin, the same one that was installed on his own phone, ticking down now on every screen. A caption beneath it read COUNTDOWN TO THE END OF DAYS? A sombre news anchor was talking to camera as a montage of images played out behind him – more riots, more roads clogged with migrating people, more cities dark and burning, and not just here but in major cities all over the world as the slow creep of panic spread. The picture cut to the smouldering wreck of the building at Marshall, then a heavily censored photo of Professor Douglas flashed up, hanging from the wall of his cabin, the word *Heretic*, highlighted on the wall next to him and a new caption flashed up: WHAT DID THEY SEE?

Shepherd drifted over to one of the ticket desks, avoiding eye contact with all the waiting passengers as he cut in at the head of the queue.

What did they see indeed . . .

'You'll have to wait in line, sir.' The man behind the counter was rail-thin and had the thickest eyebrows Shepherd had ever seen on someone under the age of fifty.

Shepherd flashed his ID. 'Government business.'

The skinny guy looked up. The eyebrows underlined the deep furrows in his forehead, reflecting the day he was having. 'OK, let me just deal with this gentleman and I'll be right with you.'

Shepherd waited while the man collected his boarding card then wheeled his carry-on away into the crowd.

'Now, sir, where do you need to go?'

'I need the first connecting flight to a place called Gaziantep. It's in southern Turkey.'

The eyebrows shot up and his fingers drummed across the keyboard. 'Best I can do is an indirect flight via Istanbul. Good news is it leaves in just over an hour.'

'OK, let's do it.'

'You have travel vouchers?'

Shepherd felt the blood rise to his cheeks. 'No. I'll pay for it on a card.'

Usually federal agents travelling on commercial flights had pre-paid tickets or documents that entitled them to fly. 'Checking anything into the hold, sir?'

Shepherd shook his head. The eyebrows shot up again in surprise. Shepherd hoped this guy never played poker for money.

The clerk finished tapping. 'That will be one thousand two hundred and fifty-eight dollars, sir.'

Something twisted in Shepherd's stomach as he handed over the card. It was more than he had anticipated and he wasn't sure if it would exceed his limit. The guy with the eyebrows swiped the card and stared at the ticket machine for what seemed like an eternity before it chattered to life and spat out a receipt. Shepherd retrieved his card.

'Boarding has already started, gate number twenty-two. Have a nice day.'

Shepherd took his passport and boarding card and moved quickly away from the desk. He shuffled through security, dumping the contents of his pockets into a tray. All he had was a phone, some loose change and a couple of credit cards. He'd had less in his life, but not much.

He stepped through the metal detector and stuffed everything but the phone back in the pocket of the coat he had borrowed from NASA. He took a deep breath and dialled Franklin's number.

'Morning.' Franklin sounded as tired as he felt. 'You made it to Charlotte?'

'Yeah, kind of. Where are you?'

'Driving home.'

'You seen the news?'

'Yep. Seems the end of the world will be televised after all. You got anything new for me?'

Shepherd ran through everything he had learned in the last few hours. It was cathartic, like a weight gradually lifting off him with every word he spoke. 'I've left the car in the long-term parking lot,' he said. 'Smith's laptop is in there and so is Williams's gun.'

'You're unarmed?'

'I didn't think they'd let me on an international flight with it seeing as they're not even letting people take large bottles of water on board.'

'What if it's a trap? What if Kinderman is drawing you out – ever think about that?'

'It's not just about Kinderman.' He took a deep breath like he was about to take a dive off a high board. 'I never did tell you about my missing two years.'

'You don't have to tell me if you don't –'

'I was homeless.' He let the breath out and imagined it drifting away in the air, carrying his confession with it. 'When the NASA funding was cut I ran out of money pretty fast. I dropped out of school, had no place to live, no family, no job. I was pretty depressed about how life had turned out and it dragged me down fast. It's a downward spiral and the lower you get, the less you care. And no one else cares either. It's amazing how easy it is to fall through the cracks and end up on the street. Then you become invisible.'

'So what happened to pull you out of it?'

'Melisa happened. You asked me who she was. She was a charity worker, here in the States on some kind of exchange visa. She found me in the stinking basement of a building in Detroit along with an assortment of junkies, winos and meth heads. I was only on the booze, which in some ways is even more pathetic. I wasn't even a proper washout.

'One day I was sleeping off a drunk when this angel appeared asking for Annie. Annie was a runaway teen who worked the streets to fund her habit and keep her pimp happy. She was also eight months pregnant. Melisa was part of the women's health programme, training to be a midwife and volunteering in her spare time. Annie had missed her check-up so Melisa had come into that stinking basement just because she was worried about her. That took some guts.

'Anyway, we found Annie unconscious, lying on a stained mattress in one of the smaller rooms in the basement people used sometimes to turn tricks. The reason she had missed her appointment was that she was in labour and had turned to her painkiller of choice. She was totally out of it, the needle still in her arm – and the baby was coming.

'Melisa was incredible. There was no sense of

judgement or disgust about what she was doing or where she was, she just got down to the business of bringing that baby into the world. And when it was born, something so small and perfect and new in the middle of all that filth, I felt ashamed.'

He took a deep breath as the memories came fast and painful.

'I was helping her clean the baby when the boyfriend arrived – a mean son-of-a-bitch called Floyd who kept in shape by handing out beatings to the women he ran and anyone else who got in his way. He saw the child and told us to leave. Melisa refused. I don't know if he was going to kill it and get Annie back on the streets and earning again, or maybe he had a buyer lined up – everything has a street-value, even a newborn baby.'

Shepherd stared out at the busy concourse but in his mind he was back in that basement room, filth, food wrappers and empty bottles on the floor, a fading *Apocalypse Now* movie poster tacked to the wall with a bright orange sun that shone no light into that dark place.

'Melisa refused to move. Floyd pulled a knife. I'd heard he'd been known to slice the face of any girl who crossed him so I reacted, grabbed a bottle from the floor and threw it at him. It caught him on the side of the head, hard enough to knock him back but not enough to stop him. Next thing I know I'm on top of him, knees pinning his arms down, another bottle in my hand. And I just kept hitting him with it. I knew if I let him get up he'd kill me and probably kill Melisa too so I just kept hitting him until he stopped moving. The bottle must have broken at some point and cut his neck. I didn't even realize. There was so much blood. It was like someone had turned on a tap.

'I can't even remember what happened next but somehow Melisa got us all out of there. She took us to the shelter where she worked and cleaned us all up. I was all for turning myself in but she told me not to. She said it was an accident, self-defence, and that I should wait until the police came looking.'

'Let me guess,' Franklin said, 'they never did.'

'I guess one less scumbag on the streets doesn't warrant too much of an investigation. So I stayed at the shelter and started getting myself back together. I kicked the booze, got on the twelve-step programme, started running computer training courses and setting up networks and websites for the charity, just making myself useful and giving myself an excuse to keep hanging around.

'God knows how but Melisa and I ended up falling in love. I guess we shared this big secret that created an intimacy and things just grew from there. Hell of a first date. We kept it all secret because of her father. He was the doctor who ran the project. He was a strict Muslim and I don't think he would have taken too kindly to the prospect of having an infidel ex-bum for a prospective son-in-law.

'Anyway, months passed and Melisa's visa was about to expire so I asked her to marry me – not because of the visa but because I loved her more than I've ever loved anything before or since. We had it all planned, we were going to slip away and just do it. Then a few days before we planned to run away something happened.

'Looking back I should have known something was wrong. Her old man called me into his office late one afternoon, said he had a job for me. There was another homeless organization we worked with way over on the other side of town and their computer network had melted down or something and they needed to fix it urgently. It was late in the day, rush hour, but I went anyway – anything to score points with my prospective father-in-law. When I got to the place the guy there didn't know anything about it so I turned right around and drove back again.

'By the time I made it back through all the traffic to the shelter the whole street was blocked off. There'd been some kind of incident. Someone had thrown petrol bombs into the place and the whole building had gone up. There were racist slogans painted on the walls too: Terrorists, Ragheads, that kind of thing – post 9/11 hate gone crazy. I tried to find Melisa and her father, checked the hospitals and everything, but they were gone.

'At first I thought they must be scared and hiding out somewhere. But when the weeks went by, then months with no word I thought maybe she'd had second thoughts about me, about living and working in a country that seemed to blindly hate Islam so much.

'I did what I could to find her, but the police weren't interested. They weren't technically missing persons and there was something suspicious about the fire. An insurance scam they called it.'

'So you joined the FBI to see if you could find her yourself?'

'Partly. Though in truth everything I told O'Halloran was also true. I do feel I owe my country a debt for everything it's done for me.'

He heard Franklin take a deep breath on the other end of the line. 'You know sometimes people disappear because they want to. Or they disappear because they're dead.'

'I don't think she is.' Through the phone he could hear the white noise of tyres in the background. 'You asked me a while back what "home" meant to me, well for me it's not a place it's a person, it's Melisa. She's where I'm trying to get to and if she was dead I don't think I'd feel what I'm feeling. Even if she doesn't love me, even if she never did, I still love her and I just want to know that she's safe. I just want to know she's OK.'

Shepherd glanced up at the Departure Board and saw *Last Call* flashing by his flight number. 'Got to go, Agent Franklin, I'll call you if I find anything useful.'

'Take care, Agent Shepherd. I hope you find

what you're looking for. And if you happen to find Kinderman and the world really is about to get smashed into a million pieces then do me a favour – keep it to yourself. I changed my mind, I'd rather not know.'

CHAPTER 89

Gabriel was woken by the sound of a bell clanging mournfully through the darkness. He opened his eyes and counted the strikes, ten in all, though there might have been more before. It had been evening when Dr Kaplan had started drawing blood. It was dark now, the room lit only by the glow of the monitors he was plugged into.

He stretched out in the bed and found his arms and legs were still bound tightly to it.

'Hello?' His voice fell away into the silence. It had to be later than ten to be this quiet. They must have taken his blood over to the main lab and left him to his rest, strapped down in his own private prison.

He listened to the sounds of the room: the faint beep of the monitor keeping time with his heartbeat, the whisper of fans keeping circuits cool and the soft bang of a door that sounded both close and also very far away as the echo bounced around inside the warren of the mountain. He looked back over at the window, his one real connection to the outside world, and felt a chill. Someone was there, a monk — standing by the door leading to the bedchamber. It was too dark to see his face, but Gabriel could make out the white surgical mask covering the lower portion of it, and above that, the lenses of a pair of spectacles reflected what light there was in the room, making it seem like the man's eyes were glowing. The heart monitor bleeped a little faster and Gabriel tried to calm himself by focusing on his breathing and doing what he could to take control of the situation. 'Good evening,' he said, as if he had met someone out on a stroll. 'You get lumbered with the night shift?'

The figure said nothing, staring at him with its luminous eyes. His silent scrutiny, the stealth of his appearance and the fact that he had not answered when he had called out combined to make alarm bells sound in Gabriel's head. He tensed his arms, testing the bindings. Too tight. He might be able to work his way out of them, given time, but his instincts told him he didn't have any.

'Are you here to take more blood?' he said, improvising. 'They said they'd be back at next bells . . .' He breathed out all the way at the end of the sentence, creating space where his inflated chest had been. He moved his right arm, the one nearest the figure, the one he would need to defend himself if it came to it. It shifted, just a little. He tried to bend his arm, breathing out further, the heart monitor racing again. It shifted a little more, but still not enough. 'What's your name?' he asked, breathing right out at the end of the sentence and trying again to loosen his arm.

'I will not give you power over me by volunteering

my name.' The man's voice was low and filled with malice.

'Suit yourself. My name's Gabriel.'

'I know what you are.' He moved closer.

Gabriel pressed himself into the bed. He saw something sharp in the man's hand. He looked around for something to defend himself with if he could get his arm free. The only things in reach were the wires connecting him to the various monitors now registering his growing anxiety.

He tried one last time to free his arm but it was no good. He looked back up at the glowing circles where the eyes should be and did the only thing he could do. He flicked the clip from the end of his finger.

A high-pitched alarm immediately split the silence. 'Technically, I just died,' Gabriel said. 'People will be running here right now to try and restart my heart.'

The eyes shifted to the door then back to the bed. 'Then pray they are quick.' He lunged forward, the metal of the blade flashing in the dark. Gabriel watched it rise up, breathing out as far as possible to create what space he could inside the cocoon of his bindings then shoved himself violently to one side as it arced down. The movement was enough to jar the bed and shift it a couple of inches so that the blade caught the side of his chest instead of the heart where it was aimed, slicing flesh and glancing off a rib before burying itself in the mattress.

Gabriel felt pain burn in his side, but put it from his mind, staying focused. The stabbing movement had brought the monk's head close to his own and he seized his chance, spitting full in his face. The monk recoiled, dragging the knife free from the mattress, too shocked to raise it again.

'I carry a mutated form of the infection,' Gabriel shouted at him, his words the only weapons he had, 'harmless to me but deadly to others. That's why they keep me here. You have maybe thirty seconds to wipe it off or you'll be dead within a day.'

The monk reached up to his face but did not dare to touch it. Beneath the wail of the cardiac alarm the sound of running feet could now be heard. The monk looked at Gabriel one last time then turned and ran from the room, heading back to the bedchamber and the washroom beyond.

Gabriel could feel blood trickling down his side and pooling on the mattress and he wondered if he had any left. The main door flew open and Athanasius rushed in followed by Thomas, Kaplan and a couple of others. 'Someone just tried to kill me,' Gabriel said, wincing as bright lights flickered on. 'He went in there.'

A loud bang echoed from the bedchamber and Athanasius ran over. 'He's gone into the private stairway,' he said, disappearing after him. 'The door's locked,' he shouted from inside, 'he must have a key.' He reappeared and looked down at the blood spreading through Gabriel's bindings then turned to Father Thomas and uttered a single word with such venom that it sounded like a curse.

'Malachi!'

CHAPTER 90

Shepherd was one of the last people at the gate but one of the first on the flight. The guy with the eyebrows had apparently given him priority boarding, another nod to the power of the badge.

He found his seat over the wing and by the window and settled gratefully into it. The sun had struggled into the sky and hung low, just below the clouds, shining straight into his face. He closed his shutter and palmed his phone, figuring he had maybe ten minutes before someone made him turn it off. He had used the time queuing at the gate to try and chase down a number for some local law in Ruin. He was going to ride the Bureau ticket as long as he could, hoping it would take him all the way before he got derailed. Sooner or later he was going to have to answer questions about the MPD searches and why he had held on to and pursued leads rather than share them. There was every chance that this particular flag might go up while he was in the air. Which meant he needed to make contact now while he still had some access and leverage.

He opened the page he had found for the Ruin City Police Department and hit a hotlink to dial the main switchboard. A foreign-sounding ring-tone purred in his ear then someone answered in a clipped, businesslike tone he understood but in a language he did not.

'You speak English?'

'Little.'

'My name is Joseph Shepherd, I'm a Special Agent with the United States Federal Bureau of Investigation. Do you have an international liaison officer I could speak to?'

'Moment please.'

Non-descript music filled his ear as he was put on hold and he watched the rest of the passengers embark. They were all dark-skinned and black-haired, Turkish people heading back to their country of birth he guessed, answering the call to go home.

'This is sub-inspector Kundakçi. How can we help?'

Shepherd told him everything he had learned about Melisa, only stopping short of revealing the real reason he was looking for her. He threw in some details about the missing American journalist Liv Adamsen, hinting that she might be in some way connected. He needed a plausible reason to be calling from an American law enforcement agency to ask about a Turkish national and this was the best he had come up with. He left him his name and number and then hung up just as a stewardess marched towards him, her over-made-up orange face a mask of stern disapproval.

'You need to turn off all electronic devices and have the shutter in the upright position until after take-off, sir.' She continued down the aisle looking for further infringements of the rules. Shepherd turned his phone off, slid the shutter back up and turned his head away from the direct glare of the sun. He was exhausted, and his nerves were shot after the unbelievable day he'd had. He'd been blown up, crossed six states in various forms of transport, discovered the brutal murder of someone he knew personally and found out that the love of his life was still alive. The flight time to Istanbul was nearly nine hours and he planned to sleep for as much of it as he could.

He closed his eyes and thought of red threads stretching tighter, to pulling him towards her. He smiled and settled down in his seat, not daring to tilt it back for fear of incurring the stewardess's wrath. He was asleep before they turned the engines on. He didn't see the only other Americans get on the plane and take their seats ten rows in front of him, a man and a woman. She glanced in his direction once before she sat down, briefly registering the man she had last seen through the sights of her sniper scope, then settled in her seat and rested her head on the shoulder of the man, cosying up and getting comfortable for the long flight to Turkey.

CHAPTER 91

Athanasius and Father Thomas reached the top of the stairs and stopped, listening to the still darkness of the upper mountain chambers. By the time Athanasius had retrieved torches and the key to the staircase Malachi had a five-minute head start on them.

'He'll get to the library long before we will,' Thomas said through grabbed breaths, 'then he'll lock the reading room door behind him.'

Athanasius nodded. 'We should make for the main entrance, it's nearer. How quickly do you think you can break in?'

'If we're not worried about tripping any alarms it will be easy.'

'I think the time for stealth has passed,' Athanasius said, and started to descend.

It took them ten long minutes to snake down the stairs and reach the library. Athanasius leaned against the wall, relishing the cold of the rock as Thomas prised the hand scanner off the wall with his pocketknife, bared two wires and touched them together.

The door slid open with a hiss and a puff of air showing that the positive pressure within the climate

518

controlled library was still active. It was designed to keep mould spores and other undesirables out of the air surrounding the priceless collection of texts. It would also be an effective way of slowing the penetration of the airborne infection into the library. Malachi was clearly being selective about exactly which parts of modernity he was turning his back on.

Thomas stepped forward and looked up, bracing himself for the shriek of the intruder alarm. 'He must have de-activated the motion sensors,' Thomas said when none came. 'That's why the lights are not working.'

Athanasius moved past him heading into the main collection. It was a strange experience, moving through the library without the usual glow of a follow light. The sweep of their torch beams revealed much more than he had ever seen before. The follow lights usually only allowed one to glimpse isolated parts, so seeing it in its vast entirety like this, the vast bookcases filled with every great thought mankind had ever had, made him profoundly sad: it was like finding a whale kept captive in a tank when it was used to having the whole ocean to roam in.

'Reading rooms,' Thomas said, shining his torch over to a set of doors up ahead. Athanasius reached the door to the reading room of the Sancti and twisted the handle. 'Locked. Do you think he's passed through already?'

Something clattered to the floor in the distance giving them their answer and they hurried after it. The noises continued as they made their way through the library. It sounded like some great creature was lumbering through the dark, bumping into everything as it made its way. They passed into the next chamber and discovered the cause of the noise. There were books everywhere, swept from the shelves by the armful onto the floor. It was like a horde of vandals had ransacked the place, pulling everything from the shelves and shredding the pages.

'Why is he doing this?' Thomas surveyed the devastation as they moved through it. 'No one loves the library more than Malachi. It makes no sense for him to do this.'

'I don't think he is in full possession of his senses. I think his world has fallen apart and this is a manifestation of it.'

They rounded a corner and saw light up ahead, coming from inside the Crypto Revelatio.

'Malachi!' Athanasius called out. 'We just want to talk.' He switched off his torch and inched down the corridor towards the light, the room beyond the arch coming gradually into view. It was in even greater chaos than the rest of the library with books and piles of paper spilling out of the door into the corridor. 'There's only one way out of there, Malachi. It's a dead-end. If you don't come out then we will come in.'

'Stay back,' Malachi's voice boomed from the chamber.

'We're just here to talk. We want to help you but we need to understand what you read in the Starmap that has made you do this to your beloved library, and try and take a man's life?'

'That is no man.'

Athanasius glanced over at Thomas who was inching his way forward along the other side of the tunnel. 'For mercy's sake, Malachi, tell us what you read.'

'It doesn't matter, it's too late anyway. You should have let me kill it before it becomes too strong.'

Athanasius reached the edge of the arch and peered into the room. It was a riot of mess, the neat order of the library turned into a scene of chaos with shelves half-emptied and the floor crammed with paper and scrolls like the nest of a huge rodent. Malachi sat at the centre of it behind a desk piled high with more paper and illuminated by a row of guttering candles.

'Tell me what you read, Malachi. Let us look at it together and perhaps we will see something different in it.'

Malachi looked up, his eyes huge behind the pebble lenses. 'You are wrong,' he said, picking up another candle and holding the wick to the flame of the last one. 'You have been wrong all along: wrong about modernizing the Citadel, wrong about allowing civilians inside the mountain.' The wick caught and he turned the candle in his hand until the flame grew brighter. 'And wrong about there being only one way out of here.'

He dropped the candle into a pile of paper and it erupted in a whoosh of flame. Athanasius leaped forward to try and stamp it out but Malachi stood up fast, heaving the table over as he did so, tipping the row of candles onto more piles of dry paper to create an instant wall of flame.

Father Thomas looked up at the ceiling, expecting the CO2 system to activate and smother the fire. But nothing happened. Malachi had de-activated that too. He grabbed Athanasius and heaved him backwards. 'We need to get out of here.'

'And you are also wrong to think you have stopped me,' Malachi shouted after them from inside the inferno, smoke rising up around him as his cassock started to burn. 'There is more than one way to kill a demon.'

CHAPTER 92

Athanasius staggered backwards from the entrance, disbelieving the horror of what he had just seen. Already the smoke was thick in the air and the fire was spreading from the Crypto Revelatio, igniting pages from spilled books lined up along the corridor in readiness.

'Run!' Thomas shouted.

'But Malachi . . .'

'Malachi is gone. He cannot be saved, we must do what we can to save the library.' He kicked a pile of books aside, trying to create a firebreak, but there was too much loose paper lying around and the flames caught them instead and sent burning embers floating through the air towards the tinderbox of the next chamber. 'Positive air pressure is feeding the fire,' Thomas shouted above the roaring flames. 'Our best hope is to get back to the control room and turn the gas extinguishers on before the whole lot goes up.'

They stumbled away from the fire, feeling the heat at their backs and tasting smoke in their mouths. The main entrance was a fifteen-minute walk away, maybe five minutes' running, but they were both exhausted and Athanasius was also in deep shock from what he had witnessed. He could not get the image of Malachi out of his mind, eyes blazing in victory, ecstasy almost, as he himself started to burn.

He turned a corner and felt cool air wash over him as he ran through the snowdrift of torn pages littering the Bible room. He was coughing from the smoke and could hear the crackle and roar of it behind him. He risked a look back. The flames had not made it into the room. He could see the glow of the fire but it was still contained in the corridor beyond. Maybe they would have a chance to stop it spreading.

Just as this thought crossed his mind a figure straight from hell burst through the door, arms outstretched and dripping fire as it ran straight at them, covering half the distance before it stumbled and fell, straight into a pile of torn pages and tortured Bibles that blazed instantly into flame. The whole room was burning in seconds, flames sucking ravenously at the air and billowing thick smoke. They were running now, all thoughts of fatigue banished by pure fear. The fire was almost keeping pace with them, leaping from shelf to shelf and room to room, roaring at their heels like a hungry predator with the scent of blood in its nostrils.

They made it to the reading rooms and hammered on the doors, rousing the few black cloaks still resident there. 'FIRE!' They both shouted, pounding on the next door. 'Run to the exit.'

The black cloaks emerged sleepy and stunned. A few, feeling protective of their domain, saw the fire and started running towards it. 'It's too late,' Athanasius shouted after them, pointing at Thomas who was already at the door of the control room. 'We're going to switch the fire extinguishers back on. Just get out and warn the others what has happened here.'

Athanasius followed Thomas into the control room and found him standing in the middle of it staring at the smashed control panels and broken screens. There would be no quick fix of the fire systems, Malachi had seen to that.

Athanasius tugged at Thomas's arm, dragging him out of the room and over to the entrance. The door to the airlock was still open and a steady flow of air was breezing through it, sucked by the conflagration now feeding on the library. The black cloaks had already gone and the fire was almost at the entrance hall now, its expansion like a slow explosion that was tearing the library apart. Thomas fumbled in the wall cavity where the scanner had been, found the wires he'd stripped earlier and touched them back together just as the smoke reached them and vomited from the door. The wires sparked and the door slid shut, slicing through the smoke and cutting off the noise of the fire.

'Will that hold?' Athanasius asked between gulped breaths.

'Only for a while.' Thomas levered off the cover of the second scanner and worked fast to strip more wires and hot-wire the second circuit. The second door slid shut, cutting off the sound of the fire entirely. Athanasius looked through the glass panels in both doors. The fire had reached the entrance now and was creeping along the desk and casting Halloween orange light over everything. It was like staring into hell.

'We have to get away from here,' Thomas said. 'When these doors give way the whole mountain is going to turn into one giant chimney and every corridor will fill with smoke.'

Athanasius remembered the last thing Malachi had said – there is more than one way to kill a demon – this must have been his plan. But he had forgotten about one thing.

'Follow me,' he said, hurrying away down the corridor. 'I know where we will be safe.'

The garden was quiet and dark when the first stretcher emerged into the cool night. The trees were all gone, burned along with the bodies, and shadows flickered on the high moonlit walls picking out the first columns of smoke leaking from the mountain as if the long-ago volcano that had formed the crater had woken again and was starting to boil.

'We should occupy the very middle,' Athanasius said, 'in case the heat causes rockfalls.'

More and more stretchers came out of the mountain and began to collect in neat rows in the middle of the garden, like eggs from a broken anthill. Everyone worked in silence, the earnest urgency of their task focusing all effort on saving those who could not hope to save themselves. Only when the last stretcher had been carried out into the cool night air did anyone stop to take stock of their situation and perform a head count. There were only five people missing, Malachi and the four doctors who had chosen to remain in the Abbot's quarters, their contamination suits protecting them against the smoke and their desire to continue their work outweighing any fear they had of the fire.

Athanasius patrolled the rows of beds, struck by how quiet everyone had become. Inside the cathedral cave the sounds of suffering had been like a solid thing, trapped along with everything else. Out here the few moans that escaped the cracked lips of those bound to their beds drifted upwards, mingling with the smoke on their way to the heavens. There was a freedom out here in the garden, you could close your eyes and imagine the walls away. He closed his eyes, and did just that, imagining himself far, far away from here, while all around him his world continued to burn.

CHAPTER 93

Gaziantep International Airport was crammed with people, noise and heat. Shepherd stepped into it feeling he'd landed on a different planet.

He'd checked his phone in the transfer lounge in Istanbul but the cop he had left a message for still hadn't called him back. On the short hop to Gaziantep he had slept again, though it had felt like the blink of an eye.

He stood in line now, sweat trickling inside his shirt and jacket from more than just the rising heat. He pulled his phone from his pocket and switched it back on, looking across the heads of the people in front of him at an armed guard standing behind the passport booth, the unfamiliar uniform underlining how far he was outside his jurisdiction. The doors that had so far opened at the flash of his badge would remain firmly shut here. But the ache he felt inside, the one that was pulling him towards Melisa was so strong it was almost painful. He knew she was here and that this was exactly where he needed to be.

The phone caught a signal and vibrated in his

hand. The countdown clock was still running on the screen, the number much smaller than it had been before, and he had one voice message from a blocked number. He called voicemail and lifted the phone to his ear, his heart beating so loud he wondered if he would be able to hear anything.

The message was short – a man's voice, heavily accented but speaking English.

'Hello my name is Davud Arkadian. I am an inspector with the Ruin police. Your number has been passed to me along with your various enquiries. I have some information for you but it would be better if we talk. Please call me when you get this message.'

He reeled off a phone number and Shepherd fumbled in his jacket for a pen to scrawl the number on his hand then copied it into the phone adding the international code for Turkey. The call would be bounced back to the States before coming here again and probably cost him about a hundred bucks a minute. He would worry about that if he was still around to get the bill.

The line moved forward. The ringing tone filled his ear, mingling with the loud beating of his heart. He recognized the Inspector's name from the newspapers they'd found in Kinderman's house. He'd been shot in the course of investigating the death of the monk and had been involved with the missing Americans he had name-dropped to lend some weight to his request for information about Melisa. It was possible he was about to be tripped up by his own subterfuge and have to listen to a detailed report about someone he had little interest in.

'Alo?'

'Hi. Is that Inspector Arkadian?'

'Yes.'

'This is Agent Shepherd – from the FBI.'

'Oh yes, thanks for calling back. Apologies for the lateness of the hour.'

Shepherd glanced out at the brightening day. 'I'm not in the States. I just landed in Turkey.' There was a pause on the line. 'You said you had some information,' Shepherd prompted.

'Yes.'

'About whom?'

'About Melisa Erroll mainly.'

Shepherd felt the blood drain from his face and he had to take a deep breath to steady himself. He glanced up and saw the guard frowning in his direction. There was a sign by his head with a picture of a cellphone with a line through it and something in Turkish that undoubtedly said 'No phones.'

'Listen,' Shepherd said, suddenly paranoid that his only lifeline to everything was about to be confiscated. 'Can I call you back in a few minutes?'

'Where are you exactly?'

'I'm at Gaziantep Airport, I'm just going through passport control.'

'Write this down.'

Arkadian was already reeling off directions and Shepherd scrawled them on his hand beneath the phone number. His eyes flicked between the message and the guard.

'Give these directions to a taxi driver and give my name when you reach the first roadblock,' Arkadian said. 'I'll see you in about forty minutes.'

CHAPTER 94

The fire took two days to burn its way through the entire collected works of mankind, and another five before the smoke cleared and it cooled down sufficiently for anyone to venture safely into the part of the mountain where the library had been.

Thomas was the first to step through the remains of the airlock. Both doors were gone entirely and the metal frames that had held them were twisted beyond recognition. He stood in what had once been the entrance, awed at the blackened nothingness the library had become. The black cloaks followed him, one of them breaking down when he saw the devastation.

'See what you can salvage,' Thomas said, 'and I will do the same.'

The control room was protected by a steel door that was still warm to the touch when Thomas tried to open it. It had buckled in its frame, jamming it tightly in place, giving him hope that something beyond it may have survived. He found a length of metal on the floor, part of a table, and jammed it into a gap in the side of the ruined door. He leaned back, heaving on the bar until the door shifted with a shriek of tortured metal. He shone his torch through the gap and hope fell away into the darkness beyond.

The fire had got in here too. Even though the door had kept the flames out the air must have still become superheated and ignited everything flammable in the room. Without oxygen it hadn't burned for long but it had been enough to destroy everything. The control systems and circuitry had all melted and fallen down through the racks, collecting on the floor in bizarre puddles of solidified plastic and wire. He grabbed the sides of the door leaving finger marks in the soot and wrenched it open, wide enough to step through. Practically his whole life's work had been contained in this room. It had been the most technologically advanced and sophisticated library preservation system ever devised but in the end all of it had been undone by a madman with something so simple as a fallen candle.

He took a breath laced with smoke and headed to the far end of the room where another steel door the size of a briefcase was set into the stone. He wiped the soot from the dial protruding from the centre so he could read the numbers then carefully dialled in the code to open the safe.

One of Thomas's initiatives had been to create a digital copy of every single item in the Great Library. It had taken nearly five years to accomplish. The entire collection – millions of books and hundreds of millions of pages – had fitted onto just eight removable storage disks and they were kept in this safe.

The door he was unlocking was fifteen centimetres thick and the rest of the safe was set into solid rock, which should have helped keep the insides cool. Even so, the fire had been so fierce that the drives might still be damaged. But as long as they were still intact he could repair them and effectively rescue the contents of the library from the flames.

He dialled in the final number, twisted the handle and heaved open the door. He stared at the glowing interior, untouched by flame or smoke and looking totally incongruous amongst the devastation. But it was empty. In truth he had half expected it. There was only one other person who knew the codes to this safe.

Malachi had been thorough if nothing else.

CHAPTER 95

It took Shepherd five attempts and an offer to pay double the fare before he finally found a taxi driver willing to take him to Ruin.

'I only go as far as roadblock,' the driver said, 'then you walk.' Shepherd took it, thinking it had to be better than walking from the airport, which seemed his only other option.

He sat in the back of the cab on worn fabric seats, breathing in the chemical scent of vanilla air-freshener and watching the unfamiliar countryside and olive trees flit past his window. Ahead of him the Taurus Mountains rose up in a jagged horizon. He tried not to think of what might lie ahead or what he might be about to learn. There could be no turning back now.

The road curved up into foothills, cutting out the sun so it seemed as though they were entering a valley of shadows. They rounded a bend and saw a long line of red brake lights ahead, lighting up the gloom and stretching away to a distant barrier manned by armed soldiers wearing battle fatigues and surgical face masks. The taxi pulled to a stop at the end of the line. There were at least twenty other cars in front of them, a few other taxis but mainly family cars laden with luggage, exactly like the ones Shepherd had seen heading into Charleston.

'Crazy people,' the driver shook his head. 'Who comes here?'

'They're just heading home,' Shepherd said.

The driver shook his head and kissed his teeth.

There was some kind of discussion going on at the barrier with the soldiers who kept shaking their heads, their eyes hidden behind sunglasses, their fingers pointing along the lines of their guns, ready to drop to the trigger if things got out of hand.

'I'll walk from here,' Shepherd handed the driver some notes and got out without waiting for change.

The air outside smelt of cypress sap and wet stone, a huge improvement on the chemical tang of the taxi. Shepherd walked along the edge of the road, his eyes fixed on the barrier ahead. One of the soldiers sensed him coming and turned the black discs of his shaded eyes towards him, twisting his body at the same time so the HK33 slung across his chest was pointing in his direction. Shepherd smiled and raised his hands over his head, one of them holding his badge.

'I'm an American police officer,' he said, arriving at the barrier and stopping short of it. The soldier said nothing. 'I'm looking for an Inspector Arkadian. You speak English?'

'No, he doesn't.' A bear of a man in his early

fifties squeezed past the soldiers and peered at Shepherd's badge through a pair of half-moon, tortoiseshell glasses perched above surgical mask. He held a hand up in greeting and showed Shepherd his own ID badge identifying himself as Inspector Arkadian. 'You're a little far from home, Special Agent.' He looked up and fixed Shepherd with sharp eyes. 'Normally we have a little more warning about international cooperation efforts.'

'I apologize for the suddenness of my appearance.' Shepherd lowered his hands and slipped his badge back in his jacket, his mind flipping through various options of what to say next. The road sat at the bottom of steep walls of drilled rock so the only way to go any further was past the roadblock. But he had no authority here and the soldiers didn't seem to want to let anyone through. 'Can we talk somewhere in private?' he said, gambling on this at least getting him the right side of the barriers.

Arkadian considered for a moment then said something in Turkish and the soldier in front of Shepherd stepped aside to allow him to pass. He stepped through the barrier and heard the clamour of voices double in volume behind him as the other drivers saw what had happened.

'These people,' Arkadian said, nodding back at the queue, 'more of them arrive each day. They were all born here. They don't care that the city is still under quarantine, they just want to go home. Especially now that this countdown has appeared on the news.'

'It's the same all over,' Shepherd said. 'Everyone getting ready for the end of the world.'

'Not quite everyone,' Arkadian said, reaching a car and unlocking it. 'For some people the world has already ended.'

He didn't elaborate and Shepherd didn't pursue it: but as they drove away from the roadblock and down an empty road he could feel the sadness coming off the Inspector like something tangible. He selfishly hoped it had nothing to do with the news he was about to hear.

CHAPTER 96

The cab pulled up outside the battered building on the outskirts of Gaziantep and Eli stared out at the noisy, busy street. He was in some kind of merchant district with warehouse shops spilling onto the streets and men milling about and haggling energetically and loudly over everything. He showed the driver the piece of paper he had written the address on, convinced they couldn't possibly be in the right place.

'Is here,' the driver said, pointing at a faded blue door set into the wall. 'Is church.'

Eli paid the man and got out, feeling edgy. They'd had to split up at the airport, Carrie following the FBI agent, him heading off to fetch supplies from a local contact Archangel had set them up with. He never liked being away from her, particularly somewhere like this where there were so many triggers for bad memories: the dry heat; the loud conversations in an alien language and eastern-sounding music blaring from somewhere; the shabby buildings lining dusty streets; the missile minarets of a mosque sticking up above the rooftops. He didn't like it – not at all – the whole place screamed 'hostile'.

He moved over to the door, scoping the street as he went, automatically looking for sniper positions and ambush points. There were too many to count and the men who had been bartering for goods started to turn their attention to him. Behind him the cab began to move away and he felt a strong urge to run after it, get back in and get the hell out of here. But then Carrie would be disappointed with him and he couldn't bear to see that sad look in her eyes or know that it was his weakness that had put it there.

He walked over to the door, sweat starting to prickle his scalp, and looked for a name or a sign, anything that might prove he was in the right place. A stack of different doorbells lined the sides of the frame with the names of businesses or individuals he didn't recognize pinned to each one. The address and instructions Archangel had given him said he was coming to a church, but there was no sign of one here. Panic started to bubble low down in his chest as he realized that, with the taxi now gone, he could be stranded here. He should have made the driver stay until he'd checked it out. Stupid! Carrie would be furious if he came back with nothing. Then he saw it, etched on the plastic case of one of the doorbell buttons, so small anyone would miss it unless they were looking specifically for it – a small cross.

He pressed the button and waited, feeling the

eyes of the street upon him. He listened out for sounds of movement beyond the thick door but all he heard was the music of the street sounding strange and unsettling to his ear. He was convinced the volume of the conversations had dropped and that they were now talking about him. He pressed the button again, wondering if the cable that ran out of it and burrowed into the wooden frame like a fat worm was even connected to anything. He felt exposed. Vulnerable. Alone. Sweat beading in his cropped hairline started to run down the sides of his face. He was on the point of turning round and walking away when a loud crack sounded inside the door making him jump. A gap opened and a round, moonlike face appeared in it. The man was dressed in the traditional long white tunic with a keffiyeh wrapped around his neck. He barely looked at Eli, his restless, bloodshot eyes sizing up the street before opening the door wide enough to let him pass.

Inside the building was dark and old and smelt of leather and dust. A staircase ran up the centre with doors leading off each landing to the various businesses that had been advertised all the bell buttons by the main door.

Eli followed in silence, keeping close to the wheezing, waddling figure of his contact until they reached the very top of the stairs and a plain door that was carefully unlocked with a set of keys kept on a leather thong around the fat man's neck.

Eli had bowed his head and prayed in some

weird churches in his time but this one was in a league all of its own. The room was tiny, about the size of a small garage, with a bedroll in one corner and a solitary window crudely taped up with old newspapers to form the sign of the cross. On the floor beneath it votive candles burned on a broad plank of wood set atop a wooden crate, their flames wavering in the disturbed air.

The man closed the door and locked it before leaning towards him and whispering with sour, tobacco breath, 'We must be careful, for we are under siege here. The enemy is outside the door. We should pray before we get down to God's business.'

He dropped to his knees facing the window, crossing himself before opening his arms wide and holding them up to the ragged, paper-edged cross.

'Lord our Father, bless us and protect us in all that we do in your holy name. And give us the strength to go into battle against the forces of Satan that inhabit your holy lands and help us to defeat those who would seek to destroy you.' He leaned forward as if prostrating himself before the Lord, took hold of the edges of the wooden board and removed it, candles and all, to reveal a neat line of weapons laid out on a blanket beneath.

Eli reached inside the crate and picked up a Ruger. It looked tiny in his hand but it wasn't for him. He checked the action and removed the clip. It only held six rounds but that wasn't necessarily a problem. Carrie was the best shot he had ever seen. For himself he took a Zigana K, a Turkish semi-automatic he had fired before, and a folding hunter's knife.

'Ammunition?' he asked.

The man turned round in the small space and flipped the bedroll over to show a hatch cut into the floorboards. He lifted the panel out to reveal boxes of ammunition as well as something else Eli had not expected.

'I didn't ask for a suicide vest,' he said, his eyes fixed on the bundle of explosives and wires like it was a coiled snake.

The fat man glanced at him. 'You are not the only soldier of God who needs a sword,' he said, handing him boxes of shells for the guns he had chosen. 'And yours will not be the only battle fought here in the days to come.'

CHAPTER 97

Arkadian turned off the road just short of a second roadblock. Beyond it the city of Ruin spread out like a ghost town. There were no people visible, no cars moving down the streets. The only movement was a military truck, crawling along the long wide boulevard that arrowed its way to the centre of the city where the Citadel rose like a spire.

'This is sort of a no-man's-land,' Arkadian explained, 'far enough away from populated areas for the air to be deemed safe by the health authority. We use it as a command centre for policing the quarantine. You're safe here but I still have to ask you to put on one of these.' He leaned into the back of the car and fished a fresh surgical mask from an open carton. Arkadian waited for him to put it on before he opened the door and stepped out.

Shepherd was struck by the sound coming from the other side of the large building they were walking towards – the shrieks and laughter of children playing, their voices tinkling and swooping like birds in the air. 'This is one of the kindergartens,' Arkadian explained. 'All the children have been evacuated from the city now.' He pushed through the entrance and went inside.

The lobby was choked with posters for mountain hikes and biking and handwritten postcards on pinboards offering guided tours of the Old Town. Arkadian walked over to a door in the far wall that opened into an office with a few desks and computer terminals. 'Welcome to the police department,' he said, moving to a desk in the corner. 'It doesn't look much but it's plugged in to all the relevant databases, all the ones you require, at least.' He pulled a second chair over and gestured for Shepherd to sit then typed in his log-in name and password. Shepherd noticed he was favouring his left hand.

'How's your arm?' he asked. 'I read about what happened.'

'You ever been shot, Agent Shepherd?'

'No.'

'It hurts more than you would imagine and it's still not properly fixed. The mornings are worst and it aches whenever the weather is about to change.'

The screen flickered and Shepherd caught his breath as a photograph of Melisa appeared.

'Melisa Ana Erroll,' Arkadian said, catching Shepherd's reaction. 'What is your interest in her, exactly?'

'I'd like to talk to her – in relation to an on-going investigation.'

Arkadian turned in his seat and stared straight

at him. 'Shall we be honest with each other?' Shepherd shook his head like he wasn't sure what he meant. 'I'll start shall I?' Arkadian offered. 'When I got your message I called a few people and ended up speaking to your partner.'

'Franklin?'

'You have another partner?'

Shepherd shrugged. 'I'm not sure Franklin would call himself my partner.'

'Well, whoever he is he told me everything, or at least enough so that I know why you're looking for this woman.' Arkadian removed his glasses and pinched the bridge of his nose. 'This is never easy and there is never any way to say it except straight. Melisa Erroll fell victim to the blight four months ago when the spread was still in its early stages. She was taken into the Citadel for treatment and apparently died three days later.'

Shepherd couldn't breathe. Part of him didn't believe it. He felt the ache inside, stronger now than ever, the red threads still pulsing and twisting.

He looked at the screen in case the photograph wasn't her. But it was.

He was suddenly aware of everything: his breathing, the way his clothes touched his skin, how his whole body felt awkward in this seat, in this room. He was aware that Arkadian was still talking, and studying him with his knowing eyes, but he couldn't hear what he was saying. He tried to concentrate until some of his words swam into focus. 'Do you need a minute?' He shook his head.

'According to the records her father contracted it first and she looked after him until he was taken into the mountain. Then she fell ill herself.'

Shepherd took a breath and felt his voice vibrating in his head. 'Is she – is her body buried somewhere?'

Arkadian shook his head. 'All victims of the blight are cremated inside the Citadel.'

Shepherd put his hand to his chest where he still felt the ache. 'She can't be dead,' he said. 'I can feel her.'

Arkadian looked at him for a moment, his eyes curious. Then he rose from his chair. 'Come with me,' he said, 'there's someone you should meet.'

Shepherd drifted after him like a ghost, down a long corridor with open doors to dormitory-style bedrooms on either side.

'Wait here,' Arkadian said, pointing through one of them to a room filled with triple-decker bunks. Shepherd went in and sat awkwardly on the edge of a bed, leaning forward, elbows on his knees, unable to sit upright in bunks that were built for kids. The sound of children playing rose in volume as Arkadian went outside then faded to silence again as the door shut behind him. The beds were still ruffled from sleep, a different stuffed toy standing guard by each pillow. The one he was sitting on had a rabbit on it. Next to the bed three small suitcases were lined up against the wall, each containing the whole world of an evacuated child.

The door opened again to let the swooping

shrieks of happy children flood back into the building. Shepherd looked up to discover a young girl standing in the doorway, her small hands clasped in front of her, her head tilted forward so her dark, wavy hair fell over her face, giving her something to hide behind. Two dark eyes peered out from behind it.

Her mother's eyes.

Shepherd stared at her, not noticing Arkadian standing behind her until she pressed herself back against his leg. 'Hevva, this is Mr Shepherd.'

'Joseph,' he said, smiling at her to try and put her at ease. 'Do you speak English?'

She nodded, a move so tiny he wouldn't have seen it at all but for the movement of her hair. 'Are you real?' she asked.

Shepherd's smile broadened at the strange question. 'As real as you.' He frowned in mock seriousness. 'Unless you're not real, are you real?'

Another tiny nod, this time with the flicker of a smile.

'I knew your mother,' Shepherd said.

'I know,' the girl said, her voice sounding older than her years. She took a step forward, those familiar eyes watching him all the way. She still seemed a little wary of him and he didn't want her to be. She was a living reminder of the woman he had loved and he just wanted to look at her.

She stopped in front of him, held out her clenched hands and opened them. Inside was a locket, held on a chain around her neck. She slipped it over her head, waves of hair tumbling over her face as the chain pulled free of it. He took it and looked at her, not sure what she meant by giving it to him. Then she reached out and – with tiny, nimble fingers – she opened it.

Tears flowed down Shepherd's cheeks when he saw what was inside. It was a tiny photo of Melisa, bordered in black, and opposite it – a picture of him.

CHAPTER 98

Gabriel continued to improve.

His occasional fits dwindled to nothing and after a few weeks he no longer needed to be strapped to his bed. But as his strength returned, so did his desire to leave the mountain and return to Liv. Dr Kaplan assured him that, though great progress was being made with his blood work, they still had not found a cure, nor had they ruled out the possibility that Gabriel was an asymptomatic carrier. He still had the virus inside him, it just wasn't killing him any more.

Rather than sitting around he made himself useful where he could. He spent a lot of time sifting through the ash and rubble in the Crypto Revelatio, hoping he might find some of the clues they needed to interpret the Starmap. But the fire had been so intense that even the clay tablets had baked to dust and the few stone items that survived offered nothing but more lost languages and further riddles to solve.

He travelled only through the upper stairwells and corridors so he would encounter no one. On his way back he sometimes took a detour to the chapel of the Sacrament with the hideous Tau silent at its centre, the front hanging open on its hinges revealing the spike-lined interior. It was a hideous place, a place where the Sacrament had been held captive for millennia until Liv had finally freed it. And it was for this reason alone that he came here, just to walk the same floor she had walked, and sit on the same floor where she had lain. Once, after sitting there a while, he had stood and spotted a long strand of blonde hair – her hair – floating down through the beam of his torch. He caught it in his hand and now kept it wound round his finger like a ring.

Weeks passed in this way. Months passed.

Then one morning, Gabriel was shaken awake as dawn had just started to lighten the blue and green glass of the peacock window. It was Dr Kaplan, black rings circling his exhausted eyes. 'Come with me,' he said.

Gabriel had not been through the main door since entering on a stretcher almost seven months previously. They turned right outside, heading away from the cathedral cave into a section of the mountain Gabriel had never been before. The corridors were wider here and well lit with doors set into the stone at regular intervals. One of them opened ahead and a visored face peered out, saw Kaplan and Gabriel and ducked straight back in, closing the door behind him but not before Gabriel caught a glimpse of the complicated laboratory set up in the room.

'In here.' Kaplan stopped outside a door with a circle cut into it and a plastic tube poking out from within. 'I think it's best I give you some context first.'

He opened the door and stood back to allow Gabriel to enter.

The room was a smaller version of the Abbot's quarters with a main reception room and another door set in the far wall. It was filled with so much equipment it made the one he had just seen look like a high-school chemistry class. There were banks of sleek, hi-tech-looking microscopes, scanners, computers, centrifuges and a large air-conditioning unit keeping it all cool, the snake of its plastic vent poking out through the hole he had seen in the corridor.

'Very impressive,' Gabriel said, taking it all in.

'The outside world has been very generous,' Kaplan replied, heading over to a large machine with a video monitor set up on a desk next to it. 'Anything we ask for gets shipped in the next day. Things move pretty fast when everyone has such an interest in our success.'

He flicked a switch and the monitor glowed into life showing a hugely magnified image of an uneven sphere with lethal spikes coming out of it. 'Meet KV292, more commonly known as the Blight or the Lamentation – the enemy. Do you know much about viral infections?'

'Only that they hurt.'

'But do you know why?'

'Not exactly.'

'What they do is invade a host and hijack healthy cells then reprogramme them to start manufacturing the virus instead.' He hit another key three times and the image stepped in until the tip of one spike filled the screen. It had a small bar across the end, making it look like a tiny, elongated letter T. 'Each one of those spikes you can see is topped off with what's known as a glyco-protein that acts like a sort of key to fool the cell's defences into letting the virus pass through its protective membrane. Once inside it releases strands of rogue DNA that find their way to the nucleus and then reprogramme it.'

He tapped another key and the picture on the screen changed to a similar-looking ball. 'This is also KV292, only we found this one in your blood. See the difference?' The ball in this image was covered with much smaller spikes making it look like a burr. 'Something is happening inside your system that knocks the ends off the spikes so they can't interact properly with healthy cells. They just float around in your blood where they get covered with antibodies until the white blood cells pick them up and digest them. They never get a chance to reproduce because they can't get inside your cells. They've lost their keys.

'Ever since we isolated you over here in this part of the mountain we've been looking for the mechanism that does it. The trouble is, with the hostile virus deactivated in your blood, the reagent that interacted with it no longer has a job to do and so has vanished. We haven't been able to find a single trace of it.

'Over the past few months we have tried everything to replicate the circumstances of a primary infection.

We screened every newly infected patient to find matches for your blood-type and then created a cocktail of your blood and theirs to see if this mystery reagent would reappear and go back to work, but it never did. Ultimately we realized the problem lies in the fact that we are always working with samples that are already fully infected. Viral infections and their reagents tend to grow and develop at the same time and at the same rate, the one triggering the other and keeping pace with it so the virus can never get fully established. This happens with things like the common cold where the antibodies start being reproduced as soon as the virus appears. If it didn't every cold would develop into a more chronic form such as pneumonia, which is what happens in immuno-suppressed people.'

He sat down on the chair in front of the screen, his weariness evident in the way his shoulders slumped inside the contamination suit. 'What we need to do is catch someone with your blood type before the virus has fully established itself and then cross-transfuse your blood with theirs. This will hopefully give us two chances of catching the reagent in action: once in your system as the infected blood starts mingling with yours, and again in the other patient as your healthy blood encounters the infection in theirs.

'However, there is a risk. If the mechanism has been completely deactivated in your system then you may end up being re-infected, with little chance of survival. There is also a risk for the other patient. This mutated form of the virus you now carry may be harmless to you but could still be very harmful to others. In trying to find a cure for the blight we may end up killing someone.'

Gabriel took it all in, the polished cleanliness of the room, the clinic quiet, the serious tone in Kaplan's voice. 'I'm assuming by the fact that you woke me up to tell me all this that you have found someone.'

Dr Kaplan nodded. 'The problem has been finding someone with your exact blood type, which unfortunately is particularly rare. You are O negative, which in Turkey is shared by less than five per cent of the population. We blood-typed everyone still healthy inside the Citadel and found one match. The reason I woke you is because this person has just exhibited the first signs of the blight.' He rose from his chair and moved across the room towards the door to the bed chamber. 'For this to stand any chance at all of working we need to act fast before it fully takes hold.'

He reached the door and opened it.

Beyond was a bedroom, two beds in the centre lined up next to each other, an array of tubes and equipment arranged around them. One was empty, the other contained a man, propped up, strapped down and breathing steadily. His eyes flicked over to the door and locked onto Gabriel's.

'Good morning,' Athanasius said. 'Forgive me if I don't get up.' He smiled but Gabriel could see there was fear beneath it. He moved over to the side of the bed and laid a hand on the monk's arm. His skin was already starting to burn.

'I admit,' Athanasius said, 'I am surprised this hasn't happened sooner. I was starting to hope that maybe I too had some form of natural resistance. But this morning I awoke for morning prayers and could smell nothing but oranges.' He shuddered and closed his eyes as something started to rise inside him. It reminded Gabriel of when the blight had first taken hold of him in the heat of the Syrian desert. He knew the torments Athanasius was starting to experience, the heat, the itching, the panic. The shaking eased and Athanasius breathed out and opened his eyes again. 'I must also admit,' he said in a soft voice that still carried traces of the tremor, 'that I am more than a little afraid.'

Gabriel took his hand, just as Athanasius had taken his so many times in the preceding months when their situations had been reversed. 'Don't be afraid,' he said. 'It's just a journey. Let's go on it together.'

CHAPTER 99

Shepherd spent the rest of the morning with Hevva, sitting by a fence in the playground like a kid himself, telling her stories about her mother, digging back into his memory for all the details he had held on to for so long. She told him stories too, sketching in glimpses of the woman he'd lost. He was amazed at how grown up Hevva seemed as she told him, in the unvarnished words of a child, how she had gone everywhere with her mother because there was no one else to care for her, and how she had helped with her work, learning to deliver babies while she was little more than a baby herself. Hearing these stories made him both sad and immensely proud. But it also posed a difficult question, one which Hevva's eerie maturity prompted him to ask.

'Do you know why your mother never tried to contact me?'

Hevva shrugged. 'She thought you were dead.'

'Do you know why?'

'Grandpa said you died in a fire.'

Shepherd closed his eyes and nodded. He was transported back to the evening when Melisa's father had sent him on the fool's errand across town in the middle of rush hour. He had thought it odd at the time and now he knew why. It had all been a set-up to get him out of the way long enough to stage the fire. The fire served as a disguise for their simultaneous disappearance, and as the basis of a wicked lie that would separate his daughter from Shepherd for ever. Perhaps Melisa had told him they planned to marry and he had taken desperate measures to ensure that never happened. The police had said the fire was suspicious, an insurance job gone wrong and they had been partly right, it was only the motive they'd got wrong. Had her father known Melisa was pregnant, he wondered – had *she* even known at the time? What must her father have shown her to make her believe he was dead? What proof had he fabricated to stop her from looking? If he had gone to such lengths as to burn down a building, he felt sure a fake death certificate would not have been beyond him. Maybe even faked-up news stories coupled with the race-hate angle to scare her away from looking into his evidence too closely.

He felt a small hand on his face and he looked up into the deep knowing eyes of his daughter. 'Don't cry,' she said, 'Mummy still loved you, even though you weren't there. That's why she kept your picture.'

Shepherd smiled and placed his hand over hers. Being with this quiet, wise girl made the painful ache that had grown inside him disappear entirely. In her he had found what he was looking for, only not in the form he had expected.

His phone buzzed in his pocket and the world outside started to creep back in. 'I got to take this, honey,' he said and he saw her eyes darken as if she knew it was trouble.

'Agent Shepherd,' a familiar voice said the moment he picked up, 'it's Merriweather, the Hubble technician you spoke to at Goddard.' He sounded anxious.

'Oh, hi.'

'You said I should call if anything came up. Well it has. Hubble has stabilized. It's in a new travelling orbit that places it in a fixed position in the northern sky.'

'Whereabouts?'

'In Taurus, right between Nath and Zeta Tauri.'

Shepherd frowned – directly between the horns. For the past few hours he had succeeded in pushing the investigation into the furthest recess of his mind: now it all came flooding back. He remembered the words of Kinderman's cryptic message: *I'm just standing on a hill looking to the east for new stars in old friends, as those like us have done since the beginning of time.*

And tonight Hubble would show up in the night sky as a new object, the sun shining off its reflectors, making it look like a new star in the constellation of Taurus. Shepherd stood up and waved across the playground at Arkadian. He needed to get to Göbekli Tepe before nightfall to stand a chance of catching up with Dr Kinderman. With the new star appearing in Taurus tonight, tomorrow Kinderman would probably be gone and he would have no idea where.

'How's the investigation going?'

'What?' He had forgotten Merriweather was still on the line. 'Oh it's – moving forward. Listen, Merriweather, that's been a great help. How you doing with getting the guidance systems back online?'

'Not so great. We could do with Dr Kinderman's help. I hope he's OK and you find him soon. It's not the same here without him.'

'Let me call you tomorrow, I may have some good news.'

'Really?'

'Yes, really.'

He hung up and turned to Hevva. 'Honey, I have to go somewhere but you need to stay here. But I'll be back tomorrow, I promise.'

The dark eyes brimmed and her head started to shake. 'You won't come back,' she said. 'Mummy didn't.'

He dropped down so his eyes were level with hers. 'It's not like that,' he said, taking her tiny hand in his. 'You'll be safer here.'

'I don't want to stay here.'

'But I can't take you, not yet. There'll be forms to fill in and tests I probably have to do so they can establish that I'm your father.'

'Problem?' Arkadian had arrived next to them.

'I need to go somewhere and Hevva doesn't want me to leave.'

'Where do you need to be?'

'An archaeological site about two hours east of here.'

'Göbekli Tepe.'

'You know it?'

'Everybody in Ruin knows it. It's supposed to be a rival shrine to the Citadel, built by the enemies of the Sancti. Why do you want to go there?'

Shepherd thought about all the things that had brought him here: the recovered data, the link with Taurus, the cryptic message from Kinderman. It was difficult to know where to start. 'It's complicated,' he said.

Arkadian looked down at Hevva and smiled. 'Tell you what, why don't I drive you there, that way we can bring Hevva along and you can explain it all on the way.'

CHAPTER 100

Gabriel never left Athanasius's side. He had promised he would go on this journey with him and, having walked that painful path himself, it was not a promise he could break. When Athanasius was not sedated he raved and howled and strained against his bindings, like every other victim of the blight had done, but unlike most he was sometimes lucid, just like Gabriel had been. They would talk in these snatched moments, and Gabriel would lie and tell him how well he was doing and how much the doctors were learning from being able to study him. In truth, they were still searching, racing against the clock to find whatever process was happening inside him before it went one way or another.

Gabriel had been unaffected by the cross-transfusion. Whatever defences his body had built were too efficient to allow the infection to take hold again. Dr Kaplan remained in quarantine too, never leaving the room for so much as a minute. He knew he had a very narrow window of opportunity to first identify and then study the reagent as it attacked and defeated the virus, and he didn't want to waste a moment of that precious time sleeping. He had a cot set up in the corner of the lab for him and the other technicians to use whenever exhaustion overcame them. There were five of them in total, each keeping their own particular brand of vigil: Gabriel, Kaplan, two technicians as dedicated and ever-present as he was, and – at the centre of it all, burning like a hot sun around which the rest of them revolved – Athanasius.

Whenever the attacks got so severe they had to sedate him, Gabriel slept in the cot too, making sure he was awake again by the time the sedative wore off. Then, one morning, three weeks after the transfusion, Gabriel woke in the cot to discover Athanasius was already awake. He rose and moved over to the side of the bed, holding the back of his hand to Athanasius's forehead. 'The fever's gone,' he said, a smile spreading on his face. 'You didn't die.'

Athanasius smiled back. 'Apparently not.'

Dr Kaplan was summoned from the lab where he was doing blood work. He stared at Athanasius from the safety of the door when he first came in. After so many months of failures and death it was like he had forgotten what success looked like. Athanasius's recovery was the final piece in the jigsaw. Kaplan and his team had successfully managed to find and isolate the reagent, but had held off from introducing it to other patients until they knew for sure it was going to be effective. They didn't want patients to have to endure the kind of drawn-out suffering Athanasius was going through if they were just going to die anyway. Better that they die quickly and suffer less than going through that. But now he was better, everything had changed.

The Blight had been conquered. They had found a cure.

And Gabriel could finally make good on his promise and return to Liv.

CHAPTER 101

Hevva fell asleep in the back of the car before they'd even made it out of the Taurus foothills and picked up the toll road heading east. Shepherd kept turning round to check on her, her face a perfect miniature of her mother's, her very existence casting a much darker light on the countdown that was still ticking away on his phone. He told Arkadian everything, finding that once he started it all came tumbling out until by the time they saw the first sign for Göbekli Tepe, Arkadian knew as much about the investigation as he did.

They turned off the main road and passed through an automatic toll barrier onto a battered track leading away into the parched, undulating countryside. There were no houses here, not even the square, flat-roofed brick blocks that seemed to be the architectural model of choice in this part of the country. There was no sign of anything at all, no greenery, no animals, only the single-track strip of black road leading them straight into the alien landscape ahead. The only reason they knew they were in the right place was the presence of a few road signs, put up for the benefit of tourists, pointing the way to the hill they could just see in the distance with a solitary tree standing sentry at the top of it.

Shepherd stared out of the window, feeling the heat coming through it despite the air-con blasting cold into the cabin. It was hard to imagine that this desolate place, burned dry and littered with broken rocks, had been home to a civilization that pre-dated the Egyptians by seven thousand years: all gone now and forgotten, ground to elemental dust by the passing of time, just like everything else in the universe.

'What if your Dr Kinderman's not here?' Arkadian said.

Shepherd looked up at a collection of tents and temporary buildings clinging to the side of the hill. 'If he's not here then it's the end of the road – for me at least.' He looked in the back where Hevva was sleeping. 'What's that thing people say – all your priorities change the moment you have kids?'

Arkadian shook his head and smiled sadly. 'I'm sure it's true – it never happened to me.'

'Me either, until a couple of hours ago. You married, Inspector?'

Arkadian shook his head. 'Not any more. I lost my wife to the blight around the same time Hevva lost her mother. That changes your priorities too.'

They pulled off the road and bounced up a dust track towards the settlement and came to a parking area big enough to cater for the strange mix of tourists and archaeologists that visited the dig. There was even a trough of straw to feed the camels. Today the area was empty but for a couple of cars so dusty they were almost the same colour as the earth.

Arkadian crunched to a stop beside them and waited for the dust cloud they had kicked up to drift away before switching off the engine and stepping out into the heat.

Shepherd unclipped his seat belt and glanced in the back hoping to sneak out and leave Hevva sleeping. A pair of dark eyes stared at him from beneath a shiny fringe of wavy, chocolate hair.

Shepherd smiled at her. 'We're just going to have a look around,' he said. 'You stay here. We won't be long.'

The eyes went wide. 'Don't go,' she said. 'You won't come back.'

'Of course I'll come back. You'll just be safer here,' he said, reaching out with a hand to stroke her face.

'If it's safer here, you stay here too,' she said.

Shepherd couldn't argue with that logic. 'I'll only be five minutes. Five minutes then I'll come right back.'

She shook her head and the tears continued to flow. 'I don't want to stay here alone.'

He looked into her imploring eyes, made huge by fear and bright with tears. 'OK,' he said, powerless in the face of an emotional child. 'But stay close and keep quiet.'

Hevva stayed so close that Shepherd kept nearly tripping over her as they made their way up the track to the buildings and the tree beyond.

Arkadian glanced sideways at them. 'How's parenthood?' he asked.

'Complicated,' Shepherd said, squeezing Hevva's tiny hand. 'I'm sure I'll get used to it. I've only been a dad for a few hours.'

They reached the edge of the dig site marked out with strings of barbed wire nailed to posts. The hill was only partly excavated, like something massive had taken a bite out of it leaving behind the monolithic T-shaped standing stones like lost teeth. They were huge and almost perfectly smooth, their size and finish in marked contrast to the broken jagged edges of everything else around them. Figures were carved on the surface of the stones, low reliefs of animals and human arms stretching round the stones as if hugging them. A wooden walkway cut right across the top of the site, suspended a few feet above it. He could see tools and buckets lying on the ground at various points, as if everyone had just stopped what they were doing and left. It was eerie, a ghost town, one that had been dead for nearly ten thousand years.

'Guess nobody calls this place home any more,' Shepherd murmured, imagining the workers responding to the growing tugging sensations inside them, urging them to be elsewhere.

'We have company,' Arkadian said. Shepherd

squinted up against the bright sky and saw a slender man standing in the shade of the tree, backlit by the sun. 'You think that could be him?'

'Hard to tell,' Shepherd said, instinctively pulling Hevva behind him. 'He's the right build. I should go talk to him.' The tiny hand tightened in his. 'It's OK, sweetheart, you'll be able to see me the whole way.'

'Take this,' Arkadian pressed something into his hand. Shepherd looked down to discover a gun. 'It's just a precaution.'

'I don't think that's . . .'

'Take it. I don't care how many Nobel prizes this man has won, he is still a fugitive from the law, which makes him unpredictable.'

The figure beneath the tree moved forward, emerging from the shadow.

'He's coming down,' Shepherd said, handing the gun back.

'Keep it,' Arkadian said. 'I'm too slow and can't shoot worth a damn since I took a bullet in my arm.'

Shepherd thought about his own less than glowing record as a marksman but slipped it into the back waistband of his trousers anyway, angling himself so his whole body was between the gun and Hevva.

The figure continued to descend the hill, picking his way down a thin gravel path that snaked its way down from the tree: a slender man with silver hair and a Nobel prize for physics on his CV, Dr

Kinderman – fugitive from the law. He reached the upper edge of the dig and did a strange thing – he waved at them.

'He doesn't look like a man on the edge,' Arkadian muttered.

'He's spent his life on the edge of the universe,' Shepherd replied. 'This probably all feels quite normal to him.'

Dr Kinderman rounded the rim of the crater and approached them, a warm, friendly smile fixed to his face, like a man just welcoming weekend guests to his house. 'You found me,' he said, his voice nasal and high, like the whine of an over-grown, over-enthusiastic schoolboy.

'Joseph Shepherd, sir.' Kinderman clasped the offered hand and shook it. 'I worked under you briefly on the Explorer mission.'

'Please.' Kinderman held his hands up and screwed his eyes shut like he was in mild pain. 'Call me William, or Will, or Bill even, but don't call me "sir", makes me feel like your father.' He let go of Shepherd's hand and dropped down to the ground. 'And who do we have here?' Kinderman brought his head right down to Hevva's level. 'Are you an FBI agent too?'

Hevva went shy and smiley and buried her face in Shepherd's side.

Kinderman stood and turned to the dig site. 'Magnificent, isn't it? A temple to the stars, built eight thousand years before the pyramids in Egypt and then deliberately buried to hide it and preserve its secrets. You can't really see it properly from here, it was designed to be viewed from up there.' He pointed back up at the tree on top of the hill. 'Interestingly enough the locals call that the tree of knowledge, always have done – even when they didn't know all this was buried beneath it. Isn't that fascinating?'

Shepherd felt like a schoolboy on a field trip with one of the better teachers.

'Shall we go inside?' Kinderman gestured to one of the larger field tents. 'It's cooler in there and I have something I want to show you.'

They filed into the tent and through a visitor's area with information posters on partition walls and a scale model of the dig site on a table in the centre of the room. There was a washroom through one door and a kitchen through the other with a stove and a table positioned beneath a ceiling fan that turned slowly, stirring the air and blowing dust into the shafts of sunlight leaking in through shuttered windows and a back door that had been propped open to let more air in.

'You wouldn't believe there were about thirty people here a couple of days ago, would you?' Kinderman said, lighting the gas on the stove. 'Yesterday there were ten and this morning just me, so I apologize in advance for the mint tea I'm about to make. I don't really have the art of it, which is a shame as it's delicious when done properly.' He put a pot of water on to boil and grabbed a bunch of mint from a bowl of water by the sink.

'I can make tea,' Hevva said.

'Are you sure?' Shepherd said, suddenly worried about the stove and boiling water in his first real moment of everyday parental angst.

'Mama showed me how to do it. She showed me how to do lots of things.' Hevva slipped off the bench and headed to the stove without waiting for anyone's permission and held out her hands for the mint. Kinderman handed it over without a word, then she dragged a chair across to the countertop and started ripping up handfuls of leaves and dropping them into a teapot. Shepherd felt a surge of pride as he watched her, though none of who she was or how she behaved was anything to do with him.

'So,' Kinderman said, moving over to the table containing the model of the dig, 'notice anything?' Shepherd looked down at it. It was perfectly to scale and even had a model tree at the top. In this shrunken form it was easier to see the configuration of the standing stones. 'They're constellations,' he said, remembering the Wikipedia entry he had read.

'Exactly, perfect facsimiles.'

Shepherd looked down at the main cluster. 'All except this one,' he pointed at the tallest stone, the home stone, which sat between two others representing the tips of the horns of Taurus. 'There is no star here, not normally – except tonight there will be, won't there, Dr Kinderman?'

Kinderman smiled. 'Bravo, Agent Shepherd, you are a worthy adversary, no wonder you found me.

And in the tradition of all great quests your triumph entitles you to some answers. What would you like to know?'

In his mind Shepherd cycled through all the things he'd been asking himself ever since O'Halloran had given him the initial brief. He decided to start at the beginning and work forward from there. 'The space telescope,' he said, 'why did you sabotage it and destroy all the data?'

Kinderman cocked his head to one side in a way that made Shepherd think of a bird. 'That's a bad question, Agent Shepherd. It is built upon two assumptions, both of which are wrong, which therefore renders the question moot.' Shepherd felt like a student again, one who was flunking a test. 'Firstly,' Kinderman continued, 'you say that I sabotaged Hubble, which implies something destructive when in fact Hubble was not destroyed, it was not even damaged.'

'What about Marshall? That was fairly destructive.'

'Yes it was, but again you are assuming that those two incidents are directly linked and that the architect of one must therefore have had a hand in the other.'

'No, I think you did one and Professor Douglas did the other but that your motives were shared.'

'Well then you are half right. I did reposition Hubble, as I have already said, but I did not destroy James Webb or the cryo unit at Marshall – and neither did Professor Douglas.'

'Then who did?' Arkadian asked.

Kinderman looked at him and shrugged. 'The same person who was sending us the death threat letters I should imagine, the one who signs his name *Novus Sancti*.'

'Cooper.'

Kinderman laughed. 'Fulton Cooper! You think someone like him could infiltrate the Marshall Space Center and blow a large part of it up without detection?'

'No, we thought maybe Professor Douglas did after being coerced in some way.'

'You knew the Professor didn't you Agent Shepherd?'

'A little – he was my tutor for a summer.'

'Then surely you know he was the sort of person who would rather die than destroy his own facility. His work was his life, he valued nothing higher.'

Shepherd felt like a green shoot shrivelling in the blinding brightness of a superior mind. All his thinking had been based on the assumption that Kinderman and Douglas were co-conspirators and saboteurs. But with that keystone gone the whole structure of his investigation was now starting to crumble. 'But if he didn't destroy Marshall then why run and hide?'

'Because we both feared for our lives,' Kinderman replied. 'And, considering what happened to the poor Professor, with very good reason it seems.'

Hevva arrived at the table with a steaming pot

of tea. She was struggling with the weight of it and Shepherd reached out to take it from her.

'You should have told someone,' he said, pouring the hot liquid into several small glasses shaped like tulips. 'The police could have protected you.'

'Protected us from whom? You just told me you thought our antagonist, the one who calls himself *Novus Sancti*, was Fulton Cooper. If the FBI cannot identify this person, then how could they possibly protect us from him? Whoever is behind all this has to be someone with a high level of access, someone inside the establishment and well connected, someone with a very clear agenda. The Professor and I both realized this. And when we both received the same letter we knew we had to act quickly. My repositioning of Hubble served as a useful diversion, a sop if you like to the black-mailers' demands to "take down the new Tower of Babel", it bought us some time. But it also served a practical purpose, one which was outlined right here ten thousand years ago then buried to protect the secrets and those who kept them.'

'The Mala,' Arkadian said.

Kinderman nodded. 'The history of the Mala is the history of suppressed truth. At the beginning of human history things took a wrong turn. Truth was imprisoned along with the relic known as the Sacrament. But the Mala knew the history of it and their enemies, the Sancti, tried to silence them. They established their Church to spread their version of history and declared that anyone who believed anything different from the word of their Bible was a heretic and should be put to death. So the Mala hid and buried their secrets underground until the time predicted when things would swing back the other way and balance would be restored. Over time many were drawn to the Mala, scientists whose findings challenged the Church, philosophers and thinkers who questioned the "truth". It was an organization that allowed free thinkers to remain free. And it still is. Without their support I would never have been able to flee from America undetected. They are like the French resistance in the Second World War, only on a global scale, providing friendship, support – even a passport under a different name.' He drained his cup of tea and smiled at Hevva. 'That, young lady, is delicious tea.'

She smiled shyly, picked up the drained teapot and took it back in the kitchen to top it up with hot water.

'In 1995, excavations started here and the first T-shaped stones were uncovered. The T is the Tau – symbol of the Sacrament, used by the Sancti and the Mala both. The mountains to the west are named for the Tau, and so also is the great constellation of the bull, which the ancients of our tribe saw as sacred, a harbinger of change. The rediscovery of these stones and the messages captured here told us that the time of change was coming. A time we refer to as the end of days. The established Church uses similar terms though they have demonized it as something terrible. But there is nothing to fear from the end of days. For every end also marks a new beginning.'

'Hello!?'

The voice took them all by surprise, puncturing the moment and making all heads turn. It was a woman's voice, American. They heard the faintest of footsteps outside then a tiny woman stepped through the door. She looked at them each in turn, smiling in a way that made her freckled nose wrinkle a little. Then a muffled shriek snapped their heads back round again.

A man was standing in the kitchen.

And he had Hevva.

CHAPTER 102

S hepherd saw the man first, then the knife held loosely against his daughter's throat. Hate boiled up inside him, but also fear. There was something in the man's eyes, something missing, that told Shepherd he would kill his daughter just as easily as snapping a twig.

'Any weapons, let's see them, nice and easy,' the woman said in her Sunday-school teacher's voice.

She was by the entrance, covering them with what looked like a toy gun. The man was behind them with a knife. Smart tactics. It made it impossible to look at both of them at the same time and ensured they wouldn't get caught in their own crossfire. If Shepherd was with a partner they would automatically take one each, but he wasn't. He was with an astronomer and a cop who had just given him his gun because he couldn't shoot straight. He felt it now, pressing into the small of his back, hidden by his jacket.

'I don't have a gun,' he gambled. 'They don't let you take them on international flights.'

The woman pointed her gun at Arkadian. 'Nice

and slow, mister police man, take it out by the barrel then slide it over.'

'I don't have a gun either,' Arkadian replied.

'You expect me to believe that?'

'Not really.' His movement took everyone by surprise. He darted right, drawing the woman's gun away from the rest of the group as he reached into his jacket.

Shepherd reacted too, only one thought filling his brain as he pulled the gun free from his belt.

A man is holding a knife to my daughter's throat.

He saw Hevva's terrified face pass through his sights as they settled centre mass of the man. A gunshot boomed behind him but he stayed focused. The man started lifting Hevva up to use her as a shield.

Shepherd adjusted. Squeezed the trigger.

The man jerked backwards as the bullet hit him and Hevva dropped to the floor. Every instinct made Shepherd want to run to her but his training stopped him.

A gun had been fired behind him.

He corkscrewed round, dropping down to make himself a smaller target. The woman was in a good two-handed stance, professional and well-drilled, her gun turning towards him, no chance of missing at this range and almost ready to fire. He willed his gun round faster, knowing it wasn't going to happen.

Scalding liquid hit her face and her head jerked away, pulling her aim wide. Shepherd's gun-sight settled on her tiny frame just as she was pulling her gun back towards him. The impact of the bullet threw her backwards against the open door, knocking the gun from her hand and out of the door.

He looked across and saw Kinderman holding the empty glass that had contained the mint tea. Arkadian was down, sprawled on the floor and not moving. Shepherd knew he should check the shooter was down and her gun made safe. He should check on Arkadian to see if he was hit. He should do all of these things like he had been taught but instead he turned and sprinted over to Hevva.

She was sitting on the floor, bright blood running through the hand she was holding to her cheek.

She should have stayed in the car.

He should have made her stay in the car.

He fell to the floor beside her and took her face in his hands, feeling the wet warmth of her blood as he checked her over, terrified of what he might find. He almost laughed with relief when he saw that the knife had just nicked her ear.

The knife-man was lying on the floor behind her in a spreading pool of his own blood. He was just about breathing but the wound was sucking and foaming. Lung shot. He was drowning in his own blood. A nasty way to go but Shepherd didn't care. 'I never knew dying would feel like this,' the man whispered as he stared up at the ceiling. 'I never knew it would hurt so much.' Then the sucking sound stopped and he was still.

Shepherd bundled Hevva into his arms and carried her over to the others.

Kinderman was standing over the woman, holding her gun in his hand like it might bite him. Shepherd could tell by the way the woman was lying, crooked against the door, that she was dead. Arkadian was still down, blood spreading out beneath him. Shepherd set Hevva down and crouched low to look into Arkadian's face. His eyes were open and he was still breathing – but only just.

'I didn't know you had another gun,' Shepherd said.

Arkadian smiled weakly. 'I didn't.'

'Then why . . .?'

'You needed a diversion,' Arkadian whispered between snatched breaths. 'Look after your little girl. Life ceases to have much meaning – when you lose the ones you love.'

Then he closed his eyes and was gone.

CHAPTER 103

T he first batch of inoculations took place the same day Athanasius woke up. All the infected in the cathedral cave, forty-seven men and women, were given the serum one after the other, almost wiping out the stocks at a stroke.

When every patient had been injected Dr Kaplan returned to the main lab and took an ampoule of the serum from the fridge. There were just twelve doses left and they were expecting new cases of the infected within the hour.

He copied all the clinical files to a flash drive then hand-wrote a note to his opposite number coordinating the medical effort outside the mountain.

Ekram,
The serum contained in this vial has been successful in curing one patient so far but we are conducting further trials on all remaining patients. I pray it is successful – we all pray it is. I leave it to you and the politicians to decide how much of it should be produced and when but my advice would be to make as much of it as you can right away. We can always destroy

*it if these trials fail, but we cannot suddenly
conjure it out of nothing if they succeed.
All the details of its makeup are contained in
the enclosed drive.
Yours, Ahmet Kaplan*

He packed the vial inside a shockproof container
and placed everything inside a padded envelope,
which he took to the tribute cave himself. He had
not been in this part of the mountain for months.
The air still smelt of smoke from the fire in the library
and reminded him of all the bodies he'd seen burned
in the garden.

No more – he promised himself – Please God, no
more.

The platform was being prepared when he entered
the cave, ready to be lowered to collect the day's
batch of infected. The wooden platform rocked as
he walked across to the box reserved for correspondence and placed the envelope in it.

He returned to the cave and watched the platform
sink down through the hatch and out into the clear
air carrying the first bit of good news to leave the
mountain in many months.

CHAPTER 104

Shepherd carried Hevva out of the kitchen and into the sunlight. He didn't want her to remain inside with the freshly slain and the smell of gunpowder in the air.

He sat her down in the shade of an awning and bathed her face, wiping away the worst of the blood then dabbing it clean with wet tissues, all the while talking to her, telling her she was fine and even starting to believe it himself as the blood washed away. Head wounds always bled more than most. The nick in the ear was all she had suffered, at least physically. She had also witnessed her new-found father shoot two people dead. He didn't want to think what the long-term effects of all that might be.

He looked into Hevva's eyes and was about to tell her to sit tight while he went in search of a sticking plaster then thought better of it and scooped her back up into his arms. There was no way he was going to let her out of his sight – not now, probably not ever again.

They found a medical kit in an office and he picked up the whole thing, figuring it would be better to get away from here as fast as possible in case the killers were not alone. Only Kinderman seemed to have vanished.

He spotted him up at the top of the hill, sitting in a chair in the shade of the tree and staring down at something in his lap. Shepherd carried Hevva all the way up, sweating from the effort. 'We need to leave,' he said.

'Indeed,' Kinderman replied, his eyes fixed on the screen of a laptop connected by a long wire to a portable satellite up-linker. 'But the real question is "where?" Look.'

Shepherd moved round so he could see the screen. 'This shows Hubble's new orbit,' Kinderman pointed at a graphic image of a wireframe globe with a circle round it. 'The other image is a direct feed from Hubble itself. That's what it's looking at right now.'

Shepherd leaned against the trunk of the tree for support and stared at the crawling satellite image of the Earth. At the moment it was showing desert, lots of brown desert, so barren it could easily have been the surface of some distant, uninhabited planet.

'I told you shifting Hubble out of position had a practical dimension,' Kinderman continued. 'Not only will Mala worldwide see it appear in Taurus tonight, it will also lead the way back to the home we all lost. Back to the origin of everything, where everything started and everything will begin again.'

'The Mala Star,' Shepherd whispered, remembering Kinderman's messages to Douglas.

They watched the crawl of brown, Hevva getting heavier in his arms with every passing minute until he had to let her slip to the ground. He was exhausted and hot and a little faint after the adrenalin high of earlier. He was anxious to get away and was about to insist as much when a thin line of green appeared on the screen, getting thicker as the world turned revealing a large patch of green with tendrils snaking out across the brown earth like the roots of a huge plant.

'There it is,' Kinderman said, with something close to wonder. 'Paradise found.' He squinted at the telemetry and wrote down the terrestrial coordinates. 'It's southeast from here, about a thousand kilometres or so, somewhere in Iraq. Less than a day's drive if we take turns at the wheel.' He hit a command button and another window popped up containing the same countdown application Shepherd had downloaded from Douglas's computer, the numbers now much lower. 'We should just be able to make it in time.'

His fingers drummed on the keyboard as he copied links to the countdown and to the Hubble feed into a website and pressed *Publish*. He turned and smiled up at Shepherd. 'Mala.org just went live – the modern way to follow a star. Come on, we need to get going. My jeep is right over there.'

'I need to grab Hevva's things from the other car.' Shepherd stood upright and felt the world lurch. He reached out to steady himself against the trunk of the tree but missed, grazing his cheek against the bark as he fell to the ground. Something sharp jarred his ribs as he hit the ground. He reached for it with his hand and it came away wet and bloody.

Oh Jesus, he thought as darkness claimed him, *damn woman didn't miss after all.*

CHAPTER 105

Seven days after the initial inoculations, the first patient recovered.

She was a forty-three-year-old bank clerk, born and raised in Ruin, who seemed more impressed by where she now found herself than by the fact that she had just survived a disease that had wiped out a quarter of the city's population.

The cathedral cave now contained over three hundred beds, most of which were occupied. Normally the numbers remained steady at around fifty, the new intake being roughly balanced by the death toll: but no one had died since they had begun the inoculations, the daily ritual of removing the bodies to the garden had stopped and the pyre on the firestone that had burned without pause since the very beginning had now gone out.

That same afternoon trucks and personnel drove into the city from the outside world, the first vehicles to have done so for more than half a year. They were laden with stocks of the vaccine, manufactured in readiness at industrial labs in Ankara, and a small army of volunteers who had already been inoculated.

The quarantined quarters were kept in place, to make

the vaccinations easier to police and monitor. By evening every living soul in the city of Ruin was lining up, waiting patiently for the salvation they had prayed for, everyone so relieved that deliverance was finally at hand that they failed to notice the creak of ropes as, down the side of the Citadel, the ascension platform began to descend with a lone figure standing in the centre of it, watching the world rise to meet him.

PART VII

The earth laughs in flowers
                    Ralph Waldo Emerson

CHAPTER 106

Shepherd woke to the vibration and hum of an engine. He opened his eyes and found a dark-eyed angel staring down at him. Hevva's face instantly exploded into a smile; he smiled back and noticed that the nick in her ear was hidden behind a fresh plaster and she was wearing different clothes. He was lying in the back of a jeep that was bouncing over very rough ground.

'Hi,' he croaked, his voice dry and raw.

'Ah, the sleeping beauty awakes,' Kinderman piped from the driver's seat. 'Just in time for our arrival.'

'Arrival?'

'Yes. We're here.'

Shepherd tried to sit up and pain shot through his side. He reached down to discover thick bandages bound tightly across his chest.

'I'd take it easy if I were you. The bullet grazed your side pretty badly. Fortunately it hit a rib, which deflected it around your body so it passed out the other side without causing too much damage. Your rib's probably cracked, which is why it hurts so much. Pretty apt though, don't you think, being saved by a rib, considering where we're headed?'

Shepherd struggled upright, feeling every bounce of the jeep jarring in his side like someone was repeatedly stabbing him. Outside, the sun was hanging low in a burnt sky above a world bleached almost white; there was nothing to see but broken land and brittle earth all around them. The only sign of life at all lay directly in front of them.

And what life it was.

The green shone in the sunlight like a bright jewel, deep and green, like a chunk of rainforest that had been dropped in the middle of this nowhere. 'How long have I been out?'

'About twenty-four hours.'

Shepherd tried to process this fact along with the growing vision of lushness that was gradually filling the windshield. 'You drove all the way?'

Kinderman picked up a bottle of pills and rattled it. 'Caffeine capsules. A lorry driver gave me some at the crossing into Iraq. You missed quite a party back there. So many migrants are responding to the homing instinct now that they've effectively thrown open the borders.'

The jeep hit another pothole, drawing a grunt of pain from Shepherd. 'Here,' Hevva said, handing him a lozenge from a different bottle. 'Place one under your tongue. It will take the pain away.'

He did as he was told. 'She's quite the nurse,' Kinderman said. 'She dressed your wound, then bandaged you up.'

Hevva shrugged. 'I used to help Mama with her work. I don't mind blood, I'm used to it.'

Shepherd felt the soothing numbness of the pill spreading through his body, melting away his discomfort. Kinderman spotted a track leading into the heart of the green and headed for it. Hundreds of different tyre marks converged on the spot, showing that many people had travelled this way before. There was a sign by the side of the road with an arrow painted on it pointing onwards into the heart of the jungle. The road followed the contours of the land, through groves of young palm trees and ferns that grew so thick it became harder and harder to see the way ahead.

They had been driving for almost ten minutes when they saw the first people. They were down by the bank of a river, washing clothes in the clear water, their children playing in the shallows. A cluster of tents were set up a little way back from the bank with more laundry drying on lines stretched out between them. One of the people looked up as they passed and raised an arm in greeting. Hevva waved back.

They followed the track along the side of the river, more arrows urging them forward. More buildings emerged from the green, mostly huts made from salvage, until they rounded a final bend and saw what looked like a small town, the outskirts made up of the same temporary buildings they had seen on their way in. At the heart of it were several solid-looking buildings constructed around a pool with a fountain of water at its centre.

'It's pretty,' Hevva said, watching the rainbows drift down in the spray.

'It's paradise,' Kinderman said, easing the jeep to a stop by the largest of the buildings. He switched the engine off and got out. Shepherd did the same, his whole body aching. He took a deep breath of the thick, perfumed air and groaned quietly as his ribs complained. There was something primordial about the place, almost womb-like with the shushing sound of the water and the moist, warm air all around them. It was so verdant and alive.

'Welcome.'

They turned to see two figures emerging from the door of one of the main buildings. The man was tall and looked Iraqi, the woman was slight with blonde hair pulled into a ponytail and eyes as green as the backdrop. She waddled as she moved towards them, her hands bracing her back against the counterweight of her ripe belly.

Shepherd stared at her, her American accent triggering a memory. 'You're Liv Adamsen,' he said.

She turned the blaze of her green eyes on him. 'That's right. Do I know you?'

He shook his head, slightly embarrassed that he had spoken her name out loud. 'Your name cropped up in an investigation I was involved with. You were listed as a missing person.'

She smiled. 'Well, I guess you found me, Mr . . .?' She held her hand out.

'Shepherd. Joe Shepherd.' He shook her hand. 'This is Dr Kinderman.'

'Bill,' he corrected.

Liv shook his hand. 'I've heard of you.'

Kinderman smiled and cocked his head to the side. 'Then you really should get out more.'

'And this is Hevva,' Shepherd said.

Hevva stepped forward and held up her hand, but instead of shaking Liv's she placed it flat on her tummy. She pressed her fingers gently in at the sides then raised her left hand and did the same on the other. Her face turned serious. 'When's the baby due?' she asked in the quiet, grown-up way she had about her.

'Not for another month.'

Hevva continued to run her hands over the dome of Liv's belly, her frown deepening. If any other stranger had done this it would have seemed like a gross intrusion but because it was this serious, small girl, somehow it seemed OK. She finished her examination and looked up at Liv, shaking her head slowly.

'The baby's coming now,' she said.

CHAPTER 107

Sweat pricked his skin, the salt irritating the ritual wounds hidden beneath his shirt as warm air blew through the open taxi window. The Novus Sanctus was tired after the flight and the heat was making him more so. But there would be no chance for sleep, there was too much to do and so little time. He checked his phone, tapping the icon to bring the countdown up on its screen. Tonight. Everything would happen tonight.

He had spent the long flight poring over the latest FBI reports, leaked to him as soon as they were updated. They didn't tell him much he didn't already know but the appearance of the Hubble images on the mala.org website had. They made him realize that it was too late now to make an example of Dr Kinderman. There was something happening out in the desert, something momentous that was tied in to the myths and beliefs of the old enemy, the Mala.

He had studied their legends and beliefs until he knew all their heresies. He was aware of the prophecy they clung to, predicting their return to power. It had always seemed fanciful to him before, but not any more, not now the established Church had been so discredited and the holy bastion at Ruin had fallen. They were preparing for their new beginning out in the desert, in their new Eden – the end of days. But the days of the true Church were not over yet, not while faithful servants of the true God like himself, and all the others like him, were ready to take up the sword.

The taxi pulled up in the middle of the street and he told the driver to wait. He would not be long and he had a helicopter to catch that would fly him into Iraq for the final part of his journey. He pressed one of the bells at the side of the door and waited. It was even hotter on the street and the cuts on his skin had become distinctly uncomfortable. But it would not be long before all earthly concerns were behind him and he would take his place with the martyrs at God's right hand. He had spent his life gazing up into heaven and imagining what it would be like, and soon he would be there.

A lock sounded inside the door and it opened wide enough for a round, moon-like face to look out. Restless, bloodshot eyes surveyed the street for a few seconds then the door opened a little wider to let the Sanctus pass.

CHAPTER 108

Liv's waters broke an hour after dusk.

She was walking by the edge of the central pool, trying to cool down a little after the heat of the day when she felt a small pop followed by an incredible, breath-snatching pain. Liquid gushed down her thighs as she crumpled to the ground, ending up on all fours, trying to breathe and calling out for help between breaths.

People came running and she was helped up and towards the main building.

'No,' she said, feeling a sudden panic as the yawning door approached. 'I don't want to be inside. I want to stay out here.'

Dr Giambanco appeared. 'Come on,' he said. 'We'll get you lying down and take a look at you.'

'I don't want to lie down.'

'I need to examine you.'

'Then bring a bed outside – it's cooler out here.'

Panic continued to flutter madly in her chest. She couldn't bear the idea of being confined, not now. There was a sail strung up for shade over a table on the beach area by the pool. 'I want to go there,' she said, walking stiffly towards it. She had a sudden flashback to a natural birth she'd once witnessed a lifetime ago when she was writing a story. Her panic rose a few notches higher as she recalled the screaming agony of it all.

I'm going to be fine – she said to herself – *women have been giving birth for ever. It's just pain – and you get a baby at the end of it.*

She reached the table and lowered herself onto one of the benches, gritting her teeth against the pain that shot up her back. It hurt so much already and yet it had only just started. She couldn't imagine how it could possibly get any worse and the thought that it would frightened her.

'Better to walk around,' said a small voice at her side. She turned, and saw the little girl who had arrived that afternoon. 'It helps the baby come and stops your back hurting so much.'

Liv stared at her like she was a small angel sent to look after her. 'How did you know the baby was coming?'

Hevva shrugged. 'I've seen a lot of babies being born.'

'Her mother was a midwife.' Liv looked up and saw the man the girl had arrived with.

'Do you mind if she stays nearby?' she asked him, smiling down at the girl. 'Can you stay? I'm a bit scared and I think you might make me brave.'

The girl nodded, looking up at her father for approval.

'If you want,' the man said. 'I'll stay close by – in case you need me.'

More people arrived carrying a mattress and sheets taken from one of the dorms inside the building. All around there was a hum of activity as stakes were found and driven in the ground to hold up privacy screens while others brought battery-powered lights on stands and set them up. They laid the mattress on the table and the doctor took Liv's arm. 'Let's get you up here and take a look at you,' he said. But Liv didn't hear him as sudden pain exploded inside her blotting everything else out.

CHAPTER 109

Shepherd walked away feeling anxious.

After what had happened at Göbekli Tepe he didn't like letting Hevva out of his sight. They had only just arrived here: everybody had been very kind and welcoming, but even so. He stopped by the water's edge, close enough for comfort but far enough so that the hiss of the fountain drowned out some of the noise coming from the makeshift maternity ward.

The stars were out already, millions of points of light speckling the night. He turned to face east where Taurus was rising and saw the new star shining between Zeta Tauri and Nath. He'd missed it the night before because he'd been sleeping like a dead man in the back of a moving car. It was odd seeing a new thing in something so familiar.

'Beautiful, isn't it?'

Kinderman joined him, his eyes tilted up to the same patch of sky. 'I thought you were asleep.'

'After all those caffeine pills, chance would be a fine thing. Besides, I wouldn't miss this for anything.'

Shepherd looked back up at the bright new speck

in the sky. 'Miss what – what did Hubble see exactly?'

'What do you think it saw?'

'I don't know. A Dark Star maybe?'

'Now wouldn't that be something! Interesting that you naturally assume it has to be something destructive.'

'It's not an assumption, it's based on the evidence of what I've seen. And you did write "end of days" in your diary.'

'Ah yes, so I did. You're being very literal though, don't you think? You're ignoring the universal law that tells us energy never dies, it just turns into something else. Therefore, the end of one thing must also be the beginning of another. In point of fact you already know what Hubble saw, because you have seen it for yourself.' Shepherd thought back through all the things he had come across since the investigation had begun but nothing came to mind that might answer his question. 'You might want to start with the one thing you are sure is connected to the question,' Kinderman prompted, ever the teacher.

'The countdown?'

'Exactly. Now in order to answer your own question you need to take a tip from Marcus Aurelius and ask: "what is it of itself?" – and don't fall into your usual trap of making assumptions.'

Shepherd thought hard. What was a countdown? It was a steadily reducing measure of time, a prelude to something, like the start of a race or the launch of a rocket. Or was it? Kinderman's question seemed to suggest it wasn't the prelude to anything at all – it was actually the thing itself.

'The countdown is what Hubble saw.'

'Bravo, Agent Shepherd.'

Shepherd reached into his pocket, looking for his phone but his hand found something else. He pulled out the small, hard object – the woman's small gun.

Shepherd dropped it back into the jacket and found his phone in another pocket. The countdown was still running, the numbers now almost at zero.

'Not long now,' Kinderman said, glancing at the screen.

Shepherd shook his head, confused all over again. 'Not long to what? If the countdown is the thing itself, then what can come after.'

'I already told you,' Kinderman said, 'a new beginning. Let me try and frame it a little. We are all effectively made of stardust: same atomic material, same physical properties, all linked by an energy and common origin, whether you call it faith or physics. For nearly fourteen billion years the universe has been expanding, from the Big Bang onwards, always heading out, always seeking the new. Everything in the universe has mirrored this inherent nature, stars, planets, even humans. As a species we have spread, conquered, always looking beyond what we already have to what we might attain, even if we risk destroying ourselves in the process: it runs through everything, from an overreaching emperor destroying his empire for the sake of one more conquered land, to the happily married family man risking his happiness for the sake of an affair. Ours is a destructive nature, often a violent one, but it's not really our fault, we are merely exhibiting the same nature as everything else, the universal urge to expand and ultimately pull ourselves apart.

'In many ways the Hubble project was no different. We have astonishing levels of child poverty on our planet and there are species beneath the deep oceans we have never laid eyes on. Yet rather than look inward so that we might know ourselves we think the answers always lie out there somewhere, past the edge of what we can see. I was as guilty of it as any. Through Hubble I was able to see further than any man had ever done before. I was gazing upon the ultimate horizon, the one beyond which nothing existed – except maybe God, if that's the way your beliefs lie – taking measurements of the very first things ever created at the instant of the Big Bang.

'I had been observing radiation and light at the very edge of the universe, taking measurements of its speed and rate of expansion. Then, just over eight months ago, there was a change. I couldn't quite believe what I was seeing, it was so – immense. At first I thought I must have made a mistake so I asked Professor Douglas to check what I was seeing and he concurred. The universe, the constantly expanding universe that has been exploding outwards at ever-increasing speeds since the dawn of time, was slowing down.

'We decided to keep our findings to ourselves, partly to prevent unnecessary hysteria and speculation and partly to buy ourselves time to try and work out what was happening. At about the same time we both started getting the postcards, which suggested someone was monitoring our work. This made us play our cards even closer to our chest.

'We classified the data and kept monitoring the furthest edge of the universe as it continued to slow. And the more things slowed down on the furthest edge of space the more we noticed things changing here on Earth. All these migrations of people heading home, the birds flying to nesting grounds out of season, this increasing urge to head back to a point of origin, it's all just an echo of the changing universe. So there is no great conspiracy or alien mind control at work. Nor is it the harbinger of some terrible divine judgement in the shape of God's wrath or a rogue planet on a collision course with Earth. It is merely the linked consciousness and impulses that drive us all, fuelled by the energy of the universe, once rushing out to ultimately tear itself apart, now rushing inwards, towards where it originally came from. Back home. To some this is the place they were born, to others it is a person rather than a place, and to others it is somewhere much further back, the place we originally came from as a species.' He opened his arms and gestured at the garden. 'Eden.'

CHAPTER 110

Liv felt she was drowning in pain.
'There's something wrong. You're almost ten centimetres dilated already and the head is presenting. This baby should be coming.' Dr Giambanco looked up from beneath the sheet draped over Liv's legs. 'Try pushing now.'

Liv was lying on the bed, sweat sheening her skin. She bore down, focusing her energy on her pelvic floor like she had once written about. The pain inside was so intense and total that it literally took her breath away. 'I can't,' she said. 'It hurts too much.'

She felt the girl's small hand grip hers, surprisingly strong for such a tiny thing. 'Can I see?' she asked.

Liv nodded, not caring who looked so long as they could make the pain go away. Hevva moved to the bottom of the bed, squirting antiseptic gel on her hands as she went. She rubbed it between her fingers and worked it to the tips in a way that spoke of much practice, then she pressed one hand on Liv's tummy and swept the other round the top of the baby's head. 'It's a stargazer,' she said. 'It's facing up instead of down. That's why it's hard to push out. The head is bending the wrong way so when you push it just gets stuck.'

Dr Giambanco peered around Hevva's narrow shoulders. 'I think she's right. We might have to do an emergency C-section.'

Liv felt sick at the thought, but the pain was so all encompassing she would do almost anything to make it stop.

'I could try and turn it,' Hevva said. 'My hands are small. I've done it before.'

The doctor shook his head. 'I don't think we should risk –'

'Yes,' Liv cut in. 'Let her try.'

Dr Giambanco nodded and moved aside.

'Could you push against the leg,' Hevva said, her serious face angled up at the doctor. 'And you,' she turned to the other medic, 'you push against the other, but only when I say.'

She turned back to Liv, squirting more gel on her hands, making them as slippery as she could while she waited for the next contraction. Time stretched and the sounds of the night and rush of the fountain filled it.

Liv breathed. Tried to relax, then the burn of the pain started rising again.

'Now. Push now,' Hevva said and everybody obeyed. Then her hands slid forward and around the crown of the baby's head.

★　★　★

The numbers on Shepherd's phone continued their steady tick down. 'What do you think will happen when it hits zero?'

'Nothing, at least not immediately. I think the changes we have already felt and witnessed will continue. The stardust in everything will respond in exactly the same way as before, only the effect will be different. I imagine we will no longer seek to conquer and discover, but become more reflective instead, our eyes will turn inward, just as Hubble has turned its gaze towards the Earth. I hope that after an entire history blighted by war and violence – manifestations of the destructive imperatives of an expansive universe – we can look forward to an equally long period of peace and calm.

'On a fundamental level, everything is bound to change: human nature, politics, science, even religion. The end of days may be upon us, but only the end of the old days, the new ones will number the same as those that have gone before as the universe contracts – fourteen billion years, the exact same time frame as its expansion.'

The number on Shepherd's phone got smaller and he could almost feel a calm flowing from it. Smaller was good. Smaller was simpler and much more comforting somehow than the concept of the infinite.

A noise made him look up, the sound of a diesel engine, approaching low and heavy like a truck. It got louder and the wash of headlamps cut through the trees, bouncing up and down as the wheels caught the ruts in the road. It swung directly towards them, the light blinding them, before slowing to a stop behind the parked jeep.

The engine shuddered to a standstill and silence flooded back. The rear canvas flaps of the truck peeled back and people started to drop to the ground, stretching their backs and looking in wonder at their new surroundings.

'More people answering the siren call of the changing universe,' Kinderman said. 'And just in time too.'

Shepherd looked down at the countdown again just as the numbers tumbled to zero and immediately started to build again with a minus sign in front. At the same moment two things happened: the ambient light levels jumped slightly as all the stars became a little brighter; and a deep, almost animal cry split the night as Liv gave one long, final push. Then there was the tiny mewl of newborn.

CHAPTER 111

The first thing Gabriel heard when he climbed stiffly from the back of the truck after the long journey was the cry of a woman. He was naturally conditioned to respond to signs of distress and cries of pain but there was something in the sound that he recognized. His senses snapped to attention and he reacted quickly, moving along the side of the truck, heading to the source. The sound had come from a screened-off area by the water's edge, with light coming from behind the screens.

He pushed past a staked sheet of canvas and squinted against the sudden brightness of the stand lights.

Liv was lying on a makeshift bed in the centre of a group of people. She looked tired and drawn but was still the most beautiful thing he had ever seen. She seemed to glow in the lights. A young girl was at her feet holding a newborn baby that squirmed and cried. She wrapped it in a towel and handed it to Liv.

A baby – Liv's baby.

★   ★   ★

Shepherd saw the man get down from the truck – and head straight for the canvas screens. Hevva was in there, he couldn't see what was happening, he was too far away. The man disappeared behind the screens and Shepherd broke into a run, his feet slipping in the soft earth of the shore.

Over by the truck someone else started to move with the same sense of purpose the first man had displayed. He was wearing a bulky jacket, like a soldier's tunic, and there was something about it and the stiff way he walked that set alarms ringing in Shepherd's head. The man reached the screens and turned briefly before disappearing behind them, the light from the truck's headlights catching his face. Shepherd stared. Shocked.

It was the Hubble control technician from Goddard. It was Merriweather.

CHAPTER 112

Liv saw Gabriel appear at the edge of the light and walk towards her. She thought it must be some kind of hallucination brought on by hormones or pheromones or endorphins or any combination of the three.

She felt the weight of the baby as it was placed on her chest and she looked down at it – this tiny, perfect being. She had never really believed in love at first sight but in that first moment she saw her baby she loved it more than she had ever loved anything in her life. She would die for it right now if she had to.

She looked back up, expecting the vision of Gabriel to have gone but he was still there, solid and real. He too had tears in his eyes and he was looking down at her and the baby.

Liv smiled and wept all at once, holding the baby's velvety head close to her mouth. 'It's your daddy,' she whispered. 'He came back.'

Then she saw movement, directly behind Gabriel.

Merriweather stepped into the blaze of light and beheld the bizarre nativity: the woman on the bed, holding the false prophet in her arms – the un-doer of everything, the Antichrist.

He stepped forward, unbuttoning his tunic and letting it fall to the floor, no longer Merriweather, now revealed as his true self – the *Novus Sancti*. He opened his arms to form the cross with his body, revealing the ritualized cuts in his flesh, and the packs of explosives strapped to his chest. In one hand he held a gun, in the other, a wire connected to the explosives.

Now he could complete his transformation and become the instrument of mankind's delivery, the first martyr of the reborn church, ending this Satanic rebellion before it had even begun.

Gabriel saw the fear in Liv's eyes and turned to see what had put it there.

He saw the bomb, the outstretched arms, the ritual cuts of a Sanctus.

His instinct was to just hurl himself forward and knock him away from Liv and the baby. But the Sanctus was too far back. Gabriel would be shot before he covered the distance. But he was also too far away from Liv and the baby and he could see by the look in his eyes that they were his target. He would move closer, to try and close the gap between himself and everyone else to make sure the bomb blast was effective. That was when Gabriel would do it.

Then someone stepped into view, and the Sanctus reacted, spinning round to point the gun at the newcomer. The gunshot was like thunder. The man fell back, thrown by the impact of the bullet. Gabriel threw himself at the Sanctus, hitting him hard and sending them both to the floor. He pinned his gun hand down beneath the weight of his body and grabbed for the hand holding the wire, digging his thumb hard into the wrist tendons, seeking the pressure point that would weaken the man's grip. In a detached part of his mind he remembered his grandfather doing something similar to save him and his mother from a grenade. He had smothered the blast with his body, giving his life in exchange for theirs, and now he must do the same.

The Sanctus roared in pain as the thumb dug deeper. He tried to twist away and brought his arm down hard on the top of Gabriel's head. Once, twice the elbow driving the full force of the blow into his skull.

Gabriel held on, weathering the blows as best he could, unable to raise an arm to protect himself. He had to keep hold of the Sanctus, if he let go then they were all lost. The blows continued to rain down and the jarring movement of them caused Gabriel's hand to slip. The Sanctus pulled his wrist free and the button fell from his numbed hand.

Gabriel kicked hard with his legs, digging into the earth and pushing them both a few inches further from the bed and the precious people on it.

He reached for the hand again but the Sanctus

had twisted it away far enough to keep it out of reach. The hand found the button and Gabriel kicked again to try and jar it free or gain a few more precious inches.

But it was not enough.

He saw the hand close around the button and he shut his eyes, bracing himself, hoping the ground and his own body would absorb enough of the blast to protect Liv and his child.

Shepherd came through the canvas screens on the opposite side to where the others had entered. The rider who had greeted them was lying on the floor, a gunshot wound bleeding in his chest. Hevva was by the bed, her eyes fixed on the violent struggle taking place on the floor. He stepped forward. Saw the hate burning in Merriweather's face, saw the bomb, the newborn baby, the mattress out of place, even the light on the stand burning like the sun had burned from the poster – all of it so familiar from Hogan's Alley and the other dark basement.

He raised the small gun he had taken from the woman and aimed it at Merriweather's head, trying to put all that had happened before from his mind.

The bullets are real – he told himself – *and so is the bomb.*

And Hevva is standing right by it.

His finger tightened on the trigger but Merriweather jerked away, swinging his other hand round. Shepherd saw the gun in it, saw it angle down towards the man he was struggling with. He took a step forward, not caring about getting shot, only about narrowing the gap and improving the accuracy of this tiny gun he had never fired.

The explosion was so loud Gabriel thought he must be dead. Even so he still clung on. He felt that if he could brace himself against death, even for an extra few microseconds, it might make a difference to the living.

So much flashed though his mind in that moment, fragments of the life he was about to lose. He saw the baby he had barely glimpsed growing into a – what? He didn't even know if he had a son or a daughter and he would die not knowing. He would have liked to have known his child and spent his life with Liv by his side. But this was not such a bad death, if his death meant life for them.

Then the echo of the gunshot rang away into the night.

And Gabriel opened his eyes.

CHAPTER 113

Shepherd sat on the edge of the water, tossing in stones. They sank beneath the surface, leaving no ripples, a tiny marker of the new universal order.

After everything Kinderman had said about the new age of peace, killing Merriweather had seemed like a particularly obscene and revolting act. He knew it had been unavoidable, but still . . .

He had drifted through the aftermath of the shooting on auto-pilot, clearing the area as if it was just a normal crime scene and backup was on its way. But he was on his own out here and he felt the sadness settle on him like his darkest depressions had done in the past. But there was one bright shaft of light shining through it all. Hevva was OK. He had saved his daughter.

Once the bomb was made safe he had called Franklin, old habits dying hard, and told him everything, using his partner like an old-time priest who might hear his confession and forgive him his sins. And when Franklin hung up, promising to call back with more news, he felt like he was all talked out and empty. He had handed on the baton of responsibility. He was free.

He stared out across the pool, the mirror of its surface reflecting the night sky. The night was cold, but he didn't mind. He had taken his jacket off and draped it over Hevva when she had curled up and fallen asleep in his lap. He sat like this for a long time, just holding her until the phone buzzed again and he answered it quickly so as not to wake her.

'It's Franklin. I'm standing in Merriweather's apartment looking at plans of Marshall, fake IDs, and a whole directory of names that includes our good friend Fulton Cooper. Seems Merriweather was something of an archiver – you should see the collection of old 45s he's got here – he recorded everything, you couldn't ask for a more smoking gun. There's also some kind of shrine in his basement, like an altar or something with a big T-shaped cross hanging on the wall – it's a proper fanatic's home-from-home.'

Shepherd nodded but said nothing.

'Listen, Shepherd, if you want me to arrange transport back, I can do that. Just tell me where you are and I'll set the wheels in motion.'

Shepherd looked up at the sky. 'I think I'll stay here a while,' he said, watching Hubble twinkling like a new star. 'It is Christmas after all. Isn't that when you spend time with family?'

'I didn't know you had a family.'

Shepherd felt Hevva stir in his arms, her head

620

nuzzling him as she slept. 'Neither did I. You should go home too, Ben – spend some time with your family.'

'I will, just as soon as I've arrested the guy behind the explosion at Marshall that nearly got us killed.'

Shepherd frowned. 'Not Merriweather?'

'No. He couldn't possibly have got there before we did and set all that up in time.'

'Who then?'

CHAPTER 114

C hief Ellery looked up from his desk as the door opened and a man wearing a black suit came in. He didn't recognize him, but he knew the Sheriff who walked in with him, a kid called Rogers, someone he'd known from back when he was still in uniform.

The suit showed him his FBI credentials, read the charges then Sheriff Rogers stepped forward to read him his rights, looking slightly embarrassed about the whole thing. Ellery looked up at the photograph of his younger self. He'd never really wanted to quit being a cop, but the Church had wanted to keep a close eye on NASA, maintaining its long tradition of suspicion regarding science in general and astronomers in particular.

Sheriff Rogers finished Mirandizing him and stepped forward, reaching for the cuffs on his belt clip.

'You don't need to do that, son,' Ellery said, rising from his chair. 'I'm too old to make a run for it or try anything stupid.' He turned to the agent. 'I'm surprised Agent Franklin didn't come here to do this himself. I imagine he would have enjoyed it.'

The agent shot him a cold smile. 'Agent Franklin's got bigger fish to fry.'

Franklin pulled up outside the large Colonial-style house, took a breath then got out of the car. He waited for the two-man arrest team to join him on the porch before knocking loudly and smoothing his hand down over his tie. He smiled at the surprised-looking woman who answered the door and turned down the offer of coffee as he walked across the hallway to where a news station could be heard playing behind a door.

He rapped once out of courtesy then pushed the door wide without waiting for an answer.

Assistant Director O'Halloran looked up from the TV. Franklin saw surprise flash across his face, but he recovered quickly. 'I was expecting your report, Agent Franklin, not a house call.'

'A draft version of my report has already been filed, sir. I sent it to Assistant Director Murray.'

The surprise returned but this time it stayed. 'Might I ask why?'

'Murray took over the covert running of Operation Fish, sir – after you tried to shut it down. It was felt that your reasons for ending the investigation into highly placed and potentially influential Christians were not entirely robust.' O'Halloran glanced past Franklin and saw the two uniformed officers waiting in the hall. 'I can tell you what's in the report if you like, though I'm sure you know how most of it goes – foot soldiers recruited and run by the Reverend Fulton Cooper through the Church of Christ's Salvation to fight the good fight against so-called "heretical scientific exploration" and the rising tide of ungodliness, Chief Ellery at Marshall keeping his eye on James Webb, Merriweather over at Goddard doing the same for Hubble – all of them controlled centrally by a well-placed puppet-master inside the FBI, feeding them information and their mission orders for the greater good of the mother church you all serve.'

'I assume your report contains proof?'

Franklin nodded. 'Merriweather kept exceptionally detailed records – I guess it's the risk you run if you start doing business with paranoid conspiracy theorists. I have all the evidence I need of the "How?" – the only thing I don't have is the "Why?"'

O'Halloran steepled his fingers in front of him so it looked like he was praying but said nothing. Franklin nodded at the arrest team and they moved out of the hallway and into the den. He stayed by the door, ready to move if he had too, remembering how it had gone down with Cooper but O'Halloran just sat there, staring ahead while they read him his rights. When they had finished he looked up at Franklin. 'If you want to know the "why?"' he said, 'just look at what's happening in the world. A judgement is coming where all shall be held to account. I answer to His law above all others. I am ready to face my Lord, Agent Franklin – are you?'

Franklin stared into his face, hardly recognizing

the man before him now that the weird light had crept into his eyes. 'I believe in people, sir. If you spend as much time on the streets as I have, it's hard not to. I used to believe in you, too, but when you chose to partner me up with a rookie on a case as important as this, even someone with Shepherd's science background, I started having my doubts. It was as if you were setting out to hamper the investigation and limit its chances of success. But in the end, sir, that's where you made your biggest mistake. You underestimated the power of people – and you picked the wrong rookie.'

CHAPTER 115

Dawn rose over the compound, lighting up the dew on the grass and the unfurling petals of waking flowers and fresh blossom that dripped between the green leaves of the trees.

Two figures emerged from the main building and moved through the morning mist that had drifted across the ground from the central fountain of water. They walked in silence, though the way they were together told their story: he, with his arm round her waist; she, leaning against him, her arms forming a natural cradle for the bundle of a sleeping baby.

They headed up the incline, bare feet leaving tracks in the wet grass that swept up the hill to the graves. The smell of loam and earth rose from the mound of freshly dug dirt where the one who called himself *Novus Sancti* lay buried next to those he had called his enemy.

The two figures moved higher to a spot where the grass covered an older grave, now fuzzed with green, a slab of granite at its centre.

'Here he is,' the woman said, resting her head on the man's chest. 'I put the Starmap here

626

because I wanted to mark it out in some way. I thought it was something you would do, if you'd been here.'

Gabriel knelt down and wiped his hand across the surface of the Starmap, clearing the dew to reveal the symbols beneath. In the middle of the second line an arrow pointed down, something Liv had always assumed meant 'King'. Now, in the light of all that had happened, she saw it was more general than that.

The Sacrament comes home and
The Key looks to heaven
A new star is born with a new <u>ruler</u> on Earth to
bring order to the end of days.

The baby began to stir in her arms as Gabriel hooked his fingers round the edge of the stone and hauled it over to reveal the symbols on the other side.

$$ \wedge \quad \underset{\top}{+} \quad \underline{\vee} $$

$$ \underline{XX} $$

$$ \underline{\top} $$

The star that heralded the end of the old had new meaning for her now. It spoke of opposites coming together and a balance being struck, for it was made up of two other symbols, the ones for the Citadel and for Eden. The symbol below also spoke of reconciliation, though this one was far more personal. When she first saw it Liv thought it must refer to her in some sinister way, the Tau with a line cutting through it. Now she realized what it was. It was the Tau and the sword combined, her symbol and Gabriel's together, creating something new entirely.

The baby wriggled and stretched in her arms, the hungry mouth searching for its mother. 'What shall we call her? I was thinking maybe Kathryn,' Liv said, referring to the wife of the man lying buried beneath the stone – Gabriel's mother.

Gabriel smiled and kissed the top of Liv's head. 'It's a good name,' he said. 'Do you know what it means?'

The baby girl yawned, unaware of the wonderful new world she had been born into.

'It means "pure" . . .'

EPILOGUE

The sun shines and traffic flows freely down the great wide boulevards of Ruin, all signs of the quarantine that held the city in its grip for most of the previous year now gone. The people have returned, the dead are remembered and life goes on.

In the centre of the city, looming above it all, the Citadel remains as dark and silent as always. It has cast its long shadow here before there was a city and will do so after the city has crumbled to dust. But those who have held sway for so long inside it and spread their influence way beyond the physical shadow of the mountain are now gone. After thousands of years withstanding everything kings and emperors could throw at it in their attempts to crack open the walls and learn its great secrets, it was a virus, one of the smallest life-forms on Earth that brought the mountain down.

But life goes on for the Citadel too.

Today the embankment surrounding the mountain is filled with people and news cameras, there to witness its reopening. Cameras have already been inside, moving through the carved corridors to reveal

629

to the outside world all that it wondered about for so long – the dormitories, the refectories, the great cathedral cave, all preserved exactly as they were when the monks lived there.

At the foot of the mountain, where the ascension platform used to rest, the mayor now gives a speech and the news cameras roam the crowd, capturing the excitement and anticipation of the first people to ride the newly installed elevators up the side of the mountain into what used to be the tribute cave. A man hangs back, hiding beneath a hat and behind dark glasses. He avoids the cameras, for he has nothing to share. He has been inside the mountain before.

A ribbon is cut and cameras flash, capturing the first elevator shooting up to the dark cave where more cameras are waiting to capture the looks on the faces of the first people to take this journey into a secret world few have ever known or seen before.

A tour guide leads them through the tunnels, explaining how the monks lived and recounting crowd-pleasing stories culled from the Citadel's long and bloody history. The man in the hat listens from the back of the group, making mental notes when the guide deviates too far from the script he helped write so he can correct him in the debrief later.

He puts the dark glasses on again as the group steps out into the brightness of the garden and the guide tries his best to paint a picture of what the barren space might have looked like when everything flourished. He moves on quickly, sensing the crowd is not that interested, and heads back inside to the grand finale of the cathedral cave. But the man in the hat remains. He removes his sunglasses and stares at a spot by the firestone where the ground has been nourished by the ash of the fire. He walks over and squats down, removing his hat to fan the dust away from the thing he has seen. The dust blows away and Athanasius breaks into a broad smile at the miracle he has discovered. It is a green shoot rising up from the grey ground straight and sharp, like a model of the Citadel in miniature.

A new life. A new hope. A new beginning.